BATTLE WITH THE UNKNOWN

Because it had helped in past exercises in the depths, I relied on my sense of smell. The Darkmaze had the same warm, musty odor it always did. The scent of leather armor and my nervous sweat hung in the air, but I recognized them as normal, and dismissed them. I searched for another smell, something unusual, something I could not identify.

There was nothing. Nothing to smell, to hear, or to feel. I was utterly alone. Without warning a paw raked my left shoulder, twisted my body and smashed my shoulder back into the wall. The blow numbed my arm and knocked me aside—had I been shorter it would have knocked me out or snapped my neck.

I rebounded off the wall, planted my right foot, and slashed my *tsincaat* through the darkness in front of me. I slid back toward my left, spun, and cut through where I had just stood. The sword connected.

My foe made no sound. It withdrew quickly, as if it evaporated, and I realized something was dreadfully wrong. . . .

BOOKS BY MICHAEL A. STACKPOLE

The Warrior Trilogy
Warrior: En Garde
Warrior: Riposte
Warrior: Coupé

The Blood of Kerensky Trilogy
Lethal Heritage
Blood Legacy
Lost Destiny

Natural Selection
Assumption of Risk
Bred for War
Malicious Intent

The Fiddleback Trilogy
A Gathering Evil
Evil Ascending
Evil Triumphant

Dementia

Once a Hero*

Talion: Revenant*

Star Wars® X-wing Series
Rogue Squadron*
Wedge's Gamble*
The Krytos Trap*
The Bacta War*

*published by Bantam Books

TALION
REVENANT

Michael A. Stackpole

SPECTRA ™ ®

BANTAM BOOKS

New York   Toronto   London   Sydney   Auckland

TALION: REVENANT
A Bantam Book

PUBLISHING HISTORY
Bantam paperback edition / May 1997

ISBN 0-553-57656-9
Published simultaneously in the United States and Canada

Bantam Books are published by Bantam Books, a division of Bantam Dou-
bleday Dell Publishing Group, Inc. Its trademark, consisting of the words
"Bantam Books" and the portrayal of a rooster, is Registered in U.S. Patent
and Trademark Office and in other countries. Marca Registrada. Bantam
Books, 1540 Broadway, New York, New York 10036.

PRINTED IN THE UNITED STATES OF AMERICA

OPM   10   9   8   7   6   5   4   3   2   1

Dedication

To Hugh B. Cave

Writer and mentor, he is an inspiration to good story-tellers. His kind writing advice pushed my development as a writer forward by ten years and his stories get in where you live. I can't thank you enough, Hugh, for your help and the enjoyment I've gotten from your writing.

Acknowledgments

The author would like to thank the following people for their help in this book's preparation:

Liz Danforth and Jennifer Roberson for having endured not only this version of the book, but the previous draft (the only virtue of which was that it was shorter and, therefore, fewer trees died to produce a manuscript). Without their support and encouragement, this book simply would not exist.

Dennis L. McKiernan for his insightful comments on this version of the book.

L. Ross Babcock III and Janna Silverstein, who thought kindly enough about this book to give me other books based on what they read here. Without their faith in my ability, this would not have been my first novel, but probably my only novel.

Anne Lesley Groell and Ricia Mainhardt for finally getting this monster into publication.

TALION
REVENANT

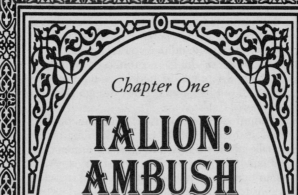

Chapter One

TALION: AMBUSH

Had Morai given the job to anyone else, the ambush would have gotten me.

The assassin waited just halfway up the hill on the camp's north side. New spring undergrowth covered the steep slope and a light breeze stirred things enough to cover tiny movements and sounds, yet caused nothing to obstruct the assassin's view of the camp. Sitting there, at the base of the big oak, he could watch everything with little fear of discovery.

His position gave him an easy crossbow shot at anything in the flat clearing below. Morai's men had stripped or scattered all the cover so I'd have no place to hide if the first crossbow bolt missed. And, if I was quick enough to figure out where the bolt had come from, the only way I could get to the ambusher was a suicidal charge up the hill, straight at him.

The only questionable part of Morai's plan was assigning Fortune the job of killing me. Fortune, the sixteen-year-old miller's son from Forest Crossing, had run away from home and decided to join the bandits who had just raided his town. The other members of the gang probably would have killed him outright or, if Chi'gandir had his way, done worse. By setting the youth out as a trap for me, though, Morai amused his men and saved the boy.

Clearly bored out of his mind, Fortune perched on a knobby root at the base of the oak. He'd waited a long time for me to walk into his sights, and after a morning of nervous, sweaty anticipation he'd set the crossbow down. After a quarter of an hour or so he took out the gold Imperial Morai had paid him for my head and inspected it. He traced the golden profile of Ell's King with a dirty fingernail and even though he'd never held a gold coin before, the novelty of it soon wore off.

Fortune, perhaps entranced by the omen of his name, flipped the coin into the air. The coin rang with each flick of his thumb, and sunlight flashed from the bright metal. With each subsequent toss the gold piece rose higher and higher until, at the peak of its gilded arc, it vanished into the oak's lower branches. Fortune caught it each time it fell toward the earth and slapped it down on the back of his left hand. He'd peel his right hand away slowly, smiling or frowning at the face of the coin showing. His guess right or wrong, he'd slide the coin into his right hand and launch it again.

One final time the coin flew from his hand as before, but then glanced off a tree branch and ricocheted to his left. Landing on the hard-packed earth, it rolled around back behind the tree and out of his sight. Fortune stretched, looked down at the clearing, and rose to a crouch. He turned around the sturdy barrel of oak and stopped abruptly.

His coin lay in my right palm.

He glanced back at the crossbow, then at me.

I shook my head slowly and his shoulders sagged. "I believe, Fortune, this is yours." I extended my hand toward him.

A handsome youth, Fortune never should have worn such

a look of abject terror on his face. Flared nostrils ballooned his noble, narrow nose. He held his brown eyes open wide enough to reduce them to flat white circles surrounding dark spots. Acrid, nervous sweat pasted brown hair to his forehead. His dropped jaw stretched his face—already thin like the rest of him—and made him look like a very old man.

I saw myself reflected in his eyes, yet I knew Fortune did not really see a tall, slender, dark-haired man with bright green eyes. His horror took him beyond my physical self and he stared at what I was and what I'd become since the ritual. He did not see a man, he saw a Talion Justice.

And he feared I was the last thing he would ever see.

Fortune reached out with trembling fingers and took the coin. He looked at it and smiled. Then he looked at my hand and dropped to his knees, tears leaking from tight-shut eyes.

Hidden beneath the coin until he plucked it from my hand, a death's-head tattoo had stared at him and had taken his breath away. The simple line drawing covered my palm and marked me as a Justice. From the fleshless jaw at my hand's heel to the skull's crown extending up to the base of my middle finger, the stark design watched him with cold empty eye sockets. Its memory forced a visible shiver into him.

I walked beyond the sobbing boy, leaving him alone with his fear and a chance to conquer it. I squatted where he had waited for me and nodded grimly. I picked up the crossbow and sighted down the bolt. The brush parted just enough for me to see the entire camp. I triggered the weapon and sank the bolt into the ashes of the bandits' campfire. A little dust and smoke rose, but nothing else moved below me.

I shivered and ground my teeth in anger. Morai knew the romance of the bandit life had attracted Fortune. Fortune's father probably had his son working hard when the boy wanted to be out courting girls or dreaming about the great warriors of legend. The bandits raided Forest Crossing, and Fortune followed them to escape hard work and reality for fame and riches.

Without question Morai knew Fortune was not suited for anything but being a miller's son. Morai also knew Fortune could not be sent away or talked out of a life on the road. If he sent the boy away, he knew Fortune would only hitch up

4 MICHAEL A. STACKPOLE

with another band, or would starve to death in the wilderness. The bandit leader realized the youth had to be terrified out of an outlaws' life, and Morai knew I could do that job.

It was a job I didn't want and one more black mark against Morai that he forced me to do it.

Part of me took pride in helping Fortune return to the life meant for him. By simply playing the boy's conception of a Justice, I could frighten Fortune enough that neither he nor his children nor his grandchildren would ever think of doing anything but milling, and milling honestly. That was good, and for that I might thank Morai. But that also meant Fortune's people would forever fear Talions—a trait too many people already shared—and I wanted no part in reinforcing that image.

Still, I knew ultimately, as much as I detested it, Fortune's fear gave me the perfect tool to set him straight. While I would have preferred to talk him into returning to his family by explaining to him the harsh realities of life on the road with Morai, the romance of the bandits' life was fairly tough armor against a commonsense approach to the problem. Some bard had even made up a song about Morai—a version of which I had heard butchered in Talianna—making him seem more noble and gallant than he really was.

Getting past that version of Morai—and the generally held whimsical notions about bandits—would require me to present Fortune with a big dose of reality, delivered in a manner that was anything but whimsical.

I returned to Fortune and towered over the kneeling boy. I let my left hand land heavily on his right shoulder. He started and the rhythm of his sobs broke. "Morai never told you I'd kill you, did he?"

He looked up at me. His red-rimmed eyes had shrunk in size, but they still brimmed with tears. Those tears washed a clean path through the dirt on his face from each eye to the corners of his mouth. He swiped a hand at the tears and smeared the grime back into place. "Not him." He halted and gained control of his breathing. "The others. They said you'd suck my soul out with that skull."

"I certainly could do that." I pursed my lips and turned away. "I have that right. You meant to kill me. Although intended murder is not a capital crime, who knows what atrocities you have already committed?"

"But I haven't done anything." Baffled innocence shot through his voice and, for a moment, set aside his fear.

I whirled back. My green eyes narrowed as I stared down at him. "And how do I know that? Forest Crossing is a dozen leagues backcountry. How do I know you didn't help murder a small merchant caravan in the two days since you left home? Do I assume that Morai, the man who collects madmen the way a Princess might collect dolls, would take in a child unless that child fit with his group? I know Morai well enough to know that's unlikely." I paused, then thrust my snarling face at him. "So what did you do?"

Fortune spilled backward and wailed like a lost soul. "I didn't do anything. Don't kill me. Please, don't. I'm innocent. Please, don't kill me."

I knelt before him and grabbed his chin with my left hand. "Understand this, little boy, you abandoned your innocence in Forest Crossing. You've ridden with a pack of human jackals. You've seen them do things, bad things, and because you were in their company, you can be held responsible for those actions."

I let him have another good look at the tattoo on my right palm. "This is a badge of my authority to deal with people like you—Morai's men. It is also a tool for me to use. If I were to press my hand against your forehead and will your soul to surrender to me, it would. You would be left here a lifeless husk, alone, dead and forgotten by everyone."

He started to cry at that prospect and gibbered words out in between sobs and sniffling. I released him, letting him slump back as I stood. He lay on the ground and his chest pounded as if something trapped inside wanted to get out.

I walked away from him and retrieved my horse so Fortune wouldn't see the disgust on my face. It wasn't for him, but for Morai in forcing my hand and for myself for allowing my hand to be forced. Some other Justices all but reveled in ripping a soul from a body, but I only used the ritual when given no other choice. Threatening the boy with it, while it did make the impression upon him I wanted to make, was using a spear to do work meant for a needle.

I'd left my horse, Wolf, down behind the hill. The black

stallion flicked his ears in my direction but made no noise. I patted him gently on the neck, untied the reins from a sapling, and led him back up to where Fortune waited.

My anger with myself grew from the realization that I'd let Morai dictate, in absentia, my actions—and not for the first time, either. That boded ill for my pursuit of him, though it continued the patterns we'd played through in the past. He intended me to harvest his men one by one while he escaped, and Fortune was the first of the lot in this go-round. I decided this would be the last time we played this particular game, but before I could continue after Morai, I needed to repair the damage I'd done to Fortune.

Fortune's unsteady approach, and the noise it created, interrupted my thoughts. Rubbery-legged and pale, he stumbled down the hill. He looked as though he might have vomited and certainly could do so again.

"Talion?"

"Yes?"

"I can tell you where they went, if you want, if that will make it right." He offered the information freely, not to save his life, but to atone for the wrongs he might have done.

I shook my head and tossed him my canteen. "Here, drink some of this; it's just water, but it will wash your mouth out." The boy drank cautiously and settled down. "Fortune, let me tell you something about the Talions. Two thousand years ago Emperor Clekan the Just created the Talions. He saw us as the instruments of his law and ordered us to travel throughout his empire. He made us independent of all authority save the Emperor or the Master of all Talions. We rode from Talianna to administer the laws and dispense justice."

Fortune restoppered the canteen and handed it back to me. I smiled and hooked the strap over my shoulder. "After rebellions shattered the thousand-year-old empire, the Talions' role in the world shifted. The Master created new divisions and the original Talions became Justices. Though the empire existed no more, the new nations agreed to let us keep peace and order when they found it beyond their abilities to do so. Chasing down a gang like the one Morai has put together, a gang that ranges over several nations, is a very good example of the duties my Master charges me with."

I smiled at him. "Killing boys who run away from home is not one of my duties." I rested a friendly hand on his shoulder and squeezed it. "Fortune, the crimes you've committed can be undone. You've left your mother terrified and worried about you. Your father, as you might expect, is angry with you, yet anguish eats him up inside. Your brothers and sisters don't know what to think and every gossip in Forest Crossing is telling every other gossip that they knew you would turn out this way."

Fortune nodded his head with resignation at everything I said. "What do I do?"

I swung into the saddle. "Go back to Forest Crossing. You're lucky in that you have a family, and doubly lucky because they love and care about you. Go home and work through whatever punishment your father gives you. Make the gossips eat their own words."

The boy swallowed hard, sniffed, and wiped tears away. "Thank you, Talion. Here." He held the Imperial out to me. "Take this, it's not mine. I've not earned it and I don't want it."

I shook my head. "Keep it. Morai would think of it as an investment. After all, without honest folk like you working to earn gold, what would he have to steal?"

The boy smiled and we laughed together. "And, Fortune, thanks for the offer, but I don't need your directions for finding the others. While you waited on the hill, I scouted all over this area. Two of them went east toward the Broad River ferry. Two others headed west and the other three, probably including Morai, started north but will have to cut west to hit any of the mountain passes. I will get them."

I reined Wolf around and started him toward the Broad River Valley. I smiled, because even above Wolf's hoofbeats I heard Fortune heading home, and the gold Imperial ringing as it flew up and down through the air.

I urged Wolf to set a faster pace than I demanded of him during our earlier pursuit of Morai's band. Though only an easy half day's ride from the bandit camp, I wanted to reach the Broad River Valley as quickly as possible. The two bandits riding to the ferry knew that by putting the Broad River between me and them they could earn a day or more over me.

I had to assume they would destroy the ferry after crossing and I knew the nearest ford lay a day's ride south. If they crossed the river I'd be forced to abandon them and probably would never find them again.

The bandits took a simple road through the Ell foothills. Broad enough for three horsemen to ride abreast, it wound through light woods that contained a few evergreen stands. The sun shined and winked through wind-rustled leaves to paint the roadway with an ever-shifting mosaic of light and shadows.

I stopped and drank at a stream where my quarry had paused to do the same thing. The muddy bank yielded footprints that easily identified one of the men to me. The footprints sank long and deep in the soft mud. Of Morai's men, only Rolf ra Karesia carried the size and bulk needed to produce the tracks. The other tracks, more normal than the giant's spoor, could have been made by at least three other men in the band, though I did know, from vast—and unwanted—experience, that Morai had not produced them.

In some ways knowing I pursued Rolf came as a relief. Red hair covered the human titan from his toes up to his big bushy beard and unkempt scalp. Those who knew him said he wasn't a cruel man, just an angry one who took his temper out on anyone who crossed him while he was in one of his "moods." Five years ago he left Karesia after nearly beating his father—a local baron—to death. Then he cut a wide, bloody swath through towns and villages in the Shattered Empire until he found himself in the black heart of Chala— an area known to all as the Black Cesspit. Morai visited the Cesspit to recruit new men after I destroyed his last band, and Rolf readily joined him.

Rolf *might* attack from ambush in the forest, but I suspected he'd wait for the open grasslands of the Broad River Valley before he attacked me. There, without the trees to hem him in, he could wield his double-bladed broadax with devastating efficacy. While I did not look forward to that fight, I felt I had one less surprise to anticipate on my ride through the forests.

I concentrated on figuring out who rode with Rolf. Rejecting Morai left me with three possibilities, and I liked none of them. Grath, the poisoner, would be little or no problem to deal with. He was not trained for or well suited to open fights. Vareck ra Daar was, like all his countrymen, mad, but he'd face me openly and try to acquit himself honorably. The third candidate, Chi'gandir, left me cold. I don't like sorcerers.

The second the thought that Chi'gandir might be riding with Rolf came to mind, I knew with a horrifying crystal certainty it was the case. The gods are perverse and enjoy toying with mortals. Not only was Chi'gandir the last person I wanted to face, but he was the one person out of the whole group who could be cruel beyond measure to Weylan, the ferryman at Broad River. I nudged Wolf into a gallop.

Chi'gandir was a renegade sorcerer of vast power but limited outlets for that power. He's a small man with a hooked nose and a bald head. No one could even accurately guess at his age, but his description had not changed in the twenty years he'd been running loose. His left eye had a diamond tattoo around it, marking him as a Tingis Lurker, which went a long way toward explaining his ability to survive and his enjoyment of cruel displays of power.

A very promising student of magick, Chi'gandir's impatience to learn the higher magicks consumed him. He left his tutor, traveled and studied the self-centered arts of the Lurkers, then found sorcerers to teach him irresponsible and destructive ways to channel his talents. They attempted to use him for their own ends, or so the story goes, but he destroyed them. Like a child given a dangerous toy, he set out playing with things and animals and people.

Known as "the Changer," Chi'gandir used his power to warp creatures. At first he did it for amusement. He added a leg or head to a newborn calf just to watch the farmers react with horror. Then he learned that he could alter people and that, if they were wealthy or powerful, they would pay well to have his enchantments reversed.

"If he's done anything to Weylan," I muttered to Wolf, "Chi'gandir will end up begging me to reverse the things I'll do to him."

Anger and fear festered and raged within me. Weylan's tragic life didn't need complicating elements like Rolf or Chi'-gandir. Weylan, despite his problems, was a good man and a better friend. Riding all too slowly through the woods, I became more and more convinced they would use him against me. Then again, if I was lucky or Weylan was lucky, Weylan and the ferry would be on the river's western shore and I'd have the bandits all to myself before the ferryman tangled with them.

Weylan exemplified the Imperial citizen Clekan created the Talions to protect and avenge. His family had operated the ferry for more years than anyone could remember: the eldest son always inherited the homestead, ran the ferry, and raised a family to take over. For centuries the heir took his wife from one of the merchant families that passed through the valley in their travels.

Until road agents got their hands on Weylan, it was a proud tradition that had no end in sight.

Ten years ago it all changed—or so the stories I had heard indicated. Weylan never talked about what happened, but folks in the district shared the story with little or no prompting. Weylan's entire family left him behind and traveled off with a rich merchant from Lacia to bring back his daughter Elverda to be Weylan's wife. While they were away a group of bandits, more numerous but less effective than Morai's pack, raided the ferry. Weylan, a handsome youth, strong from years of poling the ferry back and forth across the river, defended his birthright and killed a dozen of them before they captured him, and his captors worked on him.

The raiders bound him to a tree and deliberately maimed him. They left his body strong and straight while they smashed his teeth in and broke his face. They battered his left eye into milky white blindness and half tore off his scalp. They pulverized his nose, flattened it across his face and left him with very thick and nasal speech. It was said they watched him for several days to let the healing start so no wizard could reverse it; then they departed just hours before his family came home and found him.

His bride, Elverda, did not reject him. I don't know what her reasons were, but she showed more nobility in that act than I've seen in the rest of the world. Weylan freed her of all promises and told her to leave. She refused, so he married her and then instantly divorced her. He sent her and his family away. If tavern tales had it right, she returned with her father's caravans each spring to ask Weylan to let her stay.

Morai's bandits followed the road as it turned north toward the mountains. I turned off onto a lesser-used trail—one Weylan had shown me years past—that led more directly into the valley and the ferry itself. I started Wolf down it and murmured a prayer that it would carry me into the valley before Rolf and Chi'gandir reached it.

The instant I saw Weylan's log cabin I knew I'd lost the race. The sun still flew high in the sky, but I couldn't see Weylan anywhere. The ferry floated at the dock in front of the cabin and two horses trotted wide-eyed and spooked back behind the cabin itself.

Wolf and I raced to the cabin, but the horse shied as he got close. I jumped from the saddle, tugged my *tsincaat* from the saddle sheath, and let the horse run off. I knew only two things scared Wolf: magick and snakes. Chi'gandir was enough magic to scare anyone, and no snake was going to worry me while Rolf lurked in the vicinity. I let Wolf run off so Chi'gandir had no chance of getting hair or blood of mine. Without some piece of me to focus his spells, his magicks would be unable to affect me.

I held my *tsincaat* before me and crept cautiously to the cabin's southern wall. A faded green curtain prevented me from looking through the window, but it did little to muffle the rhythmic squeak of Weylan's rocking chair. I heard nothing else, and hoped, for a moment, that my worst fears would not be realized.

I relaxed only slightly, crossed to the cabin's porch, and pulled myself up over the railing. I lowered myself to the porch gently, so the wooden planks would not creak and betray me. I tested the door and it moved beneath gentle pressure. Shifting my *tsincaat* to my left hand and ready for almost anything, I pushed the door open.

Framed in the doorway, I stopped and could not breathe. Ten feet into the room, rocking in and out of my shadow in his favorite chair, sat Weylan.

Bright blue eyes stared at me from a handsome face, looking like matched sapphires set evenly in his head by a master jeweler. His narrow nose lent him a look of great intelligence. His long, thick, black hair hid the tops of two well-formed ears. Two even rows of white teeth flashed at me in a fleeting smile, and his strong jaw gave him a physical strength of character denied him before by his deformities.

Chi'gandir's black arts made Weylan's face perfect. Perfect, except for the tears rolling down the ferryman's cheeks.

His noble head topped an atrophied, twisted body. He'd been shrunken to proportions smaller than those of a child. The sorcerer had warped and bowed Weylan's bones like rain-soaked wood, then had swollen and knotted his joints. His ash-gray flesh hung thick and flaccid in great folds over his body the same way a father's robe hangs on his young son.

He tried to raise his right hand toward me, but that task taxed his stringy muscles beyond their ability to respond. "Talion, Nolan, friend." His voice still came clear and strong. "Kill me."

I shook my head violently and stepped into darkened, dead room. "Chi'gandir, where is he?"

Weylan did not hear the full question. The mention of the sorcerer's name tightened his face and wrung more tears from his azure eyes. "When I saw him I begged him to make me as I was. She'll be here soon and I just wanted her to see me as I was, just once." His lips quivered and he swallowed to choke back more tears. His hands tried to rise and wipe his face but they only reached his stomach before they gave up and limply flopped to his sides. "Kill me or I'll drag myself to the river and drown myself before she can see me like this."

"No!" Anger rose to my face and spat words from my mouth. "You fool, you know a sorcerer's magick only lasts as long as he lives. Where is Chi'gandir?"

Weylan's gaze flickered beyond my shoulder and a warning rose to his lips, but I'd already seen the shadow on the floor. I spilled his chair to the right with a kick as I drove forward and twisted to the left. The rough floorboards creaked beneath me when I landed—and exploded where Rolf's ax tore into the floor. Without even turning to look at him, I rolled to my feet, spun, and leaped through a draped window onto the porch.

Rolf ra Karesia turned from the doorway, ax clutched lovingly to his breast, and once again the depth of Chi'gandir's evil stunned me. Scarlet serpentskin covered the bandit and sunlight burnished gold highlights onto his scales. A forked tongue flickered in and out of the wide, lipless mouth in his

muzzled, serpentine face. His narrow, slitted nostrils ran per-
pendicular to the sharp, black-lozenge pupils in his amber
eyes. The changes melted his ears into his head, left holes
where they should have been, and welded his legs together to
form an undulating viper's body.

Rolf hissed inarticulately and writhed forward. I backed
up and vaulted the porch railing seconds before his ax splintered the wood. I retreated several more steps; then, as he
pursued, I stopped.

Rolf rippled off the porch and his torso plunged toward
the earth. His upper body teetered off balance before enough
of his lower half could reach the ground and right him again.
I rushed in, parried a weak ax blow with my *tsincaat*, and
snap-kicked the tottering monster in the head. The blow
smashed him back against the cabin, but he whipped his tail
around and almost swept my feet out from under me. I
jumped above his tail and then cartwheeled to the right out of
his range, but abandoned my *tsincaat* behind in the dust.

Rolf flicked his tail and swept the blade from his path. He
laughed, though it sounded more to me like the choking
cough of a dying coal miner than any honest sound of mirth.
He came for me slowly and, even in his bestial form, allowed
himself to relish the idea of being the first man in a decade to
kill a Justice.

I smiled at him and concentrated. I summoned my *tsincaat*, and it materialized in my grasp. I laughed when I felt it's
heavy hilt against the cold dead flesh of the tattoo on my right
palm. I thought about drawing my *ryqril* from the sheath
at the small of my back, but the daggerlike blade would
require me to get closer to Rolf than I really wanted if I meant
to use it.

Cloudy membranes nictitated up over Rolf's eyes, then
flicked back down. He surged forward and rained ax blows
down on me. I dodged the first two attacks, ducked the third,
and closed when he raised the ax over his head for the fourth.
I lunged and hit him over the heart, but the *tsincaat* skittered
wide along his scales and did not hurt him.

Seriously unbalanced, I looked up in horror. Rolf towered
over me, shifted his grip, and brought the ax haft down on
my head. I twisted, but caught enough of a glancing blow on
my left temple to stun me. Dazed, I staggered back and fell

flat. Stars exploded and cavorted before my eyes while Rolf, all red and gold like a sunset, tossed his ax aside and huddled over me.

Rolf wrapped his huge hands around either side of my rib cage, squeezed pain through my chest, and tossed me into the air. Like a parent playing with a child, Rolf caught me around my waist with a bear hug that trapped my left arm to my side. My *tsincaat* slipped from my other hand and the pain prevented me from concentrating enough to summon it again. Rolf shook me twice and then, confident I could not wriggle free, tightened his arms.

I kicked weakly against his stomach and tried to escape. My left hand remained firmly trapped in his right armpit, yet could exert no pressure on nerve centers deeply shielded by scale and muscle. I screwed my eyes shut against the pain and shuddered when Rolf's tongue played against my sweaty throat.

His fists ground my *ryqril* into my spine, reminding me how close it lay and frustrating me with its inaccessibility. I wrenched my head forward to smash it down into his face, but he held me too high up. My right fist beat on his shoulders with no effect. No other options lay open to me. Rolf himself gave me no choice.

I stared down at my palm, then shook my head to clear my mind. I looked down into his eyes, beyond the madness and anger, and tried to see what sort of man he had been. I pushed my pain away and smothered the regrets lingering from how I dealt with Fortune.

I pressed my open palm to his forehead. His flesh felt slick and fluidly warm, as if living copper or gold. I felt his brow ripple beneath my touch as the part of him that was a man tried to understand why this hand should be so cold, and why the animal in him instinctively dreaded my caress.

I breathed in and called his life to me.

Brief scenes, like pictures illuminating the manuscript of his life, flashed before my mind's eye. I felt his sense of triumph evaporate and I lived through one of his rages. I saw the world through his eyes and understood how he misinterpreted innocent acts and gestures as threats. I shared his pain and deep fear of the world.

For a heartbeat, when his life had been stripped of the evil and anger, he returned to the innocence of youth, yet retained his adult comprehension of the world. He read his own history and understood the suffering he caused. He knew why I had to take his life, and he knew he had to die. His soul fled into the skull tattoo on my palm.

I peeled my hand back from his forehead and chose to leave a black death's-head mark there. His body slackened, collapsed, and freed me of the physical pain. Life seared back into my limbs and distracted me enough that, for several seconds, I failed to notice that I'd not fallen with him to the ground. When I did notice, and looked around for the author of this strangeness, Chi'gandir contracted the spell enfolding me and held me tighter than Rolf ever had.

He rotated me through the air so I could stare at him. He strode through the cabin doorway holding Weylan by the back of his tunic. Chi'gandir settled him on the porch edge as a child might arrange a doll. Then he turned to me and gestured with my *tsincaat*, which he held in his left hand. "I always assumed, given the stories, that Justices were linked to their swords, but I never imagined such a strong link."

I nodded gently. "Give yourself up now, Chi'gandir. Kill me and other Talions will never let you rest."

Chi'gandir wheezed a nasal giggle. "Bravado hardly becomes you, Talion. It is like the ferryman's body, inappropriate and useless." Again he giggled and stroked the blade of my *tsincaat*. "Rolf's transformation took hair and blood. I wonder what I can do with you and this sword."

The tingle that stole over my body when Chi'gandir gestured at my *tsincaat* shocked away my reply to him. I felt my toes merge and lose their individuality. It started as the same uncomfortable feeling when there is something caught between my toes. It spread up through my feet as they began to flow one into the other, becoming a fertile breeding ground for fear and frustration.

I knew I had to fight him and I knew of only one way to do that. I immediately slowed my breathing, closed my eyes, and willed myself into a self-hypnotic trance. Normally Talions use the trance to monitor the extent and severity of wounds suffered, and can even limit blood flow with it, but in this case, I needed to do more with the control it gave me.

I looked within myself and cringed at the chaotic ruin

caused by his spell. Chi'gandir's magick presented a more urgent threat than the slight damage Rolf had done, so I forced my mind past the bruises and sore muscles down toward my legs. I consciously reinforced my mental self-image, down to five toes on each foot. I used the force of my will as a chisel, carefully carving away at the changes his spell had made. More easily than I expected, I broke his power and blunted his spell.

Chi'gandir withdrew and I opened my eyes. The sorcerer looked tired, and I realized I could defeat him. Rolf's transformation must have drained a great amount of energy from Chi'gandir, not to mention the job he'd done on Weylan. He had to be close to exhaustion, because I should not really have been able to block his attack on me. If I provoked him enough, he might overtax himself and his spells would fade.

Chi'gandir's left eyebrow rose, lengthening the diamond tattoo around that eye, and he slid my *tsincaat* home in his belt. "So Talions fight magick with magick?"

I snarled at him. "We're taught to deal with all sorts of minor nuisances."

The sorcerer angrily dropped a hand to my *tsincaat*. "Then deal with the river."

I shot toward the river like a stone flung from a catapult and, landing with a splash, I sank just as fast. The spellforce, though it had weakened perceptibly, still held me paralyzed while the water chilled and suffocated me. Air bubbles trapped in my ears echoed my ever-increasing heartbeat. Water washed up my nose and tickled a sneeze of precious air from my lungs. Silt stung my eyes and ground beneath my teeth. I tightened my cheeks and expelled the foul, gritty water from my mouth.

I closed my eyes, stopped fighting the river, and forced myself to ignore the growing fire in my lungs. I had to concentrate to give Chi'gandir something other than holding me down here to think about.

I summoned my *tsincaat*.

My fist locked over Chi'gandir's half-frozen hand and crushed it to the *tsincaat*'s hilt even before I realized he'd broken off his spell to work another. Chi'gandir's eyes grew wide as terror gripped him. Bubbles poured from his mouth as he tried to speak a spell. The silver-white spheres raced to the surface like sacrificial smoke rising to the heavens. The sorcerer's right hand gestured frantically, but his soaked robe just thrashed and tangled around it in a lethargic mockery of his urgency.

I drew my *ryqril* and drove it into his chest. Blood tinted the bubbles that escaped from the wound. Even though my inflamed lungs urged me to abandon him and swim for the surface, I stabbed him twice more and let him go only when confident I'd killed him.

I tugged the *tsincaat* from his belt, resheathed my blades, and struck for the surface. My lungs blazed with an ache for fresh air, forcing me to fight the reflex to suck just anything into my lungs. Part of me knew the water would quench the fire in my chest, and another welcomed any surcease from that agony. I tried to ignore all of that and worked at reaching the surface as quickly as possible.

Chi'gandir's scarlet bubbles lazily drifted past me. The surface looked so far away. Everything darkened, including the shafts of sunlight striking down into the brown water. Odd motes of light and color shimmered before me, but I could not touch them. I stretched for the surface, up there, miles beyond my outstretched fingers, and tried to grab it. My hands closed on nothing and I knew I had lost.

I took my last look at the surface. My right hand still clawed for it. The wavering, dimming sunlight bleached my flesh and let me see it as those who fished me from the river would see it three or four days hence.

Water choked my throat as my vision faded. Even as I swallowed the river and it swallowed me, a jet of bubbles lanced down from the dry world and a foolish spark of hope blossomed in a barren, dying mind.

I awoke with a start and immediately started to cough. I rolled myself to the left with a strong push off the log wall with my right hand, and vomited into the basin set on the floor at the bunk's edge. I retched twice more and managed, by begging it weakly, to convince my body nothing more could come up from my empty stomach. Exhausted, I rolled back, closed my eyes, and lay there trying to imagine how I'd escaped the river.

I felt a cool cloth on my forehead. "Marana?" I opened my

eyes and saw a woman I did not recognize sitting on the edge of my bunk.

She smiled. She was pretty. Like Marana, her hair was black, though this woman wore it short. Her dark eyes sparkled and her smile drained my anxiety. "I am Elverda." She took the cloth from my forehead and exchanged it for another in the bowl on her lap. "I am now Weylan's wife, and I understand I have you to thank for that."

I closed my eyes. I could not figure out how I was responsible for something that happened while I was a novice in Talianna. It did not make much sense, but nothing else did either at the moment. I opened my eyes again and now both she and Weylan swam into focus.

I stared at Weylan, shook my head, and stared even harder. His body had returned to normal. Once again it was tall and strong. The hands that had been unable to wipe tears from his face now rested on Elverda's shoulder and squeezed them with loving gentleness. That did not surprise me.

What did astonish me was that his face looked as I had last seen it, but now it was truly perfect because no tears rolled from his eyes. Weylan smiled down at me with an exquisite set of teeth and a strong jaw.

Confused, I frowned at him. "I, Weylan, I don't understand."

Weylan sat behind Elverda and looked at me over her left shoulder. "Chi'gandir—a name I did not know until you got here, Nolan—led the bandits who attacked ten years ago. He use his sorcery to disfigure me at that time. His people had worked me over, but I never got a look at myself until after he had done his work. My understanding of magick was and still is minimal, so I thought I was forever to be disfigured. When he returned and laughingly told the other man what he had done to me, I finally understood. He bragged that he could undo it. I begged him to have pity and reverse the magick he had worked so long ago." He stopped and closed his eyes for a moment. "You remember what he did."

I nodded.

"So when you killed him I was restored. I ran to the river and saw bubbles. I dove in and found you. You'd taken in a lungful of water, but after a difficult night you started to recover. This morning Elverda's caravan arrived and we will now live together as man and wife."

I smiled and laid my right hand on top of their joined hands. I squeezed them and then let my hand drop. I drifted off to sleep before it slid back to my side, but the happiness Weylan felt was not lost on me. It made me feel good and eased me into a good dream.

I dreamed of Talianna.

Chapter Two

NOLAN: TRIAL

I unrolled the yellowed map Orjan had given me in Tashar and squinted at the huge dolmen halfway up through the pass. Three stones supported a large, flat triangular slab. I checked the map and smiled. The dolmen was the last landmark on my map. Just up the slope, through the last narrow pass in the Tal Mountains, was Talianna. I'd made it.

I rolled the map back up and jammed it over my shoulder into my pack. I picked up my walking stick and marched forward over the uneven, rocky ground. I was so close to my goal I could feel it just beyond the horizon. The pass would open up and there it would be, Talianna, the home of the people who brought justice to the world.

A smile crept onto my face. I was eager to be done with my journey. A thousand miles and five months before, I'd left my family's home in Sinjaria and set out. At first it seemed a foolish mission. I was not even twelve summers old when I started, and the journey began without any real planning. I knew Talianna lay west and north, so I headed into the Darkesh and just kept walking.

Hiking that last mile I knew all the other miles had seemed long and lonely and dangerous. Even so, try as I might, I couldn't bring to mind the particulars of any one mile when I thought the journey would be ended prematurely. The times I came across signs of outlaw bands, as in the forests of Cela, I hid. When I found a farm or village, I traded work for space near the fire and as much food as I could get. And when I got sick I was lucky enough to meet someone like Orjan who took care of me.

The last hundred yards of the pass rose very steeply and forced me to crawl forward on my hands and feet. I carefully picked my hand- and footholds because I did not want to injure myself so close to the goal I'd worked so hard to reach. I had to make it in good health or the entire journey would be wasted.

Halfway up the slope it occurred to me that the Nolan who started the journey would never have even attempted a climb like this, nor would he have been able to complete it. I'd not filled out during the trek—there was not enough food along the way to let me do that—but I'd grown harder. I'd worked my childhood chubbiness off and I'd grown an inch or two. If I continued at that rate I'd surpass my twin older brothers and perhaps even my father.

I reached the top of the hill before I could catch myself up in thinking about my family. I pulled myself onto the hilltop and collapsed. My chest heaved and labored hard to suck in enough of the thin mountain air to sate my body. A bit dizzy, I lay back and, drunk with success, just started to laugh. Finally I regained enough strength to roll over onto my hands and knees. I levered myself up and the Tal Valley unfolded below me.

I'd never seen anything so green before. Deep, dark living green covered the valley floor. From the patchwork of cultivated fields in the south and west to the forest at the base of the mountains upon which I stood, this valley was the verdant treasure my father had promised our farm would one day become.

The natural wonders of the valley paled to insignificance, though, when compared to Talianna itself. Star within a pentagon within another pentagon, Talianna rose up, a gleaming white stone city full of strength and power. Massive white marble blocks made up the walls and buildings. The outer siege wall stood twenty feet tall, while the inner pentagon soared up to half again that height.

The central star was the most magnificent building I'd ever seen. The walls of each point sloped in and up to form a pyramid at the star's core. The pyramid itself had a flat top and a flagpole set in the center of it. A plain black flag writhed and snapped in the breeze because here, in the Tal province, it needed no ensign.

I stood there and shivered. I took a deep breath and let it out slowly through my nose. I had arrived: I'd reached my destination. I'd finished my journey and the time came for me to decide my destiny.

I opened a pouch on my belt and fished around in the bottom of it for a small, leather-wrapped packet. I untied the lacing and took out a single gold Imperial. It had been my family's treasure and was only to be used in an emergency, but even it had not been enough to save them.

It was an old coin, so old I could not read the inscription. Bright and clean as the day the mint struck it despite its antiquity, it bore no signs of use or wear. The words on the coin were old and although I knew how to read, I could not make out what they meant. Still I did recognize the face on the coin. It was Emperor Clekan, the first emperor, Clekan the Just.

I weighed the coin in my hand. I relished its coolness, and reveled in the fact that it no longer seemed heavy. I swallowed once and flipped the coin high into the air. It spun and spun, flashing spears of sunlight off in all directions. As it fell to earth again I caught it in my open right palm. Clekan's profile glowed in the sunlight.

I smiled. "It's decided. I'm yours."

A shadow blotted out the sun. I twisted to my right and caught a flash of white and brown descending through the blue sky. A high scream deafened me and something hit me hard in the back. I felt the shoulder straps on my back pull, twist, and snap as I smashed into the ground.

I landed hard on my chest and had the wind knocked from my lungs. I bounced once and flipped onto my back. I lay there, arms and legs splayed out, while I tried to breathe and scream. I tried to swallow enough air to stem the suffocating feeling in my chest, but my body would not respond. In addition to my breathlessness, my back complained of the impact and the jagged chunk of rock beneath me.

I felt someone grab my shoulders and pull me off the rock. "Don't try to move. Is anything broken?" The voice was young, about my age, and as nervous and scared as I felt.

I shook my head and opened my eyes. A sandy-haired, brown-eyed boy wearing a brown jerkin with a white hawk in flight stenciled on the left breast stood over me. With my response to his question he calmed almost instantly and that calmed me.

"I'm an Elite novice." He reached down and took hold of my belt. He lifted up, arched my back gently, and forced air into my lungs. I didn't breathe much in, but it cooled the burning in my chest nonetheless. He lowered me, then lifted again.

The numbness centered in my chest faded. I nodded at him and tapped his arm twice. He let me down and crouched beside me. "Can you feel your legs and toes?"

I took in a deep breath and exhaled slowly. I squeezed my eyes shut against the pain of sore ribs. I drew my knees up and flexed my toes. "Yes, I can."

The Talion novice rocked back on his heels and smiled. "I'm sorry for what happened. I passed my trial today and took Valiant up for a flight. He saw something and stooped. It wasn't until the last second I saw you. No one's supposed to be up in these mountains during Festival."

I tucked my legs under me and came up into a sitting position. The sharpness of pain in my back drained away, but it still felt pretty sore. That's when I saw Valiant for the first time—the blur of color I saw before he hit me did not count—and I paled.

The Elite caught my reaction and smiled. "Don't be afraid of him. He's not even full grown yet."

Valiant was an Imperial Hawk. Its belly was white and

dappled with dark brown, while the wings and back were light brown. It stood, hobbled and hooded, about twenty feet away from me and shredded my pack. From talons to the top of its head it stood about six feet high, and when full grown would be able to take cattle the way a kestrel takes varmints.

My mouth went dry. "The, ah, that's what hit me?"

The Elite nodded. He hefted my coin and flashed it in the sunlight. "I think he saw the flash and went for it. You shouldn't be up here. How did you get past the patrols keeping Festival people out of this area?" He handed me the coin and I returned it to my pouch.

"I came in from the north. I'm coming to be a Talion. My name's Nolan, Nolan ra Sinjaria."

The Talion's eyes narrowed, then he stood. "I'm Erlan ra Leth, though I've been in Talianna since just after I was born. Come on." He reached down and helped me to my feet. "You've got to sign in by the end of today or you can't try to join during this Festival."

I looked down at the valley below. "I can't climb down there by the end of the day."

Erlan smiled. "I know. I'll fly you down."

I don't know if Valiant just didn't like my weight on his back or he could smell the fear on me, but he made my first ride a rough one. My heart rode the whole way in my mouth and I was glad I'd not stopped to eat any lunch on the trail. I felt queasy as Valiant spread his wings, and I left my stomach back on the mountain when we dropped toward the valley below.

I held on tight to the saddle harness and hunched down to make myself as small and compact as possible. I heard Erlan curse the bird a couple of times, but he maintained control and got us safely off the mountain.

Erlan let Valiant glide down in a long spiral and tapped me on the shoulder. I looked at him and he pointed down. As I looked beyond Valiant's wing I saw the smile growing on Erlan's face. He knew exactly what I was seeing for the first time, and he shared my excitement and amazement.

Southwest of Talianna stood a grove of tents and pavilions. Brightly colored and clumped together like mushrooms, the largest pavilions flew flags and pennants from the different nations of the Shattered Empire. Ringing them were the smaller cloth homes of merchants and lesser dignitaries who came to enjoy the Festival.

I looked at Erlan. "The people look like ants," I yelled so he could hear me. "Everything is so small."

He smiled and nodded. "I'll land Valiant at the Mews and then we'll walk down and take care of you." He pointed first at a long, rectangular building northwest of the siege wall, then at a black pavilion between the festival tents and Talianna itself.

Erlan tapped Valiant on the head with a crop and we started down quickly. The wind whipped my hair back and forced tears from my eyes, but the exhilarating sensation of speed made the ride anything but uncomfortable. In that descent I abandoned my fear of the Hawk. How could I fear something that could let me fly?

Valiant spread his wings, splayed out the feathers, and beat them to slow us. We hovered at a dead stop bare feet above the ground, then dropped to a soft landing. Valiant cried triumphantly and Erlan scratched him on the neck before hooding the Hawk.

Erlan tossed the reins to another Elite novice and headed off toward the large black pavilion south and west of the Mews. He got a couple steps ahead of me and I hurried to catch up. He couldn't have been any older than I was, yet he walked with an ease and confidence I'd not seen in a youth before. It wasn't an arrogant swagger, like the kind one might expect from a bully who thinks he's the toughest person in the county. It was a head-held-high stride that was nonthreatening, yet was not timid or submissive.

Erlan pointed to a slightly rotund man wearing black pants and tunic. "Nolan, go over to that table and talk to that clerk." The clerk wore a tunic with the Talion Services division emblem—a hammer crossed by a quill—on his left breast. "I'll come back for you when you are done."

Erlan left me and walked over to two older Talions. He bowed respectfully and spoke with them. As directed, I walked over to the man Erlan had pointed out to me. "Excuse me?"

He looked up from his neatly kept table. His chins jounced just enough to destroy the stern nature of the stare he turned on me. "Yes, boy, what is it?" he demanded impatiently.

I fought to keep a tremble out of my voice. "I want to become a Talion."

He looked me over once hurriedly, then tilted his head back down. "Tell your parents you are too old."

I swallowed the lump in my throat. "They're dead."

He looked at me again and frowned. Was he looking for tears? His knitted brows clearly showed his frustration and annoyance with me. "Did relatives send you?"

I shook my head. I suppose it was a fair question. Any family that has a Talion in it is paid money for that person's service for as long as he remains a Talion. It was not uncommon for families to send an unwanted child to the Talions. "There is no one," I answered slowly. "I am the last of my family."

The clerk nodded and pulled a slip of paper from the stack at his left hand. He dipped his quill in the inkwell and gave me a smug smile. "You're from one of the Western Sea States, right?"

I smiled. He'd guessed correctly. "My name is Nolan."

He wrote on the tan sheet and handed it to me. "Bring that back tomorrow morning and the others will get you ready for your trial."

I rotated the paper around so I could read it. "This is wrong." I handed it back to him.

"What are you talking about?" He stared at me as if I was mad.

I pointed to the error. "It says Nolan ra Hamis. I am Nolan ra Sinjaria."

He laughed. His laughter rippled through his jowls and belly. Anger fired through me and I clamped my jaw shut. I knew what his next words would be and I wanted to jam a fist in his mouth so they'd never get out. "Sinjaria was conquered. As of this spring it is a duchy administered by King Tirrell of Hamis. You are Nolan ra Hamis."

"No!" I crumpled the paper and threw it at the table. It bounced up and hit him in his ample nose. "I wasn't conquered! I owe no allegiance to him or his puppet, Duke Vidor."

The clerk stood. Fury flushed color into his cheeks, and

the veins in his neck struggled to stand out. My eyes narrowed and I set myself to trade barbs or hit him if he hit me. Then, wordlessly, he eased back and looked down.

They surrounded me. Erlan stood at my right and the two other Talions he spoke to earlier positioned themselves at my left. The shorter one only came up to my throat. Although his seamed face and leathery skin conspired to make him look old, his jet black hair and lively brown eyes defeated their attempt. He wore brown leathers and had an Elite hawk ensign on his left breast just like Erlan.

The other man towered over me by a head, which made him very tall indeed. Whipcord lean like the shorter man, he had penetrating brown eyes and a shaven head. He had a very angular cast to his features, which would have made him look emotionless except for the smoldering fire in his eyes. He wore a black robe cinched loosely at his slender waist with a knotted cord. He had a white death's-head on the left breast of his robe—seeing it sent a shiver down my spine. He was a Justice!

The tall man spoke in a low, gentle, yet firm voice. "Is there a problem here?"

The clerk seated himself and shuffled his papers. "No, my Lord Hansur, there is no problem. The youth was confused concerning geography." The clerk reached for the crumpled ball on his desk and smoothed it out.

"I am not confused." I protested and pointed at the paper. "I am Nolan ra Sinjaria and he wrote 'ra Hamis.' "

Lord Hansur took the slip from the desk and read it. His fingers were incredibly long and well callused. He passed the parchment to the Elite beside him and stared down at the clerk. "The slip is incorrect. And it is also incomplete. Have you forgotten the information we need?"

The clerk paled and swallowed hard. "No, my lord."

Lord Hansur looked down at me. "You are Nolan ra Sinjaria?"

I nodded. "Yes."

"Family?"

"None, I am an orphan." As I answered Lord Hansur's questions the clerk copied my responses onto a new slip of parchment.

Lord Hansur paused for a second. "I am sorry for you. How many summers have you seen?"

I hesitated. "Twelve, but . . ."

The clerk would have written twelve but Lord Hansur flicked his left hand in that direction to stop him. "You do know your own age?"

I smiled nervously and glanced down at my feet for a heartbeat. "I was born very early in the fall, just at the end of the summer. I didn't see my first summer, but I didn't miss it by much either."

Again Lord Hansur paused. His eyes narrowed momentarily and he folded his arms so that his hands disappeared into the sleeves of his black woolen robe. "Understand this, Nolan, we use age to determine the difficulty of the trial for our novices. The trial will be less demanding for someone who is twelve than someone who is thirteen. You may try to become a Thirteen if you wish, but it is your choice."

I bit my lower lip and thought. Finally I shook my head. "I don't think competing as if I was only eleven would be fair."

Lord Hansur nodded and looked at the clerk. "Very well. List him as a prospective Thirteen."

I watched the clerk write that down and smiled. I wanted to be a Talion badly, but I wasn't going to cheat to become one.

"You have one last question to answer, Nolan," Lord Hansur said as the clerk finished. "What division do you want to enter?"

My heart thundered loudly in my ears and I felt fear tighten my throat. There were seven different divisions to pick from, but I ruled two of them out immediately. I couldn't be an Elite because I couldn't fly a Hawk and I knew no magick, so joining the Wizards was out of the question. My best chance would be as a Warrior or Lancer. I might be able to succeed as an Archer, and my literacy would put me a step above other candidates to become a member of the Services division. Still none of those divisions interested me.

I licked my dry lips. "I want to be a Justice."

The clerk contained himself for a second of stone cold silence, then burst out laughing. He rocked back on his stool, lost his balance, and toppled over onto the ground. He held his middle and continued to laugh.

Lord Hansur snapped a word at him that instantly strangled the laughter. The Justice said one short sentence in a language I'd never heard before, but the tone of his voice could have cut like a razor. The clerk righted his stool, bowed, and fled. Lord Hansur himself slipped behind the table and wrote the word *Justice* on the paper. He slid it over toward me. "Make your mark."

I took the quill and signed my name as neatly and evenly as I could. The lines wobbled a little because of my hand's nervous tremor, but other than that the signature was one to be proud of. I set the quill down.

Lord Hansur pressed his right palm against the parchment. When he lifted his hand I saw the death's-head tattoo on his palm, and an exact image of it etched on the bottom of the document. My mouth dropped open, and my teeth clicked when I snapped it shut again.

Lord Hansur politely ignored my shock. "This parchment is for you. Erlan will take you to Devon ra Yastan's tent. Devon will take care of you. He will give you food and a place to sleep tonight. Tomorrow morning someone will come to bring you to the Trial grounds."

The parchment fluttered like a captive bird in my trembling hands. I bowed to Lord Hansur and the Elite, then followed Erlan out of the tent.

"Well, Nolan, you sure went out of your way to impress Lord Hansur." Erlan smiled broadly.

I frowned. "What do you mean?"

"The age stuff and the orphan story." Erlan laughed and shook his head.

I grabbed the Elite novice by the shoulder and spun him around to face me. "That was all true. My family is dead, all of them."

His smile faded, then he jerked his shoulder from my grasp and squinted at me. "If that's so, how did you get here?"

I shrugged. "I walked."

My reply surprised him. "From Sinjaria? Alone?"

I nodded solemnly. "It took five months. I was sick in Tashar."

Erlan frowned. "You couldn't make it all that way by yourself."

I shrugged again. "You saw me on the mountains. Did you see anyone there with me?"

"No, no I didn't." Erlan's smile returned. "Sorry. It's just that during Festival it seems like everyone who wants to become a Talion has a reason or a story they try to use to impress the lord of the division they want to enter."

I stopped and fixed him with a terrified stare. "Do you mean Lord Hansur is one of the Justice lords?"

Erlan caught my disbelief and pounced on it like a cat on a mouse. "One of? He's the *only* Justice lord. If you succeed he'll be the man you report to." I must have looked sick or desperate because he added, "And the other man was Isas ra Amasia, Lord of the Elites. And both of them were already impressed with your ability to dodge a stooping Hawk!"

I said nothing during the rest of our walk to Devon's pavilion. A swarthy, plump Yastani, Devon greeted me with a booming laugh that made me, as nervous as I was, feel at home. He immediately turned me over to his servants, who fed me, heated water for a bath, and prepared me a rug, blanket, and pillow so I could sleep. The food was great, and reminded me of the meals I shared with one farm family I'd stayed with in Yastan. My travel caught up with me in the bath and, once I'd dried myself, I pulled the blanket over me and dropped off to sleep.

My exhaustion helped me. I slept well and didn't have the nightmare that had chased me halfway across the continent.

Devon woke me before dawn. He shook my shoulder gently. I sat up and rubbed the sleepsand from my eyes. Though I was still slightly sore and stiff, the night's rest had helped my back immeasurably.

"Nolan, get dressed. We've got some stew for you to eat before they come for you."

I pulled my clothes on quickly and sat at the table in the center of his pavillion. Devon sat opposite me and ate an apple. Before I ate anything myself, I smiled at him. "I want to thank you very much for letting me stay here. I have some money and I'll pay you for the food and space."

Devon shook his head, waved me to my food, and laughed. "No, don't think of it, lad. You are here because Hansur sent you. Besides, having Nolan ra Sinjaria as my guest has been an honor. Very few heroes try to become Talions."

A spoonful of steaming stew stopped midway between the bowl and my mouth. "Hero? I'm afraid I don't understand."

Devon laughed again. "No, I don't expect you do. Stories about you traveled swiftly last night. The clerk was from Hamis and your show of patriotism was much appreciated by the Rimahasti and Janian lords here. Furthermore it was learned and circulated that you'd traveled all by yourself almost four hundred leagues to get here."

I snorted. "More like three hundred."

Devon shrugged. "Split the difference, truth be told, but it's still quite a journey for a young man like you. And to top it all off, after all that traveling, you still have the strength and speed to avoid a stooping Hawk!" Devon's face assumed an expression of exaggerated awe. He held it until I burst out laughing, then his façade cracked and he chuckled.

I tried to look heroic, and willfully failed. "If I don't become a Talion, with that sort of story being told about me, I ought to be able to join any of the royal houses as a general or something, shouldn't I?"

"I'd settle for nothing less than Warlord, were I in your shoes." Devon calmed himself. "If you don't make it—though I have every confidence in you—come to me first."

I finished shoveling stew into my mouth as a manservant appeared and spoke with Devon.

"Wipe your mouth, Nolan. Lord Hansur has sent someone for you."

I'd hoped Erlan would be my escort, but he was not. He'd been replaced by a novice Justice. He was my height and had hair so blond it was almost white. His eyes were a deep, rich blue. He walked a bit more arrogantly than Erlan had and led me back to the large black pavilion.

Everything had been cleared from the interior and a high dais had been raised in the center of the room. Seven banners, one for each Talion division, stood around the tent's outer perimeter, and clerks sat behind tables next to each of them. I didn't see the Hamisian clerk from the day before.

My guide led me to a spot near the death's-head banner.

"Wait here until Lord Hansur is finished speaking. Then go to the banner and I will meet you there."

I nodded and he left.

The tent filled up with people over the next quarter hour. Talion novices led people into the tent and steered them toward the banner of the division the person wanted to join. Everyone looked tired and yawns passed through the crowd in waves, but I could feel the excitement we all shared. The air almost crackled with nervous energy.

The general undercurrent of muttering faded when Lord Hansur walked onto the dais. He stood tall and a black cloak swathed his slender body in shadow. He threw it back over his left shoulder and held his hand up. The black leather jerkin he wore gleamed a dull red in the blossoming dawn light, and the cold, foreboding skull ensign on his left breast blazed brightly like the rising sun. Mirthlessly it grinned and stared at all of us fools who dared presume we could become Talions.

"These are your final instructions before you undergo your trial. Please understand that you may withdraw from the trial up to the point when the trial begins. If you fail your trial you may never again attempt to join the Talions." Lord Hansur's voice touched all of us deep inside and started a panicked flutter in my chest. Part of me wanted to run and flee along the escape path he offered, but I forcefully resisted that urge. I swallowed and stood my ground while others, from strong mercenaries to hunched clerks, bowed and left the tent.

Lord Hansur waited for those recruits to leave before he continued. "There are seven banners, one for each of the Talion divisions. When I give you leave you will present the sheet you were given to the Talion at the appropriate station. You will be told when your trial will be held. You are expected to arrive here a quarter of an hour before your trial and then you will be taken to the place where your trial will begin."

The Justice lord stopped again to give everyone a chance to look around and find the banner they wanted. Some people edged toward the banners. The rest of us waited.

The Justice nodded easily as if calming a child's fear of darkness. "All of you are nervous. This is understandable, so I will explain some of what you may face today or tomorrow.

You will be tested for skills appropriate to the branch you want to enter. The trials, though difficult, seldom result in injury and only very rarely in the death of a recruit. The trial's purpose is merely to determine if you know enough and can work well enough to become a Talion. You can only do your best—and failure, in that case, is no disgrace at all."

My stomach tightened with his last words, and sweat broke out on my upper lip. For me there was no way to accept failure. A soldier who was refused by the Warriors could always find work, and a scribe would always locate a fat merchant who could neither read nor write. And even with Devon's offer to me if I was rejected, I couldn't help but feel that I'd be just a child with no direction or purpose in life. Of course I didn't think of it in those terms at that time. What I saw before me, in that tent as Lord Hansur's words kindled a torch of self-doubt, was a yawning void that threatened to swallow me the way it had my family. For me failure was worse than death, because I'd live and remember I had failed.

Lord Hansur's last words brought me back and hinted at what I'd have to do to succeed. "I will not wish you good luck, because a Talion does not depend upon luck. Have courage and trust yourself." He bowed to us, and we returned the gesture, then flew to our banners.

I reached the Justice banner before anyone else. The white skull on it was as big as my whole chest. I averted my gaze from its eyeless sockets and handed my parchment to the Services clerk seated at the desk. He looked at it, consulted a list, and wrote some numbers across the bottom. "Nolan ra Ha . . . Sinjaria?"

I nodded.

"Someone will come for you presently." He handed me back the parchment and smiled. "No need, from what I hear, for him to wish you luck or courage."

I blushed and looked down at my feet. "I'll take either if I can get them."

The clerk shook his head and turned to watch the rest of the tent. "You are a step up on all the others here. You're too young to have the desperation of the older ones." He pointed to some bent and white-haired people lined up to become Services Talions. "They're afraid of dying. They work hard all their lives and have nothing for when they can't work. For them the Talions are their last hope, and they live for the chance to be accepted by us. Those that fail will probably die before they ever return home again."

"And the others, the soldiers," he continued, "you would think they were smart enough to know they don't belong here. Some have been trained by Talions stationed in other countries and they think they are as good as the Lancer or Warrior who tried to teach them enough so they won't die the first time they face an enemy. If they were that good they would already have rank or would lead a band of mercenaries. They're here because their pride tells them they have the skills to be a Talion." He laughed mirthlessly. "Pride lies."

My snowy-maned guide from earlier returned for the second half of the clerk's discourse about the recruits. He snapped a harsh comment at the man. Though the words were foreign to me, the tone conveyed utter contempt for the clerk's opinion. The clerk whirled around with his fists knotted; then the knots withered and he replied in apologetic tones. My guide made another comment and the clerk left.

The novice Justice held the skull banner aside and motioned me through it. I walked ahead for a step or two then waited for him to catch up. "Who will deal with the others who want to be Justices?"

He shook his head and then, with his left hand, brushed back the white bangs draped over his eye. "There *are* no others, Nolan ra Sinjaria. You are the *only* Justice recruit."

He led me in silence to a smaller black tent with a white skull on the flap. The Justice held the flap for me and I entered. It took a moment or two for my eyes to adjust to the darkness. As the room lightened I saw a campaign chair, a chest, and some clothing laid out on the chest. Another Justice, a woman, sat in the chair. She waved her right hand, giving me a fleeting glimpse of the skull on its palm, and dismissed my guide.

I gave her my parchment. She read it quickly, then looked up at me. "These are your instructions. Remove your clothing and put on this loincloth and these sandals. They are the only clothing you will have in the trial. Once you have changed you will leave this tent and follow the course laid out and blazed with blue pennants. You must overcome the various obstacles in your path and collect these red strips of cloth. Gather as many as you can. You will be stopped at the end of your test and an accounting will be demanded. Do you understand these instructions?"

I looked at the strip of cloth she held and nodded. It was as long as my forearm and two fingers wide. Unless it was buried or otherwise hidden, I decided I could find something that bright shade of red fairly easily.

She stood, stepped through the tent flap, and left me alone in the tent. I quickly peeled my clothes off and tied the white loincloth on. It hung down to my knees in both the front and back. The soft, brown leather sandals laced all the way up to my knees. I tied them on tightly and wriggled my toes. Despite the chilly air that early in the morning, I felt comfortable. I mumbled a quick prayer to Shudath and walked through the rear flap of the tent.

Sunlight flooded into my eyes and a trumpet blast rang in my ears. I jumped from surprise and began running down the trail that stretched across a golden meadow ahead of me. It led down a small hill and then up to the woods that covered the northern side of the Tal Valley. I passed through the downhill quickly, still running with the nervous burst of energy the trumpet blast triggered, but settled into a more comfortable pace for the uphill. If this was to be any sort of a real test I knew I'd be running for a long time.

I realized that something about the trumpet call sounded familiar. Once my initial panic wore off, I sifted my memories and tried to recall where I'd heard that sequence of notes before. I concentrated and, almost instantly, it came to me. In Tashar, when I finally healed up enough to leave, the innkeeper, Orjan, played those very same notes as I walked away from his inn. He'd entertained me with war stories during my recovery and I knew he'd been a trumpeteer in the Tashari army. He told me how they communicated words and orders through different tunes, and those notes made up my name.

I sped up. They expected me ahead. That prospect both scared me and inspired me. I didn't know what I'd face in the trial, but I resolved to do more than my best.

Dry, dusty grassland gave way to the misty, dark tunnels of a woodland trail. Rust-colored needles from the evergreens paved the path and light green ferns lined it. The forest smelled of pine and rich, loamy earth. Sunlight tried to pierce the thick canopy of leaves, and succeeded in a few scattered places, but still failed to warm the forest's silent heart.

I ran along the path and saw nothing until a thin coating of sweat covered my body and pasted my black locks to my forehead. A wall of logs lay across and blocked my path. They had been roughly stripped of bark but were not finished and bristled with splinters. The wall stood almost as tall as me and the pair of logs lying off to the right of it suggested the height varied with that of the recruit.

I ran faster and reached for the top of the wall. My hands grabbed the top log and I vaulted myself up and over with my left hip just barely brushing the top. I was about to release and hit the ground running when I looked down.

A ten-foot-deep pit yawned open below me, ready to swallow me whole.

My left hand tightened and clawed into the top log. My left shoulder ground and popped as my body swung down and slammed into the wall. The collision jarred my teeth, exploded sparks in front of my eyes, and crunched the ribs on my left side. I hung there for a second, my body twisting like a corpse on a gibbet, and something stabbed into my left arm.

I reached back and up with my right hand and got a good enough handhold to take the pressure off my left arm. Pain shot up and down the injured arm. A long sliver of wood, as thick as an arrow, stabbed into the flesh of my upper left arm, just below the armpit, and a thin stream of blood trickled along and down my flank. I clutched the wound to my chest, felt below with my feet for any sort of a foothold, and found one with my right foot. I wedged my foot in the wall, then kicked out and jumped beyond the pit's right lip.

Once on solid ground I dropped to my knees and took a better look at my left arm. The wood had not penetrated very deep, so I gritted my teeth against the anticipated sting and pulled the splinter free. I then tore a strip from my loincloth and bound my arm up. I moved my arm around in a circle slowly, testing it easily, and discovered, although it ached and probably could not take more of the same punishment, I'd not suffered a serious injury.

As an afterthought I looked around for one of the red

strips of cloth I had to collect. Off to the left I spotted a small wooden box nailed on a tree. Inside it I could see a flag but, before I got back to my feet and approached it, a door snapped down over its front and locked the flag away. I'd lost my first flag!

I quickly examined the hardwood box and discovered a simple sand timer counterbalanced by some small weights. As the sand drained out of a small pail, the weights pulled the box lid down. The weights probably varied according to the age or expected speed of the recruit. The trumpet blast at the start, I guessed, told Talions to start the sand draining.

I started running again, faster than before, so I could regain some of the time I'd lost. That I'd missed my first flag bothered me because it was possible that I'd failed the whole trial at the first obstacle. I felt that wouldn't be fair, but I had no guarantee the trial was meant to be fair. I could only hope one mistake would be forgiven.

I ran around a hill and down into a narrow ravine. The trail ended at a stretch of icy mountain stream. It started again about twenty feet upstream and the blue pennants lined the stream shores. Up where the trail began again I saw one of the flag boxes with its door half shut.

I suppressed a smile. In Sinjaria I'd lived near the Darkesh, so mountain streams held no novelty or fear for me. My brothers and I used to relax and swim in them whenever Father didn't need us, and we were all good swimmers. Without hesitation I dove into the water and stroked toward my goal.

The cold water numbed the pain in my shoulder and I cut through it like a warship running before the wind. Drenched but exhilarated, I climbed from the stream and took my flag. I hooked it through the belt of my loincloth and started running again.

Had I not injured my shoulder, the next test would have gotten me. A half mile beyond the river, along a path that went up and down hills lying like a wrinkled blanket on the forest floor, I came to a long, deep pit blocking my way. A series of ropes hung from a log suspended above the pit by stripped-pole tripods at each end. The easy, and obvious, path across it was to swing from rope to rope, but my injury made that path impossible for me to even consider.

I shinned up one of the poles on my side and worked my way across the log holding the ropes. Midway I saw that the hook holding one of the ropes in place would shear off and drop into the pit if someone swung onto that rope. Suddenly the hole in my arm seemed not so much of a burden, because it saved me from this trap.

I located the box, gathered my second flag, and smiled, because the door on this box was not as close to shut as the door had been on the last one. I'd regained some time and that gave me a little heart. I filled my lungs with the fresh, living mountain air, fastened the flag to my belt, and resumed my run.

I almost missed the next flag. I guess it was meant as a test of observation. I'd been running for over half a league, a feat that would have been well beyond me had not my journey to Talianna trained me for it, and I felt very tired. Sweat covered me and some of it seared into my wound. It stung fiercely, as though some portion of the sliver was still in there. I knew I had to keep up my pace, to beat the timers, but I had to stop to retie the bandage and snatch at a moment's rest.

A lightning bolt of pain forked through my arm as I tightened the blood-soaked cloth. I took one end of it in my mouth and tasted the salty-sweet blood as I knotted it off. I caught my breath and then, as I looked forward again, I caught a flash of red from the corner of my eye. Instantly I left the trail.

There, at eye level but half hidden behind the thick bole of an oak, hung a box with a flag. This door stood almost as open as the last one, and suggested the pace I'd set would stand me in good stead if I could keep it up. I took the flag, tucked it for safekeeping with the others, and raced on.

I found the next and final encounter, in a small, bowl-shaped dust flat between hills. I ran around a hill and entered the arena with the morning sun full in my eyes. Silhouetted on the hilltop across from me stood several adults, and although I couldn't see their features, I thought I recognized Lord Hansur as the tall man in the middle.

Across the dustbowl from me, in a box high on a pine, sat the last flag. A Talion stepped from the brush at my right and tossed me a quarterstaff. Between me and the flag box another Talion, a novice my age, who wore the white sword ensign of the Warriors on his left breast, barred my path.

My heart sank. They'd matched me against a trained fighter with a staff. My "staff" training consisted of days spent whacking oxen who didn't like plowing straight furrows, and my only fighting experience came from the rough-and-tumble wrestling melees my brothers and I always got into. If I'd not lost the trial on the first test, I knew it now lay beyond my ability to win at all.

Desperation and anger filled me. The utter frustration at having come so far to fall so short of my goal choked me. I cried out against it in an incoherent war cry, brandished the staff, and ran directly at my waiting foe. Though I had no skill, I could certainly batter him with my rage and defeat him. At least in that I could take joy and would win a small victory within my huge defeat.

Then, as the Warrior moved to oppose me, I remembered I wanted the flag. My goal was not to crack his head, but to pull that shred of cloth from the box on the tree. I was really fighting for time and a chance to get the flag. And that battle I could win.

I raised my staff like a spear, cocked my right arm back, and threw with all my might. The staff spun like a yarn spindle and flew directly at the Warrior's face. With a look of contempt he parried my cast wide to my left. The staff skipped off his with a crack and tumbled to a rest in the dust. I veered for it and the Warrior shuffled over to block me.

As he moved, I cut for the flag box and put every ounce of speed I had left into my run. I heard him curse when he discovered my deception and he shot after me. I heard his footfalls right behind me and I imagined his breath on my neck. Exhaustion knotted my sides, but I thrust my pain aside and sprinted hard, even though I knew he gained on me with each step.

I felt him right behind me. I dared not look back, yet I knew, in seconds, he'd swing his staff through my weakening legs, trip me up and send me to the ground. He'd stand over me to knock me down if I struggled to get up off the gritty arena floor. The flag, so close, looked so far away. In my mind I had lost.

"No!" I screamed. I had not lost yet. I could not let me defeat myself.

I planted my left leg, stopped abruptly and stabbed my right leg out behind me. The Warrior impaled himself on my heel and folded around my leg like a slack sail wind-whipped against a mast. Air exploded from his lungs in a loud *ooofff* and his staff flew from limp hands.

The jarring collision knocked me sprawling forward on my face. Sand scraped and stung my chin and chest, crunched beneath my teeth, and made me sneeze. It coated me head to foot and each tiny grain seemed to weigh a pound in my exhaustion.

I slowly hauled myself to my feet. I moved as fast as I could, but my mind kept screaming that I had to move faster. I knew in my heart that the Warrior meant his groans to lull me into believing I had all the time in the world to get my last flag. I stumbled once, grinding more sand into my bleeding knees, then rose and limped toward the flag box.

Grimy and bloodstained, I grabbed the last flag. I locked it in a steely fist. My lungs burned and my body ached, but I had won. I'd gotten—no, I'd earned—my damn flags. I'd done my best and better than that. *But was that good enough?*

I bent down, rested my hands on my knees, and sucked in as much air as I could. Overhead the box snapped shut. I closed my eyes and shook my head to clear the beads of sweat running down my face. My pulse pounded in my ears and my head felt huge. Vertigo swept through me and I almost fell. Then I heard the sand crunch before me and I straightened up.

Lord Hansur stood there like the shadow of death. Behind him, a black shadow in the sun's disk, only one figure remained on the hillock. Lord Hansur held his long-fingered left hand out to me. "The flags."

I took the other three from my belt and handed all four to him. He dropped them into the sand as he counted them. To the left I could see the Warrior still rolled up into a ball, with two other Talions poised to help him, but they watched the flags fall as intently as I did. Each flag fluttered noiselessly onto the dusty basin floor, but I heard each impact with the thundercrack finality of a headsman's ax falling on the block.

The Lord of Justices looked at me. "There are only four flags here. To become a Thirteen you require five."

I crumpled inside. I could not breathe. Vertigo returned to drown me. My limbs trembled as the tension that had fueled them evaporated with my hopes and dreams. It was over, it was all for nothing. I'd done what they asked and I was rejected. I was finished.

Before I could organize my thoughts enough to remember I always had my other plan, the man on the hill spoke. His voice was not deep or commanding but all the Talions instantly paid attention to it. He spoke in the Talions' own tongue. His short statement—if inflection meant anything—was a question.

Lord Hansur, who had never turned from me, nodded. "I have been instructed to ask for the fifth flag. The flag you used to bind your arm."

A lump in my throat blocked any denial I could have offered. The fingers of my right hand trembled as I pried the knot loose and unwrapped the bloody rag from my arm. Dark brown where the blood had already dried, the rag in no way matched the other flags. Reluctantly, fearfully, I held the flag out. This was not my deception, yet I was terrified of the rebuke I'd earn for being a party to it.

Lord Hansur took the tattered strip and examined it as he had the others. Its length and ragged edges mocked the flags piled below it. Obviously torn from my loincloth, the spotty color and coarse weave proclaimed it an impostor. Stiff and twisted, it hung from his hand lifelessly. I could not have produced a worse forgery had I tried to do so.

Lord Hansur turned it over one more time, nodded, then dropped it with the others. He looked up at me and smiled. "Welcome to Talianna, Novice Nolan ra Sinjaria."

Chapter Three

TALION: PINE SPRINGS

I awoke the next morning in Weylan's cabin and, though I was anxious to start back on the trail, Elverda protested I was too weak to ride off immediately. Her persuasive argument had powerful allies in the hacking cough that racked my body from time to time—usually at the same moment I announced my total recovery—and her cooking. I agreed to stay for one more day and prayed the dry weather would hold out to preserve enough of Morai's trail so I could use it in my pursuit of him and his men.

I spent the morning writing down an

account of my actions in my journal. All Talions keep journals, though only Justices and Elites have them reviewed by their Lord on any regular basis. I also got Weylan's version of what happened at the ferry station written up. Like most people, Weylan was illiterate, so Elverda wrote what he had to say on a page in my journal and they both signed it.

That afternoon I got out into the hot sun and chopped some wood. I felt weak at first but the sun burned the remaining illness from my body as I worked. I took great satisfaction in chopping the wood because, after dealing with a sorcerer and waking up not as dead as I expected to be, finding something that worked as I anticipated it would reassured me about reality. The sharp ax split the wood with a loud, surprised crack and sent the logs tumbling back away from me.

My decision to stay the extra day provided a bonus that made the delay more than worth it. Two tinkers came to the ferry in midafternoon and I helped Weylan tie their wagon to the barge for the crossing. The tinkers, both from Kas, gladly left that work to us and, without realizing I was more than Weylan's aide, idly commented about their travels and the strange things they'd seen.

"And we even saw a Daari as we rode out of Pine Springs!" commented the elder, more rotund, tinker. "That was a nightmare. It took me back to the start of our trip."

I looked up at his comment. Vareck, one of Morai's men, was a Daari. The tinker's observation gave me one place to start looking for him. If I set out directly for Pine Springs, I'd not lose a day traveling back to the camp to pick up his trail from there.

The sun was setting by the time Weylan and I got back from crossing the tinkers. We tied the ferry to the docks, washed ourselves off in the river and returned to the cabin. Inside Elverda stirred a large pot of bubbling stew over the fire and a fresh loaf of bread steamed on the table. She ladled out a bowl of the thick, hot stew for each of us.

Over the meal Weylan told her about the tinkers and the information they'd supplied me. "Nolan thinks he can pick up their trail from there before they head north to Memkar."

Elverda nodded and smiled, but I read reluctance at my leaving in the stiff formality of her actions. I could understand that, in some ways, because she and I were Weylan's only true friends. For my part I had no doubt Weylan would well survive my departure.

Elverda stood and refilled Weylan's bowl. "The Daari, they're dangerous, aren't they?"

I hesitated, laying my brother Arik's ghost yet again, and then answered. "Yes, they are. The Daari are a very savage and superstitious people. They see the world as a demon-haunted place and themselves as the only people who can destroy those demons."

Weylan frowned. "I think I saw one once, when I was very young. He was horribly scarred on his face." Weylan shuddered and Elverda reached across the table to squeeze his right hand.

I broke a piece of bread from the slice in my left hand and dipped it into my stew. "The Daari believe that demons swallow the sun at night and then parade over the world working great evil. All the Daari are scarred at birth on the left half of their body. Each night the entire Daari population faces north as the sun sets. They expose the left sides of their bodies and the scarring is supposed to be so frightening to the demons that they avoid the Daari. In their haste to flee from these fierce folks, they do not devour the earth. The Daari even bury their dead on hillsides facing north so they continue their service to the world even after they are no longer living."

Elverda passed me a pitcher of ale. "The Daari do not often leave their country, do they?"

I shook my head. "Not since the Demon Crusade, when two thousand Daari decided to rid the world of the Talions." I showed them my right palm. "The Daari believe Talions are demon-possessed because of this mark. Our Lancers slaughtered their crusaders and captured the Prince leading the force. Since then the monarchy has avoided any overt concentrations of force. Right now the only Daari out of country are ambassadors, a few mercenaries, and one or two outlaws like Vareck."

"What did he do?" Elverda frowned. "Surely leaving Daar is not enough of a crime to set a Talion on him."

I poured ale into my cup and passed the pitcher to Weylan. "Daari elders drove Vareck out because he got a bit overzealous in his demon-hunting activities. Each Daari warrior is taught how to carve a spiritlance from a yew branch. They cover it with symbols to imbue it with the power to slay any demons possessing whomever the spear hits. The problem is the spear also kills the person housing the spirit. Vareck claimed his wife and two children were 'possessed.' He slew them and because he said they were possessed the act was not considered murder by his elders, so exile was the worst punishment they could inflict on him."

"He's killed others since, so he's mine now." I shrugged. "Local authorities normally would deal with someone like him, but since he's begun traveling with Morai, he moves fast and has eluded his pursuit."

Weylan frowned. "What would Morai want with someone like him? From the stories I would have thought Morai smarter than that."

I nodded. "So would I, but Morai has always been full of surprises. This time around he's gathered up a truly foul group of individuals, all of whom have significant bounties offered for them. I half suspect he's been paid to lure them out where they can be killed."

"Letting you take them and earn him his fee?"

"Possibly, Elverda." I hesitated. This time I'd been sent after Morai and his people because of political unrest in Memkar. The Talions in service there reported a rumor that Morai had been hired to harass and weaken various families in the Gem cartel. The people he'd pulled out of Chala certainly could accomplish that feat, which in turn could hurt the government enough that ambitious nobles could tear the nation apart and induce invasions by neighbors in an attempt to stabilize things again.

And stability is something the Master of all Talions holds sacred.

I smiled at her. "Whatever Morai is doing, I'm certain he has multiple goals and multiple paths for attaining each. Nothing is ever quite what it seems with Morai."

Our conversation turned away from things grim and ugly, and I let it go gladly. Weylan cleared the plates and we gathered the chairs in front of the fireplace. Weylan got out his lute and strummed his fingers across the strings. Both he and Elverda could play it, so the three of us sang songs long into the night. The evening passed quickly and pleasantly. It felt very good and I could only have hoped that if I'd not become a Talion my life could have been that happy.

Morning came a bit early, but other than lingering lethargy I felt very good and ready to travel. Elverda packed me some bread and cheese while I saddled Wolf. I hugged both Weylan and Elverda and promised to return to visit as soon as possible. With their wishes for good fortune ringing in my ears, I mounted Wolf and rode off.

Pine Springs lay only two days' ride from the Broad River ferry. Nestled in the foothills of the Ell Mountains, the town was the first settlement south of the pass into Memkar. Though Pine Springs thrived on the caravan trade running from Chala north and back again, the limited prosperity kept the town modest in size.

On the first night out I left the road to camp at a point beyond where the trail from Morai's camp joined the road. I found a spot back away from the road where I could make a fire without it being seen by any late travelers or bandits. The campsite had been used recently, and to my surprise I found two yew branches and a pile of shavings near the firepit. Vareck, or another Daari, had camped here.

I looked around for other signs and easily discovered another pair of tracks. This individual had harvested a number of plants from the surrounding woods. He didn't leave much behind but I knew he'd selected poisonous plants almost exclusively. That told me the man traveling with Vareck was Grath ra Memkar.

Memkar is a strange nation. To an outside observer it appears normal, if a bit crowded. Many of the families are quite large and the Memkarians are blessed with long lives. These two factors combine, though, to make things difficult for ambitious younger members of the family. Helping a relative into the grave has become an accepted method of advancement if a patriarch seems reluctant to share his power and wealth with his kin. In most cases a mild illness brought on by poison is usually enough to wrest a share of power for a relative, but the nation is so full of plot and counterplot that only the poisoner can be sure who did what to whom.

Grath ra Memkar was a poisoner. The trick to his trade

was not to get caught, because murder is still murder in Memkar. A professional poisoner has to be careful, and that word summed Grath up rather neatly.

Openly acknowledged as one of the best, Grath probably would still be working in his homeland had his last assignment not gone awry. His patron paid him for the deaths of the sire and eldest scion of a noble family. Grath managed to accidentally slay the whole family, so his employer, a noble who planned to marry into that family and acquire its wealth, refused to pay him. Grath retaliated and gave his patron a taste of the viper.

That rash act put others off and forced Grath out of Memkar. He traveled to Chala, where he poisoned thieves and extorted money from them for the antidotes. He probably would have stayed there, but Morai recruited him. Grath kept his skills sharp by visiting towns a day before the rest of the bandits would arrive. Not surprisingly, the town guards would become mysteriously ill and would be unable to harass the bandits.

That night I took very great care when I prepared my food. And, even though I did not face north as the sun went down, no demons came to disturb my sleep.

I reached Pine Springs in the late afternoon. I'd removed my black leathers and traveled in more traditional garb. I wore a dark blue linen tunic, brown trousers, and a brown vest woven of undyed wool. I was not certain Vareck and Grath still hid in Pine Springs, but it was a fair guess. Pine Springs, as small as it was, had a full city quarter devoted to taverns and boardinghouses catering exclusively to the transient trade. Those two would be anonymously safe there, for a short while anyway, so I chose not to reveal my identity before I knew where my quarry lurked.

The town guards didn't even glance at me as I passed through the gate. Following a caravan up from Chala, I reined Wolf around and rode into the east end of town. The caravan passed through the foreign quarter toward the stableyards while I stopped at the first tavern I saw. I strapped my swordbelt on, paid a child a silver Provincial to take Wolf to the nearest stable, and promised him another coin when he returned to tell me where the horse was housed.

The rough-hewn wooden door centered in the tavern's

south wall opened and admitted me into a dark and crowded common room. The bar ran the length of the west wall, ending a few feet before the stairs up to the second floor. A small stage ate into the lower half of the north wall, and above it stood the balcony leading to rooms on the second floor. They could be rented for the night or just an hour's company with one of the numerous women circulating through the crowd. A number of alcoves dotted the east wall and made me uneasy because I could not see past the thick curtains shielding them from the common room. Tables and chairs choked the common room, along with a thick cloud of sweat, the rumbling roar of conversation, and boisterous caravaneers.

I crossed to the bar and caught the bartender's attention. He was a big man—still powerful though he was running to beerfat—who'd lost the last three fingers on his right hand. "Ale." I deposited a silver coin on the bar. I held another in my left hand. "Is there a Daari about?"

The bartender set the wooden tankard down in front of me. The frothy ale sloshed over the lip, but he made no move to wipe it up. "Woman?" He shook his head. "No, we got no call for them." He grabbed for the coin, but I shifted it to my right hand before his fingers closed on it. I raised my left index finger to my lips and opened my right hand.

His eyes opened wide enough that I thought his bloodshot orbs might fall out of his head. He saw my sign to silence, thought for a moment, and then nodded. He pointed to the shrouded alcove deep in the northeast corner of the room. I flipped him the coin and smiled grimly. He nodded nervously and obviously did not like the idea of conspiring with a Justice.

I turned and leaned back on the bar. I sipped the ale so I'd not look conspicuous and found I liked the woody bite of this particular brew. I weighed and rejected various plans of action. I wanted to take Vareck quickly and, if I could manage it, without too much notice. Taverns such as this one were home to all sorts of skittish people and their reasons for being on the road might not invite unwanted attention. Caution hung in the air and an unusual action by anyone would scatter the crowd like a herd of antelope.

Before I reached any decision on a plan, the room fell

silent. A minstrel walked from an alcove more central than Vareck's and mounted a short flight of steps to the stage. She seated herself on a tall stool and intently studied her lute for a second or two, then she looked out at her audience. She flashed us a warm smile that drew everyone's attention.

Long blond hair reflected gold highlights even in the tavern's dim light. A narrow nose, high cheekbones, and bright blue eyes made her very attractive, and her smile only increased her beauty. Someone to her right called out a song title; she laughed and shook her head. Her hair fell back and revealed her bare shoulders.

She wore a white, short-sleeved blouse off her shoulders. A royal blue ribbon trimmed its bosom and sleeve, and picked up the color of her eyes. A wide brown belt drew it to her slender waist, and a brown leather skirt, made of a patchwork of squares, fell to below her knees. A pair of well-polished riding boots completed her outfit.

She strummed slender fingers across the lute's strings and filled the room with a familiar melody. "I am Selia ra Jania, and am very glad to perform here tonight. If you don't mind, for my first song I'd like to play 'The Peasant's Revenge,' " she announced in a silken voice.

She'd chosen well her first selection, because it was a song popular throughout Ell and the Shattered Empire. No one gainsaid her choice. Hard, grim men closed their eyes and remembered days when they'd heard the song at home amid family and friends.

Grime and black soil
and years of toil
this a farmer doth make.
But give the boy
a warrior's toy;
it's a soldier they take.

She sang the song perfectly in the voice of the boy's mother. She filled the words with passion and resentment at the boy's forced enlistment by Imperial recruiters. Her voice rang with the mother's pride when her son outsmarted the military wisdom of the day and earned himself a title by valorously winning a hopeless battle. Then she finished the song with just the right touch of contempt for nobility creeping into the final verse:

Awards galore,
carpeted floor,
he plans still in his keep.
For even now
new fields to plow;
bloody harvests to reap.

Thunderous applause greeted her song's finish, and she accepted it graciously. I enjoyed the song a great deal and remembered it had been my grandmother's favorite—one she always followed with a detailed recitation of the real-world facts behind it. For a moment I was able to forget who I was and why I stood in the tavern. I relaxed and clapped as heartily as anyone else.

Even though the first song was not overly demanding, it hinted at her range and abilities. I wondered if she would just sing old familiar and popular songs, or if she would try some newer tunes. Racing her fingers over silvery strings, she gave me little time to ponder my question. The notes, though I knew I'd not heard them played before, surprised me and then, as I identified them, made me cringe.

Selia smiled up at the audience. "Now a song some of you might have heard, and a song I'm proud of because I wrote it. It's called 'Morai's Song.' "

A few patrons who'd heard it before cheered and I slumped back against the bar. Jevin had heard it on a trip, hummed the melody for me once back in Talianna, and laughed his way through the words to torment me. I locked a smile on my face and endured.

Ride, Talion, ride,
But ere you reach my side,
Slay yourself my brave man,
Then catch me if you can.

Morai's man was dark and tall,
Had caused his father's fatal fall.
"The Talion's mine, wait and see
I'll nail his body to a tree."
So he waited in a meadow green,
"Come Talion, my blade is keen."
Challenged so the Talion drew his sword
And cut a man from Morai's horde.

Ride, Talion, ride,
But ere you reach my side,
Slay yourself my man bold,
And catch me ere you grow old

Cull was quick and possessed great heart,
And well versed in the killing art.
"Sword or bolt, each kills quite well
Either will send the Talion to Hell."
In an alley dark did Cull wait,
And open threats served as bait.
But he missed with the dirk he threw,
And the Talion cut old Cull in two!

Ride, Talion, ride
But e're you reach my side,
Slay yourself this noble foe,
And catch me ere winter winds blow.

Eric prince, bastard and fool
Was just another Morai tool.
The Talion's head he swore to deliver,
And promised to taste the dead man's liver.
Eric met the Justice with no fear

And passed on with a grin from ear to ear.
All the dupes with their lives did pay,
While Morai laughed and rode away.

Ride, Talion, ride,
But ere you reach my side
More men I'll get and throw to you,
And you'll never catch me when you're through.

❦

I joined the enthusiastic applause mechanically so no one would have any reason to look at me. My face felt on fire with embarrassment, and it surprised me the blush's red glow didn't bathe the back of the common room in lurid scarlet hues. I drank some ale to wash the cotton from my mouth and decided I'd wait and take Vareck whenever he decided to leave the tavern. After that song I didn't want anyone to know a Talion stood in their midst.

Vareck denied me the anonymity I desired. He burst from behind the black curtain shrouding his alcove with spiritlance firmly grasped in his white-knuckled right hand. He stared at the minstrel and jabbed the steel-tipped stick in her direction. His position gave the audience, which had fallen into a stunned silence, full view of his left profile. Hideous, twisted scars and arcane symbols puckered the flesh on his left arm and face, making him more a monster than a man.

"You lie, that's not how Morai is!" Spittle flecked his lips as he screamed at her. He jabbed a thumb at his own chest. "I know!"

Fear leached the color from her face as Selia stared at him. She paused as if trying to decide if he was just an angry drunk or a serious threat, saying nothing that might antagonize him. No one in the audience made a move to stop the Daari, and wrapping his left hand around the spear's shaft, he stalked toward her.

I stepped away from the bar. "Put the stick down, Daari, and leave her alone. She meant no harm." I kept my voice even and tried not to threaten him. I acted like a man who merely wanted to calm the situation. "Come"—I smiled warmly—"I'll buy you a drink."

Vareck whirled and snarled at me. "Stay back. I'm a bad man. I ride *with* Morai."

The people seated nearest the Daari slowly pulled away from him, and he growled at them. Everyone kept their hands away from their weapons and, if he'd been anything but a Daari, the situation would have cooled and been forgotten. But to a Daari, any insult, real or imagined, was demonspawn, and there was only one cure for that.

I swallowed hard. Vareck meant to kill her and would be as difficult as a hound with a good scent to deflect. She'd made herself a target, though she didn't know it at the time, and his peculiar view of the world told him that killing her put him one rung higher on the ladder to paradise. Nothing could deflect him from that.

Nothing but a target that would earn him even more rungs.

I took one step toward him. "I'm afraid, Vareck ra Daar, you're not bad enough." I raised my right hand and showed everyone my palm. "I ride *after* Morai."

The patrons seated around me shrank back and isolated the two of us on the floor. Vareck's dark eyes glazed over. He shifted his grip and caressed the symbol-scored spear with a lover's passion. The two blue feathers dangling by a leather cord from the spear's butt twitched in rhythm with Vareck's heartbeat. "I must kill you, Demonhost."

I shook my head. "Why? You heard the song. Morai used you. Prove you're more than just his tool."

A handsome smile slithered onto Vareck's face, but the scarred left profile ate into it like a disease. "Am I a tool, Talion? You know the saying, 'A tool is a tool unless it does the job by itself.'" He tightened his grip on the spiritlance and pointed it at my heart. "I will do the job and you will then have your proof."

He dropped into a crouch and I summoned my *tsincaat*. Vareck inched forward the shielded himself from my demongaze with his disfigurement. His spiritlance darted forward like a serpent's tongue. The steel point—a handspan in length and a third that broad at the base—had only two edges, but both gleamed razor-sharp in the weak light.

The patrons overturned the rough wooden tables and, seating themselves in the shadows behind the walls of their slender, makeshift arena, showered both of us with encouragement and abuse. A puddle of ale roughly marked the center of our strip, but drained through the worn floorboard before it could become a hazard to hamper either one of us.

Gamblers in the crowd immediately called out odds and accepted wagers on our fight. They favored me initially—for who could stand against a Talion in combat?—but my support eroded quickly enough. One bettor pointed out that Vareck did ride with Morai and his weapon outreached my *tsincaat*. Someone else noted that the spear had spells on it to counter Talion magick, and in seconds the pundits determined one silver Provincial bet on Vareck would earn half again that much if he won.

I faced Vareck, wrapped both hands around the *tsincaat*'s hilt, and set myself. I carried the blade out in front, so the *tsincaat* protected me from head to groin, and slid my right foot slightly ahead of my left. I made no move to parry Vareck's jabbed feints until he got near enough to actually hit me. He inched closer and closer, and with each shuffling step forward tension crushed in on me.

Vareck slipped into lethal range and delayed for a second. With one thrust he could reach my chest and punch the spiritlance through it. A last second shift in his attack and he could guide his spear beneath a parry to transfix my right thigh. If he was quick enough, he could even pin my foot to the floor and batter me to death with a table or chair. A legion of assaults suggested themselves to him, and he tried to select the most horrible, because a Talion should die in agony.

He made his choice and started his attack. Then he shuddered, looked at me, and saw his mistake in my eyes, just as I read it in the slackened expression of horror washing over his face. He knew, even as his spear shot forward toward my chest, he was nothing but a tool.

I shifted forward on my left foot and twisted away from the thrust he aimed at my chest. His spear slid between my right arm and body, then retreated without touching me. Vareck raised the spiritlance and tried to parry my chopping blow, but the rune-decorated haft cracked and splintered. My *tsincaat* sheared through it to cleave Vareck's collarbone and on into his chest.

The Daari lived for a second or two after he hit the floor.

His lips moved, forming a curse, but the gurgle of blood filling his lungs drowned the words. His fingers held tightly to the broken ends of his spiritlance, then went limp and let the broken lengths of wood clatter to the floor beside him.

I knelt on one knee and closed Vareck's eyes. Straightening up, I took the stained gray cloth offered by the barkeeper and wiped the blood from my *tsincaat*'s blade. Two men grabbed Vareck's ankles and dragged him out of the tavern, while a third man followed behind them throwing down handfuls of sawdust from a bucket to absorb the bloody trail leaking from the bandit.

Around me the tavern returned to near normal. Conversation started again, men tipped tables upright, and servants scurried among the patrons to renew orders and refill mugs. They kept their voices lower than before I'd revealed myself, and a few patrons seated themselves in the deeper shadows of the room, but the fight had changed no one besides Vareck and me. And the minstrel.

I looked up and tried to catch her gaze, but she only stared at the spot where Vareck fell. Her lower lip trembled and her moonshadow-pale face looked devoid of life and emotion. I grabbed one serving woman's bare shoulder. "Have you strong wine or brandy?"

She shivered and slipped her shoulder from my grasp. "Yes, Master Talion." Her dark eyes dulled with fear and her lips quivered.

"Two goblets, then. Bring them to her alcove." The woman hurried to the bar while I walked to the stage, leaped up, and filled the minstrel's view. She started and looked up at me as if I were a ghost. She opened her mouth to say something, but no words came.

I extended my left hand to her and tried to smile as reassuringly as I could. "Let us sit at your table."

She stood without my help. I dropped my hand to my side and followed her from the stage. She walked stiffly, but with a certain hint of feline grace. She lovingly cradled her lute to her chest then, when we reached her alcove and she pulled the heavy, dark woolen curtain back, she laid the instrument gently on a soft-leather traveling case. She slid onto the bench beside it and I sat facing her across the table.

The serving woman returned with the brandy in two mugs

and I paid her. I drew the curtain closed and cut the alcove off from the common room. The woolen curtain effectively muffled the conversation beyond it and left the thick, yellow candle burning on our round table to provide the only illumination in the alcove.

I gently pushed the goblet of brandy toward the minstrel. "He would not have slain you."

She fixed me with an icy blue gaze. "I saw his face, I read his eyes. He was mad!"

I shook my head carefully and deliberately. "He was Daari. He was less disturbed about your song's conclusion about Morai's men than he was about being reminded a Talion still followed him. Drink some brandy. It will steady your nerves." I sipped some of the brandy in my earthenware goblet and nearly gagged. I choked the brandy down and hastily coughed, "On the other hand, this might seriously damage them!"

Though unintentional, my distress jolted her out of remembering the look in Vareck's eyes. She smiled for a moment, then raised her cup and sniffed the dark liquid in it. She wrinkled her nose. "You a Talion and they give you the cheap brandy? They cut this with Rian wine." She shook her head and pulled the curtain aside to signal a servant.

She spoke quickly to a silhouette, then turned back to me. "If you play enough in places like this you learn what sorts of good wine and liquor hide in dusty bottles on the bottom shelf." She hesitated, and I feared she'd sink again into her memories of the fight, but she made the conscious decision not to slide back there. "I must apologize. I am Selia, and I believe you saved my life. Thank you."

I nodded and smiled. "You are most welcome." I did not introduce myself to her by name, because Talions are most commonly known as Talion, by title, or by a military rank. Most people believe this is because names have magical power, and certainly that is part of the reason behind the policy. Even more so, though, is the desire to keep Talions apart and to make us a symbol of the services we perform. It did not matter which Talion killed Vareck, it only mattered that a Talion brought him to justice. Some Talions share their real names with no one outside Talianna. Others, like me, share it with good friends.

The servant, a fiery redheaded woman, brought us two goblets and a very old bottle. She carried away the mugs, and Selia wrestled the cork from the bottle's neck. She poured, and candlelight sparked within the sweet amber liquid flowing from the bottle. She finished pouring, recorked the bottle, and raised her cup. "To a new verse for my song."

I hesitated before I touched my goblet to hers. "And to Morai's capture."

With blue eyes half shut, she drank and studied me over the rim of her cup. Lowering the cup, she licked her lips. "Don't you like my song?"

I smiled and let that answer for me while I thought about a reply and tasted the brandy. The liquor's vapors filled my head. The drink tasted strong, very sweet, and burned its way down my throat. Warmth spread out from my middle and washed all memories of the previous swill away.

I set my goblet down on the table. "I liked your song as much as I admire your taste in brandy. I marvel at the accuracy of the song, and I certainly wish I'd not heard it first from a compatriot of mine in Talianna."

Her eyes narrowed. "A Talion?" Then it hit her. Her face opened with a smile and a mischievous light sparked in her eyes. "The Fealareen! He said he knew the Talion in the song. He copied down all the words."

I shook my head with resignation. "And probably suggested the verse about Eric?" Selia nodded in reply to my question and I sighed. "Yes, it was the Fealareen. Believe me, his version of the song was not nearly as well sung as yours." Though I fought it I felt myself blushing again.

Selia straightened up and narrowed her eyes. The candle flickered and washed her face with shadows and faltering yellow light. "Does the song anger you?"

"No, I'm not angered by it."

"Do you resent it, then? Do you not like it because it makes fun of a Talion?" She watched me the way she watched Vareck. She sat poised to pounce on any hint of anger or displeasure I felt with her song.

With my left hand I picked up my goblet and swirled the brandy. I broke eye contact with her and watched as the liquid rose higher and higher toward the rim of the cup. The vortex in the cup matched the one in my head. Her questions spun around, drawing me toward an answer I did not want to know, and that surprised me. She was headed toward territory I thought I knew quite well.

I looked back up at her and shrugged. "I'm a bit embarrassed that Morai and I have provided enough material for a song, but the words don't bother me. If there is one thing I dislike it is how your song suggests Morai and I play a game of some sort with each other. I've killed almost a dozen of Morai's men in the past, and none of them have been as easy to kill as two quatrains make it sound. I don't play games with lives."

Selia sat back and pressed her hands together palm to palm, as if in prayer. She raised them to her face and rested her chin on her thumbs as she stared at the candle. A rivulet of wax poured down the candle's side and puddled on the table. Its surface had just enough time to cool and cloud before she spoke.

"I don't know if I can believe you." She saw the frown gathering on my face and opened her hands toward me. "Your points are well taken, but you are a Talion. You are used to people trembling and hiding at the sight of you. How can you not resent a song that suggests that you are not all-powerful?"

"I don't resent a song that presents a Talion as fallible because I'm not omnipotent. I don't like terrifying people."

"Ha!" she laughed. "That is impossible."

I shook my head. "It's not impossible, and you already anticipated my answer in just the way you phrased your question. But you want proof more tangible than my denial." I raised my arms to emphasize my clothing. "Surely an omnipotent Talion who desired to scare everyone in here would not degrade himself by wearing such normal clothing."

"Your point." She half laughed with a light voice. "When you spoke up I thought for a moment you might actually have been Morai. Are you sure you're a Talion?"

I laughed and wearily nodded my head. "I grew up, to a certain extent, outside Talianna. I can remember, from before I became a Talion, the stories and tales that sent shivers down my spine." I sipped more brandy. "I remember standing in a market in Sinjaria long ago when I saw my first Talion. Now I know the scrawny fellow was probably a mercenary who became a Warrior, but then he terrified me. He came no closer than ten feet from me, and never even turned in my direction, but my heart pounded and my breath came fast, short and shallow. If he'd looked at me, or spoken to me, I'm sure I'd have fainted dead way. Or worse yet I'd have run off, absolutely convinced a neighbor had reported me and my brothers for stealing a melon two summers before."

Selia drank, let the brandy sit on her tongue for a moment, then swallowed. "I'm not convinced. You know the fear Talions hold for some people, but couldn't that knowledge make having the power all that more seductive? Couldn't you be more attracted to that power because you are no longer subject to it?" A smile crept onto her face and I knew she enjoyed toying with me.

I sat back and felt the cool plaster on the nape of my neck. "What you say is very true, but . . ." I leaned forward quickly, darted my right hand out, and grabbed her left hand. She started and twisted her wrist to escape, but I held on. Anger and fear flooded her face.

I released and she snatched her hand back to her breast. She rubbed one hand with the other. "Your palm, it's so cold."

I nodded and regretted acting on impulse. "I'm sorry. It's cold, like the knot of fear I used to feel in my stomach. I knew then, and I know now, that I'd do anything a Talion ordered me to do, but I'd resent it because fear prompted my action. I've felt the fear you felt a moment ago, and I relive it whenever I see the terror I cause in someone. I decided long ago I would rather have one person work with me because I'd done him a favor and he called me friend, then have a hundred people work with me out of fear. A friend won't run when a fear-slave will."

A little of the fire crept back into her eyes. "Does that mean you *never* use fear?"

I smiled. "Given a choice I will not use it, but 'Only a fool throws away armor before a battle.' "

Selia excused herself, picked up her lute, and returned to the stage. She performed very well and by the end of her second appearance she owned the crowd. The audience loudly applauded and she took them away, for minutes at a time, from the knowledge that a Talion lurked just out of sight. I apologized for any dampening of spirits I might have caused, but Selia reported the audience's gifts of coins were quite generous so she had no real complaints.

Between her stage appearances we sat and talked. We talked about all the different places we'd visited and compared impressions of wonders we'd both seen. She recovered very well from the encounter with Vareck earlier that evening, but every once in a while I saw fear shoot through her eyes and detected a shiver running across her shoulders.

As the evening ended the tavernkeeper came over to the table. Smaller and less powerfully built than the bartender, he looked enough like the larger man, save the battle scars and maiming, to suggest they were kin. He offered me a private room—the only one he had available, he said as if pleased—but the pained expression on his face told me the real story. Inns like that were well used to packing a room with as many people as the bed and floor could hold, but no one wanted to sleep in the same room as a Talion, hence this miraculous vacancy. I accepted his offer, much to his obvious relief, and freely overpaid him well for the room. His son, the boy who had taken Wolf to the stables earlier, carried my saddlebags and gear up to the room.

Selia finished for the night and retired to her room. I left the common room shortly after she did, and quickly checked my room over for any surprises Grath might have prepared for me. Aside from fresh straw in the mattress and clean sheets on the bed there was nothing unusual about the room. I set a chair up by the door and another by the window so anyone trying to sneak into my room would trip over them, then unceremoniously dropped into bed.

I might not have fallen asleep the second my head hit the pillow, but I didn't stay awake much longer than that.

Dawn light preceded the tavernkeeper's timid knocking on the door by half an hour, so I answered the door fully awake and already dressed. The innkeeper hadn't struck me as the type to be up so early on his own account, and the woolen sleeping cap perched forgotten on his head immediately suggested something very wrong was happening. I smiled to reassure him, but he caught sight of the death's-head emblazoned on my jerkin's left breast and that scared him almost as much as the emergency that had brought him to me.

"My Lord Talion," he wheezed breathlessly at me, "the Lord Mayor's Chamberlain is below. He wishes to speak with you." He watched my face, and took no joy in the furrowing of my brows.

I waved a hand and dismissed his concern. "You have nothing to fear, I will deal with him." I had no idea what the Lord Mayor wanted me for, but the innkeeper had no place in the middle of it. I laid my left hand on his shoulder and squeezed to put him at ease. His face lost some of that pinched, cringing quality and he scurried off to tell the Chamberlain I would see him.

I'd dressed in my black leather jerkin, with a black linen shirt beneath it, black pants and my riding boots; so the addition of my weapons belt completed my uniform. I buckled it on with *tsincaat* at my left hip and *ryqril* at the small of my back. Carefully and quietly I strode from my room so I wouldn't awaken anyone else. I marched across the open balcony and without looking directly at the Chamberlain, I formed my first impression of him.

His escort, two city guardsmen, stood at attention on either side of the chair he'd seated himself in. Every buckle and badge on their uniforms sparkled. Neither of the young men, though handsome and well groomed, had the look of veteran fighters. Nothing more than an honor guard, the Chamberlain clearly used them to gild his image and inflate his own sense of importance.

An older man, the Chamberlain had aged very well. His light brown hair, with touches of gray at both temples, gave him a distinctive look of power and success. He did not slump or sprawl in the chair; instead he held his lean body upright and unbowed by the years. He wore one ring on each hand, and his hands were long-fingered and clean. Cloth of gold shined through the slashed sleeves of his deep blue velvet robe, and trimmed it at the throat.

He remained seated and did not react as I stalked down the stairs. I stopped ten feet from the Chamberlain's honor guard and gave them a smile of sympathy. They looked from me to the motionless Chamberlain as if to ask if he required their services during our talk, but the Chamberlain gave them no sign. I saw them look over at the bartender and the tavern's first few customers; then I nodded my head and freed them to get a drink.

Each took a half step away when the Chamberlain's right hand came up. They froze in their tracks. Then, continuing the languid motion with which he'd raised the hand, the Chamberlain flicked his wrist and sent both men off. The guards blushed and retreated from both of us.

I stared into the Chamberlain's brown eyes. "What can I do for you?"

"We have come in the name of the Lord Mayor of Pine Springs." He kept his pleasant voice even, yet his tone suggested he felt me an inferior. "We have Grath ra Memkar. We hold him preparatory to his execution at your hands."

My eyes narrowed and I sensed a trap closing around me. "You have him, you may execute him. You do not need me or even my permission. In fact," I smiled, "that means I can head off after Morai all the sooner."

The Chamberlain nodded understandingly. "We wish it were that simple, Talion, but we require your unique method of execution. Grath has certain information we dare not risk exposing to necromancers. We believe we have the right to request his death of you."

I shut my eyes and rubbed my right hand over my face. His request kept within the list of things a local ruler could ask of a Talion. *Occasionally* a leader would ask a Talion to pull the soul from a spy or similar individual with dangerous information, but most found other ways to make sure the necromancers never got to the body. I did not want to execute Grath in that manner, no matter what he knew, but I'd have to argue that out with the Lord Mayor, not his messenger.

I nodded. "When and where?"

"Noon today, in the square before the Lord Mayor's house." A vulpine grin snapped up any look of innocence the Chamberlain might have tried to muster.

My heart hurt. They wanted a public execution, and *that* I flatly refused to give them. "I'll be there early because I want to speak with the Mayor before Grath dies."

The Chamberlain inclined his head in a respectful nod,

collected his guards, and withdrew. Once he left the room the bartender came over and offered me a small glass of Temuri *shaisha*. I tossed the glass of liquid fire off without thinking, then signaled him for something to quench the burning in my throat.

The bartender laughed in a booming bass voice. "Thought the *shaisha* would get your mind off that pompous ass. I was hoping your Grath would kill the Chamberlain out of spite before he was caught."

I gulped down some of the ale in the tankard the bartender handed me, coughed, and frowned at him. "What? You knew Grath was working here in Pine Springs?"

The bartender took a step back, then relaxed as the tone of my voice revealed surprised with no hostility. "Aye, I did and so did most of the rest of the town. He and the Daari came in a while back, three, four days now, and Grath read the political situation like I can read Dhesiri track. There's two factions in town; the one that's out of power is close to replacing the one in power and probably will the next time the full Council of Merchants meets. Grath offered his services to the Chamberlain to deter some of the opposition in return for enough money to buy passage for himself and Vareck safely through Memkar." The bartender shrugged. "Anyway that's what the Daari said one night when he'd drunk himself deep into his cups."

I nodded and sat there stunned. I had no doubt Grath could sort out local politics and offer the right people his services. Morai probably had recruited him as much for his knowledge of Memkari politics as his skill as a poisoner. I also found it easy to believe a man like the Chamberlain would make use of Grath to solidify his own position, but the temerity of the Chamberlain to come and demand I kill Grath so none of this information would get out—that was nothing short of incredible.

I narrowed my eyes, sipped the ale, and let the world fade from my consciousness. The Lord Mayor wanted Grath's execution to be a public spectacle, and probably hoped it would reinforce the image of his power in the minds of his people. I nodded slowly as a plan crept from the crueler reaches of my mind. Indeed, the Lord Mayor and his people would learn something that day about power.

· · ·

At my request Selia joined me for my audience with the Lord Mayor of Pine Springs. At first I thought he might be nothing more than the Chamberlain's puppet, but my first look at him shattered that myth. A bulbous man with thinning black hair, he wore both a moustache and gaudy clothing that gave him a foppish demeanor. Even so, the look of animal cunning in his dark eyes told me who really controlled Pine Springs.

The Lord Mayor sat in a chair upon a dais in his private chambers. His Chamberlain stood at his right hand, and a few other advisors stood at his left. Through the window to my right I saw the guardsmen force the crowd back away from a hastily erected scaffold.

I bowed my head to the Mayor. "Your Honor, I would like to present Selia ra Jania. I brought her here as my witness to what we discuss, though I have her pledge she will tell no one what was said unless my Master requires testimony of her."

The Mayor looked at her and dismissed her as inconsequential or easily murdered and watched me. "We are pleased you have agreed to execute the prisoner."

Muscles bunched at my jaw. "I have not agreed to execute Grath in the manner I believe you desire. I will kill him, but I will not rip his soul from him."

The Mayor skewered the Chamberlain with a look of pure venom, then leaned forward and pointed a finger at me. "You will use your power on him, Talion, you have no choice. We will not have the secrets he learned—information garnered by deception—pulled out of him by some necromancer."

I breathed out slowly to calm my rising ire. "I understand your concern, my Lord Mayor, but you can burn his body, or chop it into little bits, or boil his brain to get the same effect. I will oversee whatever method you want to use, and I will make certain your secrets are safe."

The Lord Mayor shook his head with increasing vehemence. "Your assurances will not do, Talion. We desire no chance of reconstruction possible. Who knows what spells he's already had cast upon him to enable a sorcerer to bring him back to life?"

I forced myself to laugh derisively. "So, you believe witch-wife rumors and faery tales. That cannot happen. . . ."

"It cannot happen if you pull his soul from his body." The Lord Mayor knew he had me trapped because, whether or not his request was genuine, I had, ultimately, no choice but to honor it. "You will go down there and execute him now!"

I turned to Selia. "Please note I have offered alternatives to this ritual execution, and the Lord Mayor has rejected them." I spun back and faced him. "Put it in writing to my Master that you have given me no choice but to pull his soul from his body and seal it." I stared at him. "You disgust me."

The Mayor glared back at me. "But you must do what we tell you to do." He dictated the message to a secretary, then signed and sealed the message himself. He handed it to me and I tucked it in my jerkin.

We left the Mayor's chamber behind two guards and passed through a throng to reach the scaffold. I waited for Selia to reach the top of the platform before I climbed up. Behind me came the Mayor and the Chamberlain. Grath already waited for us on scaffold.

I felt sorry for Grath when I saw him. A slight man, one well built for court intrigues and unnoticed poisonings, Grath had been bound with heavy chains that shortened his stride into a clanking shuffle and forced him to stoop. The instant he saw me he knew why he'd been betrayed by his employers. He snarled at them and shook his head.

He cast a sideways glance at the Chamberlain and the Lord Mayor, then spat on the ground. He looked up at me and I nodded almost imperceptibly. I wanted him to know I'd have taken him cleanly, and that I'd give him a quick death. I also wanted him to know I shared his opinion of his former clients. That's a great deal of message to put into a moment's worth of movement, but Grath returned the gesture and I knew I'd been understood.

I waited for soldiers to wrestle two chairs up onto the stage for the Mayor and the Chamberlain before I began. I walked to the edge of the planking and stared out at the sea of heads. Although clouds shrouded the sky with a promise of rain, and the chill wind puckered the flesh, people packed the courtyard and had even climbed out on the roofs of the buildings surrounding the square. I raised my right hand and waited until the murmur died before I spoke.

"I am a Justice. Many of you have heard I took a man in

the foreign quarter last night. That is true. He attacked me. I slew the Daari with my blade." I half turned back toward Grath. "This man was the Daari's companion, and the Chamberlain informed me this morning of his capture. The Lord Mayor tells me Grath ra Memkar has learned some important secrets, and he has given me no choice but to execute the prisoner."

Many people nodded in agreement, but no one shouted a comment or otherwise drew attention to himself. Bile boiled up in my throat and I almost broke off the course I'd set for myself. I really didn't want to use the citizens of Pine Springs so badly, but I refused to execute Grath just to satisfy the whims of a dictator.

I lowered my voice. "Before I do what your Mayor forces me to do, I wish to apologize to you." My words shocked silence from the crowd, but an explosion of thunder burst in to fill the void. A light drizzle started to fall and I continued. "I want to apologize now to you all because I will be too busy to apologize to each of you later. Please understand what I do is not personal, it is a duty forced upon me."

The people below me watched each other nervously and sought support. They'd come to watch a Talion kill a poisoner, but now the Justice apologized to them for actions he would take. My words confused them and worried them.

I frowned and looked puzzled at them. "Do you mean you do not know why I apologize? Do you not know what I must do after I pull his soul from his body, as your Lord Mayor requests?" I stared down at them, and they up at me like drowning sailors bobbing in a storm-racked sea. Rain fell harder and mingled with the tears on some faces. Disembodied voices demanded an explanation from me.

I nodded solemnly. "When I pull his soul from his body, in just retribution for the murders he has committed, I will see everything he has seen, and I will know all he knows." I pointed to Grath. "I will see any crimes he has seen, then I will be bound to execute those criminals in the same manner. I will absorb their knowledge and have to act upon it. I will do this until I see no more evil."

I shook my head ruefully and pulled the Mayor's letter from my jerkin. "I would not have it so, but your Mayor gives me no choice in the matter."

Thunder cracked again and the crowd surged forward to slam into the scaffold's base. The platform pitched and both Selia and Grath fell to the wooden planking. The Mayor stood, then stumbled, but the Chamberlain managed to keep his feet when he rose from his chair.

The Chamberlain angrily stabbed a finger at me. "You cannot do this."

"Quiet, puppet, your master has given me my orders. I have no choice but to obey him." I stared down at the Mayor as a sheet of rain scourged him, and a lightning flash highlighted the fear on his face.

"No, Talion, you do not have to execute him." The Lord Mayor levered himself up from the stage. "I rescind my command."

That quieted the crowd for a second, but I dashed their hopes with a harsh laugh. "Oh no, my Lord Mayor, you cannot change your order. I gave you a chance before, and you ignored it. Now I suspect you or your Chamberlain of having reasons you do not want me to take Grath's mind. No, I must obey your order because"—I pointed at Grath—"his memories are the key to evil in this town!"

The crowd, goaded by a fork of lightning slamming into the tower atop the Mayor's residence, pressed forward again and tilted the platform. The Chamberlain drew a dagger from within the sleeves of his wet robe, leaped over the fallen Mayor, and dove at me. He screamed an inarticulate cry and slashed wildly as I backed from his attack and spun. I lashed out in a roundhouse kick with my right foot, caught him behind the ear, and smashed him into the crowd waiting below.

The people beneath the Chamberlain scrambled out of his way, or pulled themselves from under his body as quickly as they could. I heard one man say "His neck is broken!" and that message passed through the crowd to release their tension and give them a moment's pause. The death they'd all feared at my hands appeared among them in a tangible form and momentarily refocused their concerns internally.

"Hear me, citizens of Pine Springs!" I shouted. I pointed to the Chamberlain's dead body. "There is your evil. I have found it, and taken it, without needing to use extreme methods. The suspicions I had earlier, those that prevented me from accepting the Mayor's gracious offer, have been satisfied. You should consider yourselves lucky that a town of this size harbors evil so easily dealt with."

The crowd melted away as if the downpour eroded them. I stood and watched them like a statue until they vanished, then I turned and glared at the Mayor. "You and I both know some of what the Chamberlain wanted to keep hidden. Poisoning, and conspiring with a poisoner, is a capital crime in Ell. None of my superiors would fault me for taking you here and now, and many of them will chide me if I don't. But I think you deserve another chance."

The Mayor, still on his knees from his earlier fall, reached out and grabbed my rain-slicked jerkin, then released me. "I'm sorry, I meant you no offense or disrespect. I was wrong. Yes, anything. I will do anything."

"Good." I pointed to Grath. "Behead him, then strike his chains and bury him below this spot in the courtyard. You'll build a monument here. That monument will remind you that all power is nothing if it is wielded selfishly."

"Yes, Talion, yes, I will do it. . . ." The Mayor's sobs swallowed his words. Then wind and rain blasted all nobility from him. I turned from him and descended into the nearly empty courtyard.

One street away Selia called out to me. "Talion."

I stopped and waited for her. She fell in step with me and we walked in silence until we reached the transients' section of Pine Springs. There the rain eased and a shaft of sunlight lanced through the clouds.

"Talion, would you have done what you threatened? Would you have gone through this town and slain everyone?" Fear tinged her question, but she asked it honestly.

I reached out, with my left hand, and touched her gently on the shoulder. "Does it matter what I would have done? I am only here to administer justice. I think Pine Springs has had enough of that, with any luck, to last them for generations."

Chapter Four

NOVICE: FESTIVAL

Sweaty and bleeding, I stood there and looked over at the rising disk of the sun. The man who had spoken no longer stood on the hilltop. He'd vanished, and along with him went the last remnants of my fear. Relief flooded through me, a chuckle—that I smothered immediately—started in the pit of my stomach, and I suddenly felt exhausted.

The two Talions before me lifted the Warrior and carried him out of the dust-bowl. Lord Hansur waved a hand to indicate I should follow them, so I did. We walked a narrow, twisting trail up a hill and I discovered another small dust flat where a tent and some chairs had been set out. The white-blond novice who guided me before led me to one of the chairs.

"I am Lothar ra Jania. Like you, I am a Thirteen."

I smiled and gladly took the goblet of watered wine offered by a Services Talion. I gulped it greedily and some of it poured down my chin and chest. It stung when it hit my scrapes, but the wine's coolness was worth the pain.

I nodded to the server. "Thank you." I offered Lothar my hand and he shook it firmly. "I am Nolan ra Sinjaria. But are we supposed to call each other by name? I thought all Talions were known by title?"

Lothar smiled and revealed even, white teeth. "That is for those outside. The lords are known by their names, and Talions serving in a foreign court are often known by rank, but it is not forbidden for us to give our names to others. Here, among Talions, we use our names. It would be rather confusing otherwise."

I smiled, visualizing the chaos if Talions only answered to that title in a city full of Talions. "Where in Jania are you from, Lothar?"

The novice Justice turned and barked a command to the azure-robed Wizard examining the Warrior I'd kicked. The Wizard turned enough for me to see the pentagram on the left breast of his robe and replied in the same tongue to Lothar. Lothar nodded and turned back to me. "He'll be over here in a moment to fix you up. Your question, where am I from, ah, I'm from Trisus, the capital, but I've been in Talianna since I was six months old."

"Oh." I rubbed my left arm and checked the splinter wound. The bleeding had stopped, but the injury still stung. "What did you say to him?" I asked, jerking my head toward the Wizard.

Lothar shrugged. "I told him you needed his services more than that laggard Warrior. A Justice would not have fallen for either one of your tricks."

I frowned. Lothar's voice carried contempt for the Warrior, and with it I felt some judgment of me implied in his comment. "What language did you use, and what did the man say to Lord Hansur when he was counting my flags?"

Lothar signaled the Services Talion to pour me more wine, which I gratefully accepted. "I spoke in the Tal dialect. It's said the language has not changed since the Talions were formed. You'll have to learn it." He paused and refused to meet my eyes. "I do not know what was said to Lord Hansur."

If he was lying I couldn't tell. I still felt uneasy, and if I was now the same rank as Lothar, as we were both Thirteens, I didn't want him feeling I'd not earned my place. "I take it from your remark about the Warrior you do not feel I should be a Justice, that I failed my test?"

Lothar's face brightened and he laughed. "No, no, don't take it as that. Making it to Talianna from Sinjaria by yourself is enough proof for me that you belong. And seeing you here, exhausted and torn up, I know you earned your flags. No, my anger is with him." He stabbed a finger at the Warrior seated across the campsite. "You would have beaten him in any event, but you would not have humiliated him if he had not underestimated your abilities."

I drank more wine and felt relieved that Lothar did not judge me harshly. The Wizard left off the Warrior and crossed to me. He quickly examined my arm, poking it none too gently, then smiled. "No need for me to spell you back to health. Just wash the grime off and bind it with a clean bandage. It will bother you for a few days, but you will heal."

Lothar stood and led me out of the clearing. We crossed over two more hills and I discovered we were very close to Talianna. My course had taken me in a long loop. We quickly marched down a trail back toward Talianna, but paused just long enough for me to dive into a stream and clean myself off.

The trail took us on the north side of Talianna, between the siege wall and the Mews, where we passed through the gate on the eastern side of Northpoint. Two Warriors stood guard duty there but neither one challenged us. Through the gate we headed south and east toward the Eastgate in the second pentagram.

Between the siege wall and the Citadel itself, the street looked like it might in many a large city, with one major difference. "Lothar, the streets are incredibly clean here." I looked around in total disbelief. I could see no piles of garbage, dead animals, or broken cobblestone anywhere.

The novice smiled. "This is Taltown. It is home to the families of Talions, the Tal farmers, and all the businesses needed to support them. The Master allows people to live here only if Taltown is kept as clean and orderly as the Citadel itself is maintained."

"Hmmm. And anyone can live here?"

Lothar thought for a moment. "Yes, just about anyone. There are no beggars—they get put to work on the farms. Once a criminal the Justices were hunting came here and hid out. It's said he tried to become a Talion, a Justice in fact, when the next Festival came around."

My eyes flew wide at that. "What happened?"

"Where you found a Warrior he met the Lord of Justices. He did not get the required number of flags."

We walked around and through crowds of people buying and selling various wares. I'd been to a market before, once, in Sinjaria, so not much was new to me. Still there was an overwhelming number of Talions in the crowd, and that took getting used to.

Twenty-foot-tall, massive oak-and-iron doors closed off Eastgate. A smaller, man-sized door stood open at the base of the left door. Lothar explained, "Normally these doors are open, but when Lancers pass their tests they have the annoying habit of riding through the hallway and into the mess hall to celebrate."

I smiled and followed Lothar through the door. We stood in a long, dark tunnel that formed the base of the Star. Early-morning light streamed through the door, and it cut enough of the gloom to let me see the murderholes above us. Anyone mad enough to lay siege to Talianna, and lucky enough to get this far, could be shot with arrows or flooded out with burning oil from above. I'd heard of such things in my grand-mother's stories, but actually seeing them sent a chill through me. For the first time in my life I connected the horror of death with the reality behind tales I used to enjoy listening to.

Lothar led me on through the corridor and stopped at the door in the southern wall. "We'll get you some supplies in here."

I followed him through the door and stopped instantly. The room was considerably larger than the house I'd grown up in. Shelves lined the walls, filled the interior, and reached all the way up to the twelve-foot-high ceiling. Neatly folded clothing packed every shelf and displayed a rainbow of colors. My mouth dropped open and I drifted toward the nearest shelf, ignoring Lothar and the Services clerk he was speaking to.

"Stand still, boy!" The clerk's command froze me in place, and jerked my extended hand back from the velvet robes on the shelf before me. "How can I size you if you keep moving? Lothar, shelf thirteen, middle pile, for pants and shelf fourteen left for shirt." The clerk, an older man shorter than me, with brown eyes and white hair ringing his head, squinted at my feet and held a pair of boots out toward me. "Well, here, take these. And get some stockings and underclothes there on shelf three. Shelf three. You can read, can't you?"

I took the boots and turned a full circle before I saw the shelf I wanted. "Yes, I can read." I took a pair of stockings and some underclothes. "Should I try these on?"

The clerk's eyes widened until they were almost all white. He snapped something at me in the Tal dialect. Lothar stifled a laugh, jammed my shirt and pants into my stomach, and steered me out into the hallway quickly.

"What did he say?"

Lothar laughed. "Don't worry about it, you don't look like you've got any goat blood in you to me." He opened a door in the south wall and we stepped out into a grassy courtyard. "This is where we'll do some of our training. We live over there, and the Thirteens have rooms on the upper floor this year!"

We walked through an arched doorway in the east Citadel wall and ran up two flights of stairs to the third floor. The hallway was ten feet wide and tiled for its entire length. Every fifteen feet along each wall, staggered so they did not open onto each other, doors dotted the length of the corridor. There was a doorway at the far end of the corridor, and there was one directly behind us.

A clerk with a slate stood at the far end of the corridor. He spotted us and stalked down the hallway toward us. He said something to Lothar that I could not understand, but the scolding tone was easy to recognize.

Lothar frowned at him. "Say it in the common dialect; Nolan cannot understand us." Lothar added an edge to his voice and the clerk hesitated.

"Finally, Lothar, you appear." The clerk sniffed and checked something off on his slate. "The others have had

their choices. You'll have to room with this one, this Nolan."
The clerk's grin was meant to be cruel, as if pairing Lothar
with me was a heinous punishment for his tardiness.

Lothar stiffened, then took one step forward. He towered
over the clerk, and he cowed a man easily thirty years his
senior. "It clearly did not occur to you that I might have
planned this. If Nolan failed I would have a room to myself.
With his success I am now roomed with an interesting addition to our company."

The clerk recoiled, then narrowed his eyes and spat something back at Lothar in Tal. Lothar answered quickly and
sharply. I caught "Hansur" in Lothar's riposte, and whatever
else he said combined with that name to batter the clerk. He
pointed to a doorway and left. Lothar stalked down the
hallway, and I followed in docile silence.

Our boxy room was fifteen feet wide and ten feet deep.
The window looked out onto the grassy field we'd crossed
coming into the building. A bed sat against each of the side
walls, along with a big clothes chest and a wardrobe for
hanging cloaks and storing boots. An oak table sat beneath
the window, with chairs on three sides of it, and a fourth
chair beside the door.

Lothar threw himself onto the bed in the far corner, with
the head against the window wall, leaving me the bed in the
opposite corner of the room. "The clerks will bring up more
clothes for you, and put them away later. Cloaks and ceremonial clothing get hung in the wardrobe. Boots and sandals go
in the bottom of it. Anything else gets stored in the chest.
They'll also bring your stuff from Devon's tent. Anything you
don't want will be given to children in Taltown."

I nodded and sat on my bed. When I started unlacing my
sandals Lothar got up, left the room, and closed the door
behind him. I changed my clothing quickly. Everything fit
well, especially the boots, but had some room to let me grow
before I'd need new clothes. The clothes were black and
made of a material lighter than wool but just as durable. I
knew enough to know it was not silk, and I found it very comfortable. I tucked my pants into the tops of my boots and
studied myself in the mirror behind our door.

I'd certainly changed in my journey. Leaner and bonier, I
looked something like the scarecrow I'd stolen my last tunic

from. I knew, from what Grandmother had said of Father, and the way Hal and Malcolm had filled out when they looked as gaunt as I did, I'd be a big man. My face had the same, strong features as my father's, but my green eyes, from my mother's side of the family, burned away the weary look I always remembered my father having.

Not just a vastly different Nolan stared out at me from the glass, but a totally new Nolan stood there. I smiled at the white death's-head ensign on my left breast. In the Talion uniform I felt taller, stronger, and no longer a child. The smile dulled a bit with my realization that becoming a Talion novice was but the first step in my plan, and the knowledge that I'd have to work hard to stay a Talion to accomplish my ultimate goal.

Before I could lose myself in a morass of painful memories and heaven-blown plans, the door opened. I stepped back and Lothar smiled. "You look good. Definitely grist for the mill."

"He must have insulted Allen *after* he got his clothes." Lothar stepped aside as a girl walked into the room. She was smaller than either of us but could not be described as delicate or fragile. She moved like a cat and took in everything in the room with a single glance. Then she looked me over.

She narrowed her brown eyes so they were reduced to dark spots edged with white. Her hair was very black, and because of its length, lost definition in some of the darker places. She was pretty, but the predatory look on her face chilled me just a little bit. Finally she pursed her lips, nodded quickly, and turned to Lothar. "I believe he made the journey."

Any comment I was about to make died as Lothar crossed to his bed and another novice walked into the room. He was huge, taller even than Lord Hansur, and had the bulk to match his height. And if that was not enough to shock me—the boy who thought himself a world traveler—the novice was not even human. His gray-green skin showed off the white fangs protruding a half-inch or more over his lower lip. His hair was black and as long as mine, but failed to hide the slightly pointed tips of his ears.

All deep and rumbling, his voice boomed like thunder. "Of course he made the journey, Marana. The tale's too fantastic to be a lie." He growled the last word and smiled. He flashed a set of teeth I'd only imagined seeing in a nightmare.

My jaw dropped open and the only reason I didn't run from the room was because the giant demon blocked the door. Lothar caught the abject terror in my slackened face and started laughing. The girl joined Lothar's laughter and, after a puzzled look flitted across his face, the demon joined in.

His warm, hearty laughter brought me back to reality. *I cannot fear anyone who can laugh that openly.* I recovered myself and started laughing with the others.

Lothar, holding his stomach, rolled up into a sitting position on the bed and nodded toward the girl. "Nolan, this is Marana. Marana, this is Nolan ra Sinjaria." We bowed at each other and Lothar continued the introductions. "Nolan ra Sinjaria, I present Jevin the Fealareen."

The word *Fealareen* exploded like a dropped clay jug and explained the depth of my fear at seeing Jevin for the first time. Like any child in the Sea States I knew that across the Runt Sea lay the Borrowed Lands and the Fealareen Haunts. Fierce mountain giants who lived in and on the mountains, the Fealareen tended flocks of demonsheep and did a host of other things the storytellers only hinted at darkly. Every twenty-five years the leader of the humans in the Borrowed Lands and the Fealareen leader would meet in a contest—a ritual contest created, maintained, and adjudged by Talions—to see who would control the Borrowed Lands until the next contest. The stories of what the Fealareen did to the human inhabitants of the Borrowed Lands when the humans lost the contest were quite horrible, and seeing a Fealareen firsthand lent more credence to those tales than I'd ever given them before.

Still, unless the Fealareen controlled the Borrowed Lands, none of their kind could leave the mountains. As near as I knew, Queen Briana still reigned over the Borrowed Lands, and easily had another ten years before a Ritual would be held. According to all tradition and legends, Jevin could not be standing before me.

Jevin's smile remained on his face and he bowed toward me. I returned the bow, making mine just a bit deeper than his; then I extended my hand to him. He hesitated and looked into my eyes to search them for fear or mockery. His black irises produced a penetrating gaze but he found no fear in me. We were the same—both far away from where we should have been. We had no need for fear or animosity.

He grasped my hand firmly and I returned the grip. In that moment we forged a lifelong bond between us. I broke the grip and smiled at everyone. For the first time in months I felt like I might actually have found another home.

"Now what is this about me insulting Allen? All I said was 'Should I try these on?'"

The three of them fairly exploded with laughter. Marana shook her head. "You couldn't have said that!"

Jevin stared out at me from between his fingers. "No, you couldn't have said that. You are still living."

That started all of them cackling again. I frowned and spoke over their chuckles. "I don't understand."

Jevin gained control of himself first. It took a great effort and was the first evidence I had of the great self-restraint governing the Fealareen. "Allen has been fitting people for clothing for thirty or more years. He can tell, at a glance, what will fit you. He takes great pride in his skill, and even suggesting he might be wrong is a grave insult indeed."

"Oh." I grinned sheepishly. "I will have to apologize to him."

Lothar agreed. "Best do it soon or your clothing will be a random selection of things Allen has collected over the years."

A sharp peal rang through the corridor outside the room. I turned and saw the others stand at attention and straighten their clothing. I dropped back into a line with them and stared stern-faced at the doorway.

Lord Hansur appeared in the doorway. He spoke in the Tal dialect to the others. They bowed and filed past him into the hallway. Then he looked at me. "May I come in?"

"Yes, my lord."

He walked in and closed the door. He surveyed the room and frowned a bit at the rumpled condition of Lothar's bed. "I see Lothar has gotten you some clothing and secured you as his roommate."

I nodded. His voice was not flat and emotionless, nor was it commanding, yet I felt compelled to answer or acknowledge everything he said. It was my first experience with the Call.

"Very well, Nolan, come with me. You are to see the Master." He opened the door and the bell rang again. Lord Hansur waved me out into the corridor first then shut the door behind us. Novice Justices stood frozen at attention up and down the corridor while we passed to the stairway. Once we started down the stairs the bell rang twice and the normal sounds of living returned to the hallway.

"I believe, Nolan, you are aware I am the Lord of Justices." Lord Hansur paused and returned the bows of two novice Warriors who had stopped on the stairs to let us pass. "That means I control all the Justices in Talion service. Justices answer to me or the Master. Justices are special, and you have been accepted as one of them. Do you understand?"

I nodded.

Lord Hansur studied my face a moment before continuing. "A Justice is trained and able to do everything any other Talion can do, with the exception of High Magicks and some strictly clerical duties. A Justice must fly a Hawk as well as an Elite, be more at home in a saddle than a Lancer and a better fighter than an Archer or Warrior. Mastering all these skills is difficult even when a Justice is trained from birth for his job. For you the task will be almost impossible."

We reached the bottom of the stairs and turned into the corridor that led past the storeroom. We headed into the Star.

"Your training will not be easy. In addition to exercising with Lothar and the other Thirteens, you will be trained with some of the younger Talions. You will learn the Tal dialect and become fluent in it. You will study Talion history. You will make up the twelve years of training you have missed."

Lord Hansur's words should have terrified me, and probably would have if he had given me any room to doubt. His sentences were statements of fact. He gave me no choice but to succeed. I felt as if, because I *had* passed my trial by however a thin thread of chance, I was capable of all he said. That gave me confidence and made me determined not to fail Lord Hansur.

The corridors we wandered through looked all the same. Yellow ovals glowed high upon the walls with a magical luminescence to light our path. The doors were all made of iron-bound oak planking and had no marks on them. I had no way of telling where we were, or how far we'd come. I soon learned an enchantment on the Star made finding certain rooms impossible unless the traveler had a legitimate need or was desired at his destination.

Lord Hansur glided through the maze without making a sound. Thrown back over his left shoulder, his black cloak did not hide the death's-head ensign on his left breast, but I could not imagine that anyone who saw him could mistake him for another. His bearing and aura of power were unique. Even blind and half dead I would know him.

Lord Hansur stopped before a bronze set of double doors. They looked heavy, but he merely brushed the center with his left hand and the doors opened on well-oiled hinges. Lord Hansur bowed toward the center of the room, then stood aside and let me see something so grand that nothing I had ever seen before could even begin to compare with it.

A huge cavern of a room, the Master's Chamber was dark, unnaturally so, and the lamps hanging down from the ceiling were dimmed, as if they hung further away than they truly did hang. A thick strip of carpeting ran from the doorway to the throne. It was elaborately woven with a gold dragon pattern yet, in the half light, the red, greens, and golds of the carpet could barely be seen. Other works of art, like tapestries and statuary of various sizes, mediums, and subjects, stood arranged around the room to create an impressive display, but the darkness shrouded their intended beauty.

The Master's throne dominated the room. It stood on a black basalt dais six feet tall and looked as if it had been sculpted from a single block of ivory. I knew, instantly, that was impossible, because no source of ivory in the world could produce a block that large. It was carved in the shape of an animal's skull with its mouth open; two enormous fangs as thick as my thighs jutted down from the tapered, fleshless snout and propped the throne's roof up. A dark purple jewel glimmered between the vacant eye sockets, set deep into the skull as if it had grown there. The carving was otherwise unadorned and might have been dismissed as an incomplete effort because of its stark simplicity and clean lines, but its sheer size and the menacing authenticity of the teeth were impressive enough to rank the throne as a masterwork.

Then, after I'd completed my appraisal of the throne, I realized the truth, and it took my breath away. No artisan had labored to create the throne—nor could human hands have created something that exquisite. The throne, in fact, was a dragon's skull!

Lord Hansur strode into the room. Thick ropes of incense smoke broke and swirled around him. The air was heavy with it and I recognized the acrid scent in an instant. I'd smelled it once before—I was very young at the time—when a magician performed a ritual to save my grandfather's life. I associated the scent with death, and a shiver rippled down my spine.

Suddenly my awareness of the room faded. I looked up and focused beyond the trappings of the Master's throne. I saw, seated on a simple wooden chair beneath the jewel, the man who was the Master of all Talions.

From the stories told me as a child, and from my brief association with Talianna and the Talions, I expected the Master to be a mountain of a man. I was prepared for a hero, a man bigger than Jevin and quite capable of killing the creature in whose skull he now sat. Yet even as those thoughts entered my mind I caught myself, because the converse was also true. I would have easily been satisfied with a small man. Someone tiny, quick, and deadly like a mongoose would have been perfect to guide the Talions. Either of those images would have made overwhelming sense.

The man who sat in the throne was neither a giant nor a compact assassin. He was just a man. He sat in the wooden chair within the dragon's jaws as if he was uneasy with the image they projected, or as if he thought, just possibly, the jaws might close and swallow him up. His face was one I'd seen a thousand times and places before. It was completely ordinary and quite unmemorable. He could have been anyone, or no one.

I bowed to the Master. He stood, returned my bow, and seated himself again. He stood shorter than me, and his hair appeared dark brown except where the lamplight burned red highlights into it. His eyes were dark and he was slender, but the blockiness of his build and his height did not emphasize that fact. On the street, out of a Talion uniform, he would be unremarkable and impossible to remember. It dawned on me then that almost as valuable as being known as a Talion might be the time when a Talion is not believed to be anything but an ordinary man.

"Come forward, Nolan." The Master's voice, warm and friendly, sounded like that of an uncle or a friend's father. I recognized it instantly but I could not bring myself to ask the question I needed to have answered. I entered the room and the doors swung shut behind me.

"I understand that you have no living kin. Is this true?"

"Yes, Master."

"You know the families of all Talions are paid for their kin's services. Had you come to us as a child your parents would be paid for the work you will do for us. In your case there is no family to give the money to." The Master leaned forward in his throne and clasped his hands together. "Under normal circumstances, with an orphan, we would send the money to your sovereign, but I have heard you do not acknowledge King Tirrell of Hamis as your ruler. Is there someone else you would prefer to have the money sent to?"

I nodded carefully to conceal the anger and hurt burning through me at Tirrell's mention. "Sir, there is an innkeeper in Tashar, a man named Orjan. He took me in when I was sick. I would like the money to go to him. His inn, the Red Fox, is on the Cold River near Patria."

The Master smiled gently. "As you wish. Aside from clearing that matter up the only other thing I have to do is congratulate you on succeeding in your trial. You performed admirably for an outsider being tested as though he were a year older than he is."

I bowed deeply out of true respect.

The Master inclined his head to return my bow. "If there is nothing else you may go."

I hesitated. Inside I wanted to burst. He had the answer I needed, but I did not have the right to ask the question. His praise had been sincere, but was he testing me? I opened my mouth, the words on the tip of my tongue, then shut it again.

"Nolan ra Sinjaria, is there something you wish to ask me?"

I nodded and swallowed hard. "You spoke to Lord Hansur and gave me my fifth flag." A thin curtain of smoke drifted between us and I could not read his face as I spoke. "Why? I had failed."

He watched me as he considered his answer. I stood there and felt very alone. I had tried my best, but I had failed. An exception had been made in my case, and I needed to know it was because of more than pity for a child who made a fool's trek halfway across a continent or a boy who stood up to an enemy and refused to admit defeat in a war long finished. That type of person could be found anywhere in the Shattered Empire. I needed to believe there was a good reason for the Master's action, and I wanted to know what it was.

The Master stood and walked down the half-dozen steps to the carpet. "Understand this, Nolan. I am not often called upon to explain my choices, and certainly never by a novice."

I bowed my head. "Forgive me. I meant no disrespect."

He smiled and snorted a half chuckle. "I know that, and because that answer is so important to you I will explain at least part of my motivation." He seated himself on the steps rather unceremoniously. "When you reached the end of the trial you had gathered all the flags you could have gotten, save the one from the first obstacle. You were injured in that first challenge, yet the test did not trap you. If it had you would have fallen in the pit and never gotten out without help. You realized your error and saved yourself. You learned something in that test, and you'll not be caught by that sort of thing again."

The Master licked his lips and leaned back. "Even in the last test, torn and tired as you were, you did not give up. You remembered what your goal was, and your opponent did not. You beat him, though he was a better fighter, because he beat himself.

"If you wanted to be a Lancer or a Warrior I never would have spoken for you and accepted that bloody rag as your fifth flag. The qualities you have are not needed in soldiers. They must just fight and follow orders, and while our soldiers are the best in the world, they have no use for your talents. A Justice, on the other hand, constantly needs to learn. He must be able to recognize when he makes a mistake and has to act decisively to correct that mistake. You can do that, and that is why I spoke for you."

I smiled. The pressure inside me drained away and I finally

felt I'd honestly earned my place as a Justice novice. "Thank you, sir."

The Master nodded, then leaned forward. "Bear something in mind, Nolan, and remember it always. The rumor will fly, from the Warriors down at the site, that you did not pass the test but were let in anyway. Whatever Lord Hansur may have suggested as the difficulties you will face, you can double them. Any novice who has been held back for continued training because he failed a test will hate you." The Master smiled and shot a glance at Lord Hansur. "Justices are often disliked by other novices because you are all special, but they will focus on you. You are different, you are from the outside. They will see no way you can truly be one of them.

"Because you are from outside you know more of the world than they do. Remember what you learned before, and temper what you learn here with that knowledge. Some people think the world is centered around Talianna, but you know better than that. Use what you know, and share what you know, so you can make yourself and the Talions better."

I stood still as the Master rose and walked to me. He placed his hands on my shoulders. "Remember, Nolan, that unlike them, unlike those who feel Talianna is their birthright, you chose to join us. Never doubt you made the right choice."

A Services clerk led me from the Master's Chamber and pointed me in the correct direction back toward my room. I passed down the hallway leading to the storeroom and I stopped in to apologize to Allen. He grumbled when he saw me, but smiled when I finished and handed me a black jacket with a stiff, high-necked collar, buttons at the right shoulder and down the right flank, and a death's-head over the left breast. Then he shooed me out of there, complaining he had real work to do.

I returned to my room without getting lost and found Jevin and Lothar talking. Both wore jackets like the one I'd been given. Jevin had buttoned his all the way up but Lothar's hung half open. Lothar smiled. "Good, you're here. Now we only need Marana."

I shot Lothar a quizzical glance.

"Get into that jacket." Lothar reached up and started buttoning his jacket the rest of the way up. "Tonight Jania is holding a celebration and my uncle Rudolf is the host. Marana, Jevin, and you will accompany me this evening."

I shrugged the jacket on and looked over at Jevin as Lothar finished. "Jevin, do we go as his friends, or his *entourage*?"

The Fealareen snorted and grinned wolfishly. "His friends, or so it has been represented to me." Jevin turned and looked at Lothar with the cruel smile still on his face.

Lothar opened his mouth to reply, but Marana spoke from the doorway and cut him off. "You must forgive him, Nolan. During the Festival Lothar's kin come and visit. This reminds Lothar he is a noble and from time to time he even tries to act like it." Lothar reddened and she continued. "During the rest of the year we disabuse him of that notion."

Marana wore a jacket similar in cut to mine, but a knee length riding skirt completed her uniform. She'd braided her long hair with a royal blue ribbon and it looked quite attractive. She smiled and curtsied before Lothar. "Are we presentable, m'lord?"

Lothar winced. "I'm sorry. My family is still not used to the idea that I'm a Justice. They expected me to be a Warrior or Lancer so I could return to Jania and command the troops stationed in the capital, Trisus." He studied our faces to see what effect his plea had. I was sympathetic, but the other two were granite-faced.

"You say that every year, Lothar." Jevin's tone was very disapproving.

Marana nodded in agreement. "And he'll probably say it in the years to come." She shook her head slowly, then looked up. "So why should it spoil our fun?" Jevin joined her laughter and we all headed out to the Janian celebration.

The monthlong Festival started back when the Emperor formed the Talions. He invited the Imperial nobles to Talianna so they could see for themselves the skills of the Talions. At that time all Talions were Justices, Wizards, Elites, or Services—the other three divisions were not created until after the Empire crumbled—so the nobles got a good look at the troops who would oppose them if they revolted.

As the tradition developed, the Festival became a time

when delegations from various countries could meet in decidedly neutral territory and talk about alliances, trade agreements, and other diplomatic matters. Each nation that could afford it took to hosting a celebration once during the Festival, and each country made it a display of copious wealth and national pride. Full Talions could attend as many of the celebrations as they wanted while novices were restricted to that celebration hosted by their home nation, and one or two others after they passed their trials.

Lothar proudly led us toward the Janian pavilion. It was really a large grouping of tents; a huge central one surrounded by rings of smaller and smaller tents all colored yellow. People streamed in and out, and while I saw no one being actively discouraged from entering, the celebration seemed restricted to important people and nobles from other nations.

"Each year one or more of Lothar's relatives hosts the Janian delegation." Jevin pointed to a huge blond man with a thick blond beard in the middle of a crowd. "That's his uncle Rudolf."

I nodded to acknowledge Jevin's words, but I was a bit beyond understanding what he said. We'd just entered the central pavilion and I was stunned. I'd never seen so much food in my whole entire life.

The first ring of smaller tents held tables and mountains of food. Every fourth tent was home to casks of wines, ales, and liquors from Jania and the finest vineyards elsewhere in the Shattered Empire. Other tents held nothing but fruit. I recognized some of it by description but some shapes and colors and fragrances were so alien I could have easily believed the Fealareen or the Xne'kal were hosting the feast. Not as exotic, but equally astounding for quantity and variety were the tents filled with breads, cheeses, and pastries. There were more sweets gathered there in one place than any child could dream of. Lastly, being roasted on spits over open fires and paraded about by straining servants, were sides of beef and pork, and a whole flock of fowls. The wind carried the aroma of cooking meat to us, and Jevin smiled broadly.

I shook my head at the wonder of it all, and a shiver ran up my spine. There, in one place, for one evening's revel, was gathered more food than my father had produced in all the years on the farm.

"Lothar!" The bass voice boomed over the murmured din and silenced all speakers. I saw tall men back away as a wave of motion rippled through the crowd and Lothar's uncle waded into view. He darted free of the crowd and swept Lothar up in a bear hug as if his nephew were an infant.

Lothar reddened as he dangled helplessly. He shouted out a curse in the Tal dialect and twisted to get free. Rudolf laughed and held him all the tighter. "They've taught you to swear in an improper tongue. That archaic speech is meant for lawmakers, not gutterkin cursing!"

"Uncle Rudolf, put me down!" Lothar tried to put command into his voice, but in his position, and with the help of a well-timed squeeze, he squawked the sentence out. Rudolf abruptly released him and, unable to get his feet under him to remain standing, Lothar fell to the ground.

Lothar caught himself on his hands and feet before his back could hit. Scuttling forward two feet, he swept his right leg out and around through his uncle's legs. Anticipating the move, Rudolf easily kicked his feet forward, above the scything leg, and leaped over his nephew's attack. A smile spread across his face, but only for a second as Lothar reached up with his right hand and caught his uncle's right heel. The novice Justice pushed off with left arm and leg and unceremoniously dumped his uncle over on his back with a thump.

Stunned to silence, the crowd just stared. All conversation had lapsed as the mock combat started, but now no one even dared draw a breath. Jevin got a bit grayer than before, and others in the crowd were bright red from embarrassment, or absolutely ashen-faced with dread. My heart pounded wildly and I stared at the two Janians: the youth with fists balled and planted on his hips, the elder flat on his back and defenseless.

"Damn, Lothar, that was quick!" Rudolf slapped the carpet and sat up. "I'll have to remember you've learned to feint for next year."

He started laughing, a deep echoing laugh that spread through the crowd faster than nasty court gossip. Lothar extended a hand and helped his uncle up; then they hugged each other. There was genuine pride and pleasure on Rudolf's face. Rudolf then released Lothar, straightened and brushed off his dark blue velvet and satin jacket and trousers, and approached Marana, Jevin, and me.

Lothar attended his uncle. "You remember, Uncle, Marana and Jevin." Lothar nodded his head toward me. "This is Nolan ra Sinjaria. Nolan, my uncle, Count Rudolf ra Blackwood ra Jania."

The Count bowed to Marana, took her right hand, and kissed it. "You are even more beautiful this year than you were two years ago, my dear."

Marana smiled and curtsied. "Your Lordship is most kind."

The Count moved to Jevin and clapped him on both shoulders. "You are even bigger than I remember. If you ever stop growing, and they send you from here, come see me. The Steel Typhoon will find a place for you among us."

Jevin smiled politely and bowed. "I would be most honored to serve in the Steel Typhoon."

As the Count turned to me pieces of a puzzle started dropping into place. The Steel Typhoon was famed throughout the Shattered Empire as a heavy cavalry unit without equal, though many Imperianan groups disputed that claim. And it was lead by a Janian count, often called Blackwood because there are so many nobles in Jania one could only reliably identify one by naming his demense. But Blackwood was also the Janian king's only sibling, which made Lothar a prince!

The Count bracketed my shoulders in massive hands. "I have heard of you, Nolan, and I am pleased at least one Sinjarian refuses to acknowledge Hamisian rule."

I bowed. "Thank you, my lord." Silence hung in the air for a moment, as I knew I should answer his comment in some other way, but the thousand responses that crowded my brain all seemed cynical or bravely stupid. Finally one thought, one safe thought, presented itself and I offered it. "I believe, Count Rudolf, more Sinjarians would deny Hamisian rule, but they do not have the luxury of being out from under King Tirrell's thumb. This far from Hamis I am safe in my denial."

The Count stepped back and narrowed his eyes. His smile became more cautious and he unconsciously stroked his beard with his right hand. "Well said, Nolan. If you ever wish to be closer to Hamis to restate your denial, you will always be welcome in Jania to do so."

I bowed again. "I thank you very much, my lord."

Count Rudolf's grin spread openly across his face again and he draped his right arm over Lothar's shoulders. "Enough politics! You're hungry and Lothar has to see his aunt Tedra, or she'll thrash me more solidly than he did." He waved his left hand to take in the whole tent. "Enjoy, please, you are honored guests."

He turned and led Lothar off through the crowd toward a dais. Uncertain as to what to try first, the three of us drew together in a small circle and studied the tents like mules set between two equal piles of hay.

My stomach growled and protested any delay in eating something. "Eat or drink first?"

Marana reached out, took my right arm and Jevin's left, and steered us toward one of the bread tents. "First we eat some bread so the wine doesn't go straight to our heads." Jevin groaned, remembering a painful past experience. "Then we'll sample something of everything before Jevin runs off to eat a cow."

Jevin frowned. "We tried that last year." He leered over the crowd in the direction of the cooking pits. "I barely got a taste of meat last year."

"That's because you guzzled a tankard of Janian brandy, said grain and fruit were for rodents, then passed out before you reached the pits." Marana stabbed a finger into Jevin's stomach. "If Lothar and I had not gotten you back to your room, Lord Hansur would have had your head."

Jevin sighed. "Perhaps prudence is a wise course. Lead on, my lady."

Marana led Jevin and me through the tents and picked out things for us to try with the same sharp eye my mother had employed when buying things at a market. There were over twenty different types of apple, and I tried slices from all of them except two varieties with blue-green flesh. Marana introduced me to *chado*, a tear-shaped fruit with a rough green skin, soft green flesh, and a central seed twice the size of a plum. It tasted rather bland plain, but there was a spicy paste made of it that a servant spread over a piece of bread for me, and that tasted very good.

The wine tents were an adventure. We tried a little of everything, though Jevin abstained from Janian brandy, and I discovered I liked the sweet or dry wines. Jevin and Marana both prefered the heartier reds, but I didn't like the after-tastes they left in my mouth. There were also a whole legion of fruit wines and nectars to try, and the others agreed with me that *syeca*, a fiery orange-flavored liquor, was the best of an excellent lot. It was not until later that evening I learned that both *syeca* and the wine I liked the best were the product of the Sinjarian province Yotan. That made me very happy.

We reentered the main tent just as a troupe of Janian dancers began performing in an open space before the dais. Lothar, Count Rudolf, and Countess Tedra were seated in the tall chairs on the dais. Servants with their arms full of pillows scurried through the crowd passing out cushions so everyone could be seated for the performance. Beyond the dancers, back in a small tent, other entertainers awaited their turn center stage.

Marana left us and wandered through the crowd toward an open area near the dais. Jevin and I skirted the crowd and headed over toward the open cooking pits. Jevin clearly thought more of food than he did dancing. While I was inter-ested in seeing everything, the meat smelled good to me and I noticed I could watch the dancers from outside with no trouble now that the crowd was seated.

Jevin coaxed a steaming haunch of half-raw meat from a cook while I settled for a well-cooked half chicken. We wan-dered a short ways and seated ourselves on empty wine casks. We watched the show while eating. Jevin tore into his meat with an unholy vigor. His white teeth flashed in the torchlight as he gobbled down great chunks of flesh. For my part I was a bit more conservative in my attack on the chicken, and I hunched awkwardly over so anything I dropped would hit the wooden platter lying across my thighs instead of staining my new clothes.

Lothar and his family had their backs to us. I could see little more of Tedra than her long blond hair. Still, as she turned to comment to her husband, I caught a glimpse of a classically beautiful profile, from straight nose to strong chin and high forehead.

The dancers were excellent. They wore red and gold satins and swirled about in a riot of color in time to the music of three musicians behind them. Then the four men formed a line and went through a series of solo dances, each one different and characterized by an accompanying violin-and-pipe piece. Then the four women swung into a lively country dance that combined speed, precision, and complexity into an intoxicating display of their skill. Finally the eight dancers all whirled through a series of steps that had the partners constantly changing in a seemingly random pattern, but whenever the music stopped for a beat or two—again at irregular intervals—the dancers were somehow still paired with their beginning partner.

Jevin nibbled the last thread of meat from a bone and tossed it over onto a garbage pile with careless abandon and an artful flourish. At the same moment the dance stopped within and the eruption of applause seemed as much for his skill as the dancers. We both laughed at the idea.

When the applause died, and a pair of fencers took the floor, Jevin turned to me. "I'm glad I don't have to sit out here all alone this year."

I frowned. "Why would you sit alone? There's plenty of room inside."

Jevin shook his head. "I'm afraid I make some people uneasy."

"I can understand that." I started to talk about my brother Arik, but the words stuck in my throat. I coughed and switched away from painful memories. "I'd think Lothar would make sure that didn't happen."

Jevin patted my left shoulder. "Don't blame Lothar, there's nothing he could do. I make them uneasy, and they do the same to me. And Lothar's not being insensitive. Every year someone from his family comes to Festival, and he really enjoys seeing them. Last year Countess Tedra and some cousin whose name I cannot remember hosted the celebration. This year Count Rudolf was able to attend." Jevin smiled. "Lothar was disappointed last year when the Count could not be here, so this year he was very excited when he saw the Blackwood banner flying over the Janian pavilion."

"Why didn't Count Blackwood attend last year?"

Jevin shook his head. "He couldn't. He was with the Steel Typhoon patrolling the Eallian border in case King Tirrell was not satisfied with Sinjaria." Jevin saw me stiffen and looked down. "I'm sorry."

I smiled weakly. "Don't be. I only wish the Steel Typhoon could have swept Tirrell's forces out of Sinjaria."

Jevin shrugged. "That would have been impossible. You have to remember that Ealla was formed when the eastern lords of Jania revolted and broke with Jania during the Shattering. Even after a thousand years they fear Jania and would fight to the death to avoid being reconquered. They'd never consider granting a Janian force safe passage."

Words stuck in my throat. I felt angry because no one had saved my country and my family. I was angry with Hamis for conquering us, and I was mad at Ealla for barring any aid Jania might have given us. Most of all I felt angry at myself. "It's so frustrating, Jevin. And so silly. I'm angry at myself because I survived."

The Fealareen sighed and a milky white membrane nictitated over his eyes as he squeezed my shoulder. "You are not alone in that, my friend. At least you know why you are no longer in your homeland, and you exercised some choice in that matter. I was sent here as an infant, exiled from a place seen fit for only my kind." Jevin looked away, toward the east, and I shared his longing to head back home.

Then he turned back and smiled. "Let us not dwell on the morose during a celebration. Tell me of your family, of the good times. Tell me what life is like outside Talianna."

Chapter Five

TALION: MORAI

"That's most interesting, Talion. I would not have thought Talianna a place of such broad training." Selia, mounted upon a bay gelding, reined her horse around the end of a log fallen across the woodland path we took and watched my profile for a reaction. The sunlight, where it pierced the green, leafy forest pavilion above us, burned white highlights into her hair. A gentle breeze rustled the leaves, both cooling us and making enough noise to make me nervous.

After Grath's execution I stopped at the tavern long enough to change into some dry clothing. I wanted to head back for the pass just west of Pine Springs as soon as possible. Even though the rain would have wiped out Morai's trail, I knew that pass was the one he'd taken. Like the Pine Springs pass it led to Memkar, but it was a harder trail, full of twists and turns ideal for bandits and ambushers.

When I'd gathered all my things together, and the tavern-keeper's son Drew had fetched Wolf for me, I found Selia ready to leave as well. She asked if she could accompany me and, while I wanted to refuse her, I guessed she had it in her mind to follow me to Morai, so I welcomed her along. With her riding in my company, I could keep her safe, and she was certainly more talkative than Wolf.

"Selia, you think of Talianna as a big military camp. Everyone does. Warriors are forged of steel, Justices are demons in human form. We're not supposed to understand philosophy or have a grasp of more than military history." I watched the trail up ahead of us and slowed our pace a bit. The trail wound up and around a hillside, then disappeared into a woody tunnel of darkness. "We *are* instructed in more than purely martial disciplines."

"My apologies. I've never spoken with a Talion who is so candid about his life." Her smile was genuine and friendly. "It's a very enlightening experience."

I shot her a sideways glance and snorted a laugh. "I certainly hope so. We've ridden for two days and other than comments about the weather or food the only thing you've done is ask me questions about Talianna." I turned in the saddle and faced her smiling. "If I didn't have this death's-head on my jerkin I'd think I was the minstrel and that you were the taciturn and mysterious Talion."

Selia threw her head back and laughed. "I can see your point. Shall I tell you about myself?"

I bowed my head and faced forward again. "Please do. I'll need the time to rest my voice so I can tell Morai to stop running." I also needed to concentrate on the woods and watch for Morai and his compatriots. They traveled at a slower pace than we set and we were no more than a half day behind Morai, Brede, and Tafano.

"Very well, Talion, I will tell you my life story." She shifted, sat a bit taller in the saddle, and hooked a strand of blond hair behind her right ear. "My full, true name is Selia ra Jania ulPatria."

That remark caught my attention much as finding a scorpion

in a boot might. I jerked my head around and studied her. "You're ulPatria?"

She reined her horse up and fixed me with a very surprised stare. "Come now, Talion, you can't be superstitious about the ul!"

I recovered quickly and shook my head. "I don't think I am, but not many people run around admitting they are ul as openly as that. And, given who we're chasing, these woods are fairly thick with them."

She frowned and gently dug her heels into the gelding's ribs to start him walking again. "Morai is ul?" There was a bit of disappointment in her voice.

I grinned and shook my head. "No, not him. Brede ulRia."

Selia sighed with relief. "He is not truly ul." And though she didn't say it I could tell she was relieved Morai had no such simple motivation for his actions.

"How can you refuse to claim Brede? He was royalty and he's been disinherited. And you certainly can't deny his litany of crimes rivals that of the greatest ullords."

Selia shook her head violently. Through a curtain of blond hair I could see tightly closed eyes and a grim, thin line of a mouth. "I can't believe you'd judge the uls by a few distorted legends. Talions—Justices in particular like yourself—should understand how the truth could get twisted into fearful and unfounded stories."

I snorted. "Oh, then none of the bloody tales are true?"

She opened her mouth to protest, thought, then closed it again. "All right, I'll concede first blood to you, but the fight's not over. Might I explain?" She took my nod as agreement to both points and continued. "You know from the legends that ul families are those families of nobles who were ousted from power during the Shattering. Rebels or other nobles drove the rulers out and their families, when they escaped, were left to wander the Empire and beyond looking for aid. Since virtually all the provinces had new leadership and proclaimed themselves sovereign states, no one looked favorably upon the uls. Just harboring them could be seen by a neighbor as a hostile act, so the disinherited families had to keep moving and remain constantly vigilant against attacks."

I laughed lightly and relaxed. We'd reached the top of the hill and the trail below wound through a grassy meadow where any ambush would be difficult to stage or execute. "Selia, you make it sound as if the old nobles just kindly left their nations when asked. As I recall there were many brutal civil wars at that time. Even today tyrannicide is still considered justifiable."

She smiled. "Your point is well taken, but your caution is a sword that cuts with both edges." Some of the anger I'd sparked left her and she relaxed into a more comfortable, storytelling mood. "Do not assume, Talion, that all the provinces fell in violence. Patria is a perfect example. The King realized neither of his legitimate sons was competent. After destroying the corruption in his government he turned the power structure over to the rebel Marcherlords. He even arranged for his two sons to be executed so they could not be used by others to seize power. On his deathbed he legitimized all his children, creating the ulPatria, but they never made any stab at power and settled elsewhere in great peace."

I frowned. "Having his own sons slain does little to make the King a hero in my eyes. No offense intended, but that's just another story of court intrigue and murder."

Selia nodded her head. "It is that, but it's hardly the bloodiest tale from those times. Take Hamis as an example. There Prince Roderick killed his father and eldest brother to take the throne. His other elder brother, Uriah, was out of the country at the time, and remained in exile for over three decades. Roderick's own son Roderick, after years of putting up with his father's mad plans for assassinating Uriah, killed his father. He invited Uriah back to Hamis to heal the family rift. Uriah returned and Roderick murdered him.

"The legends have it that Uriah fathered a family while in exile, and that the House of Hamis is always afraid that an ulHamis will come to reclaim the throne. The ulHamis are one of the few families that have a legitimate blood tie to the current Throne House."

I controlled my emotions concerning Hamis and dismissed them with a laugh. "I've yet to hear a story from you that does anything but strengthen the case for Brede being ulRia. He's disinherited nobility with a record of bloody crimes so horrid that the King sealed the records and outlawed the name 'Brede' within Ria's borders."

Selia shivered with disgust then smiled ironically. "Actually,

Talion, the Bastard of Ria has no claim to the throne. As you will recall his mother, Queen Candra, confessed in the King's Court that Brede was the product of an adulterous affair, even though that admission made her life forfeit."

I nodded slowly. Again our trail took us into a dark woods, where it slithered through high, shadowy tunnels of over-arching trees and around brush strewn hillocks. I had a bad feeling about this stretch of the trail, and as the time was right, I suggested we stop for a rest and some food. We dismounted and let our horses graze while we ate some of the bread and cheese we'd brought from Pine Springs.

If someone waited to ambush us, I was content to let him lie in wait a bit longer during the heat of the day.

"Selia, you know as well as I do that Queen Candra's testimony was a lie. It was the only way her son could be kept from the throne without a civil war." I finished the last of my cheese and tossed a crust of bread to a chipmunk daring enough to pop up on the end of the fallen tree I was using as a bench.

The minstrel smiled. "Can't have it both ways, Talion. If he was a noble they couldn't have disinherited him, and if he's not a noble he can't be ulRia."

I bowed my head to her. "Now you've blooded me. I do acknowledge that not all uls have a family history drenched in blood, and that grouping Brede with any people is a grave insult indeed. Still, and getting back toward my original surprise, you don't strike me as typical of the ul. Uls roam the Shattered Empire in great colorful caravans. They stop wherever they want and set up little tent-and-cart villages. They claim that they have enough blood of each royal family in them to have a right to any land they want. They tell fortunes, sing forgotten songs, and keep ancient traditions alive. Was your life like that?"

She shook her head, growing a bit more quiet. "No, my life was not like that at all. Truthfully, most uls do not wander with the ulbands. Those are for the footloose, the ones who prefer lamenting their losses to trying to build a new life for themselves. I actually pity them, for they cling to an old way of life, hoping for something to sweep away a thousand years of history so they can lead again. What they do not realize is that if they were capable of leading they never would have been thrown out of their homelands in the first place, or they would have long since made a new life elsewhere."

I nodded. "Interesting observation. In many ways they are like those who refuse to try the tests to become a Talion."

"Exactly. They were deposed because they could not effectively rule. My father was not caught in that trap—of hoping for something beyond hope. My father is a good man; an artisan in Trisus, the capital of Jania. He crafts the finest musical instruments ever made. He made my lute." She smiled proudly and swept crumbs from her lap.

I stood and untied Wolf's reins from the tree where I'd hobbled him. I swung up into the saddle and patted Wolf's neck. He turned his head enough to stare at me with his left eye and let me know that a friendly pat on the neck was not suitable recompense for so short a stop.

I saw Selia had mounted up, so we headed out. The trail here was wide enough for us to ride abreast, so we did. "I assume if your father made your lute he also taught you to sing?"

She stiffened. "No." Sucked down by sorrow, her voice dropped an octave.

I was watching the trail in front of us intently; as a result I did not react to her statement immediately. I turned to look at her, but her long golden hair shielded her face from me. "I'm sorry for whatever I said. I meant no offense."

She brushed her hair back from her face with the same motion that wiped a tear from her eye and gave me a brave smile. "My father cannot talk. He was not born mute. In fact, as my mother tells it, he had a beautiful singing voice. He grew up in Trisus, apprenticed to an artisan who made musical instruments, but really wanted to be a minstrel. He applied himself very hard to learning how instruments worked, how to make them do whatever he wanted, and he learned how to sing. My mother said he would work from dawn to dusk in the shop, and then sing half the night away in taverns or at celebrations."

I frowned. "Few men are able to do what they love and still afford a family. With a wife and child his life would have been complete enough for most men. What happened?"

Selia stared off into the leafy canopy above us, and the smile got a bit stronger. "He was not married at that point. He was hired to sing at a wedding feast in Trisus, which he saw as a chance to show his skills off to a host of willing patrons. My father went gladly, as most of the nobility in Jania would attend even though the marriage was a strained, arranged affair. The groom was a minor noble and the reluctant bride was the daughter of a merchant who had the money the noble needed to bring his family back into prominence.

"The bride was rather melancholy at the feast. She had not wanted to marry the noble, but her father urged her to do so because he wanted titled grandchildren. The noble asked my father to sing a song to cheer his bride and lift her spirits so she could at least *appear* to be pleased with the arrangement. My father had a song that never failed him when he wanted to please a woman, so he sang it. He sang his heart out. It's said a dozen ladies of nobility fell for him that night." Selia hunched over in the saddle to avoid a low-hanging tree branch.

"Unfortunately," she continued, "one of them was the noble's new bride. She couldn't take her eyes off my father, and she looked far too happy to suit her new husband. The noble knew everyone felt the forced union a shameful fraud, and what little honor his family had left burned in him for satisfaction.

"So while everyone else congratulated my father on his fine voice, the noble brooded. My father was the center of attention and the feast seemed to be more in his honor than the host's, and the host's wife was more than properly attentive to my father. The noble was not pleased and his rage finally exploded. He said the song offended his wife's honor and he would duel with my father to gain satisfaction."

I sighed. "And the noble stabbed your father in the throat, ending his career."

"No." Selia grinned broadly. "If this was a song that would be the ending, but life seldom works out so simply. Lord Joachim was not as good a fighter as he thought, and my father had some training in swordplay because of a mercenary uncle who thought Father ill prepared as a minstrel to head out traveling. Father fought the noble to first blood and won by inflicting a small cut on the back of the noble's right hand. My father then dropped his guard. The noble advanced and lunged at my father. Father dodged away from the blade, but caught the sword's guard in the throat.

"My father never sang again. I never heard him raise his voice above a whisper, yet even a whisper was painful for him." Selia smiled. "In his eyes, in the fluid grace of his hands when he plays a lute or a dulcimer, I have seen what it must have been like to *hear* him, but that has not stopped me from wishing I could have listened to his songs or have sung with him."

"I can understand that desire. What happened to the noble?"

"The noble claimed he did not feel the cut on his hand. He paid my father three hundred Imperials, a fine levied by a brash, young Count Rudolf ra Blackwood, the ranking court member in attendance."

A picture of Lothar's uncle flashed before my eyes. "Three hundred Imperials is not much reparation for what happened to your father. He should have had more for that night and his injury."

Selia smiled—a cruel smirk that blossomed into a bright grin. "He did. The woman was my mother. She bore three children, all of them sired by my father, not her husband. I think Lord Joachim knows we are illegitimate, but he says nothing. My mother controls him, and does as she pleases. Lord Joachim is a laughingstock among the nobles of Trisus. Everyone believes he has been dealt justice."

I nodded in agreement with her verdict. I stopped Wolf. We'd just come up a hill, and the trail entered a small clearing before plunging again into a thicker stand of woods. In the morning the sun would have blinded any rider coming up the hill, but after we took the time for our lunch, only shadows greeted us.

Wolf's ears flicked forward a half second before I saw the motion. I slipped my left foot from the stirrup and kicked Selia off her horse. She grunted, folded forward over my foot, and fell back off the gelding as the crossbow bolt hissed through the air and tugged at her shoulder. She dropped from sight before I could see how badly she had been wounded. In the same motion I twisted from my saddle and fell off Wolf to the right. Leaving my *tsincaat* in the saddle scabbard, I rose, ran forward, and dove into the brush wall to the right of the trail.

I caught a glimpse of Brede, the Bastard of Ria, before a root caught my ankle and dumped me to the ground. He'd only ever been able to kill something tied up for him and had no illusions about honor or fairness—hence his attack from ambush. I gathered myself into a low crouch, trusting in the fact that my lack of helplessness would put him off killing me immediately.

Selia was very right, he could not be ulRia. For that he had to at least be human.

"Come on, Talion, come to me." Brede filled his voice with forced levity. He had to be trying to reload his crossbow, and his anxiety made that task difficult. Under normal circumstances reloading a crossbow would present no one a problem, but usually the archer is smarter than the bow and he does not have a Talion, a Talion he just tried to murder, in such close proximity.

I pushed on through the scrub and reached an area that was relatively clear of underbrush. The evergreen trees in this stretch of woods had blanketed the ground with pine needles—all orange-brown and dead—that smothered any undergrowth and strangled most sounds. Because the lowest branches were six feet over my head, nothing but tree trunks blocked my vision. Many of the recently trimmed branches littered the ground and gave me a cold feeling in the pit of my stomach. Brede, or Morai for him, had chosen well the site for this battle.

I ran to a tree and stood with my back pressed against it. The rough bark felt smooth beneath my leather tunic. Few enough of the pines had sufficient girth to hide Brede, but I still could not see him. A breeze threaded its way through the grove to steal any sound that might have pointed me toward Brede's haven. I crouched low to make a smaller target and armed myself.

Out of the pouch at my belt I drew my sling and a stone. I looped one leather thong around my hand, placed a stone in the pocket, grabbed the second thong, and whirled the sling. Prepared, I rose up and looked out around my tree. From behind a thick tree fifteen yards ahead and off to the left, Brede did the same thing.

Simultaneously we let fly. His bolt thudded solidly into my tree and scattered splinters of sappy wood into the air. My stone tore bark from his tree and just nicked his right ear before he ducked back to safety. Without a second thought I cut around my tree and headed straight for him. I knew I was much better suited to unarmed combat than any Rian bowman, especially when he was trying to reload his crossbow.

I advanced unopposed and that only struck me as peculiar when I rounded Brede's tree and stopped like a wagon with a broken wheel.

Brede stood there grinning like the fool he felt I was. At his feet lay one crossbow and in his hands he cradled a second. The bolt in the second crossbow had a nasty looking head with twin razor edges spiraling around like ivy on a post. It was designed to drill into its target—usually large game like deer—and core a hole large enough to let the target leave a blood trail if it ran off. He aimed that bolt at my stomach but did not shoot.

"Morai told me you'd fall for that trick. 'Keep a bow loaded at all times, Brede, and you'll have him.' He didn't think I could do it." His grin was mirthless, like the bolt, and a look of ecstasy flashed through his large brown eyes.

I held my right hand out, moving it slowly and easily, and let the sling slide through my fingers to the ground. "Brede, give me the crossbow. Give me the crossbow and we can get this over with easily. You don't want to kill a Talion."

He narrowed his eyes and flared his nostrils. He did his best to live up to the Rian stereotype of stupidity and bovine looks. "Why not? Think of the reputation I'd have."

I shook my head gently and tried to swallow. "You'll have a hundred Talions after you, and you don't want to end up like the last man who killed a Talion. They say he, or most of him anyway, is still alive in a dungeon in Talianna. Even you don't want to endure that much torture."

Brede grinned and his eyes went blank as he thought back to fond memories of times in the foul torture pits of Ria. His attention wavered for a second and that gave me all the time I needed. I concentrated.

My *tsincaat* came to my hand just as Brede triggered the crossbow. I lunged at the bow and tipped it away from me.

The bolt slammed into the *tsincaat*'s blade with a loud ringing sound and raced up to the crossguard. It tore the *tsincaat* from my grasp—utterly numbing my right hand in the process—and sent the blade flying back over my right shoulder.

Brede was stricken. He screamed in rage and charged forward with his crossbow raised like a club. I dodged to the right and side-kicked him in the stomach, though with considerably more force than I'd used on Selia. His quiver of bolts sailed off and rained quarrels all over the ground.

Brede reeled backward and slammed into his tree. He dropped the crossbow, then fell to his knees. He reached down, grabbed a bolt, and clutched it like a knife. Scrambling to his feet, he rushed at me again. Anger masked his face and flushed his skin to a bright red shade.

I sidestepped his clumsy low slashing attack and this time planted my right foot on his chest. I heard a crunch and sympathetic pains rippled through my chest, but Brede didn't even notice. He dropped back two steps and turned to charge me again.

I fell back as the bolt slashed past my face. I planted my right foot in his ample stomach and grabbed his shirt with my left hand. Deliberately continuing my fall, I rolled onto my back and dragged him with me. As he came over the top of me, I kicked up and sent him flying over my head. He sailed into his tree, glanced off it, twisted, and fell to the ground. He tried to rise once, but a ribbon of blood trailed from his mouth and he lay back down, very still.

I stood, shook my numb right hand, and tucked it in my left armpit. I was puzzled, because my kick might have cracked some ribs, and the tree might have bruised his shoulder or arm, but that should not have stopped a man as big as he was. I cautiously walked over to the body, taking care to see he was not trying to trick me, and, with some effort, managed to roll him over with my right foot. Brede had fallen on his bolts. Two of them had twisted their way into his back, doing to him what he would have done to Selia and me.

The Bastard of Ria was no more and I felt sorely tempted to record his death in my journal as involuntary suicide.

I broke his neck to prevent any chance of revivification.

Normally that was not a worry, but even the Talions did not know the full extent of Brede's crimes and who his friends were, or how powerful they might truly have been. I recovered my *tsincaat* and sling, then walked from the grove back to Selia.

Wolf and the gelding grazed in the small clearing somewhat away from where Selia sat. She looked a bit pale and had torn her tunic away from the top of her right shoulder. She winced as she gently probed the gash on her shoulder with her bloodstained left hand.

I dropped to one knee. "Let me take a look."

"Why?" She smiled a bit and her lips trembled nervously. "I think my ribs hurt more than my shoulder."

"Ah, I'm sorry for that, but I had no choice." The bolt, probably another one of the bleeders, had stitched three cuts across the top of her shoulder just above the collarbone. It looked worse than it was and I had no doubt her ribs did hurt more.

"You don't think he poisoned the bolt, do you?" She asked the question hopefully, and a great deal more calmly than I would have if our roles were reversed. She was very brave and I smiled to reassure her.

I stood and walked to Wolf. "No, I don't think it was poisoned. Brede would have prefered you to scream and suffer while he killed me. You know how some people hum or sing to themselves while they work? From what I understand of him, Brede liked a stranger accompaniment."

"Ugh."

"Yeah, not the sort of music you want to add to your repetoire, I imagine." I took a crusty green bottle and a rag from my saddlebags. "This will clean the wound up and prevent you from getting bloodfever."

I knelt beside her again. "Tell me what happened to your father after the fight." I wanted her to concentrate on anything other than the wound so I could treat it without interruption.

"My father immediately won the sympathy of all Trisus. No one who was anyone would order an instrument made if he did not offer the job to my father first. At least the first orders were sympathy orders, but after that—OUCH!—they came for his talent. . . ."

"Sorry, I forgot to tell you this stuff would sting." I poured more of the liniment on a cloth and wiped the wound clean. She cried out again and Wolf nickered in sympathy. The cut cleaned up nicely and closed easily enough that I didn't think she'd carry much of a scar away from the wound. I wrapped the shoulder in a clean bandage torn from the rag.

"Your father knew his craft, then?" I helped her stand. The color returned to her face and she walked without any problem to her horse. She mounted easily. I placed the bottle back in the saddlebags, climbed into my saddle, and we set off.

"Yes, he did know his work. It seemed that all the energy he put into his singing now went into his instruments. He created instruments to be his voice. I remember sitting spellbound as he told a story through song with each character performed by a different instrument. The performance was wonderful. He's wonderful."

I smiled. "Good, I'm glad for him, and for you. I'd like to meet a man of such ability."

"You cannot unless Jania lifts the interdiction." Selia laughed. "I find it hard to believe a nation would ban all Talions and call Talions of their own nationality home. The Talions must have grossly insulted the Janian Royal House."

I shook my head. "Nations do that from time to time. They kick us out for fifteen or twenty years, then call us back in. It's not common, but it's not unknown either."

Selia rode with the reins in her right hand, her left hand probing the bandage.

"Is it hurting?"

She shook her head. "It really was Brede?"

"In the flesh."

She raised her eyebrows. "The wound doesn't seem to hurt enough to have been caused by him."

I smiled and tried not to think about how much the bolt he had aimed at me would have hurt. "You're one of the lucky ones. He did not have you and a room full of tools at his disposal. The bolt was meant to cripple or kill slowly, though two worked quickly enough on him."

The tall, forest trees kept the trail moist enough to retain hoofprints, and those we followed were very fresh—less than six hours old. Tafano's big horse—the only creature capable of hauling him and his armor around—made the deepest hoofprints. A lighter horse, probably faster than any horse I'd ever ridden, was Morai's mount and, because the larger prints sometimes obliterated the smaller ones, I knew it led the way along the trail.

We covered another mile of the forested trail as it wove in and around hills. Finally we topped one hill flecked with granite fangs and fingers, as if some huge stone monster were digging itself out of a grave. A hundred yards down the shadowed trail, the tunnel opened up into a brilliantly lit meadow. The very bright sunlight initially burned all color and detail out of the meadow, but bees and butterflies swam into view quickly enough and lent an air of tranquility to what I was uneasily certain had to be another trap.

Unfortunately, I was not wrong.

We cautiously rode into the meadow and stopped in the warm sunlight. Off to my right, leaning against a maple tree, stood the stripped trunk of a small pine. Tafano had chopped all the branches off and sharpened the narrow end. Despite its crude manufacture, it was clearly meant to be a lance.

Across the meadow, riding from a darkling copse, came Tafano. Bright silvery armor encased him, and green peacock plumes garnished his full helm. He carried a real lance with finely shaped shaft of oak and a brightly polished steel claw on the end. The claw, a three-pronged lance head designed to look like a metal eagle talon, existed solely to shear through my chest and tear my heart out. The sight of it set my stomach roiling.

"Selia, listen carefully to what I'm about to say. Tafano will charge me when I pick the lance up. If he wins, and he's much better at this than I am, ride fast in the other, *any other*, direction."

Selia nodded and reined her horse off to the left. I pulled a pair of leather gloves from my left saddlebag, then leaned down and picked up the pine lance. Tafano raised his lance above his head and pumped it upward three times. I imitated his gesture, found the proper balance point for my lance, and hugged the butt end of it to my ribs. We spurred our horses forward and galloped at each other.

As I thundered through the meadow at Tafano, a thousand lessons echoed through my head. We'd pass each other on the left and target the other's shield or chest. Tafano, with a glittering triangular shield on his left arm, gave me a choice of targets—a choice I denied him rather reluctantly. I noticed he cocked his head to the right, so much so that he could only see me with his left eye, so I hunkered down even lower in the saddle to make myself a difficult target to hit without full depth perception. Even with that added advantage, though, I did not honestly think the battle would last beyond the initial pass.

Imperianan warriors, as a class, are simply the best heavy cavalry in the world. Most of them learn to ride before they can walk, and some of the nobles wear mail once they start walking. An Imperianan is a demon on horseback, riding only the best-bred and best-trained warhorses in the Shattered Empire outside Talianna. Their warriors are even well versed in infantry battling with their massive greatswords. In fact, if most of them were not so arrogant because their nation had once been the capital province of the Empire, their customs and abilities might well have been widely admired.

Wolf raced forward with his ears flat back against his head. Sunlight slithered across Tafano's armor and leaped away flashing from the curves and joints of his silver carapace. The plume rising from his helm—far too brilliant a green to be lost in the dark woods behind him—danced and bounced like a cat's paw striking at a dangling piece of string. I would have laughed, but the extended claw tore all possible humor from the situation.

I twisted in the saddle and eluded the lance's tempered grasp while I stabbed out with my own lance. It struck home on Tafano's shield, then exploded into a cloud of splinters with a loud, wet crack. Tafano rocked slightly in his saddle but sped past, fully recovered before the tip of my broken lance even hit the ground. Disgusted, I threw aside the butt end of my lance and rode to the end of the field where Tafano had begun his charge.

I reigned up short. Morai blocked my path.

I nearly smiled at him, because, standing there so boldly, he looked very much the roguish hero Selia's song made him out to be. He wore a blue silk tunic and red silk breeches

tucked into the tops of high riding boots. A red silk headband
circled his brow and got lost in the tangle of dark hair, though
the ends emerged to float gently in the light breeze coursing
through the meadow. He wore a neatly trimmed and fashionable moustache that combined with his clothing to make him
appear more a noble out riding than a criminal pursued by a
Talion. His eyes, a brown so light it appeared gold, sparkled
as he smiled.

"Greetings, Talion, it has been some time." He bent down
and brought up another pine lance from it hiding place in the
long grass. "I assume you can use this?"

I couldn't help it, I had to smile. "If you have no immediate need for it, I would like to borrow that lance." I looked
back over my shoulder at the mountain of man and horse on
the field. "I can't promise I'll return it in good shape."

Morai shrugged. "No matter." He waved a hand and
encompassed the whole forest with the gesture. "I can always
make another."

It wasn't until he held the lance up to me that I remembered how small he was. I was easily a head taller than he was,
and Tafano was at least that much taller than me. Still I knew,
from people like Morai and Lord Isas, that judging a man by
physical size alone was a bad mistake.

I turned Wolf so we faced Tafano again. "You realize I
will be back for you."

Morai nodded. "I expect it. Bring your compatriot with
you when you finish Tafano. Oh, did you notice how he held
his head?"

I smiled. "Is he half blind?"

Morai shrugged and rubbed the knuckles of his right fist.
"Temporarily. We had a disagreement this morning. His right
eye is swollen shut."

A low laugh rumbled in my chest and Morai joined me.
"Thank you for your assistance."

"Could I do less?" Morai's smile brimmed over with
memories, and I blushed.

Turning from Morai, I raised my new lance and pumped it
three times in the air. Tafano returned the signal and again we
started our horses hurtling toward each other. Grass and
trees flashed past in a blurred wave. Each hoofbeat pounded
up into me and started a sympathetic rhythm pulsing in my

temples. I ground my teeth together and stinging sweat seeped into my eyes.

I waited until we were close enough that Tafano set himself for impact and, with pressure from my knees, I cut Wolf to the left. For the barest of seconds we sped directly at Tafano and his mount and I envisioned the tangled, broken, screaming mass of horseflesh and man we'd become if I allowed us to collide. More pressure and Wolf moved left again. We would pass on the right.

Tafano twisted his neck even further in a futile attempt to spot us. At the last second he tried to bring his lance up over his horse's head and strike out blindly at us, but his attempt was too late and far off target. Sweeping past on his right I stood in the stirrups and, wrapping two hands around the lance's butt, I swung it like a massive club.

The blow caught Tafano square in the chest, dented his breastplate, and snapped the lance cleanly in two. His lance arced up into the air and sailed from his slackened grip as the Imperianan reeled in the saddle and tipped to the right. Somehow he kicked free of his stirrups and avoided being dragged by his horse. Even so his fall from the saddle was heavy and hard. Accompanied by a loud, metallic din, he rolled up into a silver ball.

I vaulted from Wolf's saddle as soon as the horse had slowed enough for it to be safe, summoned my *tsincaat*, and slapped Wolf on the rump. He headed off, wary of Tafano's horse, and nervously watched while I circled toward Tafano. The warhorse moved at me and effectively cut me off from his fallen master.

"Tafano ra Imperiana," I shouted. The armor stirred and straightened itself. It looked for all the world like a metal warrior arising from a steel egg. "Tafano, send the horse away. Let this be between us."

The Imperianan shucked his gloves and pulled off his helmet. Blood ran from his nose and ears to streak his brown moustache and beard with scarlet. His right eye was swollen and blackened but his left one burned with an intensity that cut at my spine like a cold grave wind. He spat blood. He tried to rise, stumbled, and caught himself on one hand and one knee.

He spat again. "Rasha, kill him." He stabbed a finger at me, coughed and sat down abruptly.

The horse charged at me to ride me down, but I dodged out of the way. I circled back across the path he had taken, forcing him to turn even more for another pass, but he stopped in midturn and watched me. The stallion had been ordered to kill me and he would do so unless I killed him first.

"Tafano, call the animal off."

The warrior laughed. "He is as much a weapon to me as my sword. You are dead, Talion." His laughter continued, then dissolved into a racking cough.

The horse started forward again. This time he was cautious and herded me gently. He played with me and for a second lost all sign of being anything more than a high-spirited horse. Then he charged quickly and I barely dove from beneath steel-shod hooves.

I rolled to my feet and wrapped both hands around the hilt of my *tsincaat*. "This is the last time, Tafano. Send Rasha away or anything I do to him I do to you!"

Tafano looked at his horse. "Rasha," he commanded, balling a fist and slamming it into the ground, "*stomp him!*"

Blindly obedient to his master, Rasha charged and reared up in front of me. Eyes wide and nostrils flared, he kicked out at me. I dodged back as a hoof slashed past my left ear. I brandished my *tsincaat*, but the horse ignored it and kept coming. He reared, then stomped and jumped forward. With each motion he drove me back.

I retreated from five attacks before I had the pattern. On the sixth assault, as two hooves pounded and tore the ground at my feet, I dodged left and forward. Rasha reared and just missed my right shoulder with a futile kick as I rushed along his flank. Even as the horse roared furiously and twisted to bite at me, I slashed through the powerful muscles bunched on his gaskins and he went down in a dusty heap.

I reeled away from the horse and my mouth soured. The animal lay there and thrashed, screaming. Blood spurted from his hindquarters, yet he still pawed the ground with his forelegs and tried to drag himself toward me. I wanted to turn away from the pitiable sight, but I had to respect the fierce determination in the beast's eyes. The horse would never surrender while he had a duty to perform, making it clear to me that I, too, had a duty to perform. Numbed by his suffering, I circled the horse and pressed my right palm to his broad, starred forehead. In seconds I took Rasha beyond all pain.

I laid Rasha's head on the ground and heard the squealing protests of dented armor as Tafano tried to get up again.

"For that, Talion, you will die very slowly!" His voice was weak but full of venom and arrogance. *I* had to pay because I'd done something I'd begged *him* to remove from me.

Utter rage flashed through me like fire across a puddle of lamp oil. I spun, pounced on Tafano, knocked him to the ground, and rained blow after blow on his face. I shattered his aquiline nose and pulped his full, noble lips. I kicked his hands from beneath him as he tried to rise and I stood with one foot on his chest until his struggles taxed his strength so heavily that he could not rise against the weight of his armor.

Tafano lay there in the hot afternoon sun like a beetle trapped on its back. I stalked over to Rasha and tugged Tafano's greatsword free of the saddle scabbard. Twice the length of my *tsincaat*, the blade was as dull as an old paring knife. It needed no edge because it cut through nothing; it *smashed* through anything it hit. A warrior wielding the sword in battle could crush armor and shatter the bones beneath it. It was a terrible weapon, one that granted lingering death as opposed to something more swift and merciful, but at that moment I could think of no more perfect weapon in the world.

I looked down at Tafano and studied his blood-smeared face. He stared at me with his left eye. There was no fear there, only anger. And the grand arrogance of his people.

"I warned you. What you forced me to do to the horse . . ." I took one solemn step toward his feet and raised the greatsword. I held it there, for a heartbeat, and brought it down as Tafano raised his head just in time to look, and just in time to scream.

The armor over his thighs dented as easily as a tin tavern cup hurled against a wall, and his legs broke as simply as my lances had. Tafano clawed at the ground and threw great clods of grass and earth into the air as he writhed in pain. Then some god showed Tafano the mercy he'd denied Rasha. The Imperianan fainted.

• • •

Tossing the greatsword aside, I summoned my *tsincaat* and
stalked across the field. Morai sat on a log back beneath the
growing shadows of the forest. Selia sat beside him, and they
were laughing. Something inside of me, something touched
by the horse's death and the events in Pine Springs, just
snapped. "Enough, Morai, enough. I'm tired of chasing you
all over."

The both of them stopped and stared at me as if I were an
intruder in some noble's love garden. Selia started to speak,
but Morai laid a gentle hand on her forearm and she stopped.
He stood. "Whatever do you mean, Talion?"

I stared at him with disbelief. "I've got at least a dozen
warrants with your name on them in my saddlebags." I
looked back toward Wolf. "You're wanted in every nation
west of Imperiana—Memkar just being the most recent. Go
read them for yourself."

The bandit laughed easily and shook his head. "You know
I eschew reading those things."

I snorted and rubbed my left hand against my sweat-slick
forehead. "Them, and anything else, you illiterate fraud."

Morai shrugged easily, then stared at me. "Talion, are you
serious?"

I screwed my eyes shut and tried to massage away the pain
throbbing through my head so I could think clearly, but it
was no use. "Yes, Morai, its over. It was one thing for you to
head up a pack of bandits stealing things here and there.
Selling your services to nobles who want to overthrow their
government is another thing entirely."

"But common banditry was getting boring. At least when
intriguing you meet a much better class of people."

"That may well be, Morai, but you can't be allowed to
bring governments down."

A hint of irony threaded its way through his reply. "Better
a bandit than a power broker, is it? Is that because upsetting
peasants is preferable to upsetting nobles—perhaps because
the nobles can read?"

I opened my eyes just a bit. "You know better than that.
I've chased you before this, remember?"

"You have, Talion, and your point is well taken. I'll heed
your advice." Morai smiled, held his hands up, then clapped

them together once. "As I was telling Selia here I'd decided to abandon political intrigues and leave off banditry. I will leave this area and become a jewel thief. There's always some bauble worth stealing somewhere."

I shook my head. "No! I mean it has to stop—all of it. Your career is over. This is the end, Morai."

The smile on his face melted into a thin, grim line. "Swords, then?" I nodded, and he drew a pair of gloves from his belt and pulled them onto his hands. He freed his swept-hilt longsword from its scabbard—which had been belted to a low tree branch—and scythed through golden grass stalks with some idle cuts.

He looked up at me and moved to my left. A breastwork of long grass stood between us. "If you want me, Talion, come and get me." He struck a guard and waited.

I took three steps toward him and the ground fell away beneath my feet.

I hit the bottom of the pit in a shower of branches and grass clods. I coughed out the dust and spit out the grit grinding and crackling between my teeth. I'd broken nothing in my fall and my pleasure in that turn of events shattered the dark mood that possessed me. I stood and saw that the hole was too tall for me to jump out of, and the walls too weak to support any attempt to climb out.

Morai did not laugh when he looked over the pit's edge at me. "I am truly sorry I had to do this to you, Talion. I did not want to fight you. If I killed you your Master would send more Talions after me. That would be inconvenient."

I laughed and dusted myself off. "Others would be more bother than I have, I imagine. Had the possibility that I might beat you arisen?"

Morai smiled. "Yes, and it was dismissed in due course." He pointed at the pit. "I estimated that you could collapse a wall of the pit, digging with your sword . . ."

"*Tsincaat.*"

"*Tsincaat* in four or five hours. In that time Selia and I will be long gone. You won't hear of me for a month or two and then who knows?"

Selia appeared at the edge of the pit. She smiled weakly and a bit apprehensively. She tossed my canteen down to me.

"I thought you might like that. I've hobbled Wolf in the shade where he can get some grass."

I smiled back at her. "Thank you. You are going with Morai of your own accord?"

For a second she was shocked, then she smiled at my concern. "Yes. Accompanying him is my choice."

I looked over at Morai. "Let her get hurt and after I take apart those who hurt her, I'll find you."

"I will take good care of her, Talion." He held his hand out to her and she took it. "Just so you know, I didn't take my people in to Memkar because the nobles who purchased my services were buffoons. Their enemies found them out, which is why a ship burned and sank on Lake Tiakly with loss of all the conspirators on board. I'm not above exploiting political fantasies, Talion, but I have no intention of triggering wars to enrich myself."

I nodded up at him. "I believe you, oddly enough."

"As well you should. You know I've never lied to you." Morai tossed me a quick salute. "And I wish you the best until we meet again."

I'd worked at the pit wall for the better part of two hours before the first shadow passed overhead and blotted out the sun. I heard a Hawk cry and Wolf whinny in response. I redoubled my efforts to collapse the wall and climb out in four or five seconds. The task was impossible and I cursed Morai for it. I knew I was doomed.

Two smiling Elites looked down at me and laughed. I was covered with dust and dirt that my sweat transformed into a muddy coat. I'd tossed my tunic and jerkin up out of the pit earlier and it was impossible to tell that my pants and boots had once been the same dark shade. I rubbed my right forearm across my brow and succeeded only in transferring the dirt on my arm to my face.

"I told you, Erlan, it couldn't be mantrap. It caught a Justice." A young blond Elite looked across the pit at Erlan and they both burst out laughing.

I growled. "Don't tell me you Elites couldn't find something else to amuse you between Talianna and here."

Erlan stopped laughing and smiled at me. "Careful, Nolan, or we'll leave you there." Erlan dropped to his knees and reached a hand down for me. "Tadd, get my legs so I don't slide in there with him."

The joking Elite complied with Erlan's wishes and they had me out quickly. I stood and scraped as much of the dirt from me as I could. Beyond Erlan I saw two Imperial Hawks hooded and hobbled in the middle of the meadow. One was preening itself while the other was trying to get to Tafano's horse.

"Can I feed Fleet some of the horse?" Tadd walked toward his Hawk.

"Go ahead." I turned to Erlan. "Can you ride with Tadd back to Talianna, or ride Wolf? I need about two hours to catch Morai."

Erlan shook his head. He pulled a sealed letter from inside his jerkin and handed it to me. It had the Master's personal seal.

I broke it open and walked a pace or two away from Erlan. The message read: "Return to Talianna without delay. Stop shaving." I extended the message to Erlan. "The Master weaves with invisible thread."

Erlan shrugged his shoulders and refolded the paper. "Who can tell the Master's mind? Tadd has orders concerning Wolf he's to open once we leave. You'll fly Fleet and I'll take Val back. We're to leave now, and I was told to use any means necessary to get you there."

I shot Erlan a sidelong glance. "That sounds like words from Lord Eric's mouth."

The Elite nodded. "He told me I would not be disciplined if I had to use physical force on you."

"Oh. I'll feel threatened if you wish."

Erlan laughed out loud and caught me with a playful cuff. "Let's go."

I got my saddlebags and swordbelt from Wolf. I led him to the Hawks. Tadd held the reins while I sat down and pulled off my riding boots. Erlan tossed me a pair of soft-soled boots used for riding Hawks and I put those on while he stowed my boots in the saddlebags.

Tadd swung up into Wolf's saddle. "Hey, Nolan, that guy over there is still alive."

"I know." I pulled a shirt on but did not button it up.

Tadd looked a bit puzzled. "I can take him to a town. They might be able to fix him up."

I shook my head. "No, leave him." I climbed onto Fleet's back and reached up to unhood him.

"But he's in pain. He's struggling to get out of that armor."

"Tadd, leave him." My voice was harder than before.

Tadd turned toward Erlan, who had mounted Val. "But leaving him in such pain is cruel."

I used the Call. *"It's justice, Talion."*

Tadd turned back and faced me. The motion was slow. My words dragged him around and he resisted it as much as he could. He lost the fight.

I slid my *tsincaat* into the saddle scabbard. "Tafano had his cavalry ride through a Bosal village, killing anything that moved. He's caused untold suffering and pain. He chose to defend himself with that horse over there, refusing to call it off when I asked. I had to cripple it before I could kill it."

Erlan and I took to the air. We left Tadd staring at Tafano. I knew he'd leave the meadow alone, but I could only hope, when he left, he'd understand.

Chapter Six

NOVICE: FOURTEEN

My heart rode in my throat, squeezed up there by the nervousness that tightened my chest and tied my stomach in queasy knots. Although, as Fourteens, we'd spent enough time around the Hawks to believe ourselves Elites instead of Justice novices, the birds were still unfamiliar enough to make flying solo a difficult experience. And now, after only two weeks of solo flights, our instructor expected us to stoop a Hawk at a target!

Our instructor, a grizzled old Elite with no hair and a scar on his upper lip that gave him a perpetual sneer, had forced us to straddle sections of logs and pretend they were Hawks until he satisfied himself we all had the commands memorized and instantly available. He stalked through the ranks and screamed out a command. If novice hesitated or gave the wrong signal, a stinging blow from the Elite's quirt rewarded him. Though one of the best in our group, I got hit twice and could still feel the last lash tingling on my right arm.

After a morning of instruction in the middle of a hot field the Elite Fourteens flew their Hawks out to us and dismounted. Soon after their arrival three Lancers leading twenty old, broken-down nags appeared. Each horse had a stick and straw dummy tied into the saddle to serve as our targets for the afternoon's exercise.

I picked Valiant as my mount. Erlan turned the reins over to me and scowled. "You hurt Valiant and you better march back to Sinjaria before I get my hands on you."

I smiled at his concern and pulled myself into the saddle. "You just better hope Val doesn't like me better as a master, Erlan ra Leth. Might get away from me and I don't believe you quick enough to dodge his attack."

I signaled Valiant to fly and he spread his wings. With two powerful sweeps of his wings we cleared the ground. Leaving the earth always pressed me down into the saddle, and this time was no exception. Still I maintained a strong grip on the reins and with gentle touches of my quirt I let Valiant know I was in command and intended to stay that way. I flew him a bit to the south, well clear of other Hawks taking off, then signaled him to climb and join the instructor and the others in formation.

All the Justice Fourteens were in the flight. Marana, Lothar, and I flew younger birds, as did most of the other Fourteens. Because of their heavier weights, Jevin and one big Imperianan novice, as well as the instructor, had to fly older birds. The older birds required more strength to handle, but had better training than the younger Hawks so were a bit easier to control.

Cotton-mouthed, I really wished to be on the ground riding a horse. While a horse cannot match the speed of a Hawk, the drop to the ground is much shorter. And horses don't eat meat. Hawks have a nasty tendency to land near a fallen rider and feed as if nothing was out of the ordinary. My threat to Erlan, while offered in jest, was an Elite's nightmare.

Down below, the Lancers organized half of the Elites and gave each of them two horses with straw men in the saddles.

The other half wandered off with two Lancers across the golden meadow below us. In theory the birds had been trained to take riders and spare the horses. Our task was to guide the Hawk so it sighted the target and restrain it from attacking the horse in the event the Hawk decided it wanted the larger, edible target instead of the straw man.

We circled over the field waiting for a Lancer to release a target horse. A Lancer waved at one of the Elites and a horse slowly trotted away from the group below. It wandered aimlessly into the meadow, then headed across to where the other half of the Elites stood waiting. A whooping cry from a waiting Lancer sped the horse up and prevented it from grazing or stopping.

Our instructor pointed at Jevin, and the Fealareen raised his quirt in acknowledgment. He reined his bird out of our formation and looped it back toward Talianna in a pass that let the Hawk's shadow drift behind the horse. Then he turned his Hawk back, let the bird sight the target, and gave it the signal to attack.

His Hawk screamed and collapsed its brown and black fletched wings. It fell from the sky with the speed of a priceless crystal goblet falling just out of reach. Jevin gripped the reins and saddle tightly, and his black hair flapped back behind his head like flashing raven's wings. He leaned back, almost lying flat on the Hawk, to make the drop faster. Only his head leaned forward so he could see.

Jevin hauled back on the reins bare seconds before impact, pulling his bird away from the horse's neck. The bird screamed again, plucked the dummy from the saddle, and turned skyward. Scenting no meat or blood, it cried out indignantly and dropped the dummy. Jevin flew over behind the horses and landed his hawk.

The next horse headed out. The instructor pointed at me.

I turned Valiant out of formation and spiraled him a bit lower. I knew a fall from even that height would kill me, but it made me feel better. My target wandered in a circle that brought it close to some trees, so I positioned Valiant for an attack from the rear, not broadside as Jevin had. Valiant bobbed his head several times to let me know he had the target sighted. I tapped his wing with my crop and we were off.

Valiant folded his wings and we dropped fast. It felt like my stomach still circled up above, and I couldn't catch my breath. The wind tore at me. It whipped my hair back—snapping it like a flag in a storm—and clawed tears from my eyes. The target blurred and swam through the tears. I leaned back as far as I could and guided Valiant in at the target.

We came in just a little to the right of the target. At the last second I pulled back and to the left on the reins. Valiant screamed and unfurled his wings. He turned hard with his left wing fully straight and stretched out to catch as much air as possible, and his right wing half collapsed. We spun sideways as Valiant snapped his right wing taut and guided us across the horse's path. I never saw the horse because I was suspended parallel to the ground with Valiant's wings reaching from meadow to sky and blotting out any view of the target. Still, straw and shreds of a red cloak flew all around me and I laughed. Valiant screamed defiantly, straightened out our flight, and glided over to where Jevin had hooded his Hawk.

The others accomplished their attacks with seeming ease. Her long black hair a tangled cape behind her, Marana looked terrifying. She could have been a *jelkom* gathering bad children up for sale to the Dhesiri. Lothar, on the other hand, looked very heroic. His bird leveled off early and glided through a swoop that picked the rider out of the saddle without the horse noticing or being spooked. Others in our group did well: a couple missed their first attempt, but succeeded in the end.

The Elite instructor addressed all of us once he'd landed. "You all did an adequate job here today. Lothar was the best of you. His attack could have removed the last in a line of soldiers without alerting the others in the troop. Nolan's attack, while very pretty and daring, is not a tactic a newly trained rider should use. It is just as likely to cripple the Hawk as it to succeed. Remember that."

He looked hard at me. I nodded and blushed.

"Justices tend to think of a Hawk as a fast, feathered horse, but it is a weapon. It is an unpredictable weapon that will eat you as easily as it will eat a target." He waited a moment to make sure we understood the gravity of his warning; then he waved us away.

He ordered us to run the four miles back to Talianna. We passed the Elites coming across the meadow to get their birds. The Elites would fly them back to Talianna as we ran in, and, although the distance was really short compared to our normal training, all of us thought the Elites had life easy.

"Well, Nolan, did you apply to enter the wrong branch of the service?" Lothar ran up next to me. We were both in the middle of the pack. We knew it was a good position to be in to sprint the last leg of the run to Talianna and "win" the race back.

"Me, an Elite? You heard the instructor. By this time I'd have ruined fourteen Hawks." I spat as Lothar laughed. "The birds are fine, but I prefer caring for a sword to a bird. Swords can't eat you."

Lothar laughed. "Call your sword a *tsincaat*."

I frowned. "Why the formality? They won't be *tsincaats* until we pass the final tests and get through the Ritual of the Skull."

"Practice, Nolan, practice." Lothar shook his hands out and wiped his palms on his tunic. "Even after a full year of training you're the worst of any of us at speaking High Tal. You need the practice."

"Finde thee thys any the better?" High Tal was a chore because all the words were older and harder to pronounce. The syntax made the tongue slow and precise. That precision and deliberateness was what Talions wanted, however, so I was forced to learn the language.

"Better thou hast become, Nolan, but ye speake with over-much haste for proper speech." Jevin pulled up along the two of us. Despite the mile we'd already covered, his deep voice contained no trace of a wheeze like mine or Lothar's.

"Thou art a mountain demon, Jevin. Thou canst correct me amidst a run, yet thine voice hast nary a hint of strayne." Sweat rolled off my forehead and stung my eyes. *"Must we speake High Tal when I hath not the breath for a good, common curse?"*

Both Jevin and Lothar laughed.

"What could be funny during a run?" Marana caught up with us and fell in beside Lothar. I saw Lothar's pleased grin and smiled myself. Lothar had confessed to me an interest in

Marana and she'd hinted a certain affection for him in a conversation just days before.

"Nothing," I said. "Someone once told these two they were funny and they actually believed him." We had one more hill before everyone would start sprinting to Talianna. The Elites flying back to the Mews passed overhead. "Marana, you look like a *jelkom* on that Hawk."

"Stooping to drag off bad children like you?" She laughed and clapped her hands with delight. "Did I scare you?"

"No, I wasn't in that saddle. Besides, Lothar looked enough the hero to frighten you off." My comment broadened Lothar's grin, and Marana read it clearly.

"He'd have to catch me first." Marana put her head down and sprinted off to reach the base of the hill before the rest of us. Lothar headed after her, knowing full well that if she could keep running into Talianna the lead she'd build up on the hill would leave her unbeatable in the race. Jevin and I looked at each other, shook our heads, and moved a bit toward the front of the pack. My body protested but I shook my arms free of knots and ignored the rising, fiery pain in my thighs.

The two of them disappeared over the top of the hill— Marana a good twenty yards in front—while the rest of us were three-quarters of the way up the rise. Jevin and I topped the hill with four others, three boys and one girl, in front of us. They had run out in front most of the way, so they were ready to be passed. We obliged them and dropped into long-legged lopes that swallowed distance like a wolf bolting meat.

Marana still led Lothar, but both of them had fallen off the pace a bit. Clearly the hill had taken its toll. "Jevin, if we can keep a sprint up we can take them."

"I'll match you stride for stride, then pass you at the last." He smiled his predator's smile. That smile only came out when Jevin truly competed. In any contest where he could hurt someone he held back, but in this race he would give no quarter.

I bobbed my head in an imitation of Valiant. Jevin laughed and we ran. With each stride I reached out for more and more distance. My legs became iron springs hurling me forward faster and faster. My chest pumped like a bellows and my skin flushed scarlet. Distance evaporated and Jevin shadowed me.

Jevin and I flew past Lothar and overtook Marana easily. Their lead would have won the race had either of them started early and reached the hill well before the rest of us. As it was, the hill drained them. While their lead would hold the rest of the pack off, it did nothing to stop the Fealareen or me.

We rounded a long right-handed curve and raced in toward Talianna. I was on the inside and I knew the road ran straight past the Mews to the gate in the Siegewall to Taltown. The first of us through the gate would win, and I meant for that novice to be me. I also knew Jevin would pace me until the last ten yards, where he'd sprint past and win.

I smiled my own wolf's grin at Jevin. *"Fare thee well, mountain demon."* I put my head down and sprinted.

I saw everything along the road as a blur, but I could feel everyone's eyes watch us. My lungs worked hard, sucking air in through clenched teeth and blowing it out my nose. My arms pumped furiously. My fingers splayed out like claws. They tore at the air to shred it and pull me along through it. My legs stretched and I flowed forward. There were no jerky movements, no jarring impacts with the ground. There was only fluid and I ran like rain whipped before the wind.

All the while I heard Jevin behind me. Where I sounded like a man on the edge of collapse, his breath came easily and reminded me of the low growl of a hunting wolf. I used that image. I imagined him stalking me. I let remembered folktales consume me. I caught up the terror of being chased by a Fealareen or a *jelkom* and used it to fuel my legs. I welcomed the panic and gave it free rein. The fear ripped through me and boosted me forward. I made no effort to curb it, and even let it play over my face, because I knew Jevin would never hold himself back and would use any tool he had available to win.

I shot a last glance over my shoulder. Jevin hung there like a nightmare beast lurking in my shadow. A new wave of terror surged up through me and I increased my speed yet again.

Two Lancers at the gate saw us coming. They exchanged a couple of words then turned to clear the way. They knew

Jevin and I would not stop for anyone or anything. Thankfully even Lancers could understand the importance of a race, even if it was just for the sake of the race itself.

I shot through the gateway first. I tried to stop but my momentum carried me across the courtyard. I literally ran up the wall for two steps before my speed was spent, then I bounced back down to the ground. I turned and slumped against the wall. A couple of seconds later Jevin joined me.

Neither of us could speak. Our chests heaved and sweat covered us like dew on a morning field. I stood first, having spied the distant dots that had to be Lothar and Marana, and tugged at Jevin's arm. He looked at me, puzzled, then understood. With energy from the gods alone know where, we struggled off to the Justices' wing of the Citadel. Though the stairs were worse than the last hill, we climbed them and reached Lothar's and my room on the third floor.

I collapsed on my bed while Jevin appropriated Lothar's bunk. We lay there, very still, until we heard voices. Both of us smiled and sat up, as if we were not the least bit tired. I made notes in my journal while Jevin studied the chessboard on our table where Lothar and I were engaged in a game.

Lothar and Marana, hand in hand, slumped in the doorway.

"Who dragged whom across the line?" I asked innocently, and glanced at their intertwined fingers.

They looked at me with withering glances. Jevin and I simultaneously sank back on the beds and the four of us dissolved in laughing fits.

Hawk training comprised an afternoon each week. As Fourteens we also took on other duties. Along with the Fifteens and Sixteens we had to patrol the Citadel walls and accompany Services clerks on their various inspections of Taltown. While the duties were simple, they added to our training. We had learned to fight; now we had to learn how to deal with people without using violence.

The rooftop patrols were organized by wall, and members of every division except Services and Wizards had to stand guard. The leader for any patrol was selected ahead of time, and it was that Talion's responsibility to make sure his force was assembled and vigilant. I think if I had been a Warrior or

Lancer leading a group I'd hope I didn't get any Justices in my patrol.

The night after the race Jevin and I had to stand watch from midnight until dawn. We'd gotten enough sleep to rest our bodies, but we were still giddy from the race. Others, including the Lancers at the gate, had come by at supper and commented they'd never seen men run so fast. That did nothing in the way of deflating our egos, and made us very resistant to discipline from anyone who was not yet a real Talion.

A Lancer Fifteen, Gaynor ra Borrowed Lands, led our patrol. He was as tall as me, and we were taller than all in the patrol except Jevin. I had reached a full six feet but had not filled out yet. Jevin both was taller, by at least another foot, and had bulked out to adult proportions. Gaynor was somewhere between us. His head was shaved except for the black mane running down the middle. Like most other Horseheads he was cocky, and the chip on his shoulder for Justices in general and Jevin in particular did not bode well for our watch.

He ordered us into formation and accepted the post from a tired Warrior Fifteen. The Baton of Command in his hand, Gaynor proceeded to brief his troops. "Talions, we have a sacred duty to perform tonight. We are to protect Talianna from any invasion, any violation, no matter how trivial. If needed we are to sell our lives dearly, crying out only to warn others of the danger."

I rolled my eyes skyward and felt sick. I turned to Jevin and whispered, "It would sound better from horseback. He really needs to be a lord for this speech." Jevin and I both chuckled.

Gaynor's gray eyes blazed fury. "Do you Justices find something funny in my speech?" His voice carried the force of a reprimand but he was only a Lancer.

Jevin snorted. "Nothing beside the absurdity of it in light of the fact that there are no troops within sixty leagues of Talianna." Jevin's answer, delivered with a serious, respectful look on his face, wrenched a chuckle out of me and started two Warriors quivering with restrained laughter.

Gaynor walked back toward us, but stayed away from Jevin. "Fine, Talion. Then perhaps you'll find watching the far end of the wall not too much of a chore. And your fleet friend may accompany you."

I bowed with ceremony. "As my lord commands."

Jevin and I broke formation, each picked up a spear from the wall rack, and walked to the far end of the roof without waiting to be dismissed. The post was the least desirable because it put us across from the stables and right above the manure pile left from mucking out the stables earlier in the evening. Luckily a breeze blew most of the scent out and away into the night.

The night was warm and the bright stars filled the sky. I easily picked out the Great Bear and the Dancing Turtle. I could only see the masts of the Ghost Ship because Tal was further north than Sinjaria. Sighting a familiar series of constellations always made the night seem more comfortable.

"Jevin, why is Gaynor afraid of you?"

Both of us sat on the roof and leaned our backs against the inner citadel wall. Jevin turned his face to me, but I could only see his fangs and eyes in the darkness. "I suppose it is the same reason you were afraid of me this afternoon. Does that answer your question?" Pain threaded through his reply.

I touched his shoulder. "Jevin, what do you mean? I don't understand." Already I'd forgotten the fear coursing through me because it had been just a tool to help me win a race. It wasn't real then and it ceased to exist the second the race was over.

"Nor do I, Nolan." Jevin turned from me and I watched his silhouetted profile against the starlit sky. "When you looked back at me I saw the raw terror I've seen during a couple of Festivals. People fear me because I am Fealareen, without knowing me or who I am."

I could feel his betrayal, and I felt like I'd been hit in the stomach with a brick. "Jevin, I'm sorry. I don't fear you. I know you hold yourself back when you might hurt another person, and I knew you would not be holding back in that race. Imagining you as a monster or wolf hot on my heels— which you were at the time—was just a way to convince my legs to work faster. I never imagined you would notice, much less be hurt by it."

He started to reply, but I held up a hand and cut him off. "Ever since I swallowed my fear the first day I saw you, I resolved to be your friend. In battle you will be horrifying. You're big and strong, capable of destroying foes. But you can only let yourself loose on enemies, you'd not hurt friends. Like it or not, until I go outlaw, I will not fear you."

I felt the tension drain from him. "Nolan, thank you. I cannot judge people. You've all been raised on tales of *jelkom* and Fealareen. We're not seen outside the Haunts. I'm as much a freak as that two-headed colt born last spring. It was lucky because it died. It did not have to go through a life of people being afraid of it."

I nodded and scanned the stars. "I know a bit of what you're talking about." I swallowed my way past the lump in my throat and brushed a tear from my left eye. "My little brother Arik had a clubbed foot. People thought him demon-cursed or god-blessed. People wanted to burn him or have him touch them to heal their illnesses. No matter what they believed, though, people were afraid of him."

We were both quiet for a second, each of us lost in thought of places many leagues to the east; then I spoke. "Still that doesn't explain the depth of Gaynor's fear."

Jevin laughed lightly and all his teeth showed in the night. "No, Gaynor is a special case. Remember, Gaynor is from the Borrowed Lands. To you the Fealareen are just monsters in stories but to him we are reality and death for his family."

I frowned. "Gaynor was brought here at the same time you were. Neither one of you knows anything about your homelands."

Jevin smiled uneasily. "Gaynor has put our library to good use. He knows his homeland used to belong to the Fealareen. We used to graze our flocks there in the winter. A thousand years or so ago, human settlers began to flood into the area. They were mostly refugees from Tingis, the Tortured Province, but they took our best lands. At first we did not mind, we lived together with relative peace.

"Then a leader showed up and he offered to fight the Fealareen king for domination of the lands. An agreement was struck: every twenty-five years both leaders would meet in a series of Ritual battles and the winner would have dominion over the Borrowed Lands for the next quarter century. The Fealareen have a tendency to raid the area when they are in power—making them no different than the counts and barons elsewhere—and the citizens of the Borrowed Lands are in dread of their leader losing."

Jevin shook his head. "Gaynor has decided he was sent from the Borrowed Lands to watch over me and prevent me from threatening the Shattered Empire!"

I looked away and swallowed hard. He was not the first Lancer to assume the weight of the world was on his shoulders, but he was starting younger than most. "When is the next Ritual?"

"Eleven years."

I did some quick math in my head. "That means you left the Haunts during the last Ritual."

"A month later. I was born the night my father died in the Ritual. He was beaten for the second time. His defeat at the hands of Queen Briana would have led to his execution by the Fealareen had he survived the Ritual. Because of his loss I was cast out." Part of Jevin cried out for an explanation of his exile. I read it in his posture and heard it in his voice.

I smiled and tried to steer the conversation back away from Jevin's quest for an answer he'd never have. "I think you have that wrong, my friend." Jevin turned and stared at me. "You weren't exiled, you were sent out to keep an eye on Gaynor."

That forced a smile back on Jevin's face. He looked up and over me back toward where Gaynor marched from post to post requesting reports and encouraging his men. "Gaynor would just love that idea."

I nodded. "So, we've decided why Gaynor especially hates you, but why does he hate me or any of the rest of the Justices? Did you and Lothar do something to him years ago?"

"No, not that I know of or can remember." Jevin tipped his face skyward and calm seeped back into his body. "His hatred probably springs from our being Justices and the Justices' position in the factional struggles in Talianna."

I considered his remark for a moment. In the two years I'd been in Talianna I knew there were tensions between the different branches. All the military branches were jealous of each other, and no one liked the Services. Elites and Justices really comprised a small percentage of the total Talion population, but our political power was considerable, so we were viewed as either arrogant or far too influential for our actual worth. Wizards, with their subdisciplines and ethereal differences, were too preoccupied with magick to pay attention to the fights, but they were far too powerful to ignore or anger.

"Jevin I think I understand what you mean, but . . ."

The Fealareen chuckled, a low, evil chuckle. "It is rather simple, Nolan. I'll just apply labels to things you've already seen and understand. Until the Empire fell apart the duty of the Talions was clear. We were the Emperor's instrument of Justice.

"After the Empire fell apart, thought about the Talion role in the world changed. One faction wanted to reconquer all the lands and forge a new Empire with Talianna as the capital, because they felt without an Empire the Talions lost all legitimacy. Without an Empire we would wither and die. Once the Empire was rebuilt, and the Master was acknowledged as the new Emperor, we could continue our work."

I knitted my brows in concentration. "Obviously we did not take that route, so there must have been another faction that was more powerful or made more sense."

Jevin nodded. "Yes and no. The other main faction believed Talions should act as guides. They hoped, through subtle pressure, we could keep the world from falling apart. We could prevent a total collapse, as happened with the old Empire of Kartejan, and keep the world civilized. The guide faction wanted Talions to help keep the Imperial laws alive and to act in a positive manner."

I closed my eyes for a second and thought. "You mean by training troops and having Justices bring the lawless down we could keep everyone on an even footing and prevent total barbarism from swallowing up the world?"

Jevin nodded. His bobbing head eclipsed the rising Wolf Moon. "Those are still the two biggest factions in Talianna. Two others split off. One advocates doing nothing more than keeping the peace. The other says all men are guilty of something, and that only terror and fear can keep people honest. Many Justices end up adopting the latter view, especially after they've tracked down a series of ruthless killers."

I shivered. "Unless I miss my guess Lancers want to reconquer everything, and Justices believe in guiding?"

"In a nutshell. Add to that the feeling among Lancers, Warriors, and Archers that Justices exert more of an influence on policy than they should and you can understand why Gaynor feels the way he does."

That made sense to me. The Master made all policy decisions but he consulted with the lords of the different divisions in regular meetings. With Lords Hansur and Isas in agreement, and His Excellency, the head of the Services, backing them, they formed a small but powerful faction that could block the ambitious plans of the military divisions.

Before I could make a comment, our political discussion ended abruptly. A black wave swept up over the Citadel wall and splashed over us. A muddy concoction of horse manure, urine, and straw from the stables, it stank enough to drop me to my knees as I tried to stagger over and see who had thrown the stuff up at us. I fell forward and spat even as Jevin stood and looked over the roof's edge.

Two clumps of manure hit him, one in the chest and the other in the face. He spun away and dropped beneath the wall. "Damn, Nolan, those were Lancers!"

I shuddered and shook my head to clear it. I got my legs under me and stood. I stumbled two steps to the left and leaned heavily against the inside Citadel wall. I spat again to rid my mouth of the sour taste.

Gaynor marched to our position. "Having some trouble, Justices?" He wrinkled his nose. "You stink."

Jevin's fists clenched and unclenched; then he lunged at Gaynor. I stepped forward and firmly planted a hand in Jevin's chest. I felt his heart racing and pounding against his ribs, but something within him recognized me and he stopped. "No trouble, Lancer, beyond that which you caused us."

Gaynor balled his fists and puffed his chest out. "You accuse me of some duplicity in this when it was your own slovenly manners and lack of vigilance that permitted this outrage!"

Anger burned off the weakness in my knees and cleared my head. I shoved Jevin back and stood nose to nose with Gaynor. "Perhaps I should remind you, Gaynor, that we are in your command and to have two of your men so attacked does not reflect well upon you." That put him off a bit, because he'd clearly not considered that angle for viewing this incident. "I just want to add that if you ever feel you need to test your belief in your superiority I'm ready and willing to meet you any time and any place."

I inched even closer and Gaynor gave ground. I couldn't blame him, because I smelled horrid.

Gaynor straightened himself and sneered. "Clean your post up then go clean yourselves. I'll file the report on this evening, Nolan, and while I may be criticized for my actions, there is no way either of you will escape a reprimand for your frivolous attitude. Even those who want to be Justices must play by the rules."

Lord Hansur called both of us into his room after we had cleaned up. Though the sun had stolen over the horizon only an hour before, he already had a two-page report on our actions. He invited us to sit on campaign stools while he read the report. The dark woods of his desk and the shelves lining the walls lent the room a powerful, brooding sense that made me uneasy.

Finally Lord Hansur, sunk deep in a high-backed chair, looked up from the report. "Well, novices, did you openly defy his authority?"

"Yes, my lord." My answer earned a scowl from Lord Hansur.

"Let us be more specific. Did you comment and laugh during his instructions to you?"

We answered together. "Yes, my lord."

"Did you relax at your post and ignore what was happening in the courtyard below?"

"Yes, my lord."

"Did you threaten to beat the Lancer to a pulp?"

I shook my head. "No, my lord. I merely offered to meet him later if he felt the situation needed resolution."

Lord Hansur shook his head. "It was kind of you to offer, Nolan, but this report has resolved the situation itself."

I swallowed hard to get my heart back down out of my throat.

Lord Hansur rose from behind his oak desk, turned, and stared out the narrow window in the wall behind him. "I can understand your chafing under the command of a Lancer, especially that one. I can understand that he might have it in for you, Jevin, and that he might resent you, Nolan. I know he could have been hard on you—as hard as a Lancer could possibly be on a Justice—and that you bristled at this treatment. Still this does not excuse your action."

He turned and riveted us with an iron stare. "Patrols are not organized for the protection of Talianna. If there was a threat we would not have half-grown boys guarding us." Jevin and I both blushed. "Patrols are to teach you to work together. They are a basic military operation, and they are performed to teach you both to accept commands, and to understand how others command."

He sat again. "I have to discipline you. Gaynor reached Lord Eric very early with this report and I was forced to sit through a discussion of respect and the lack of it among the Justices for the other divisions. Lord Eric also suggested there was no military discipline in the Justices and that for a force that is supposed to do anything any of the other Talions can, there is no way we can be thought of as martially competent."

I looked down at my feet. I wished I could melt and run down through the cracks in the floor. "We understand the difficulty . . ."

Lord Hansur frowned hard. "Do you, do you really understand the difficult situation you put me in? I have to prove you are capable of planning a military operation and executing it. That means I cannot tell you what to do. And even if you and Jevin manage to research and come up with a historically brilliant campaign, Lord Eric can dismiss it as impossible to verify, or can suggest that any campaign using Talions would be assured of success because there are none who can stand against us."

Lord Hansur sat silently and the silence settled over the room like a thick blanket.

Jevin spoke. His voice, though kept low and soft, shattered the quiet like a Hawk's scream. "It appears, my lord, that Nolan and I must accept sole responsibility for our actions, and be disciplined if we cannot prove to Lord Eric's or your satisfaction that we do grasp the importance of military planning and execution."

Lord Hansur nodded. He turned to me. "Nolan, are you willing to join Jevin in his attempt to prove the accusations about you incorrect?"

I nodded.

"Even if it means being dismissed as a result of failure?"

That took both Jevin and me by surprise. My stomach felt full of wriggling snakes, and Jevin paled to an ashen gray. We nodded.

Lord Hansur smiled as if he'd expected this outcome since the beginning of our meeting. "Very well. I expect your plan in a sealed envelope by the end of the day. The plan should be executed two weeks from tonight."

Jevin and I rose and bowed, then turned and left the room. We barely concealed the smiles on our faces. The night Lord Hansur picked was moonless, and Gaynor commanded that night's patrol.

Although we'd done dozens of exercises in planning over the past two years, no military campaign we'd designed ever saw so much extensive work put into it. Jevin and I haunted the library and pored over maps by the hundreds. We even got permission to fly two Hawks out toward the area where the Justice Fourteens were supposed to camp out on the night of our operation. Everyone who knew something was up clearly assumed we planned to ambush our comrades to prove our understanding of military strategy and tactics. That won us our first victory and proved we understood the value of intelligence and counterintelligence.

Lord Hansur scheduled the Justice Fourteens for a field exercise west of Talianna on the night of our operation. He threw that in as an extra wrinkle, to make our job more difficult, but we turned it to our advantage. After questioning Allen about the terrain in the camp area we managed to cajole some rope and rock-climbing gear out of him so we could surprise our comrades by coming over an unscalable cliff at them.

Jevin and I planned to work alone originally, but it was difficult to keep our mission a secret. We invited Lothar and Marana to join us, and we told them we trusted them completely, but even they did not know our true target until that night. They liked the plan we told them about and they agreed to it enthusiastically.

Lothar's opinion of our plan changed, that evening, when we told him what we were really going to do. "You're going to attack Talianna?"

I smiled easily. "Yes. Look, if a couple of Lancers can sneak up on Jevin and me and do what they did to us it should be easy for us to slip into Taltown and enter the Citadel."

Lothar looked at me like I was utterly mad, but before he could protest I turned to Marana. "You're still with us, right, Marana?"

She smiled easily and shouldered a coil of rope. "Sure. This should be an adventure."

I smiled at Lothar and his eyes blazed back at me. Marana's involvement gave him no choice, which I knew as well as he did. I tossed him a bag full of clothing.

"Never again," he mumbled. Jevin and I chuckled and led the way back toward Talianna. Our team walked well behind the other Fourteen groups and none of them noticed our departure. Part of the field exercise required each team to navigate to the campsite by the stars and a complex set of directions given us by Lord Hansur. In following the directions we'd find a number of hidden landmarks and had to write down the symbols we found on them. By looking at our individual course assignments and the symbols we wrote down our instructors could determine if we knew what we were doing or if we found the campsite by accident.

Our journey back to Talianna went off without serious incident. We alternated the position of scout and moved as quickly as possible while trying to be silent. Two groups of Lancers rode past us, but we hid well enough at the road's edge to escape detection. While they probably wouldn't have paid us any attention even if they *had* seen us, we wanted surprise in our operation and we took steps to insure it.

We came in toward Talianna from the west and cut up toward the north near the Mews. We left Jevin hidden in the shadows near the northwest corner of the Siegewall with our gear, while we changed into Elite tunics and quickly joined with Elites heading back into Taltown from feeding and caring for their Hawks.

"Damn birds get so testy when they molt," I commented aloud as we reached the gate.

Marana agreed. "And they can't be flown with any sort of speed. I hate it."

The Warriors warding the gate looked at us, saw a bunch

of Elites returning from the Mews, and let us pass without a second thought. We wandered casually into Taltown and headed off west. We reached the corner of the wall and, there in the shadows between a bakery and a small home, I pulled some string from my pocket. I tied it to a stone and sent it sailing up over the wall.

Jevin tied his climbing rope to my line and tugged twice on the cord. I pulled the slender rope over to our side, where the three of us held the rope as Jevin climbed up over the Siege-wall. Once on top, Jevin, dressed in his totally black nightsuit, dropped our supplies and then lowered himself over the edge of the wall. He let himself hang down to his full height, then released. His total drop was a little over six feet, so he landed soundlessly.

The other three of us pulled our nightsuits on over our uniforms and headed west. We successfully passed from the north wall to the south wall of Taltown and reached the manure pile easily. As we expected, from personal experience and two weeks of intelligence gathering, the novices at that end of the roof had moved away from their post. They talked and laughed with the pair of guards at the next station over.

Lothar arched a padded grappling hook over the lip of the wall. It hit with a muffled clank that sounded like thunder to me, but none of the novices paid it any attention, if they heard it at all. Lothar pulled on the rope to test how well the hook had set itself. It slipped once, and Lothar stumbled, but then the hook caught and held firm. Lothar signaled me all was clear, and my mouth went dry.

I climbed the rope first. Lothar held it at the bottom so I could pull myself up and virtually walk up the wall. Still the climb was difficult. I'd gotten only halfway up the line when it went slack and I fell against the wall. I tightened my grip and felt the fire starting in my shoulders, but I could do nothing to lighten the load on my arms.

My heart stopped pounding thunderously after a moment or two, and I heard the two novices patrolling above me. Each scraping step echoed louder and louder. Their voices were just loud enough for me to hear, but I couldn't make out any words. I calmed myself, forced air in and out of my lungs, and relaxed the muscles I didn't need to keep me on the rope. Below me Jevin, Lothar, and Marana had vanished, and from my vantage point, nothing looked out of the ordinary in the darkened street.

Finally the voices receded and Lothar stepped from the shadows to grab the end of the rope. He signaled me to come down but I shook my head and completed my climb. My shoulders burned with pain by the time I finished and elbowed my way over the crenellated wall. I dropped into the shadows, checked the hook, reseated it to my satisfaction, then waited.

Marana followed me up with no trouble. We moved forward, up and away from the hook, toward the novices. I looked over at Marana but could see nothing but a narrow band of flesh around her eyes. The nightsuits, complete with gloves and hoods, made us invisible unless one knew where to look.

I heard Jevin come up over the wall; then I felt Lothar touch my hip to signal his readiness. The four of us crawled forward and got close enough to the four novices—two Warriors and two Lancers—to hear their discussion. My heart leapt, and I suppressed a laugh. They were talking about what Gaynor had done to Jevin and me.

Like dust borne on night breezes, the four of us flowed forward. I swept up and grabbed a Warrior from behind. I pressed a dowel of wood into his back and clapped my left hand over his mouth. *"Were this steele and not woode, thou wouldst be dead. Act as it were soothe."*

We'd decided to use High Tal to make the guards think this was a training exercise organized by their lords. Because of my difficulty with the tongue I had practiced my little speech for days. The novice stiffened, then slumped as if he'd fainted. I didn't know if it was an act or not, but he was still breathing so I left him and advanced.

We took one more pair of novices before Gaynor came into sight. He marched along like a lord making his rounds and praised his men for their obedient and vigilant service. He looked very self-possessed. Baton tucked under his arm and a sneer of contempt riding confidently on his lips, he came toward us like a man with an appointment with destiny.

We overwhelmed him quickly. *"Thou arte our captif. Do nothing or thou wilt be as dead in thys exercise."*

He stiffened for a second, debated resistance, then surrendered. We led him back to the station above the manure. *"Ye will climb down the rope, and wait for us at the bottom."* Gaynor turned to protest my command, then seized the rope and quickly started his descent. He knew he would reach the ground before us and be able to escape.

Seeing hope flash in Gaynor's eyes, Jevin laughed and drew a real knife. Remorselessly he sliced through the rope suspending Gaynor over the manure pile.

Under the cover of Gaynor's sputtered screams of outrage the four of us climbed down the interior Citadel wall. As Gaynor's patrol responded to his screams by raising an alarm, we ran across the exercise fields and fought our way up the stairs to our rooms. Other novices poured down and out of the Citadel as we did, so intent on seeing what the fuss was all about. In our rooms we took off our nightsuits and hid them under our mattresses. Jevin put on an Elite's vest and we joined the stragglers running down the stairs.

Absolute chaos reigned in Talianna. The patrol's panic spread to the rest of the novices and then on into some Lancers who heard one of their own had been attacked. Full Talions shouted orders and tried to station novices in places they'd be useful. We ignored the commands shouted at us and joined the mass exodus of Elites toward the Mews. No one at the gate stopped us and none of the Elites noticed when we headed off west. And though difficult, we even managed to get all the symbols correct on our map to the camp-site, though our instructors noted our tardiness and assigned us the early watch.

The next day Jevin and I had a note from Lord Hansur. It read: "I believe you understand military operations. No further demonstrations will be necessary."

Chapter Seven

TALION: SHARUL

❦

Talianna lay over four hundred leagues to the northwest. Despite the urgency of the Master's message, I convinced Erlan that a stop at the Broad River ferry was not out of order. Hawks flat refuse to fly in the dark, so our first day could only be a short flight, and we landed in the meadow near the cabin just as the sun started to set in the west.

Weylan and Elverda were more than happy to see me and they accepted Erlan as if he had visited many times before. The Elite delighted in showing Elverda the Imperial Hawks close up while I spoke with Weylan. He admitted that living with another human being did take a little getting used to, but they both looked very happy to me.

Despite Elverda's protests that she had nothing special to fix for us, the dinner she served was delicious. Weylan had caught some fish and she had baked bread earlier in the day. They had fresh milk from a cow they'd added to the ferry since I'd left.

Weylan smiled. "Elverda said some fresh milk would be nice so I convinced a tinker that the cow he'd taken in trade would not cross on the ferry at all well, and he consented to trade it for passage throughout the next three years."

After dinner we talked and sang well into the night. Erlan recited an Elite poem that I'd heard a number of times in my youth, but he made it come alive. It told of an Elite and the special relationship between him and his Hawk. Like most tragic poems it ended with the hero and his faithful mount dying in a glorious battle, but the tragedy to this poem was the pain in the Elite's voice that he'd die earthbound and would never again soar with the winds and chase the clouds from the sun's face. Erlan presented it very well, and both Weylan and Elverda cried at its ending.

We headed out early the next morning. Fleet was interested in Weylan's cow but I reined him away from it and we flew off toward Talianna. Before noon we let each Hawk take an antelope and after we hooded and hobbled the birds Erlan managed to steal enough meat for us to eat. We rested for a short time and then were off again.

At night we chose not to head for any settlements or even isolated farms. Aside from the way stations the Talions maintain for Elite couriers—many of which appear to be nothing more than a normal farm—no place really has the facilities to care for an Imperial Hawk. Very few farmers are eager to put the Hawks in their barns, and I can't blame them for their reluctance. The way stations south of Talianna were a bit off line of our course, and a couple of Elites Erlan preferred to avoid staffed the only station even close to our route.

Luckily the weather remained warm and dry. We chose all our campsites for water and cover and, if we had to make a choice, we opted for a defensible position. Even so, nothing out of the ordinary happened on the journey, and three and a half days after we left Tadd and Wolf in the meadow we reached Talianna.

The view of the Tal valley from the air—when it is not

choked with Festival visitors—is deceptively peaceful. The valley looked very much like any of the other valleys we flew over, and carried with it no hint of the power seated there. A patchwork of small plots with even rows—by this point in the spring, filled with half-grown plants—carpeted the valley floor. The outlying buildings looked quite common even down to the drying laundry flapping in the light breeze nearby.

Everything looked perfectly normal, if you ignored Talianna.

Talianna rose from the valley floor like a piece of earth-bone. Brilliantly white and surrounded by verdant fields, it appeared less built by man than an ancient structure uncovered by erosion; much as gold nuggets are sometimes discovered in a streambed. Pennants snapped and canopies rippled above merchants' stalls in Taltown. Once again I felt at home and proud to belong in Talianna.

Erlan and I flew one pass over Talianna. The Hawks easily recognized Talianna below them and stretched their wings out to show everyone their power and majesty. Fleet bobbed his head once, having selected a target below, but I jerked his reins sharply to the right and broke off any stoop. The bird cried out and followed Valiant to the Mews. We landed without further incident.

I hooded Fleet and tossed the reins to a young Elite. "Feed him, but be firm." The Elite looked at me curiously. I frowned. "Fleet wanted to stoop on the crowd."

Erlan looked over at me from where he was hooding Val. "These birds get nasty when they molt."

I slid from the saddle and joined Erlan's laughter. I knew many Elites made "feints" on targets both in Talianna and on the road, but I was not going to criticize that practice standing in the Mews. Actually I should have anticipated Fleet's action, and I did remember that he broke the attack off the instant I pulled him away from it.

I shouldered my saddlebags and headed down the hill to the Siegegate. I'd been more than three months away from Talianna, between one assignment and the next. Though winter blanketed the valley with one last snowfall the day I left, the ground had been bare weeks before that so the valley did not look that much changed to me. It felt good to be back, and would feel better if I found Marana waiting for me.

Bored with their duty, the Warriors at the gate decided to be difficult. It bothered the larger one that he'd not seen me leave the gate earlier, and he wondered why I had saddlebags when I had no horse. *"Who art thou?"* he demanded. His voice, along with his look, marked him a Rian who'd managed to win entry to the Warriors as an adult. That accounted for his arrogant challenge, but did not excuse it.

I stiffened. My eyes blazed at him. No Warrior watching the gate had any reason to demand anything from a Justice and my exhaustion eroded my restraint. I balled my right fist even as his partner shouldered through the stream of people pouring in and out of the gate.

His partner saw the Justice emblem on my jerkin, and could see from the sweat stains that I'd been traveling for a long time. I saw he even noticed that I'd not shaved for days—as per the Master's message—and he suddenly concluded something was unusual here, and with a Justice that meant only one thing. Still the Rian only saw a disheveled Justice and decided it was his duty to force me to conform to the rules and regulations of the service he had worked hard to join.

"Who art thou?!" The Rian's voice rose to a bellow, as if his volume could bludgeon me into submission. He ignored the hoarsely whispered advice offered by his partner and put a hand out to stop any effort I made to go around him.

Slowly and deliberately I raised my right hand and opened my palm so both of them could see the skull. The smaller Warrior blanched immediately and withdrew, but a mask of uncomprehending anger still possessed the Rian's face. Because I stood within the shadow of Talianna—as the itch beneath the tattoo reminded me—I could but utter one word, so I filled every syllable with all the rage boiling up inside me. *"Sharul!"*

The Rian stood there dumbly then jumped back as if a viper coiled on my chest to strike at him. "He's *Sharul*, Niles, *Sharul*!" The other Warrior nodded with disgust at the Rian's display of surprise and waved me past them both.

Sharul. Unclean—or rather "one who needs cleansing." A Justice who has taken lives through the Skull is prohibited from speaking any but that one word when he enters within the shadow of Talianna. Until I completed the Shar ritual I could not speak with or touch another human inside Talianna, lest they have to complete a ritual of their own. I would not eat or drink. I did not exist as a living human until I had undergone Shar.

Enough of the crowd had heard the two Warriors and my reply to know I was *Sharul*. They cleared a path for me to the Eastgate. The people stood and stared, with little children poking their heads out from between adult legs, in awe and horror of me. I looked at the crowd and tried to recognize people I knew, but as my gaze touched theirs people turned away and secretly made signs or breathed prayers against evil.

Everyone saw me as a monster because I could kill in a way that repulsed them and confused them. They would rejoice if I destroyed their enemies, but were terrorized when I walked among them while *Sharul*. Yet let me be two minutes outside the Shar chamber, wandering around Taltown, and they would carry on as if I were a favorite customer or very good friend.

That reaction embittered a number of Justices, but I learned early on to accept it. People are fickle, but they try to view everyone in a positive light if given half a chance. I decided long ago to give them that chance.

I entered the long, dark tunnel into the Star alone. The shadows swallowed me and cooled me while my footsteps echoed and heralded my arrival. At the far end of the tunnel, before the doors that led to the supply corridor, a clerk stood and bowed. I paused and returned the bow. He did not meet my eyes and said nothing to me. He respected the great burden I bore while *Sharul* and would do nothing to irritate or inconvenience me.

My saddlebags slipped from my shoulder almost accidentally. I ignored them and proceeded beyond the clerk; my long strides greedily devoured the distance between me and the Shar Chamber itself. I knew the clerk would clean the saddlebags and deliver them to the room I had been assigned. The only part of my luggage that would not make it to my room would be my journal. The clerk would deliver that to

Lord Hansur so he could review my performance even as I cleansed myself.

All the doors between me and the Shar Chamber stood open so I had to touch nothing. No one walked the corridors, which saved my friends the awkwardness of refusing a greeting, and afforded me the luxury of silence. I did not find the isolation disquieting. It settled my nerves and let me gather my thoughts in preparation for Shar.

I turned the last corner and took a dozen fateful strides through the half-light to the door of the Shar Chamber. The doors themselves are narrow, only two feet wide for each of the double doors, but are cast of bronze and look heavy and strong. Magical runes, arcane symbols and designs of great antiquity and importance, scarred the doors' surfaces, but darkness swallowed all but one of them. Inscribed on two halves of a circle in the center of the doors, the simple line drawing of a skull that matched the death's-head on my palm glowed with a coruscating red light.

I reached my right hand up and out and pressed my palm against the skull sealing the door. The perpetual chill in my palm abated for a heartbeat, as if the Shar Chamber returned that part of me to me; then it went cold again and I felt a tremor in the doors. They rang with a click from inside. I felt pressure against my hand, so I lowered it back to my side.

The doors slowly, evenly, swung open and out toward me. Incense smoke drifted out like mist to spill over me in the first step of the Shar ritual. No evil spirit or demon bound to me by chance or deliberate curse could abide the smoke and would be banished by it. Furthermore, the symbols worked on the doors barred them from entering the chamber because even the Shar ritual could not cleanse their black souls.

I let one wave of the sweet smoke wash totally over me from head to foot before I stepped forward. The doors closed silently behind me and would admit no one else for Shar until I completed my ritual. In the next three hours I would see or hear no one. I would be alone with my conscience and if I could not justify the actions I'd taken in the past three months I would never leave the Shar Chamber alive.

I stood in the first of several smaller chambers and alcoves set within the Shar Chamber. Incense choked this first chamber. The acrid smoke poured into and filled the narrow space from censers set high up on the walls. Though the heavy smoke burned my eyes and lungs, I forced myself to breathe and purged my body of any evil spirits lurking within my chest. Breath wheezed in and out as tears rolled down my cheeks, but I passed from that chamber only after I satisfied myself I harbored no supernatural evil inside my body. The doors in front of me—smaller doors cast in brass—opened at my touch, and I stepped through into the Shar Chamber proper.

The Shar Chamber's vaulted ceiling glowed with a gentle amber light that wavered and flitted unbound from spot to spot. It played through the stony arches like lightning trapped within a thunderhead, yet never made a sound or flashed brightly to the floor below. A pool of steaming water dominated the center of the chamber. Multicolored tiles arranged in a pattern that seemed random to me lined the pool. I'd often marveled at the delicate design but whenever I tried to follow the pattern consciously I found myself drifting off and remembering the true purpose of the chamber. I am certain there is a very subtle enchantment woven into that design, but it never seems to matter enough to me after Shar to inquire about it.

Lastly, and oddly foreboding in this place of peace and sanctuary, across the pool stood the black slab. The cold stone reflected none of the vault's light. If not for the gold inlaid circle and skull in its exact center, the slab would seem to be nothing more than a slice of midnight bound by sorcery and trapped inside Talianna. The last phase of the Shar ritual took place in the chamber beyond that slab.

I stepped to the right and knelt in the first alcove. Here I removed all my clothing and separated it into two piles. I placed all leather items including my boots and weapons belt in one pile while I sorted all cloth items into the other. I picked the cloth items up and placed them in a small, wicker basket. Services clerks would come later, remove those clothes and have them cleaned or burned.

Before I picked up my weapons and leather to move to the next alcove, I took a small, earthenware jug from a hollow in the wall and uncorked it. The scent rising from it was heavily spiced and full of wine, but it could not disguise the cloying underscent of an emetic. I choked it down and promptly threw it back up again—along with anything remaining of my breakfast—into a basin to my left. I took a small swallow of water from a goblet deeper in the hollow and rinsed my mouth out before I wiped my face and replaced the jug where I first found it.

I picked up my leather apparel and weapons gear and carried it to the next alcove. There I drew my *tsincaat* and *ryqril* and set them aside. Kneeling on the cold stone floor, I poured liquid from an urn onto a cloth and, beginning with my jerkin, cleaned my leather. The liquid smelled of vinegar and removed the salt stains and other grime easily. I set each piece, when done, aside to dry. When I had finished cleaning the leather I unstoppered a squat brown jug and rubbed everything down with a polishing oil.

Though part of me knew how much time passed as I knelt there and worked, I did not consciously keep track of my time. Working on the leather, cleaning and polishing it, was certainly symbolic in the Shar ritual, but it was something else as well. It was a simple task that had a beginning, middle, and end. Unlike so many of the tasks I was asked to perform as a Justice, this task started at one point and would end at another, and at any point in the process I knew how close or far I was from finishing. Success was easy to measure. Such a simple job did not annoy me as it did others because, for me, it provided a reference point within reality and reassured me that while I dealt with good and evil, and the vast gray area in between, there were jobs that could be finished and finished well. In its own small way it confirmed the possibility of progress, and how any task that could be started could also be completed.

I rose and left the leathers neatly folded in a pile with my boots beside them. I took up my weapons and slipped barefoot through the open archway into the next small, round alcove. There I knelt again, this time beside a pot of jeweler's polish, and worked on the tools of my trade.

I took great care to clean the blades. I lavished upon them the deep cleaning I would have given ordinary blades. I dragged the polishing cloth along each edge, searching closely for the nicks I knew would never appear, and waited for even the tiniest tug or snag. I studied both my *tsincaat* and *ryqril* for any signs of rust or weakening. There were none, because the blades were perfect, and would remain so until I died.

I settled the *tsincaat* and the *ryqril* in the rack at the alcove's edge and passed to the next alcove. It had a stout, wooden door that opened at my touch and closed behind me. I stepped into an utterly black room. I stood and waited.

The room's heat built slowly and seeped into my body. First sweat beaded up on my nose, then rolled down from my temples. My black hair caught the heat, trapped it, and felt hot enough for my head to burst into flames. Sweat moistened my armpits and slicked my flanks while it streamed down my chest, thighs, and buttocks. Soon I stewed in glaze of my own perspiration and could taste the salty fluid on my lips.

The internal heat rose as soon as my outer body surrendered any attempt to keep me cool. Blazing warmth waded through the torrents of sweat washing down my body and seared into my lungs. My nostrils burned with every breath and the back of my throat dried like a drought-bled riverbed. I calmed myself and forced myself to breathe slowly past my swollen tongue to save my lungs. I shut my eyes against the heat and the sting of sweat. Though my body begged me to leave the room, I resisted because this part of the ritual was not complete for me.

I set aside the physical discomforts and withdrew into my mind. There, with cool deliberation that mocked the inferno torturing my body, I painstakingly reviewed my conduct over the last three months. I relived every incident, every hour of time I spent away from Talianna. I checked all my actions against my responsibilities as a Justice, then checked them again against my own personal code of conduct.

As a Justice I was allowed leeway in my conduct, and it would be ludicrous to suggest I held myself to a stricter standard than my masters demanded, but ultimately I had to live with my decisions. I was determined to make sure the choices I made were ones I could freely justify to myself and feel good about.

I don't think I'm special in this regard. I am merely a man who realizes he is capable of mistakes, but I am also a man who is willing to take responsibility for those errors. That is a decision I made long ago, and it is one I have chosen to live with. I have my own code of justice and I work within it. After all, if I do not control myself, how can I be asked to dispense justice to others?

I decided that nothing I had done while chasing Morai was unjust. I was uneasy with how I left Tafano, but the memory of his horse's death stole away any guilt I might have felt. Satisfied by, but not totally pleased with, my conduct, I left the hot alcove.

The Shar Chamber's air struck me like a punch, wrapped me up in an icy blanket, and tried to peel my skin off to get at the warmth inside me. The air was not really that cool, but it was terribly cold in comparison. I descended into the steaming pool immediately, and only after the water had rewarmed my flesh did I notice that my leathers and weapons had been removed from the chamber.

The deliciously warm water had been lightly scented with a spicy perfume I long ago commented that I liked. The comment had been made in passing to a clerk, and it had instantly become part of my record. Somewhere, hidden deep within the Services archives, a file existed concerning each and every Talion. It contained notations about his habits, preferences, and dislikes so the Services clerks could do everything to make his life pleasant. Of course, the records could be, and occasionally had been, used to make an arrogant Talion's life an exercise in slow torture.

I interrupted my bath to drink down a goblet of watered wine. It quenched my thirst, and I managed to keep it down by drinking it slowly, before I returned to the bath and scrubbed every inch of my body. The week's worth of grime and bird scent, which had been loosened in the sweat chamber, washed off easily. After I'd scoured myself, I lay back in the water and floated in perfect warm comfort for far too little time.

Finally, and reluctantly, I stepped from the pool and used two thick, white towels from a chest to dry myself. I combed my hair as best I could without a mirror and refolded the towels. From the same chest I took the two pieces of clothing that signified my physical purity. I tied a white strip of silk around my forehead and belted on a white silk loincloth. The ends of the loincloth extended just past my knees and were decorated with a black skull front and back.

I positioned myself in front of the black slab of stone and touched its golden center with my right palm. Silently, slowly, the stone withdrew upward into the wall like a shadow shrinking from the sun. A small dark chamber carved from the same shaderock lay beyond the receding door. I entered it and was entombed.

Across from the doorway stood a solid altar with a wide base and sharply sloped sides that narrowed to a top about two handspans wide. Seamlessly and smoothly chopped into the front of the altar was a cube open at the front and top. Shining radiantly, a skull carved of crystal sat within the alcove. A perfect replica of the death's-head tattoo on my palm rose in relief upon its brow. Behind and above it, illuminated by the white-argent glow, I saw the hilts of my *tsincaat* and *ryqril*. A Services clerk had sheathed them in the altar's flat surface.

I crossed to the altar and knelt. The fabric of the loincloth rustled and the sound thundered through the small room. I waited until all echoes of sound faded and all the while stared into the sightless sockets of the skull. With silence restored and at peace inside myself, I raised my hand and pressed my palm to the forehead of the skull.

My flesh felt like I'd raked my palm across a cactus or caught a glowing ember and held it tight. The skull itself radiated cold as my tattoo always did; in fact my own flesh seemed more a part of the skull than it did a part of me. I felt something flow into my body, ripple like a snake along my arm and coil into my brain. I could feel it slithering through my thoughts and retracing the same pathways I traveled in the hot room. It examined what I had done and judged my assessment of my own actions.

I felt no pain, no fear, no joy. It observed me as I might observe quarry from afar. I could not hide anything I had done, but I felt no need to hide. I was content with myself and my actions.

It began to withdraw and I felt it pulled something with it. Flashes of Rolf's life brushed past my consciousness, followed quickly by visions of the horse's life. The skull drew these other lives from me, took their life force away and cleansed me of the ghosts that might haunt me. This last phase of Shar left me totally clean.

It left me and I withdrew my hand from the skull. I breathed a deep sigh. I stood and pulled my weapons from their slots in the stone. In response to their removal a panel of stone to the right opened up. I walked through it into a corridor. The wall sealed itself up and in a small basin carved from the wall I found a wooden disk with a room number on it.

Services assigned me a room on the uppermost floor of the Justices' wing. While I felt somewhat sorry for the Fifteens who got moved into other rooms for the duration of my visit, I was more concerned over the fact that I was housed in the Justices' wing, as opposed to being given a room in the Star. This meant I'd get another mission quickly. I would be in Talianna long enough to be briefed and then sent out. That, coupled with my orders not to shave, clearly suggested I was in line for a covert mission where my identity as a Talion had to be obscured.

The residents of the upper floor peeked out of their rooms at me as I walked down the hallway. What they saw was a tall, lean, well-muscled man with a fair amount of black hair on his chest. The gold Imperial-sized scar on my left shoulder came from a wound I got too far away from magicians who could heal it properly, which in and of itself was remarkable, and the four days' worth of black stubble gracing my chin certainly marked me as different. Clad only in a Shar loincloth and headband and carrying my weapons unhomed I made, at best, an unusual sight.

I reached the room assigned to me and pushed the door open with my right foot. The interior looked exactly like the room I'd left behind three months earlier. My Tashari blanket, a gift sent from Orjan, even rested diagonally across the mattress as I'd last tossed it the day I was ordered out in pursuit of Morai. My clothing, including the newly washed clothing I'd had on the road and those items I'd left in Talianna, hung in the wardrobe. Other personal items—my razor a notable exception—were arranged on the dresser top in the same order I had left them when I last packed to leave.

I leaned back against the doorjamb and laughed aloud. After the disorder of months on Morai's trail, constantly facing the threat of death or injury, the image of Services clerks scurrying about to get my room, whichever room that turned out to be, arranged exactly as I had left it three months ago forced me to chuckle. It also gave me a feeling of belonging, of literally having a home, and a place to return to after so much time.

I took the swordbelt from the bed, slid my *tsincaat* and *ryqril* into their sheaths, and hung the belt in the wardrobe. Then I lay down on the bed, waited, and watched the door. I did not have to wait long.

As I had done as a Fifteen displaced from his room by a visiting Talion, the Fifteens quickly knocked on the doorjamb and entered. "Talion, we hope our room will be adequate for your stay." The speaker was a tall, thin boy. His roommate was short and stocky.

"I think it will suffice." I shifted a bit, as if moving to avoid a lump in the mattress, but they did not grimace. The whole exchange was a little game Talions play with those who will replace them. These youths knew the game well and waited for the next round in which they could ask their "guest" about the outside world.

As a youth I'd very much enjoyed listening to Talions tell about their adventures, and as a Justice I enjoyed sharing stories with the novices. Still there was something about these two boys and the eager light burning in their eyes that made me uneasy. I narrowed my eyes and watched the smaller novice blush. I was in trouble.

"Talion, we would be honored if you would share with us some insights about the world." The taller novice's delivery was flawless and very respectful.

I nodded slowly and kept watching the other novice. "What would you have me tell you about?"

The smaller novice squirmed a bit, but was too pleased with himself to be upset. "Perhaps it will seem trivial to you, but we will soon face our Journey and we wondered if you would tell us about your Journey year."

Oh Jevin, you bastard! "I'd rather tell you about something more recent." I thought I could skirt the Fealareen's ambush but I walked right into the second half of his snare.

"Yes, tell us about Morai. Wasn't he the one who. . . ?" asked the tall youth. His roommate choked back a laugh.

I frowned and cut him off. "Yes, he was. But that was

another day, another time." Both of them recoiled and were afraid they'd overstepped their bounds, which they had, even if it was at Jevin's suggestion. I hated having one story about me outlive all the others, especially when it described a set of circumstances I could have done little to alter. "Does everyone know that story?"

Both of them smiled sheepishly. "Yes."

Before I could start a countercampaign against Jevin, a chime rang throughout the building. It signaled the evening meal and, as tightly as Jevin had woven his trap, it came not a second too soon. The youths darted out of the room; then the shorter one stopped and poked his head back in. "Will you be sitting with us?"

"Perhaps. I must see if others have plans for me."

He ran off and I shut the door. I changed into more suitable clothing. Instead of leathers I donned a black silk robe with a skull embroidered on the left breast. The robe had been cut to just below waist length and I belted it with a white silk sash. I selected some black silk trousers, put them on, and tucked them into the top of my boots. Actually a regulation uniform, Allen and his seamsters custom-made it for me from material I'd purchased during one of my missions. It was comfortable, light, and did not sap the feeling of well-being I had after Shar.

Properly dressed but without weapons, I walked through the quiet, empty hall, down the stairs and through the supply corridor. I walked to the Star's north wing and came into the mess hall. As can be easily imagined of a room filled with hundreds of hungry people, it was chaos.

The huge room took up the whole of the Star's north point. The kitchen, located in the extreme north corner, was staffed by Services personnel and novices under punishment. Long tables filled the rest of the room and fourteen individuals crowded around each one. Each of the identical tables had a Sixteen at both the head and tail to maintain some sort of order. The tables were grouped by branch, starting at the north end with Justices, Wizards, Elites, and Archers, then widening out to accommodate the Warriors, Lancers, and Services. All Talions, except those on exercises, watch or special duty, ate at the same time.

The lords of each branch, His Excellency, and the Master

sit and take their meals at a table set upon a dais in the northermost point in the room. On occasion one of them will rise to address the assembled multitude. The room has excellent acoustics which makes such a task relatively easy, though such addresses are usually kept short and come before food is actually served.

The rules in the mess are quite simple and every novice learns to work around each one to his own benefit. Take one and pass the rest. If you finish a dish and someone wants more, you go get it. No throwing food. Everyone takes turns scraping and stacking the plates. On the surface it would seem that so simple a set of rules could not be misinterpreted or twisted, but the rules are, and more than once it has been suggested that Justices, not Sixteens, should supervise the tables.

Services Talions wheeled carts laden with bowls and platters between the tables. They deposited one dish for each part of the meal at the head of the table. After a Sixteen took his portion, he passed the dish on, generally heading it the long way around the table from any novice who bothered the Sixteen for some reason. For a simple system it worked as well as could be expected, though feeding troughs had been offered as a viable and more orderly alternative.

I looked across the room toward the Lords' Dais. Tables beside it were usually reserved for Talions back from the field. I smiled as I recognized Jevin and quickly crossed to his table.

"Jevin, how are you?"

The Fealareen smiled a full grin, stood, and clapped me on both shoulders. "They said you had returned, but no one told me you had left Shar." I could see that he was dying to ask if my hosts had interrogated me yet so I gave him no sign of their first attempt. Jevin waved me to the chair across from him. "Sit, Nolan, sit. What a night for you to return. We're having liver!"

I grimaced then quickly scanned the nearby tables. "Marana's not here?"

Jevin wolf-grinned. "You'll have to cool your ardor, she's off on a mission. She left quickly about a month after you did. I've had no word since then, but I just got back last week."

A cook wheeled a cart to our table. I took the bowl of liver and selected a small charred portion of the meat. The cook winked an eye at Jevin and produced a portion of raw beef liver. Jevin smiled, a membrane nictitated up over his eyes for a second, and he licked his lips.

"Did you have much trouble tracking Morai?" Jevin asked his question between gulps of liver.

I shook my head, both to answer his question and to comment on the enthusiasm with which he devoured the meal. I had a hard time choking liver down even when it was burned black. "I can't eat this stuff."

Jevin laughed lightly. "You eat it cooked. You might as well boil leather for boots. Liver is meant to be eaten raw."

I spooned some green beans onto my plate and passed the bowl to Jevin. He looked at the beans the same way I had looked at the liver. "We're even. Want some applesauce?" I passed it to him and he emptied what little I'd left him onto his plate.

"How did Morai get away this time?"

"Why, did you have a bet with someone on his method?"

"No, I heard some Elites laughing about a Justice . . ."

I cursed. "Damn that Erlan." I paused. "Morai dropped me into a man-trap pit easier than if I'd been blind." I shook my head. "I thought I had him. He was standing there, large as life, and the ground just dropped out from under me."

Jevin sat back and wiped his mouth with a tablecloth. "You did get the others?"

I narrowed my eyes and stared at him. "You could rephrase that, old friend."

Jevin nodded and chuckled. "How did you get the others?"

"Thank you." I wiped my mouth. "Rolf and Chi'gandir died at the Broad River ferry. I killed Vareck in Pine Springs and I had Grath executed by Pine Springs' Lord Mayor. Brede ambushed me and the minstrel whose song you butchered, Selia ra Jania, and died in the woods at the base of North Pass. Tafano wanted an honorable duel but set his horse on me. I broke his legs. I don't know if he's dead, and I don't care." Memories of Tafano's horse, while not as acutely painful as before Shar, took my appetite away.

Jevin shook his head. "That was a nasty crew for Morai to

be running with. You could have been killed if they'd jumped you all at once."

I smiled. "Yeah, I would have been in trouble but Morai divided them up when he got word I was on their trail. He kept Brede and Tafano with him, knowing he could arrange it so they would fight me one on one. He knew the others, paired off as they were, would be hard-pressed to work together and get me. Still Rolf and Chi'gandir almost did the job." I forced another piece of liver down, knowing I'd be very hungry in the morning if I did not. Applesauce helped the taste immeasurably.

"I got sent after Rostoth ra Kas."

I nodded. "That should have been little more than a training exercise for you. He's only a slasher, not a cunning murderer."

"You aren't kidding." Jevin speared another piece of liver, this one barely cooked, from the bowl. "He would have been easy but they wanted me to bring him back alive!"

I rocked back in my chair. "Alive? That's odd. I wonder what they want with him?"

Jevin shrugged his shoulders. His mouth was too full to comment but the gesture told all.

I watched my friend eat. I'd always marveled at his ability to wolf down mountains of food. No matter how much he ate, though, there always seemed to be room for more. And there was not a single ounce of fat on that gray-green body of his.

I leaned back in my chair. "So, there has been no word from Marana?"

Jevin shook his head. "She came in from her last mission on the Daar-Thran border: some Daari cultists raiding Thran villages for sacrifices. She cleaned it up with her usual efficiency, apparently leaving the surviving cultists with the impression they had angered a nasty *jelkom* with their antics. They'll not be a problem for a long time yet."

I shivered. Despite her problems I hoped my love for her would turn her away from her own savage side. What I did to Tafano was not easy for me, but for her it would have been a matter of course. Marana reveled in the mystical terror the Justices held for common people. For all I knew her way was better than mine, but for my own sanity I had to hope that was not the truth.

Jevin continued eating and spoke between gulps of liver. "She did not need Shar, so she was sent out almost immediately. All I know is that she headed east. Rumors suggest she went out because there was trouble with the last Black Wagon."

That surprised me. The Black Wagons were sealed wagons that traveled into and out of Talianna very infrequently. Elites usually escorted them and I'd never heard of any problem with a Black Wagon before.

Though many tales got told of what the wagons contained, and many guesses were made whenever one rolled in or out, no one aside from the Master or His Excellency knew for certain what the wagons carried. I always assumed, because it was easiest, the wagons contained gold or prisoners. It *was* within the realm of possibility for someone to have attacked the wagon, but the person organizing the raid would have to be very brave, very stupid, or a traitor: a renegade Talion. But there were no renegades, unless you counted the recalled Janian Talions. . . .

Before I could ask Jevin any questions about the wagon, he stiffened and swallowed quickly. He stood and bowed. I turned, rose, and repeated his action.

Lord Hansur smiled and returned our bows. "Nolan, have you finished eating?"

Whether or not I had finished, his question signaled the end of my meal. "Of course, my lord."

Lord Hansur nodded to the Fealareen. "Jevin, you will excuse us."

"Yes, my lord." Jevin bowed and sat. He waited until Lord Hansur turned his back before he speared the last of my liver. I followed Lord Hansur away from the table and chuckled. Some things never changed.

Jevin had not changed and neither had Lord Hansur. His face was perhaps a bit more seamed and thinner than when I first met him, but his body was still the same tall, lean, wiry skeleton that looked frail but was not weak. Some of the other lords showed their age, but Lord Hansur did not. He was ageless; as ageless as the skull tattoo on his palm.

We left the mess hall and walked through the Star's corridors to Lord Hansur's rooms. Lord Hansur shut the door behind me, then crossed around to his desk and sat. He waved me to the chair facing him, and then he picked up my journal.

He leafed through the book. "Your conduct was satisfactory, if a bit strange in Pine Springs. In the future I would prefer you to deal with the politicians in private. I realize there have been no bad repercussions because of your actions, but I am sure you can share my dread for a day when an offended noble decides to slay those who remind him of his humiliation at your hands."

I bowed my head and rubbed my left hand over my face. "You are correct, my lord. I will change my behavior in the future."

Lord Hansur smiled gently. "I can also understand what you did to Tafano, but I submit that was not the wisest thing you could have done. If he heals you will have a very big problem on your hands."

I marveled at Lord Hansur's evaluation method. He did not rant as some other lords did. Coolly he reminded me of the unnecessary risks I'd taken and advised me against them. In effect he suggested what actions he felt I should avoid, but he did not expressly forbid any action. He retained control of me, but did not put me in a situation to resent that control.

I found it interesting that he handled each Justice differently, if tales told by other Justices of their evaluations were true. Whereas I might be praised for an unusual solution to a dangerous situation, another Justice might be chastized for having gotten into such a situation in the first place. Each Justice was measured against the standard of the laws we enforced, but more importantly each Justice was judged against himself. Lord Hansur asked for the best from each of his Justices, and he got it.

"Nolan, Morai's escape is a minor problem. The fact that he has eluded you so many times is not as bad as it might seem. Because he has escaped you, men believe him immune to your power and are willing to join him. He keeps them in line, curbing their baser instincts, and brings them out where we can get at them. If I did not know he allowed us to get his men so he'd have an easier time splitting up the loot, I'd imagine he actually worked for or with you."

I smiled sheepishly. "I only wish he did work with me. If he did I would've been out of the pit when the Elites arrived."

That brought a smile to Lord Hansur's face. "I must apologize for that. Your immediate return was necessary. A situation has arisen, one that you are uniquely suited to deal with. You will be briefed on it in the morning."

"My time is mine until then?"

"Yes."

I rose and he handed me my journal. I turned to leave but his voice stopped me.

"You might take Jevin into Taltown and have him show you the newest braising pit. A businessman all the way from Gull came here to treat us to culinary delights beyond, as he put it, 'your reach, my Lord Talion.' "

I laughed aloud. "That ought to be worth some time." I bowed. "Until the morning, then."

Lord Hansur returned my bow and I left. I found Jevin in another room down the hall from mine. Despite his protests that he could not eat another mouthful, no matter how well the Gull merchant prepared marinated liver, he came with me. We found the stall with ease, though getting through the press of people was less simple.

I shouldered my way past two Lancers, and one considered starting a fight, but that was before he got a good look at Jevin. The merchant, and two children, were doing a brisk business. The merchant took the money and the children delivered the wares. Most people brought their own platter, or paid a silver Provincial deposit on one of the merchant's wooden plates.

"What will you have, my lords?" The merchant's chubby cheeks were bunched around the corners of his wide smile.

A thread of smoke passed by me and made my decision simple. "I would like half a chicken. Jevin, do you want anything?"

"Nolan, I couldn't."

"I'll buy. . . ."

The Fealareen grinned wolfishly. "Well, only to be polite."

I laughed. "Of course. . . ."

Jevin looked at the merchant. "The usual, kind sir."

• • •

I slept well that night. The chicken was delicious, and I have to admit the merchant's treatment of liver actually made it palatable. With my belly full I drifted off into a thick slumber and remembered none of my dreams.

Morning came none too quickly, and I awoke refreshed. I stretched and got out of bed. A note sealed by the Master lay on the table in my room. It read: "Feed yourself, then come prepared to my chamber." The "prepared" meant only one thing: he wanted me fully armed and ready for combat.

The directive puzzled me, but that was not unusual. A normal Talion like myself is not meant to know what the Master is thinking. I'm meant to follow orders and do my job. If I have to think while doing it, well, that's part of the job.

Since I had been called for an audience I decided to eat only a light breakfast. I ran to the mess hall, stopped to tell Jevin I'd not be eating with him, and walked back to the kitchen. I grabbed a bowl of stew and ate it while standing, then returned to my room. I quickly brushed all my leathers and donned them. Instead of the sleeveless leather jerkin I'd worn on the road I opted for a full-sleeved, padded jacket. A leather tab on each sleeve extended far enough to cover the back of my hands. I strapped on my weapons, which included buckling my spurs onto my boots. Fully prepared, I headed to the Master's Chamber.

The iron-bound oak doors of the Master's rooms swung open before me. No incense choked the room this time. The Master sat in his dragonthrone and Lord Hansur stood beside him on the dais. The other lords and ladies: Fletcher of the Archers, Isas of the Elites, Kalinda of the Warriors, Cosima of the Wizards, and Eric of the Lancers stood on either side of the dais. His Excellency, Lord of Services, was not present.

The carpet had been peeled back from a trapdoor. The broad wooden door stood upright like a Warrior prepared for inspection. It opened onto a black void.

"Justice Nolan." With a voice just a trace weaker than I remembered it, the Master addressed me solemnly.

"Yes, Master."

He pointed to the opening in the floor. "The Darkmaze."

"Yes, Master."

"If you can, kill whatever you find down there."

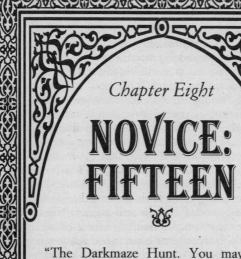

Chapter Eight

NOVICE: FIFTEEN

"The Darkmaze Hunt. You may have heard of it, Nolan." The Sixteen spoke particularly condescendingly to me. He was from Hamis.

I nodded my head.

He smiled. "Good. The exercise is simple. You enter the maze ahead of us, hide, and we will try to find you. If we cannot, you win." His tone clearly suggested that I could only delay my discovery, and that too long a delay would make it rougher on me when they finally tracked me down.

I groaned inwardly. Occasionally our lords allowed the Sixteens to make up exercises to run us Fifteens through. Their drills generally involved a great deal of body contact—"good-natured rough-housing"—and, if nothing else, an object lesson in avoiding a more organized, larger group of foes.

"Hope I don't make it easy for you!" I lurched up from the old, wooden bench, sprang past the startled Sixteens, and dove feet-first into the Darkmaze. Their shouts of outrage and threats of revenge chased me into the black pit.

This was by no means my first visit to the maze that lurked like a stagnant shadow-pool beneath the Star. Like my other visits to the maze, this one began in one of three holding rooms. Other exercises ran from simple races through the maze to team competitions and mock battles in the dark.

From my first trip into the maze I decided to conquer my fear of cloying darkness and learn as much as I could about my surroundings. I discovered many pits and trip blocks that made reckless dashes through the maze very foolish. I uncovered narrow passages and tunnels that worked around often traveled intersections or led out of cul-de-sacs. I saw each visit as a chance to use what I had already learned in the Darkmaze, and an opportunity to learn more about the maze itself.

I landed on my feet and crouched to absorb the impact of the drop. The air was dry, musty, and full of the dustcloud I raised with my landing. I stifled a sneeze and headed deeper into the maze. I felt along the walls with my left hand and chose branches that took me to the left.

During my last run through the maze I found a pit near the south wall of the maze, but I couldn't find any tunnels that approached it from the other side. That was unusual, and although I relied upon a strictly mental map of the Darkmaze, I felt certain there had to be something beyond the pit.

I couldn't ask anyone if they'd ever discovered anything beyond the pit, because the Lancers and Warriors considered mapping the Darkmaze cheating. They enjoyed reacting to unusual situations, it seemed, and they guaranteed themselves plenty of surprises by refusing to learn the maze's layout. Most other novices followed the Lancer practice because they didn't want to take the time to learn the maze, and if any of them were in the same situation I was, of having half-memorized it, they surely would not mention it for fear of Lancer ridicule.

I reached the pit quickly and fished a handful of stones out of my pocket. I dropped the first into the pit and listened for it to hit bottom. It landed after a short drop, so I estimated the pit was only twelve or fifteen feet deep—enough to trap a foolish novice, but not really enough of a fall to hurt someone badly. I arced the second stone gently out into the darkness, and, waiting for it to hit the far side, I got a big surprise.

It clicked against the far wall far more quickly than I expected.

I stopped for a moment and thought. The pit itself could only be six to ten feet across, which made for a substantial amount of room between it and the Star's south foundation wall. I was convinced there was something beyond it, and unmindful of the exercise I was trapped in, I was determined to see what was on the other side.

I smiled and quickly banished the thought of leaping through the utter darkness to the other side. I had no guarantee that some sort of ledge jutted out on the pit's far side. Without a ledge I'd jump out, hit the blank wall solidly, and bounce back down into the pit. Even if a ledge did exist on the other side, it might not be wide enough for me to land safely upon. In addition, the pit's builders might have set wooden posts out in the darkness across the pit to stop anyone foolish enough to jump where he could not see.

I reached out and touched the right wall with my right hand, and the left wall with my left hand. The corridor was narrow enough that I could straighten both arms. I shuffled forward until I toed the edge of the pit and braced both my arms against the walls. I inched my right foot forward and smiled as I felt a toehold. I secured my foot in it and started forward with the left foot.

My shoulders started aching immediately. The toeholds bore some of my weight, but I really hung from my arms. The toeholds just kept me up as I shifted an arm forward and braced again. With agonizing slowness I crawled forward. Had I been able to see myself hanging spread-eagle in midair I might have laughed, but the pain in my shoulders was not funny at all.

When only a foot or two into the pit I heard the Sixteens drop down into the maze. A couple of them called to me to surrender, and others laughed, but fairly soon I heard the Hamisian novice's voice and the others fell silent. He issued orders, neatly splitting the maze into quadrants, and started the search for me.

Another foot forward and I hoped I'd half finished my journey. My limbs started trembling with fatigue. I gritted my teeth against the pain and tried to speed my pace up. I heard searchers behind me and, as I had done racing with Jevin, let fear flood through tired muscles and convince them to do what I could not beg them to accomplish. My progress quickened and I reached the pit's far side—and a six-inch-wide ledge—just as two Sixteens entered the corridor behind me.

One novice advanced quickly and almost fell into the pit. "Whoa!" he cried. I heard him clawing at the wall and the laughter of his companion when she grabbed his belt and dragged him upright.

"I told you there was a pit down this way. Remember last year when Gaynor fell in?" Her remark almost forced a laugh from me.

"Yeah, sure, I remember." He took one last deep breath, then growled, "Come on, he isn't here." They turned and marched back the way they'd come.

Sitting on the ledge, which was a precarious balancing act, I noticed there was far more than six inches of hollow below the ledge. I reached back with my feet and could not touch the wall, which surprised me. I slowly moved to the pit corner and wedged myself in position so I could lower my body and try to touch the back wall with my left leg. I braced my right hand against the pit wall and rested my left hand on the ledge, then lowered myself slowly and reached out. I still couldn't touch the back wall, but on the side wall, down at my right side, I felt a solid foothold.

Quickly I twisted, dropped down into the pit, and hung by both my hands from the ledge. I never really considered what I'd do if I found no passage down there. While dragging myself up to the ledge would not normally have been difficult, crossing the pit tired my arms and they let me know right off they were not ready to haul me back up to the ledge any time soon.

Luckily I felt another ledge about four feet below the original ledge. I reached up with my feet and discovered the cavity was at least two feet deep, and probably more since I couldn't touch its back wall. Gently I lowered myself down and lay back in the hole I'd discovered.

A lump on the floor pressed uncomfortably into my back. I rolled up into a sitting position and reached back with my hands to examine the stonework. I felt a wheel half-embedded in the floor along the left wall. It had ridges that made for good fingerholds, and the wheel spun forward and back pretty easily. I rotated it backward, toward the pit.

Something ahead of me in the darkness made a grating sound. I felt a cool breeze rush over me and head toward the pit. Confused, curious, but most of all scared, I crawled forward. After ten feet of dusty pathway that gently sloped down, I felt cool clean smooth stone. Beneath my left hand I found another wheel.

I spun this wheel forward and heard a stone panel slide down behind to cut me off from the maze. I realized, as the panel shut with a gentle thud, that I might have trapped myself. Anxiously I spun the wheel in the opposite direction, just a little, and the panel slid up again a short way. Satisfied I could escape if I wished, I closed the panel and stood.

I placed my hand against the left wall and started forward. My fingers brushed against a series of raised bumps carved into the wall. A split-second wave of nausea washed over me as a *leechspell* sucked energy from my body and triggered another spell. For that moment I went from being scared to being utterly terrified.

My fear evaporated as light glowed from a series of white disks set in the wall. The light came up gently and gave my eyes time to adjust to it. In it I saw that the raised bumps I'd brushed were magick runes of the written symbols for light and dark. By running my fingers along them from left to right I produced light. Reversing the order would shut the light off. At that time, though, I'd have sooner cut my right arm off.

I stood—alone and unwatched—in the Talion treasury! The narrow room ran deep to the south and was stuffed to overflowing. Gold and jewels spilled from barrels and chests burst from the sheer weight of treasure! It was a miser's paradise; a riot of incalculable wealth. My body trembled worse than it had halfway over the pit, and I knew if anyone caught me in here, the Master would put me to death.

Even with that dire a punishment hanging over me, I could

not force myself back into the Darkmaze. I staggered over to one chest of gold coins and gingerly reached my hand into it. The bright coins made a ringing rasp as I touched them. They were cool and sent a thrill through my body, but that elation condensed and froze into terror as I realized the significance of these coins.

Clekan's smiling face flashed in the light and mocked me. All the coins in this chest matched in age and beauty the Imperial my family treasured. Still, none of these coins showed even the slightest wear from use or commerce. My family's coin was worth more than the value of its gold because of its rarity and antiquity, but here sat a whole chest full of them!

Reverently, I set the coins back on the pile and wandered deeper into the room. Something struck me as very strange here. My fear and curiosity fought, and curiosity won only because I already knew I was doomed. If I had to die, I reasoned, I might as well solve this mystery first.

I slowly identified the out-of-place elements and defined the room's mystery. One thing made itself apparent almost immediately upon reflection: wherever I was, it was not the Talion treasury.

The way the treasure had been sorted and stacked was perfectly in keeping with Talion ideas of order, but the decay suggested a long period of neglect. All the chests and barrels were old, very old. Their collapse and the subsequent mess was most unTalionlike in its disorder.

I worked on that problem as I wandered. I sorted through the various coins, searching for the youngest available. I saw no coins from any of the kingdoms of the Shattered Empire, and that disturbed me. All the coins were from the Imperial era, and after a thorough search I settled upon the coins stamped with Kiritan the Mad's profile as the youngest series of coins here.

I took note of the style of box I'd pulled Kiritan's coin from and continued my search. I studied the other piles of treasure and decided the jewels and jewelry had suffered the least. Little more than rust remained of steel weaponry, and the fabrics crumbled to dust when I walked near them and stirred the air. Finally I located a couple more boxes similar in style to those containing Kiritan's coins.

I lifted the boxes down from atop a cask of tarnished silver coins and, despite the gold latticework caging the boxes themselves, their relative lightness surprised me. I plucked a gold spoon from a nearby pile of loot and carefully sprang the latch on one box with it. As I forced the lock a needle shot out and would have skewered my hand had I not taken my precaution. From the look of the needle, it once had been covered with poison.

The first box held a crown. The cloth part of it long ago fell to dust, but the jewels still sparkled and the intricate designs worked on the golden ribs and spires were still distinct. The other box, also with a poison needle in the lock, held another crown. I studied both crowns and did my best to memorize every detail I could.

I walked to as far back in the room as I could get and saw a doorway in the southernmost wall. I knew it stood well beyond the Star's foundation and guessed it extended below the Archers' quarters in the Citadel. I searched behind two piles of gold coins and located another set of runes and a door wheel in the floor. I doused the lights and opened the stone door.

The door opened into a narrow passage, which I followed blindly south for a considerable distance. It sloped down, heading toward the Tal River. At its terminus the air was quite moist and I found a trapdoor leading up. I could not open it but I felt fairly certain it opened into the grove of apple trees overlooking the Talions' burial field.

I retraced my steps and thought about what I would do with the information I had learned. It seemed obvious to me that no one knew of this treasure trove and what it contained. I saw nothing to indicate it had ever been visited since the collapse of the Shattered Empire, but I still had a hard time believing the Masters since they did not at least know about it.

But, I asked myself, if they didn't know anything about it, was it up to me to tell them about it? There might have been a reason the treasure was buried, and if I let the fact slip that I knew of it, I might ruin some careful plan laid down by a Master a thousand years ago.

I decided, as I stalked past barrels of treasure, to study the problem and try to learn where all the treasure had come from. I would start by learning anything and everything I could about the Darkmaze, and the collapse of the Shattered Empire. If the Master at that time wanted knowledge of this treasure hidden, I'd certainly see the signs when my study became difficult. And if I learned something different, I could tell the Master about this store.

I climbed up the rope ladder hanging down from the staging room I'd entered through. I smiled at the assembled, dour-faced Sixteens. My smile died when I met the reproving gaze of Lord Hansur.

"They thought you were dead. They could not seem to find you."

I smiled. "I'm sorry. I thought I wasn't supposed to be found."

Lord Hansur stared at the Sixteen from Hamis. "That is something they, apparently, forgot."

The library at Talianna sat in the middle floor of the Star, right below the observatory level. Small rooms, often used for instruction, were located along the north and south walls. The center of the Star contained the stacks of bound and unbound manuscripts that made up the library. The west wall had desks for studying and several Services librarians scurried about between them and the stacks to find books and shelve them.

The books in the library were mostly histories, both national and personal. There was a vast section of journals kept by Talions through the ages, but they were written in High Tal and my command of that tongue, even after three years, was not very good. The national histories were written in the common dialect, and allowing for the age of the text, were nearly understandable. I found a history of Talianna itself, begun after the Empire was shattered, written in common, and used that history for my starting point.

I visited the library in the free hour after the midday meal. I read as much as I could but made no notes because I did not want my work discovered. I trusted my memory enough to carry important details around, and I found the research exciting enough to make memorization easy.

The Talianna history hinted at things that took place

during the fall of the Empire, and gave me a fair idea what the treasure was, but did nothing to explain how it got where it now lay. Relatively swift, in comparison to the life-span of nations, and very bloody, the Shattering touched the lives of every man, woman, and child in the Empire. The very existence of ulbands pointed out that many people refused to acknowledge the new order, and many leaders lost their positions and lives amid savage civil wars, but nowhere was the collapse as savage, or as shrouded in mystery, as in the fall of the Emperor himself.

The Empire's central problem developed well before Kiritan assumed the throne. The provinces had long sought independence, but the Emperors had countered this desire by granting more privileges and powers to the individual provincial rulers, dropping their tax rates and still providing protection in the form of Talions. These concessions decentralized the government and reduced the Emperor into a figure to be respected, and a force that could be called upon in an emergency, but little else. This worked well to preserve the Empire's integrity, but caused trouble in the provinces. By wielding power in a tyrannical manner, some provincial rulers created unrest in their own provinces and sowed the seeds that would make their families ul during the Shattering.

Kiritan the Mad ascended to the throne upon the death of his father. He hated the idea of an Empire where he was nothing more than a figurehead. He tightened his grip on the reins of power and the provincial nobles, in turn, were forced to tighten their control of the provinces. This heightened the strife in the provinces, so the minor nobles and other mistreated people quickly rebelled. The Mountain Warlords declared independence first and, in their shadow, Azealtia, Hanrith, and the Free States of Aziz revolted.

Kiritan acted immediately. He sent Imperial troops east from what was then the capital—the present-day Imperiana—through Jania, toward the mountains. The Janians protested and fought the Imperial troops. The eastern lords of Jania revolted and formed Ealla. Instantly Hamis and the other nations around the Runt Sea broke with the Empire.

This open eastern revolt pulled troops from the west, so Temur and Boucan wasted no time declaring themselves independent. Zandria and Juchar, knowing troops would march over them to get to the rebels, allied with the rebels so the battles would be fought in Daar or Venz.

The Empire broke apart like a ship in a raging sea. Any warrior with a gang of men would take land and declare himself a noble. He would ally with the strongest leader he could find and they would forge a nation. The nations secured their own borders, looked at neighbors with envy, and watched for any signs of weakness. If they saw an opening, they struck.

Imperiana was born when a number of ulLords fled toward the capital. Kiritan promised them their old holdings if they could keep the core of the Empire alive. All of them realized the Empire was a dream that had faded, and they divided the central province into their own domain. More a figurehead than he had ever been before, Kiritan quickly found himself trapped in his own palace.

Kiritan decided the time had come to use the Talions. No one had been foolish enough, even with war in the air, to try to take Tal. The Talions pushed their borders out, established No Lords' Land, and sent a message to all the warlords within striking distance: "Leave us alone and your army will not be destroyed."

Simple and succinct, the message worked.

Kiritan got word to Master Vaughan demanding Talions be sent to rescue him. The task should have been easy. A half-dozen Elites, at that time the Emperor's bodyguard company, could have flown him and his family to Talianna. Kiritan, though, wanted his treasure moved with him.

From that point things got a bit hazy, but the general outline, as nearly as I could make out, followed something like this: the Rebel Lords sacked the Imperial Palace and carried Kiritan's treasure away from it. Kiritan and his family escaped the palace and fled west. The exact manner and location of Kiritan's death is still unknown, but the accepted finish to his story is that he was captured by a Xne'kal party in Woodholm and his head graces one of their altars. The treasure, which the lords who took the palace carted off, just vanished into thin air, and many dreams of conquest—meant to be financed with the booty—just evaporated.

In several Talion diaries dating from that time I found gaps in reporting that covered roughly the dates of the sacking. From other references in the various journals—

obscure and obtuse allusions to a most exciting incident—I pieced together what probably happened to the Emperor's treasure, and how it ended up below the Citadel.

Master Vaughan knew the conquering lords would never rest until they had sacked the Imperial Palace and taken the treasure. Each of them wanted a piece of the treasure to pay for his war and to build up his portion of the province. The one who got away with the most, one could assume, would be able to gather an army and possibly carve out a new empire.

The Master sent Talions disguised as normal fighting men into Imperiana and directed them to assist in sacking the castle. They helped carry the treasure free of the Imperial capital. Where Talions made up the masters and men of a detail hauling treasure back for their lord, they rerouted the treasure to Talianna. If a lord had his house troops carry the treasure home, very nasty and highly skilled "bandits" struck and looted the caravan.

All the histories spoke of Vaughan as a wise man despite his relative youth. All during the civil wars he kept the Talions neutral, except when a group of men went renegade and sacked at will, killing innocents and destroying defenseless villages. He had those bands hunted down and slaughtered— reiterating the Talions' right to dispense justice anywhere while keeping them clear of politics.

As the wars ended he also extended invitations to the most promising of generals and other fighters to join the Talions— skimming off the best leadership from the nations and reinforcing the Talions at the same time. He then made a practice of assigning these new Talions back to the emerging nations to train their old troops.

Very quickly the Talions became the seat of all military science in the Shattered Empire. If a king wanted his troops to be the equal of his neighbor's he had to hire a Talion to train them. And that meant he had to agree to allow Justices to travel through his country to hunt down and destroy criminals.

Vaughan made the best out of a very chaotic situation. He took away from the lords, in leadership and money, the ability to wage a sustained war. By assigning individuals to the lords to train their armies he could keep the armies at even strengths and thereby make decisive victory highly improbable. In one generation he changed the tasks asked of Talions; created the Warriors, Lancers, and Archers; and insured the stability of the new nations. As a testament to his vision, the stability he established, though weakened somewhat by time and ambition, had largely survived to the present.

Getting the treasure into Talianna without notice might have been a bit trickier, but Vaughn managed it. He stationed most troops out in No Lords' Land and issued orders sending everyone off on a carefully planned series of patrols. He told the unit leaders that with the palace's fall he feared the new lord would come after Tal—their journals show they agreed with him—and ordered the total evacuation of Taltown. In a remarkably short time Talianna lay virtually empty.

I had to guess at the next step because I found no mention of it at all. The Talions returning with the treasure must have been given specific traveling orders to weave them through the network of patrols without being seen. They brought their loot into Talianna, hid it in a room that probably once served to store food in case of siege, and then the Master used the Call to insure secrecy concerning their action.

The one thing I did have a solid piece of evidence about was the origin of the Darkmaze. I had nothing as good as the journal of a Services mason putting it together, but I noticed almost immediately that none of the Talions' journals mentioned Darkmaze training at all until after the Shattering. The Darkmaze had not been built until after Kiritan's death and, though Vaughan ordered it built, it saw completion only after his premature death.

Trying to guess what Vaughan would have done with the money had he lived was impossible. He died from food poisoning, which was not really suspicious, though he did refuse magical attention and insisted he was fine the night before they found him. It was possible, I thought, that he'd killed himself so the treasure never would be discovered.

I decided he wanted knowledge of the treasure hidden because there would always be those Talions—around then as well as now—who would want to use the money to reestablish the Empire. That philosophical split, born during the Shattering, still existed in Talion thinking today. I paled at the thought of the Talions starting out to put the Empire back together again. I felt sure Master Vaughan had shared my feelings.

His simple plan insured peace. I decided I would not jeopardize it.

I closed my last book and started to get up when Marana seated herself across from me.

"You aren't leaving on my account, are you?"

I smiled. "No."

She pointed to my chair. "Then sit." Half an order and half a plea, she gave me no option but to obey.

I sat. "Where's Lothar?" I looked around the library. "I don't see him anywhere."

Marana frowned. "Why should he be here?" Her unbound black hair slid forward to hood her face.

I blushed and stammered defensively, "Well, you know, the two of you are, um, have been together for a while and, ah . . ."

Marana rocked back, laughed, and covered her mouth to kill the sound. I glared at her and a deeper shade of scarlet burned onto my face. She reached out and laid her right hand on my left wrist so I'd not flee. "I'm sorry, Nolan, but the sight of you nervous is so alien."

My head sunk, and I stared at the table for a moment, then raised my head and nodded resignedly. "I know, it's like seeing Jevin excited about eating oatmeal." My blush faded and Marana squeezed my arm. "You and Lothar always spend a lot of time together so I just expected to see him here with you."

Marana smiled and nodded her understanding. For the first time I really saw how much she'd changed over the past two years. She'd gone from being a pretty girl toward becoming a beautiful woman. Her brown eyes were full of life and her smile was enough to melt even the most committed misogynist's heart. Part of the reason discussing her relationship with Lothar so embarrassed me was because I envied him very much.

"It's a fair question, Nolan." She grinned and rolled her eyes to heaven. "He got another letter from Jania and he's composing a 'suitable' reply. He gets more communications from home than anyone else. If all of us got as many letters, we'd get no training done in . . . Oh, Nolan, I'm sorry!"

I'd stiffened at the mention of family and clenched my jaw to choke the lump back down in my throat. I knew if I said anything my voice would crack so I just looked over at Marana and forced a smile on my lips.

Marana took both my hands in hers and leaned forward. "I should have thought, Nolan, I didn't mean to hurt you."

I squeezed her hands and swallowed. "It's fine, I know you didn't mean anything by it. It's just me, I should be over it by now. . . ."

Marana frowned. "Hush, don't ever say that. Your family meant and still means a lot to you. They loved you, and if you forget that you'll be worse off than you are now. After a time the pain will fade, but you don't ever want it to be gone."

I forced a chuckle and nodded. "Thank you. During Festival, when Lothar's kin descend on Tal as if it's a province of Jania, I feel so lonely. I know Jevin does too. At least you have Lothar. . . ."

Marana smiled and shook her head. Her hair rippled like a curtain in a gentle breeze. "When Lothar's relatives are here they have him. Just like you and Jevin, I'm an orphan as well. So, while Lothar writes his relatives, I come up here and try and learn everything I can about Temur, my homeland."

I nodded slowly, and reluctantly let Marana draw her hands away. Her search for information about Temur was as important to her as my solving the mystery of the secret treasure was to me. Rumor had it, fairly well substantiated, that Marana had been brought to Tal by merchants who found her left out on a hillside in Temur. Female infanticide was not all that common a practice in the Shattered Empire, and normally such a child would have been refused to prevent others from dumping unwanted children on the Talions, but His Excellency agreed to take Marana for reasons known only to him.

"So, what have your studies told you? Have you figured out who your parents were?"

A second of displeasure flashed over her face; then Marana sighed and opened a small journal. "It's dreary stuff, really. Temur is a flat grassland nation. We herd cattle and live in migratory tribes. There are nine major tribes, each named for a point on the compass, and countless clans within the tribes.

It's a great mess, with vendettas and blood alliances back and forth in a complex web of relations."

I paused for a second and organized the information in my own mind. "So, have you figured out what tribe you came from?"

She shook her head. "It's too tangled a web to unravel from the outside. His Excellency won't tell me where I was found, which would make the search simple, so I can only go by general clues and make assumptions. By my coloration I should be a member of the Amar clan, and my name, Marana, is common in the clan. But right now the Amar are not one of the major clans in the South tribe, so it is unlikely they would have sent me away because they could use daughters to marry off and make alliances with stronger clans."

I frowned. "If the tribes take their names from the compass points, doesn't it get complicated? I would think a war against a neighboring tribe would create confusion, turning the South tribe into the South-southeast tribe."

Marana smiled and shook her head. "If you can believe it, the system is odd enough to handle all that so such problems do not arise." Marana turned to a map she had drawn. "The city here in the center is Betil. It is home to the ninth tribe— the Betil tribe—and the Emir of all Temur. The Betil once conquered the whole nation, then split it up among the defeated tribes. All the tribes send representatives to Betil to adjudicate any disagreements between tribes."

I raised an eyebrow. "Yeah, but I understood there were wars between tribes. That sounds like it would do away with war."

Marana shook her head. "There are wars, but before another tribe can take over a new territory, the representatives meet in Betil and award the new territory to the conqueror. It prevents the wars from getting truly too savage." She raised a hand to silence my coming protest. "Sure, warriors run out and get killed, but the wars don't carry the destruction to the civilian population. The Tribal Council awards the contested province to the winner and the tribes exchange lands. Those who don't want to move can stay and join the new tribe provided they are allowed to do so by the Tribal Council."

"What happens if they are not given permission?"

"The Tribal Council declares them dead and no one is permitted to trade with them until they bow to the Council's will. All in all the practice really prevents any cities aside from Betil springing up. The lords of Betil like this because it makes their city the commercial hub of the country."

I smiled and looked up at the ceiling as I absorbed the information. The paint was cracked. "That's complicated. Temuri history must be a mess."

Marana smiled somewhat proudly. "Aside from Betil's conquest of the nation a hundred years before the Empire collapsed, Temuri history has been a case of each tribe getting used and discarded by outsiders. The Temuri are excellent horse archers, which makes them a nasty light cavalry. Outsiders have promised them great riches if they will come out and fight in support of their 'ally.' Each tribe that has done so has been betrayed. The oldest saying in Temur is 'Trust a man only as far as your bow can shoot.' "

I laughed and squeezed Marana's right hand with my left. "You Temuri are generous. In Sinjaria the saying went, 'Trust a man to the length of your sword.' "

"The Fealareen trust men only when we have their hearts in our hands." The friendly smile on Jevin's face betrayed his deep and menacing voice. I started and pulled my hand from Marana's. "Come on you two, we have fighting practice in five minutes. You'll be late."

Jevin, already in his practice leathers, walked quietly and calmly from the library. I don't think he noticed the redness on my face, but I caught Marana's grin out of the corner of my eye.

Even though we sprinted to our rooms and changed quickly, Marana and I were late, so we were formed into a fighting team. Jevin and Lothar were another team. Lothar had waited for Marana and expected Jevin to choose me as his partner. In the normal course of events we often paired that way, and our two teams usually ended up fighting each other as the "best of the best" when we fought in two different exercise groups. This time the instructor, a Sixteen, took great pleasure in splitting our usual teams.

We used padded leather for armor and blunted weapons in fighting practice. The instructors and judges decided the lethality of each blow landed and applied the results to the fight. While Justices would seldom work in teams, the instruction gave us insight into how teams might work together to oppose us. Most important, to me, it showed where a fighter might let his guard down if he fought with an ally at his side.

I'd not fought with Marana as my partner before. She was about half a foot smaller than my six feet, but was very quick. I knew from opposing her that she might be out of range in one second and then in, attacking, and back out in the next. She relied on finesse: she knew all the points on a body where the arteries passed close to the surface, and she practiced hitting the blood vessels with quick slashing attacks. Suffering within limitations placed on them by the judges, many of her foes simply bled to death before they could even hit her.

I was not surprised when Marana and I were placed in a preliminary circle of fights that did not include Jevin and Lothar. The instructor clearly believed we'd be the best in our circle, and that Jevin and Lothar would defeat everyone in their group. The other teams knew that and did their best to knock us out of the running fast.

The first two teams, knowing I relied on power more than speed, attacked Marana first. I took a lesson from her, moved quickly, and adapted my style to defeat enemies who expected me to stand and exchange sword cuts. My first victim went down quickly when, after one passing slash, the judges ruled I'd broken his spine.

Marana finished his partner by using my normal fighting style to oppose him. She exchanged sword cuts with him; then she slipped her blade between his legs and, as the judges ruled, sliced the artery in his left thigh apart. He hopped around on one leg for a half minute while Marana avoided him, and a judge finally ruled him unconscious from loss of blood. When he fell Marana dispatched him with an elaborate thrust to the chest that had all the observers, and the victim, laughing for a minute or two. "Had I known I'd die so picturesquely," the dead man quipped, "I'd have given up immediately!"

As others in our circle fought, we watched Jevin and Lothar destroy their first opponents. Both of them closed on their foes like thieves descending upon a caravan. Fierce and powerful, they forced their opponents back with feints and bluffs before any blows actually landed. Lothar, with a series of feints and cuts, "broke" the sword arm of his foe, then "crushed" his skull. Jevin brutally parried a blow, knocked his opponent's blade flying, then pushed the startled boy down on his back and placed his blade at the youth's throat.

The judge declared his victim dead and Jevin looked over at me. "That'll be you, Nolan, just remember."

I looked over at Marana, rolled my eyes skyward, and we both started to laugh. "We'll see, mountain demon, we'll see."

Our other fights went as easily as the first. Without consulting each other we switched styles back and forth and constantly threw our foes off balance. We adapted ourselves to their styles. If they sunk back into a defensive posture we attacked quickly and without pause. If they swept forward we defended until their flurry of blows spent itself; then we aggressively counterattacked and vanquished them.

If I was in trouble Marana appeared, and vice versa. We matched each tactic the enemy employed with one of equal or greater strength. I could leave Marana to parry the blows of both foes while I circled wide and attacked from the flank or rear. Without a word spoken between us we would switch opponents, surprise and kill them. We made a very effective team.

Jevin and Lothar were equally efficient. They powered through their foes easily, though each of them got killed at least once. The worst wound we sustained came when I lost my left arm from the elbow down. My foe had not expected me to parry with a bare arm, and my riposte took him through the chest so I thought the exchange worth it. Still our lack of deaths made Marana and me the favorite to win the day.

Both teams had a chance to rest while others fought. I dipped water from a bucket in the Citadel wall's shadow and drank deeply. Jevin walked up behind me and rested a heavy hand on my left shoulder. "Don't drink so much, Nolan, it will only slow you down." He smiled and took a dipper of water himself. "You don't want a belly full of water, *or anything else*, distracting you during the fight."

A rivulet of sweat ran a cold course down my spine. "Jevin,

Marana and I were just talking. She's Lothar's lover, and he's my friend. You know me, Jevin, I'd do nothing to hurt either one of them."

The Fealareen drank and nodded. He wiped water from his chin with the back of his left hand. "I know you, Nolan, and what you say is true. I merely suggest you remember those words and don't let anything distract you. As good a friend as Lothar is now, he'd make a worse enemy."

I smiled and gently punched Jevin in the shoulder. "I understand. Thank you, Jevin."

He grinned enough to let his canines show white against the green-gray of his lips. "I just want to make sure you are back as my partner next time."

I laughed and danced out of striking distance. "Just so I won't kill you all the time, right?"

The four of us entered the fighting circle and bowed to the judges and then each other. We were all somewhat giddy, because Lord Hansur came out to watch the final fight and a few Justices—full Justices back in Talianna from assignments out in the real world—offered each other wagers on our chances of success. In their estimation Jevin and Lothar were a two-to-one favorite.

Jevin and Lothar lined up so Marana would go against the Fealareen and Lothar would fight me. Though better than me at swordfighting, Lothar's hideous overconfidence made him vulnerable. "Marana," he said, "Jevin will keep you occupied until I can dispatch the farmer and go after you. To the victor go the spoils. . . ."

She shot him a withering glance, but backed it with a smile so he laughed it off. If she'd looked that way at me—without the smile—I would have run, further and faster than I did with Jevin on my heels.

Lord Hansur gave the signal and we closed. Lothar came at me, decided to attack with power, and clearly expected to crash through my guard. I cut to my right, evaded his blow, but did not counterattack. I let myself move just a bit slower than I had in the earlier fights. I let my left arm hang wearily and acted as if the earlier fights had exhausted me.

Lothar smiled wide to give me as close to a predatory smile as he could muster. "You're mine, Nolan. *Thou art dead.*"

He came again and I dodged at the last second. I slashed

back at him, caught his left shoulder, and the judges ruled his left arm impaired. His smile died and he gnawed his lower lip. After a swift flurry of blows that came far faster than I could parry, he hit *me* on the left shoulder. We were even.

"Come, Nolan, let us fyghte without guile." His voice was low and cold. I'd heard that tone before: when we spoke harshly to the Services clerk on my first day. He used that tone to command inferiors, and with it commanded me to lie down and die.

I frowned and concentrated, because I knew if I did not think my way through the fight I would lose to his superior skill. But before he could read the concern on my face, I forced myself to grin at him. *"Defeat me, if thou art able."*

Despite the armor and the bluntness of the blades, two fighters can hurt each other. The blows can leave nasty bruises. Lothar and I struck hard. We made each cut count and hurt to prove who was best.

Out of the corner of my eye I saw Marana. She held her own against Jevin, but his superior reach kept her at bay. The agile Fealareen easily danced away from her attacks. She parried his cuts or faded away from them, but she just could not dart in quickly enough to actually hit Jevin. A blind man could have read the frustration on her face.

The fight was a stalemate.

The second I realized we were too evenly matched for one side to win decisively, I decided to do something about it. I moved so Lothar and Jevin fought virtually back to back. Lothar smiled, glad to have his ally behind him and confident that Marana could not get at him through Jevin. *"Now, Nolan, thou art dead."*

I smiled. *"As are thee."*

Lothar launched a sweeping cut at me and I rushed forward into it. He caught me on the left side and the blow crushed my left arm against my rib cage. Even so, my momentum carried me forward into his body and knocked him backward and down into Jevin's legs. Surprised and unbalanced, Jevin fell back and ended up on top of Lothar.

Marana leaped in and quickly dispatched both of them.

Lord Hansur laid his hand on the judge's shoulder and usurped the right to pronounce the verdict. "Nolan, you are dead. The blow would have carried through your arm to your vital organs."

Lothar, regaining his feet, beamed. "I got you, Nolan. You walked right into the blow. Even you should have seen it coming."

"And, Lothar, he got you," snapped Lord Hansur. "Both you and Jevin are dead by Marana's hand." Lord Hansur waved us back and, when we seated ourselves on the circle's edge, addressed the assembled novices. "You just witnessed a good victory. The object of the contest was for the *team* to win. Nolan realized there was a stalemate and acted to break that stalemate. Lothar's victory was short-lived."

Lothar grumbled. "But he died from my attack. That was stupid. He just helped Marana win as if he was just her second sword."

I frowned. "A tool is just a tool, unless it does the job by itself."

Lord Hansur raised a hand to silence both of us. "Your points are well taken. Remember this fight. Self-sacrifice is impractical, but Nolan took an action that resulted in victory for his team. Remember that a stalemate is a stalemate as long as no one acts. A man who you fear will kill you is often afraid of the same treatment at your hands. There are times when two men in such a position both defend to prevent injury and deny victory to themselves. The person to act in that situation, if he has the required skills, will break the stalemate and be the victor."

Lord Hansur turned and walked away. The Justices followed him. They shook their heads but smiled at all of us. From comments made by other Fifteens about what they had overheard the two of them say, our martial abilities had impressed them.

Jevin slapped my back with his right hand. "An interesting tactic, Nolan, and quite effective. I'll be glad to have you back on my side."

Marana walked up and kissed me full on the lips. My face burned crimson and the thrill the kiss sent through my body was greater than the one I felt in tricking Lothar during the fight. "Thank you, partner, for the sacrifice," she murmured.

My words tangled in my throat so I said nothing.

Marana walked to Lothar's side and took his hand in hers.

The fury on his face died, and he blushed because his jealous anger shamed him. He smiled. "Don't get used to that, Nolan, or we'll be bound for the *Cirhon* to settle this."

I held my hands up and surrendered. "I don't want that, Lothar." Jevin's comment about Lothar as an enemy ripped through my mind. "After today the only outcome of such a fight would be both of us lying dead!"

Marana slipped her arm around Lothar's waist and hugged him. We all started to laugh and the four of us led the other Fifteens back to our rooms.

Chapter Nine

TALION: NEKKEHT

I dropped through the hole, hit the Dark-maze floor, and rolled forward to the right. I stood quickly, pressed my back against a rough stone wall, and unconsciously called my *tsincaat* to hand. My heart pounded loudly in my ears and drowned out any sounds my quarry might have made. I closed my eyes and concentrated. My heart rate slowed.

I breathed in slowly and silently. I kept my eyes closed. I'd long ago learned that if I left my eyes open I would concentrate too much on *seeing* in a place where nothing could be seen. With my eyes closed I focused more attention on hearing, touch, and smell.

If you can, kill whatever you find down there. The Master's words whispered through my mind with each heartbeat. This was no idle exercise. The Master could order me to kill anyone or anything up above if he just wanted to see something die. His instructions had purpose and with his words came the possibility that, in the Master's judgment, I might not be able to kill whatever I found hiding in the darkness. This did not set me at ease.

Because it had helped in past exercises in the depths, I relied on my sense of smell. The Darkmaze had the same warm, musty odor it always did. The scent of leather armor and my nervous sweat hung in the air, but I recognized them as normal, and dismissed them. I searched for another smell, something unusual, something I could not identify.

There was nothing. Nothing to smell, to hear, or to feel. I was utterly alone.

Without warning a paw raked my left shoulder, twisted my body, and smashed my shoulder back into the wall. The blow numbed my arm and knocked me aside—had I been shorter it would have snapped my neck.

I rebounded off the wall, planted my right foot, and slashed my *tsincaat* through the darkness in front of me. I kept the blade level and aimed the cut at waist height, but met nothing before the blade rang loudly and sparked when it struck the wall. Instantly I slid back toward my left, spun, and cut through where I had just stood. The sword connected.

My foe made no sound. It withdrew quickly, as if it evaporated, and I realized something was dreadfully wrong. I could smell nothing. No matter where I hit it I would have drawn blood. I'd felt the blade cut through something, dammit!

I touched the cold steel tip of the *tsincaat*. It was dry.

A shiver ran down my spine. That was impossible. After enough fights the sensation of hitting flesh becomes all too familiar. I knew I'd cut it, and while I was sure the wound was relatively deep, I was willing to accept that it might have been a flesh wound. Still there should have been blood.

What kind of creature does not bleed?

It came for me again and caught me with a shoulder in the stomach. Its arms locked around my waist in a fierce hug that jolted even more pain than Rolf's had through me. The tackle carried me back ten feet and blasted me into another maze wall. My head smacked into the stone and stars exploded before my eyes.

It kept me pinned against the wall and tried to bite through my armor on the left side of my chest. With each driving step it wrung more pain out of my back, and my ribs protested in earnest. I brought a knee up into its chest but the weak blow had no effect on the creature at all.

Its tackle had not trapped my arms. Though in too close for me to stab it with my *tsincaat*—my body pinned my *ryqril* against the wall—I attacked. I raised both hands, wrapped them firmly around the hilt of my *tsincaat*, and crashed the hilt down on the back of its neck. I heard a distinct crack, and it released me, but did not drop unconscious. It melted away again.

It seemed human, or human-shaped, but my blow would have killed most men easily. Someone like Jevin might have survived the broken neck, but he wouldn't have been moving at all, and besides, whatever had tackled me was not big enough to be a Fealareen. The Master's orders echoed again through my mind, and dread sucked my stomach in on itself.

First, I knew, I had to stop acting like a target. So far it had hit me twice before I knew it was coming. I had to assume that it could see in the darkness, and that meant it had magic of some sort. Ferocious, it attacked without thought to its own safety, so I had to assume it was unintelligent or insane.

The more I thought about it, the more doomed I felt.

Immediately I dropped into a crouch, my left knee touched the ground, and I gave it less area to hit. With my right hand I raised my *tsincaat* and leveled it to skewer anything charging at me. Then, to test whether or not it could see in the dark, I slapped my left hand against the stone behind me.

It was blind. It charged the sound.

Once I'd gone boar hunting and I took the charge of an adult male on a boarspear. Its assault dwarfed the boar's attack. My blade slid home until only the crosspiece stopped the creature from running itself all the way up my arm. It battered me back against the wall, but before I could be trapped, I abandoned my *tsincaat*, twisted, and raked my spurs across its upper chest as I rolled free.

I rose into a crouch, but it was gone. And it had taken my *tsincaat* with it.

I nearly panicked. Stronger than anything I'd ever faced before, it escaped no matter what I did to it. It did not bleed, it did not react to my attacks, and it made no noise. For a half second I thought it might be a vampire, but they are rare and so utterly evil that I couldn't imagine the Master permitting one into the Darkmaze, nor risking a single Talion's soul to try to kill it without some sort of warning about the nature of his foe.

No, this was something very special, and very deadly.

I stayed low, scurried through the maze, and called to mind all I could remember from my novice days. I stopped at intersections and strained my ears for any sound of it. I toyed with the idea of calling my *tsincaat* but, mindful of what I'd done to Chi'gandir, I decided against it. Besides, as far as I could tell from the fight's progress, the blade was of little use against the creature.

Suddenly, from behind, steely fingers dug into the back of my neck. They drove into my flesh like nails through soft wood. I cried out in pain but the fingers choked the sounds off. It lifted me up and twisted in a valiant effort to wring my neck. If the sweat pouring out of me by the gallon had not spoiled its grip, it might have succeeded. Instead it merely strangled me.

I knew I'd black out if I couldn't break its hold. I grabbed its wrists to take the weight of my body off my neck. Then I kicked back with both feet and smashed my spurs into its thighs and groin. I heard no reaction from it, but I felt a tremor ripple through its arms so I kicked again and it lowered me to the ground, but still did not slacken its grip.

With my feet on the ground, I let go of its right wrist and drove my right elbow back into its rib cage three or four times. I heard and felt ribs pop and grind, yet my foe did not give up. It hung on like a leech. It started to force me down, to lessen the effectiveness of my blows, but it made no sound nor gave any indication that I'd hurt it in any way at all.

The years of training I'd undergone as a novice saved me. I dropped faster than it intended and reached back between my legs for its right leg. I got a handful of cold fleshy ankle and pulled it forward as I leaned back. I hoped to snap its knee by sitting back on it. The creature anticipated the move and turned sideways so it could bend in the direction of my attack, but its defensive action broke the death grip on my neck.

I rocked forward as it pulled free and slithered its leg back behind me. I dropped to all fours and kicked back with my right leg. I hit the creature dead center with my heel, and heard more ribs pop, but again had no sign I'd hurt it. Not content to stay that close to it, I used the kick to somersault me forward and into the intersection ahead of me.

I spun, rose to a crouch, and tried to catch my breath as I prepared to take its charge. It came as it had before, as I hoped it would, in a low tackle. I grabbed it by the shoulders, rolled back and planted my right foot in its stomach. When my back was flat on the gritty floor, I pushed off and sent the creature flying into the wall across the intersection.

It hit hard, and for a second I thought it was dead because I'd heard the hollow sound made when a head hits something more solid than it is. But, like a reoccurring nightmare, the scrabbling sounds of the creature getting up on its feet again followed the wet smack. It was slower this time, though, and made some noise, so I swept forward and just started kicking.

Bones snapped with each kick, yet it kept coming. It grabbed my right leg and pulled me down. On my knees I warded its hands off and hammered it with fists and elbows. I broke both its arms in three or four different places and shattered both of its thighs before I rose and stepped away from it. Even so I could hear its fingers clawing the ground in an effort to drag its broken body after me.

I shuddered and stumbled my way back toward the point where I had begun the test. I caught my breath then yelled at the door above me. "It is finished."

The door opened and a rope ladder dropped down. Wearily I climbed it and pulled myself out onto the floor of the Master's chamber. As an afterthought I summoned my *tsincaat*. It was clean of blood or flesh.

The Master looked at me. "Did you kill it?"

I nodded, exhausted and trembling as my body calmed down. "I broke every bone in its body. I did not wait to see if it died. It could fight no more."

The Master frowned. He looked at Lord Hansur. The Jus-

tice Lord nodded and entered the Darkmaze. No one spoke
during his absence, but I had the distinct feeling I had failed.
I'd been asked to kill the thing down there, and I'd destroyed
it, but that was not the same as actually killing it.

There was only one way to be certain of killing anything.
The tattoo on my right palm burned. I *had* failed.

Lord Hansur climbed up the ladder with the body thrown
over his shoulder. Without a sound he laid it at the Master's
feet. When the body sagged to the ground, and yellow torchlight played over the face, I recognized it instantly. Jevin had
been sent out to bring this man, Rostoth ra Kas, back to Talianna alive!

I stared at the dead man and shuddered. I knew what I'd
tangled with down in the darkness, and there was no way
Rostoth could have put up that savage a battle. Rostoth ra
Kas was just a man, and any one of the wounds I'd inflicted
should have killed him instantly. He had a hole in his stomach
where he'd impaled himself on my *tsincaat*, and I broke his
neck when I hammered both hands down on it early on. *Tsincaat* cuts and spur slashes crisscrossed his body, and his
head was misshapen from the collision with the wall toward
the last.

I could make no sense of it. Everything I'd done, I'd done
to a common bandit, but he survived it to keep coming. The
evidence of his body utterly defied any logical explanation,
and once I realized that, I knew the solution. I looked up and
asked, "What enchantment? It had to have been magic, and
magic cast here. Otherwise Jevin never could have dragged
him back here without killing him first."

The Master looked up when I spoke, and nodded in agreement with my conclusion, but the other lords said nothing
and paid me no attention at all. I suppose I should have been
flattered, because they gathered around the body like Guild-
masters studying a Journeyman's masterpiece. I appreciated
the approving look on Lord Hansur's face, and accepted the
anticipated sour grimace supplied by Lord Eric.

Lady Kalinda turned from the corpse first and walked over
to me. She bowed her auburn-maned head, and I returned
the gesture before she spoke. "I am impressed by your
fighting ability. Any of these wounds would have stopped an
ordinary man."

I narrowed my eyes and scratched at my beard. "Thank you, my lady." Those few words were high praise, and I knew a number of Warriors who would have killed for that sort of recognition. Kalinda personally taught me swordsmanship when I became a novice, and because of her able instruction I quickly caught up in skill with the other Justice novices my age.

The other lords and lady broke away from the body. The Master looked from it to me and then to each of them. "Is Nolan our agent?"

Lord Hansur made his reply first. He held his right palm up to indicate he was *Sharul*, then nodded his head in agreement.

The Master next looked at Fletcher ra Leth, Lord of the Archers. He was a bit shorter than me and wore his light brown hair cut very close to his head. Aside from the arrow ensign on his tunic, the bracer on his left forearm was the only indication of his branch. His blue eyes studied me; then he nodded. "Yes, Nolan is suitable."

Isas ra Amasia, Lord of the Elites, stood silently and looked around the room. He blinked his eyes slowly and rotated his head as one of his hawks might have done. He looked from me to the body and back. He nodded.

Kalinda ra Thele was next. She smiled. She was a huge woman, powerfully built and fast in combat. She was an excellent tactician, which earned her leadership of the Warriors. "I believe Nolan is capable of destroying it. He is our agent."

Lady Cosima, leader of all the Wizards, raised a bony hand to her mouth and cleared her throat. She was tall and thin and her flesh was almost transparent, as if she did not wholly exist in this world. Her eyes were dark pits and I felt her look right through me. A silver clasp gathered her long white hair at her neck and yet did not detract from her handsomeness. She turned to the Master. *"Suffice, he will."*

Eric ra Imperiana, Lord of all Lancers, wore his salt-and-pepper hair in the mane style—head shaved except for a strip down the middle where the hair is grown long like a horse's mane. He stood shorter than me and had a stockier build, but he did not run to fat. Though I admired his ability at strategy and tactics, I did not really like him as a man. He was utterly intolerant of insubordination, which made sense when dealing with a strictly military unit, like a Lancer company. However, his view of order often bled over and resulted in many Justice or Elite novices being punished for actions he did not like, even though the novices were not under his jurisdiction.

It was no secret: Lord Eric did not like me. He turned to the other lords and ladies. "You all seem to forget that Nolan did not *kill* the thing. Lord Hansur did. If we send Nolan are we going to send Lord Hansur to finish the job?"

I clenched my jaw and forced myself to breathe in and out slowly. Justices are the only Talions below the rank of lord who go through the Ritual of the Skull and have the ability to pull a soul from its host body. Most other Talions view this ability as a "magic death touch," and have little idea of the responsibility that comes with the death's-head tattoo. I felt angry that I was being criticized for not using the tattoo when my instructions were so vague.

I was proud that my first line of attack was not to pull the soul from a victim; a sword cut struck in anger can be healed, but a soul pulled in error cannot be replaced. In addition, using the tattoo takes time and concentration. The battle with Rostoth left me short of both, and even if I'd thought of using the Ritual on him, I doubt I would have there in the heart of the Star.

I saw the others turn and look beyond me, so I shot a glance back over my left shoulder. His Excellency, Lord of Services, filled the doorway. He was as tall as I, yet was twice my size. Black robes swathed him, and his black hair was combed back to accentuate his widow's peak. Despite his obesity no one questioned his brilliance and iron-willed dominion over everything that organized the Talions.

"My Lord Eric does have a point," he began. "Still the delicate problem we are faced with does call for the reexamination of facts that point yet again to Nolan. Only Nolan, with his grasp of the local dialect, can adequately disguise himself in this situation. Similarly he has area knowledge that will make his background seem real enough."

Lord Eric's nostrils flared. "We have others from that region. I have two men from that locale who could fill that role, and can be trusted." He glared at me. "Trusted to follow and execute orders; and who know when something is dead!"

His Excellency smiled. "Granted, but could they grow their hair out in three days? Can they *actually* kill the thing, or could they merely do to it what Nolan has done here?" Lord Eric started to reply, but His Excellency cut him off. "And have they the skills needed to pass for what we want them to be, or would our carefully constructed deception collapse when you were unable to give them direct orders?"

His Excellency crossed from the doors and stood amid his peers before the Master's dragonthrone. "No, Lord Eric, Nolan is the only obvious choice for this job. He has the skills and abilities. He had the background and knowledge. And he has motivation. . . ."

Listening to the discussion made me very uncomfortable. I knew, had I not been there, the words they used would not have been any different, and everything said seemed to speak of at least one previous debate, but my presence made me a focus for Lord Eric's discomfort. He had to know I would say nothing of this argument when I left, but my just being there while His Excellency trapped and crushed him as he, Lord Eric, might trap and crush a group of rebels with a Lancer company, had to irritate him. And while I certainly enjoyed the praise His Excellency seemed to heap upon me, I knew well enough that he could turn on me and savage me in an instant if it suited his enigmatic purposes.

The conversation lapsed and silence drifted in to fill the space. Lord Eric calmed himself and bowed his head. "I yield to the wisdom of the Master and my assembled peers. The *Hamisian* Justice will be our agent."

The Master allowed himself a thin smile. "I thank you for your agreement. Those who wish to stay while we inform Nolan about his mission may do so, the rest of you are released." Only His Excellency seated himself in a huge chair—the only one suited to supporting his bulk in the whole room—and Lord Hansur departed for the Shar Chamber. The others headed for the door, having recognized the Master's invitation as courtesy only, but then Lord Eric stopped at a chair and sat. Only Lady Cosima seemed to notice, and she rewarded his action with a blazing glare, but she left the room nonetheless.

While they left I crossed the room, closed the trapdoor to the Darkmaze, and rolled the carpet back over it. The Master gave me leave to get a chair, so I did. I did not assume it would work, but in an effort to put Lord Eric at ease, I selected a chair that sat slightly lower than the one he chose.

Once I'd seated myself, the Master began. "Nolan, what you faced down in the Darkmaze was not Rostoth ra Kas. It was a *nekkeht*. A *nekkeht* is an undead creature. You are the first Talion of your year to know of *nekkehts* and, in fact, there are no Talions within five years of your age who are aware of their existence. This information is very secret and *you will not share it with anyone.*"

The Master's last command burned into my brain. He used the Call. It is a technique taught all Justices and lords to allow us to focus our voices very specifically. At my level of skill I could use it to discipline Tadd or direct bystanders away from a criminal, but I could not compel behavior or force someone to act against his will.

The Master, however, is far more skilled than I ever hope to be. By using the Call on me the Master literally made it impossible for me, even under torture, to reveal anything I was about to learn. That impressed upon me the gravity of the situation and importance of the information. The Master also honored me by sharing this information that was not known by Talions even five years my senior.

The Master allowed my eyes to clear, then continued. "During Shar you release into the Skull the lives of those you have taken through the Ritual. Those lives are trapped in the Skull to, among other things, prevent hauntings and, as some believe, to delay rebirth. The souls are trapped for a time until the Skull wishes to release them or when we need them.

"Early on we discovered that trapped souls lost their identity—literally forgot who they had been—but did not lose their vitality. We call these *rhasa* souls. Wizards studied the phenomenon for centuries to learn how and why this happened. The only answers they came up with were these: the length of time it takes for a soul to be cleansed is linked to the age of the person who lost it, and the life force of an animal and a sentient creature do not differ."

I understood what the Master was telling me only because I likened it in my mind to a shirt that gets bleached. Without stains, dyes, or designs, a shirt is a shirt. The number of washings needed to get a shirt clean might differ with the age or filthiness of the shirt, but in the end it would just be a shirt. That was simple to comprehend.

The difficult part was realizing this explanation concerned souls. I knew what it felt like to draw a soul from a body, but my impressions of each soul differed. Still, stripped of the memories, I could imagine them being the same. Even so, the suggestion that Talions had studied and manipulated something most religions held sacred disturbed me.

My feeling of dread increased as the Master continued. "Our first attempts at using souls were directed at healing wounds and curing diseases. Progress was spotty and frustrating because of the utterly unpredictable results. Some patients did well for a short time, but then the energy evaporated and left them exhausted and worse off than they had been before. Worse yet were the cases where the soul used was not wholly free of personality and the patient would go mad as two minds competed for one body."

The Master paused to drink from a goblet on the small table at his right hand. I felt sweat slicken my back and roll down my temples. Growing up in Talianna I heard many rumors about deep, dark secrets that were supposed to be held in the strictest of confidence, but of this soul-play I'd heard nothing. I glanced over at His Excellency, but I could not read his face or even begin to guess what he was thinking. I felt as if I was being initiated into a conspiracy I wanted no part of at all.

The Master wiped his lips with a white cloth and spoke again. "Wizards experimented with dead animals to see what effects the introduction of a *rhasa* soul would have on dead tissue. They discovered the animals became strong, quick, and easily trained. Because the soul was not natural—not bonded to them at birth—the creatures died again within days, but during their new life they were very powerful indeed."

I gnawed my lower lip. I guessed at what was coming next, and it set my teeth on edge. I knew most of my revulsion with anything that sounded even close to necromancy came from childhood fears of *jelkom* and the horrible things they could do with dead bodies. Part of me realized those stories were just that, stories, and my childish fears embarrassed me. On the other hand I'd just fought something that was dead, and I couldn't kill it, which lent new, adult credence and validity to the things I'd learned to worry about as a child.

The Master read my thoughts, or seemed to. He paused to let me think and did not rush, despite Lord Eric's tiny displays of impatience. When he began speaking again he proceeded slowly and let me work past each objection I had, one at a time. He knew, as I did deep down, that I would absorb the information and learn to use it to complete my assignment successfully.

"The Wizards placed souls in dead bodies of all types. We learned certain things and reaffirmed things necromancers had discovered years ago. For example, a body dead for over a week has lost enough brain through decay to make any sort of real thought impossible. On the other hand, training can survive death as long as the body remains in decent condition."

The Master looked away while he searched for a suitable example. He smiled and continued. "Revitalizing a skilled swordsman gave us a *nekkeht* skilled in the technical points of fighting. It could no longer outthink a foe, but when faced with untrained or unskilled enemies, it would destroy them."

The Master pointed at Rostoth. "We obtained the best results when we stripped a body of its soul and placed new souls in the body immediately. It gave us a trainable *nekkeht* capable of following a limited set of orders. It became an agent that felt no pain, was unstoppable, and, if captured or discovered, would die without revealing anything."

The Master smiled at me. "You really did better than expected against the *nekkeht*, Nolan, especially when you battled it physically and without the Ritual."

His Excellency and Lord Eric both watched my face. I found the information overwhelming, repulsive, and, worst of all, seductive. The ability to create a warrior that could do things no *living* person could meant accomplishing impossible tasks. A *nekkeht* could be used to bring supplies to a caravan trapped by snow in a high pass or rescue miners trapped by a cloud of poison gas deep inside the earth.

The possibilities were endless and very important. My uneasiness started to evaporate until I remembered that not all uses might be helpful or peaceful. I suddenly felt cold.

"If I understand what you have told me, the Wizards can

implant multiple souls in a body to create a superior creature that can be trained to accomplish a task?" I reached back and rubbed the bruises on my neck with my right hand. "I also gather that these *nekkehts* are sometimes used on very sensitive tasks where the conditions might be harsh and any connections with the Talions should be avoided."

His Excellency smiled. "You do understand some of this, but your discretion does us discredit. *Nekkehts* are not used, generally, as assassins. Assassination is not a tool we need to employ covertly because coercion works so much better—why kill a man when you can, by virtue of compromising information, use him over and over again? Most *nekkehts* are used to recover certain cargoes from sunken ships or to destroy man-eating animals in remote regions. Growing up you must have heard the ironic stories of a wanted felon and a rogue mountain leopard killing each other—two 'outlaws' finishing each other off in the wild."

I bowed my head to His Excellency. "I apologize and meant no disrespect, but I needed my worst fears laid to rest. I have heard those tales and did think them 'just' in my youth." I turned to face the Master again.

"Recently," he began, "we needed a *nekkeht*. The nature of its mission is not important, but what happened with that *nekkeht* is. We ordered the apprehension of one particular felon, but a different man was brought in. Because he was a Lurker, and appearance was rather distinctive, no one detected the difference. The Lurker played his part well. He was prepared, killed, and revitalized. We sent him on his way in a Black Wagon."

I raised an eyebrow. "The Lurker you wanted was not the one you got? And he willingly let someone pull his soul from his body?"

The Master nodded. "Someone anticipated our need for a *nekkeht*. The Lurker was an adept and was very skilled in the meditative techniques practiced in Tingis. He allowed himself to be pulled free, then he projected his soul from the Talion's body to avoid capture. His skill allowed him to retain control of his body even when infused with five *rhasa* souls. While the Justice who had taken his soul was undergoing Shar, we packed the body in a Black Wagon and sent it out. The wagon was two hours gone from Talianna before the Justice realized he no longer had the soul in him."

I looked down and stared at my feet. I could see all of it happening. The Justice assumed the soul was trapped in his body, and did not check to see if it was or not until he tried to empty the soul into the Skull. By then it was too late. "Once the *nekkeht* was clear of Talianna, he exerted control and used his new power to escape."

The Master nodded, rose, and beckoned us to follow. We walked behind the throne and through a doorway I'd never known to exist. The Master led us into a bare round room with large doors leading out toward one of the exercise yards. In the center of the room sagged the wreckage of the Black Wagon.

I'd once seen a tin box in which a Wizard tried to trap a demon. In theory the box had symbols on it that rendered the demon powerless. They didn't. The demon dented the box's sides out and clawed rents clean through them. The two of us dispatched the demon before it could win free, and I swore nothing would impress me as much as the condition of that box, but the remnants of the Black Wagon pushed the tin box from my mind.

The Black Wagons were built by layering steel plates over wooden frames. They had very heavy suspension and were made to transport anything through hostile territory without damage. They had to be drawn by six draft horses and carried food, fodder, water, and repair equipment that made each of them virtually self-sufficient for at least the trip from Talianna to its destination. Only the Elites who drove them knew what they hauled, but no Black Wagon, in my memory, had ever suffered more than a broken wheel or a lame horse.

The shattered ends of wooden ribs blossomed through gaping holes in the steel plating. At points the plates were just warped, and at others they were ripped and peeled back. Some dents clearly showed the outlines of a fist or foot. The roof was humped like a camel and a kick aimed straight down through the floor broke the forward axle cleanly.

It reminded me of a toy battered and smashed by an angry child. It had literally been destroyed from the inside out.

The Master stood the closest to it and looked as though he carried its full weight on his shoulders. "We lost three Elites.

The driver and his partner were killed when it reached through the front viewport and crushed their spines. The third died when he stooped his Hawk at the *nekkeht*. It dodged the attack and broke the Hawk's wing. The bird slammed hard into the ground; its rider broke his neck when he hit."

I shook my head. "The fourth Elite returned here to tell you what happened?"

The Master nodded. "He wanted to head out after it, but that would have been futile." He walked back toward the throne room and we joined his exodus. I followed last and took one final look at the wagon. I shuddered and rubbed my neck again.

We all returned to our chairs and I leaned forward. "Forgive me, but I assume from what I heard earlier that a plan to find and destroy this *nekkeht* has already been organized. This means, I would guess, that you have a good idea where it is, and what it is going to be used for."

The Master actually smiled. He nodded at His Excellency.

The rotund man shifted in his chair, cleared his throat, and half closed his eyes. "Before we get into any details of your assignment, we must make sure you understand how the *nekkeht* has to be destroyed. Its destruction is the focus of your mission. If you cannot accomplish that, anything else you might be able to do will make no difference in the great scheme of things. You must understand this first, very important point."

I sat up straight and nodded solemnly.

His Excellency continued. "While your destruction of Rostoth's body did eliminate it as a viable assailant, such treatment will not work on this *nekkeht*. With the extra souls, and the ability to control them, this *nekkeht* can heal its own injuries. In the same way that you have been trained to concentrate to deaden pain or stop bleeding in a minor wound, the *nekkeht* can employ the energy in the extra souls to speed healing almost as fast as you can wound him.

"If it had the training to concentrate on what it was doing, Rostoth could have healed almost all the damage you did in the time it took Lord Hansur to finish it. Physical destruction will not eliminate the *nekkeht* you are to pursue."

I looked down at my right palm. "To kill it I must drain it of its souls."

His Excellency raised a cautionary hand. "You will have to do more than that, Nolan. You must drain it while it is physically active or engaged in some task that prevents meditation or concentration. If the *nekkeht* can project its soul out and away from your attempt at draining it, it might be able to battle you for those souls."

I nodded. "Also it would still retain the knowledge of *nekkeht* and that is something I need to prevent?"

"Bah!" Lord Eric exploded. His voice was harsh and his tone derisive. "How can we expect him to do this? He questions the obvious!"

I turned and snarled. "I am a Justice. I have to ask questions so I can understand all I am to do. I cannot do what the Master wants if I do not know his wishes."

Lord Eric narrowed his eyes. "You failed to slay the *nekkeht* before even though the command was clear."

My fists knotted in frustration. "I did what I thought would kill the creature. I've not stopped to make sure life has drained from each person I've had to kill before I moved on to the next. For all I know a dozen criminals recovered from their wounds and are all planning to get me the next time I ride from Talianna."

"They'd be led by Morai, I have no doubt!"

Lord Eric's words struck me like a gauntlet in a duelist's hand, but I did not rise to the challenge. I let a breath out slowly and turned to the Master. "What is more important, stopping the *nekkeht* or preventing knowledge of *nekkehts* from becoming common?" I forced my hands to relax and wiped them on my pant legs. "Who can be trusted with that information? If a village learns of it do I burn the village?"

Lord Eric rose from his chair to protest but the Master waved him back down. "Lord Eric, Nolan's questions are justified." The Master gave Lord Eric a moment to calm himself before he answered me.

"Your primary task is to destroy the *nekkeht*. In addition, the death of any confederates who understand what has happened would be appropriate. The destruction of innocents would be up to you, subject to your assessment of their ability to repeat the series of events that started this whole regrettable scenario. Certainly a whole village should not be destroyed, but the death of an inquisitive soldier or minister would not be too much if it would keep the secret intact."

"Thank you for the clarification. I hope your trust in my judgment will not be put to the test." I looked over at His Excellency. "I remember something being said earlier about a limit on the time the extra souls stay with the body."

His Excellency pursed his lips. "There are too many hidden factors to make any assessment of time limit possible. Because of his skill the Lurker may be able to keep the souls with him indefinitely. Still, in the past, the souls have never remained for more than eight weeks."

Unconsciously I stroked my growing beard with my left hand. "I have to assume the *nekkeht* is being used as an assassin. If it was out after some hidden treasure you could create another *nekkeht* to oppose it. You'll put me close to the intended victim and I'll stop it before it kills." I nodded, but inside I knew it was easier said than done. "Who is it?"

His Excellency steepled his fingers. "King Tirrell of Hamis."

I sat back and closed my eyes. They wanted me to protect the man who had taken my nation. My family was dead by his hand, and they wanted me to stop someone from killing him. I shook my head in disbelief. "No, I can't do it."

Lord Eric stood up, ready to explode. The Master watched me. He waited for an explanation, but words stopped up behind the lump in my throat. Only His Excellency did not react. He just sat there, stared at his fingers, and worried me.

I looked up at the Master. "I cannot do it."

Lord Eric sputtered with frustration. "We go through all this just to have him refuse! This is utter madness. Master, order him to comply and be done with this nonsense."

"No!" I shouted. "With all due respect, Lord Eric, I am a Justice. My work calls for judgment, not blind obedience to orders. The Master would never order me to hunt down my own kin. If I cannot be sure I will be able to complete a mission, I have the right to refuse it. If I have any reservations at all I might hesitate at a crucial moment, and that would kill me and the assignment at the same time."

Lord Eric's face flushed bright red. "Such insolence! If you were in my command . . ."

"Don't you understand, I'm not under your command? I'm a Justice!" I turned to the Master. "I'm not the only one who can do the job. There are other Justices . . ."

The Master spoke in a low voice. "We sent another."

I stopped. Suddenly I went cold and felt as if someone had just walked on my grave. "Marana?"

His Excellency replied to my question. He'd been waiting. He'd baited the trap, and I'd blundered into it like a blind, hungry mongrel cur. "She was killed in Hamis three weeks ago. We just got word from the Lancer Captain attached to the court. She was cremated because there was not enough left of her to send back for burial."

As crude and brutal as his description was, it did not shock me. I felt nothing. I was absolutely numb. I tried desperately to recall a mental picture of Marana, but all I could remember was my terror in the Darkmaze and knew her last moments had been full of it.

I stared at His Excellency. *You bastard, you calculating bastard. I swore "never again," but you did it.* I covered my face with my hands to snatch a moment's refuge and get a grip on myself. I pulled my hands away, bowed my head to the Master, and forced my reply past the thickness of my throat.

"I will do as you ask."

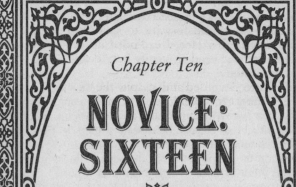

Chapter Ten

NOVICE: SIXTEEN

I could not breathe for fear the steam I'd produce would alert them. Though the icy wind snatched away every word they spoke, I knew they stood only a yard or two from where I lay hidden in a frozen snowbank. I knew because I could feel the vibration of their steps as they punched through the snowy crust. In a second or two they would discover where I'd burrowed beneath the crust, but by then it would be too late.

I'm sure I smiled but my face was too numb to feel it. These Fourteens had been hunting us, Marana and me, for the past three days. This group's leader was an Elite, and he took great delight in making order and sense out of the tangle of tracks Marana and I struggled to create in eluding them. Late in the previous day we shook them, which pleased us because they nearly tracked us to our camp, and through the night we labored to prepare this welcome for them.

A black-booted foot crashed through the snow beside me. I grabbed it and rolled forward to spill the Fourteen connected to it onto her face. I exploded up out of the snow, roughly cuffed her head to signify her "death," then turned on her companion.

That Fourteen whirled and, despite the look of surprise on his face, swung his walking stick at me. I caught the blow with my left hand, stepped in, and drove my fist rather ungently into his stomach. He doubled over, more to move with the blow than because I'd hurt him, and that left him open. I slapped him across the head as I'd hit the first Fourteen so he flopped wordlessly to the snow.

I knelt and recovered the pouch full of snowballs the first Fourteen had almost crushed when she broke through the crust. I looked back along the track these two had made up the small hillside overlooking the roadway through this section of forest. I could see no one but, now above the snow, I could hear snatches of conversation—more noise than words. Beyond them, in the snowbank opposite mine, I knew Marana waited. I couldn't see her, but I knew she could see me, so I made a sign and arced a snowball back toward the voices.

Luck guided the throw. "Hey!" I heard someone shout. Then he added, "Uh-oh! I'm out."

A couple of other people shouted; then the first of them ran up the hill, and straight into another snowball. I hit him in the forehead, and the look of astonishment on his face as the snowball exploded into hundreds of fragments drove a chuckle from me. He reeled backward as if I'd hit him with a rock—probably hoping for a reduced ransom price because of his acting—and spun out of sight.

Two snowballs curved up over the hill edge but both flew wide of the mark. I took two steps to my right, getting closer to the road itself, and threw two more snowballs. I hit no one but, from the cursing I heard, I came close. More of their snowballs flew over the hill in retaliation, but again they did not hit.

Then I heard new screams of outrage. I sprinted forward, running a dangerous straight line course toward the Fourteens, but I expected no resistance. They had their hands full.

I started down the hillside and waved. Marana stood alone amid the scattered bodies of seven Fourteens. The pair that looked most unhappy had fallen when Marana stepped from the snowbank. They lay flanking her outline. The other four looked a bit more affable, and one claimed he would have fought, but when he saw the facial expressions on his two comrades he couldn't stop laughing.

Someone yelled to the two Fourteens I'd killed and they wandered down to join us. The group huddled against the wind and waited for us to set their ransoms. Marana and I were generous and asked the standard six Imperials for each. A couple of them grumbled about having to do extra duty to buy back into the exercise, but the others just shrugged it off.

They turned to depart, but the Elite hesitated. He was the one I'd eliminated with the blindly thrown snowball. "Not bad." He grinned as he looked the ambush point over one last time. "I'll remember this for next year." He rejoined his squad and turned back one last time. "See you tomorrow!"

The lords designed the Winter Game as an exercise to make Justices resourceful and independent of support. They divided Justice Sixteens into pairs by lot and sent them out to survive for a month in the Tal Mountains. In addition to battling the elements and gathering food, all the Thirteens, Fourteens, and Fifteens headed out, one set per week, to harass the Justices and try to capture them.

A simple economy governed the drill where the novices earned Imperials by performing tasks in their camp, gambling or capturing Sixteens. The novices in on the capture of a Sixteen got to keep a share of his "treasure," and a Sixteen's treasure was created from the ransoms paid, up to a maximum of eight Imperials, by each novice the Sixteen killed. A captured Sixteen would be held with a ransom equal to half of whatever his treasure had been before that final encounter and, while he could escape if the opportunity arose, an unsuccessful escape doubled his ransom.

Our success or failure in the activity was measured by the number of Imperials we'd earned, though many people acknowledged that keeping score that way just rewarded

those who gambled well. I'd always felt just surviving my
week hunting Sixteens was enough, but as a Fifteen I got
greedy, and that was to make this year's Winter Game very
difficult for the Sixteens.

Marana tapped my shoulder and pointed toward the sky.
"It'll snow soon, Nolan, we ought to get to our camp so the
storm can cover our tracks."

I nodded my head and set off up the mountain. We'd been
told what our "territory" would be two weeks before the
exercise, and Marana and I located several different sites for a
camp. We decided the best one was a cave high up on the
mountain. It was bound to be very cold, but it was sheltered
and one chamber actually twisted around to be out of sight of
the cave mouth and remained relatively still despite storms
raging outside.

Wind roared across the broad snowfield spread out below
our campsite. We worked across it as quickly as possible and
reached the cave mouth just as the snow started falling. I
pulled open the white canvas sheet we'd hung over the
entrance and Marana slipped in. I knelt once I entered and
tied the canvas back down to a stake wedged in a fissure.
Though the wind plucked at and battered the canvas, the
cloth kept most wind and snow out.

After ten feet, the four-foot-wide entrance tunnel opened
into a large chamber. The large airy chamber had a crack in
the roof that let a few flakes of snow drift down in. Below it
was a fire-blackened wall and a store of wood. I assumed,
when I first saw it, that shepherds used the cave during
summer storms, but I found nothing else to indicate this
might be the truth.

Off this large chamber lay a smaller room. Because it
would be easier to heat, Marana and I elected to stay in there.
The smoke from the small fire we dared risk was drawn out
through the natural chimney and the smoke presented little
or no threat as long as we kept the fire small. The floor was
just stone and somewhat uneven, but every night I'd been too
exhausted to notice or care, though I awoke stiff in the mornings. Nothing either one of us had done seemed to make it
any better.

Marana had already shed the white canvas suit she wore
over her furs to enable her to blend in with the snow. The

suits had little or no value beyond camouflage, but neither one of us considered going out without one.

I peeled my snowsuit off and then removed my furred jacket. I wore only a cotton tunic beneath the jacket and the sweat I had worked up in the walk to the cave steamed. Marana looked at me and laughed. "You look like a demon."

"That from a *jelkom*?"

She grimaced, twisting her face into a horrible leer. "Boo!"

I smiled and threw my jacket at her. "I'll be frightened if you really want me to be."

She wrinkled her nose, then narrowed her eyes in a mock threat. "Just start the fire, or I'll give you something to be scared of."

I drew the knife from my boot top and whittled slivers of wood from a dry log. Once I had a fair pile of tinder I twisted the knife around and used the top of the blade to strike sparks from a piece of flint I dug from my nearby pack. On the third try I got a spark that ignited the tinder and quickly a yellow flame sprouted up. Little by gently I fed larger and larger twigs and slivers into the fire and soon had a tiny pleasant blaze crackling away.

"Makes me feel warmer already." I let the fire catch solidly before I got up, filled a small pot with snow at the entrance, and returned. I wedged the pot between two of the stones that surrounded the fire.

"Be sure to stir it." Marana looked up from where she was skinning the snowshoe hare we'd snared earlier; because it was still frozen, the work was relatively bloodless. "I know, Marana, I won't scorch it like I did the other day." I drew my knife again and swished the melting snow around. On the first morning I'd gone out to get more snow, saw some Thirteens below, and stayed to watch them while the water burned. Marana kidded me because even she knew snow would burn; she was from Temur where, unlike Sinjaria, it never snowed.

This time the snow melted quickly—without burning—and quite soon I had a pot of boiling water. I rummaged around in my pack and found my cache of tea leaves and tossed some of them into the pot. The water darkened and the springtime aroma of the tea filled the cave.

"That smells good, Nolan." Marana touched my shoulder

and I smiled up at her. She'd removed her furs and steam rose from the cotton clothing she wore beneath.

I reached over and flipped my bearskin sleeping rug at her. "Get this on or get closer to this fire before you freeze to death."

She caught it, wrapped it around herself, and sat down beside me. "The rabbit is ready to burn."

I force a smile. "As I recall it is your turn to 'render inedible' our meal." Worse than burning the water I'd managed to actually cook a rabbit we caught two days before. Marana felt like Jevin about cooking: if the gods intended man to eat thoroughly cooked meat, animals would carry their own firewood. I'd done a very good job of cooking it, and even sacrificed some of the salt I'd smuggled out of Talianna on it, but Marana was not pleased. She ate it, though, because bad food is better than no food at all.

I leaned over, pulled a wooden bowl from my pack, and poured some tea into it. The tea steamed and I inhaled the sweet warmth. I smiled and sipped gingerly. Despite my caution I burned my tongue.

I stood and bowed to Marana. "The fire is yours." I walked away toward the larger cavern with steaming bowl in hand. "I'm going to look out at the storm."

Marana crawled around to where I'd been sitting and vanished from sight as I moved on. The canvas cover tugged at its moorings and snapped, but held firm. I drank more tea, let its warmth spread from my belly up and out, then knelt and unfastened the corner tie.

Snow swirled and fell like wind-tossed autumn leaves. Already our tracks had been covered by drifts and the storm showed no signs of abating. If we chose not to leave the cave there would be no clue as to our whereabouts. For the time being, anyway, we were safe.

I retied the canvas in place and sat back. I listened to the wind shrieking outside and I hoped the others had found equally good shelter. Jevin was paired with a blond Sixteen girl named Vedia and I didn't envy him.

Vedia was Marana's roommate and she decided that if Marana had a lover, so would she. She made a play for me, but I escaped by telling her I'd been betrothed at birth to a girl back in Sinjaria. I don't think she believed me, but soon enough she was chasing after Jevin. I never kidded him about her, because he agonized a great deal about whether or not he would hurt her feelings or how she would take a particular action on his part.

Lothar suggested he just kill her and be done with it, but Jevin rejected that as a viable plan. He'd managed to avoid her, as much as that was possible when we all trained together, and it looked as if she would give up on him when she was drawn to spend a month alone with him in the wilderness of the Tal Mountains.

Lothar was, depending upon how you look at it, in a better and worse position than Jevin. When I was drawn to be Marana's partner, Lothar offered to head out alone. His request was not all that uncommon, and there was an uneven number of Sixteens anyway, so he got his freedom. Lothar's mood was subdued before we left Talianna, but he clearly felt he'd do great things during the Winter Game.

I raised my tea bowl in a silent salute to Jevin and Lothar, then drank the last of the tea. I'd been lucky enough to confiscate it from a Thirteen. Bringing anything in the way of foodstuffs to the Game was strictly forbidden, but we all smuggled things in anyway. In the hunter camps food could be bartered for Imperials. All the Sixteens, on the other hand, thought of the smuggling as the first test of survival. The Services clerks who searched us before we left, while disapproving of smugglers, were not very good at their jobs.

Marana poked her head out and called me to dinner. She'd done a very good job roasting the hare. "I hung it so your side would be done to your liking while my half would still be palatable." She split the beast down the middle and plopped my half in my bowl. It still smoked.

We said little as we ate. This was the first time we'd returned to the cave before dark and had enough energy to actually enjoy the food. My half of the hare was a bit overcooked, but the charred parts made it crunchy and it really did taste good. I told Marana as much, and even shared some salt with her to prove how much I appreciated her cooking.

After dinner I washed my bowl out with the remnants of the tea and gathered snow for more. Once I'd brewed it up I poured both of us a bowl just in time to let the weariness of the two and a half weeks we'd already endured catch up with us.

Marana seated herself cross-legged at the edge of her deerskin blanket. She closed her eyes and leaned back. The flickering firelight caressed her throat and shone off her now-unbound long black hair. "Mmmm. After so many hours in the snowbank I thought I'd never be warm again."

I gulped down a big mouthful of tea. It coursed down my throat and settled in my stomach. The heat radiated down through my thighs and out across my chest. It felt very good. It burned the cold from my muscles, and with it went the numbness. I enjoyed actually *feeling* again, even when what I felt most were aches and pains.

"Nolan."

"Yes?"

Marana nodded toward the fire. "Look into the flames."

I did. The flames licked, embraced, and consumed the wood we'd fed them. One log was a fairly aromatic wood and filled the cave with warmth and life. "All right."

"When I look into the flames I see things. Do you?"

I mumbled my reply. "Yes." Even after four years such a simple questions locked words in my throat.

Marana continued without really having heard me. "I see celebrations in Temur. I can see the young warriors dancing the Sworddance. I know I've only seen it performed once at Festival, but this brings it back. See them, the blades flashing as they whirl around each other in mock combat."

I looked over at her. Though her eyes focused distantly, leagues beyond here and the fire, her face was filled with enthusiasm and joy. She looked far more beautiful than she ever had before. She turned and caught me staring at her. She smiled. "Nolan, what do you see in the fire?"

I stiffened. "Faces."

She missed my initial reaction and pressed me. "What kind of faces?"

I hesitated. "Faces of the dead."

Even the pain creeping into her expression could not kill her loveliness. She opened her mouth to speak, but her lower jaw just trembled and no words came out.

Outside my control my voice filled the silence. "My family all died during the war. Only I survived. I could not bury them. I'd been sick so I was not strong enough to dig graves. Since I could not commit their bones to the earth, I made our house into a pyre and I watched to make sure it did its job."

I pointed my quivering finger at one guttering flame. "There, that's Arik. He was five years younger than me. He had a clubfoot, but you'd never know he was different. By the gods, he was always so happy. If he couldn't play a sport with me or Hal or Malcolm he'd yell and scream encouragement to us." My throat thickened. "Those bastards rode him down and speared him like a pig."

I shut my mouth before my cry could escape. I knew the fatigue and feeling of being hunted again brought the images to mind and the tears to my eyes, but I could not stop either. I buried my head in my arms and started to cry. I wanted to choke back the tears but I couldn't. The tears burned hot against frostbitten cheeks and my chest shuddered with sobs. I couldn't get Arik out of my mind. I just kept seeing his happy, smiling face twisted and broken in death.

I didn't notice Marana until her hug became so tight that I couldn't breathe. I twisted around and sat up to return her hug. She slipped into my arms and felt so small and delicate, yet so full of strength.

"Nolan, I'm sorry." She squeezed a bit tighter, then drew back just enough to look at me. She knelt there, took my face in her hands, and brushed tears away with her thumbs. "I didn't know. I never would have asked. . . ."

I half closed my eyes and gently shook my head. "Not your fault. I'm tired, I'm sorry." I tilted my head and kissed the palm of her left hand. "Thank you."

I relaxed my arms so she could escape, but Marana did not withdraw. I looked up into her eyes and saw the pain receding to be replaced by something else. She lowered her mouth to mine and we kissed.

The kiss might not have been enough to waken a sleeping princess or turn a frog into a prince, but it unlocked feelings I'd kept hidden away since my family was slain. The part of me that hungered for more emotional support, like that I'd known growing up in Sinjaria, carried Marana straight into my heart. The piece of me I'd ignored in my haste to become a Justice and exact revenge for my family's murder exerted itself and told me this was good and right.

We made love that night. It was gentle yet playful and full of tenderness I'd not have imagined in either of us when we trained or stalked Fourteens. It left both of us tired but pleasured, and full of nervous energy.

Marana and I lay in the dying firelight afterward, warm and comfortably entwined in our sleeping skins. I talked to her of many things, shared with her deep dark family secrets, and recounted family stories and jokes. I told her things I'd been forbidden by my grandmother to tell anyone outside our blood kin—with my family dead the confidence seemed not as important as the act of sharing did right then and there.

I banked the fire so the coals would last until morning. I crawled back between the furs and we talked some more until we both fell asleep.

And not once, awake or dreaming, did I think of Lothar.

The next three days do not stand out well in my mind. They all flowed into each other because the sky remained overcast, it snowed constantly, and I'd never been so happy in all my life. The giddy joy and excitement kept me emotionally charged all the time, and consequently I acted utterly irrational and made life hell for the Fourteens hunting us.

When not out harassing the Fourteens with suicidal forays that worked only because of their audacity, Marana and I talked and loved. We interrogated each other and learned the other's most personal secrets. We compared our impressions of things that had happened over the past three years, and laughed or blushed as embarrassments were called to mind again.

The more we talked, the more I became convinced Marana was the one woman meant for me. We agreed on so much. Looking back, we decided when we'd first been attracted to each other, and recalled all the things we did to hide that fact from each other. At times one of us would answer a question the other had not yet asked, as my mother often did with my father, so I knew what we had was blessed.

Our happiness bled over into our luck. We survived traps prepared by our pursuers, foiled their ambushes, and even raided them when they stopped to take lunch in a sheltered grove. Again and again we melted into the blizzard pouring snow down over the mountains after devastating a patrol. We even dared and successfully managed to ambush a patrol pursuing Jevin and Vedia.

Our love made us invincible.

The fourth morning brought a change, both in the weather and our pursuers. I woke and slipped from the furs without waking Marana. Clad only in boots and fur trousers, I walked to the tarp. It hung slack and motionless. I knelt and slipped the knot at the corner. Raising it I walked out and stood in the morning sun. A very clear blue sky arched over me.

A gust of wind raised goose bumps on my flesh and puckered my nipples. I breathed in through my nose and felt the mucus freeze. My eyes teared and the left one froze shut. I pressed my rapidly cooling fingers to it and used the last of their warmth to melt the ice.

Despite the bitter cold I did not retreat, but dropped into a low crouch. There, far below, a line of Fifteens broke from the woods. Working together in a pack of thirty or more, they swept the area looking for tracks. They'd started early and undoubtedly would pick up some Sixteens before the day was through.

Marana and I were lucky. For the moment we were safe, because the previous night's storm had covered all our tracks in a fresh layer of powder.

I returned to the side chamber, squatted next to the fire, and woke Marana. "We've got trouble."

She sat up and sleep evaporated slowly from her face. The furs slipped down around her waist and I silently cursed the Fifteens. She stretched and rubbed sleep from her eyes. An instant later she was awake and the tactician in her was alert and already thinking. "The Fifteens?"

I nodded and threw her the woolen tunic she'd worn the day before. "It's bright and clear out there and they're hunting in a pack." I growled and poured myself some tea. "The ones who went past here were Lancers, I think. Voices carried enough to hear a comment or two about not having horses."

She pulled the tunic on. "Typical."

I frowned and sipped the tea. It was weak, because my supply had run out the night before and I'd scraped the pouch to get as little as I did that morning. "This does not please me."

I passed the bowl of tea to Marana and shrugged my furred jacket on. "They'll sweep the areas and return, in force, to the places where they don't pick up any Sixteens. With them working together it'll be tough."

Marana nodded agreement with my assessment of the situation. "That's what you get for bragging."

"I wasn't bragging, it was one of Erlan's friends." As Fifteens, Jevin and I arranged with Erlan and the Elites to hunt in large packs. Like the Fourteens we'd captured this year, the previous year's hunting had been bad in small groups. When we ran in packs the Sixteens could not attack us. Apparently someone remembered the stories of our success the year before and had decided to use our own plan against us.

If I had my numbers right approximately two hundred Fifteens were out searching the mountains for only forty Sixteens. That meant five Fifteens hunted for each Justice, and that held true as long as no Justices had already been captured. Surviving was going to be difficult.

Marana and I got a warm breakfast. We cleaned up the cave and decided to chance hiding our gear in the main cavern where the shepherds had stacked their wood. We covered the equipment with logs. We also took the tarp down and hid it.

Dressed in our snowsuits, snowshoes in hand, we looked out over the unblemished snowfield below us. The Lancers had passed and their track was plain at the base of the slope. I turned to Marana.

"Do we attack or run?"

She smiled, a fair imitation of Jevin's wolf-grin. "Can you see any reason, lover, that our luck won't hold out?"

I thought for a moment and banished all thoughts of failure. "No." I swept a hand out over the pristine white expanse below us. "To the wars, my lady?"

"A favor first, kind sir." She slipped her mittened hands around my neck and pulled my mouth down to hers. We kissed long and deeply. "Just to keep you warm."

I smiled. "Let me know when you get cold."

"That I will, lover, that I will."

• • •

We took an hour to get down the hill and reach the Lancers' tracks. They traveled east on a march that would take them toward Jevin's territory. That worried me, but even if I knew where Jevin laired, I could not get there before the Lancers. I hoped Jevin could elude them, even if he had to abandon Vedia to do it.

Marana crouched beside me. "It looks as though they came here straight from their base camp. Their tracks are crisp so I'd guess it's not far away because none of them are tired yet."

I nodded. "I'd really like to know where they are. We might see if we can find a place they've searched and move our camp there."

Marana smiled and unlaced her snowshoes. It took me a second to understand; then I joined her. We tied the snowshoes on backward. In doing so we could walk along the Lancer's back trail and the tracks would be too confused for anyone to follow clearly. It would look like we walked to this point and vanished. by the time anyone figured out what we'd done, our scouting mission would be over and we'd be long gone.

While backtracking the Lancers was easy; approaching the Fifteens' base camp unseen was not. The Fifteens had not posted any guards—no one would dare attack the camp—but the bustle of activity therein meant there were eyes looking everywhere at one time.

I first noticed none of the Fifteens wore snowsuits. When hunting in packs that made sense because they wanted to drive their quarry before them and trap them, not sneak up on them. It also meant their hunting packs would not end up pursuing one of their own people. Marana and I quickly took advantage of this strategy, doffed our snowsuits, and buried them. To casual observers we would appear to be Fifteens.

They'd set their horseshoe-shaped camp in a clear meadow. A large tent sat in the middle of the smaller tents that made up the horseshoe. The large tent served as headquarters and mess hall in one. The smaller tents, half dug into the snow, were the tents the Fifteens used for housing. Each tent could comfortably fit four people and there were sixty of them. The extras, over the fifty needed to house the Fifteens, were meant for captured Sixteens.

The number of people still in the camp suggested that only two-thirds of the Fifteens were out hunting. The other third remained in the camp working. That realization made me very uneasy, because it meant they'd adopted our strategy from last year. The best hunters went out and took the chances while the poorer people stayed behind to earn Imperials so they could ransom the good hunters.

Lastly, and worst of all in my mind, the camp was orderly and well organized. This meant to me that the Fifteens had a Lancer or Warrior leading them. As much as I might not like Lancers, I did respect their tactical abilities and I was reluctant to have a strategy that Jevin, Erlan, and I cobbled together last year used against me this year, especially after a tactician plugged all the holes in it.

Marana and I found a place to watch the camp from the woods surrounding it. We hid beneath the branches of a big pine tree. The snow had drifted up to meet the lower branches, but around the trunk a saucer-shaped depression afforded us cover from the wind and let us watch unobserved.

What we saw was not good. By midday six Justices had been brought in. Four had their heads down because they had been captured by the Lancers and some Warriors. The last two had been taken by Justices so they were not so downcast. The Fifteens guided the prisoners to a tent at the edge of the horseshoe and posted a Lancer to stand guard in front of it.

Four more pairs were brought in through the afternoon. The people who'd worked earlier in the day were sent out two hours before sunset and by dusk they came back bringing another three pairs. Finally, as the sun infused the snow with a bloody red hue, the last two groups came back, and they also had prisoners.

It took an even dozen to drag Jevin and Vedia in. Four of their captors walked in front of them and the other eight, because they'd been killed in the struggle, walked behind. Their ransoms would be applied against the Sixteens' ransom, but I doubted it would be enough to free even one of them.

Jevin looked very tired. Even with dusk darkening the landscape, I could see he was pale. His shoulders slumped forward and, for the first time ever, he looked *defeated*. Vedia did not appear as bad off, but she kept looking up at Jevin and saying something to him. I couldn't catch the words, but from her hand motions, and Jevin's wearily nodded replies, I guessed she was apologizing for getting them captured.

A full score of Lancers made up the last group, but only two of them preceded their captive. Lothar walked proudly and held his head high. His snowsuit was shredded and several of the Lancers limped, so I safely assumed his pursuit and capture had been difficult on both sides. I grinned and looked forward to the telling of that tale.

It never occurred to me, at that point, that Lothar and I would never be friends again. Lothar was so self-sufficient and capable, how could he need someone else the way I did? I was sure Lothar would see how happy we were and would give us his blessing. We were his friends, after all, he should be happy for us.

At that moment, though, even those thoughts did not pass through my mind. I fought a grin rising to my lips and looked out over the camp again. I ignored the growl in my belly. It was possible to do something about our captured compatriots, and if we succeeded, by the gods, it would be beautiful!

I turned to Marana and pulled her close. I kissed her gently, then smiled. "How would you like to free them all?"

She readily agreed and we started planning a premature end to the Winter Game.

The physical task of freeing the Justices was simple, on the surface of it. All either one of us had to do was to walk across an enemy camp, kill two or three guards, open the tents, and tell our compatriots to run. The chances that any one of us would get very far were decidedly slim, and the penalty of doubling a ransom for a failed escape was very severe.

The other option was to ransom our friends. Each captured Sixteen had his snowmask nailed to a post in front of the large tent. Attached to it was a strip of cloth with the amount of his ransom on it. A Sixteen who wanted to ransom his partner had to capture a novice and send him in with the instructions to transfer his Imperials over to his friend. The captured Sixteen then could buy his freedom.

Marana and I probably each had two hundred Imperials from ransoms, which was a healthy sum, so we might be able to add enough to Lothar's treasure to purchase his freedom, but that left the rest of them stuck. We'd have to capture everyone in the camp three or four times over to earn enough ransom because of the Imperials surrendered to the Sixteens earlier by the less experienced Thirteens and Fourteens.

There was a third way, technically, and upon it hinged our whole plan. Just as I'd plundered the tea from that Thirteen, a Sixteen could take any Imperials a captive had in his possession at the time of his capture. Under normal circumstances no one carried the coins with him. All the accounting was done by someone in the camp, but various individuals did take their coins to use playing cards, so from time to time a captive actually had Imperials with him.

As Fifteens, the only way we could get everyone to agree to hunt in packs was to promise an even split of all Sixteen plunder. We appointed one Archer as our treasurer and he kept the money in his possession. In the middle of camp it was quite safe, and at the end of the action we divided the spoils up evenly. The system worked quite well, but until we actually split the loot, it belonged to the Archer as far as the Winter Game was concerned.

Last year we'd garnered over six thousand Imperials, and the two hundred Fifteens had lost none of their seventy-two hundred Imperials earned during that week, so we ended up with almost two-thirds of the Imperials in the Winter Game. That was the highest total ever brought in by Fifteens, and placed fourth behind three very high Sixteen totals from Games over a century old in the race for highest total ever.

If these Fifteens were playing the same game we had, and everything told me they were playing it better than we had before, somewhere in that camp one person had a stack of Imperials. And if we wanted to free the other Sixteens, and set our own record for money brought back by Sixteens, those Imperials had to become ours.

The Elite walked into the woods toward the latrines. I stepped from behind a tree, clapped a hand over his mouth, and dragged him back. "If I let my hand slip down and touch your throat you'll be dead. You don't want that."

He shook his head rather violently.

I smiled to myself. I'd watched him working hard in the camp and refusing good-natured calls to join another card game. He had no Imperials to ransom himself, and I used that against him. "Good. Answer my questions and you'll survive. Are there any passwords or countersigns for entering the camp."

Shake. No.

"You've got a leader. Warrior or Lancer?"

Shake then nod.

"He's a Lancer?" I thought quickly of the Lancer Fifteens capable of handling and organizing the rabble below. "Serle ra Imperiana?"

Nod.

"Good." I forced the words out while my stomach roiled. Serle was Lord Eric ra Imperiana's nephew. I almost hesitated and backed away from the plan, because I didn't want the Lancer lord angry with me. While he protested what Jevin and I did to Gaynor, he'd berated Gaynor for his stupidity. The last thing I needed was for Lord Eric to hate me.

I pawed the Elite's throat and settled him back on the ground. He looked up at me with eyes full of betrayal. "I'll ransom you myself. Stay quiet and hidden here, otherwise I won't be so positively disposed toward you." After being slain he could do nothing but work for six hours anyway, so he had no reason to hurry back to the camp, and even if he had the money he was bound by the rules to say nothing of where or how he'd been slain.

Marana jumped a female Justice and made her the same deal I'd made with the Elite. I walked back into the camp first. The only guards I saw were stationed around the Justice captives' tents, but if anyone had been watching people head out of camp they would have seen the same number come back in.

The horsehair standard stuck in the snow in front of Serle's tent made it easy enough to locate. Halfway down the arm with the captives' tents, and across from the tree where Marana and I had spent the day, a lantern burned in the tent and I counted five silhouettes.

Marana and I crossed the camp independently. The Elite's

friends called to me as they had to him, but I waved them off using the same hand motion he had. They laughed and ignored me, as everyone else did until Marana met me in the shadows. Shadowy outlines against the snow, we did not hide because, in our furs, we looked like everyone else in the camp.

The Fifteens did well when they chose Serle to lead them. Sure, he'd not posted guards around the camp, but that would have been a waste of time since the Sixteens would never attack the camp. Instead of keeping people up through the night without reason, he rested his troops for the next day's hunting. He'd planned for everything he could think of, but overlooked the two flaws in his plan.

The first he could do nothing about: his personal vision of life and the way it works. He was a Lancer, which meant he believed in his own invincibility and infallibility. In addition he was from Imperiana. That added lots of national pride and a confidence that nothing could possibly defeat him. He'd applied those properties to organizing the Fifteens, and had netted all but a handful of the Sixteens because of that application. Still his planning skipped over a mission like ours.

The second mistake was one he should have known about. He forgot that Sixteens do know more than Fifteens. He forgot that Justices know more than Lancers. He forgot we had been trained to use the Call.

Marana and I slipped behind his tent. Fifteen feet away from where he counted Imperials, we stood close enough to hear them click against each other. The Fifteens had done very well indeed, and one of Serle's companions commented that if this pace held true they would break last year's record.

I looked at the tent and Serle's profile. *"I don't like it. I don't trust that Serle. He's a Lancer, and worse yet he's from Imperiana."*

Marana smiled. *"I won't believe he hasn't pocketed a few Imperials for himself unless he lets me count them myself."*

Silhouettes moved in the tent. Serle stood and pulled on his furs and others took up the count.

I reached out and squeezed Marana's shoulder. *"Counting the coins would not tell you if he stole any. You'd have to frisk him. He'd probably enjoy that."*

Marana winked at me. *"I might like that too."* She lowered

her voice to make it all throaty and seductive. Serle moved a bit faster and left the tent. He marched out toward us with his hood down and his brown hair standing erect.

We both acted startled and turned to face away from him. He kept his voice low. "It's no use, I heard you."

I stammered and stamped my feet. "Sorry, we were just talking. We've all been hunting and I can't afford to fail . . ."

Serle slapped me reassuringly on the back. "I understand. Come on in and at least take a look at our treasure. You can even count the Imperials if you like, though you'll find it a tedious task." He turned to Marana. "And you can even see if I've pocketed any . . ."

He guided us back to his tent. He went in first and wove his way back to the open cot at the rear of the tent. In the center stood a table where a fortune in Imperials climbed toward the pitched roof. It looked as though, as usual, the Thirteens and Fourteens returned to Talianna with practically nothing.

Serle's tentmates looked up when we walked in. I nodded and then killed the two closest to Serle. Marana got the other two. They all paused, then dropped back onto their beds and remained silent. They all watched Serle, waiting to see his expression when he turned and realized he had led two Justices into the heart of the camp.

I grabbed him and clapped a hand over his mouth. I felt him shudder when Marana dropped her hood back and he recognized her. "You have a choice. You can fail this exercise, or you can be disgraced and fail this exercise. It's your choice."

He tried to be stoic, but the fear in his eyes betrayed him. He looked at me and bowed his head. I dropped my hand because I knew he would not cry out.

"From what I saw on the post outside the ransom for the captured Justices is, all totaled, almost four thousand Imperials. On that table you have over eight. We'll deduct four to pay for our compatriots. Agreed?"

Serle nodded. His blue eyes were as pale as I'd ever seen eyes. I sympathized with him because I could imagine how I would have felt in his position a year before. I pawed his throat and he slumped back.

"The remaining four thousand is to go to Marana and me.

Once my fellows are free, I will consider six transferred to you for your ransom." I also gave him the names of the two Fifteens we'd jumped to enter the camp and told him to credit them. "And, of course, you'll say nothing of this, and raise no alarms."

Serle sighed and nodded. His compatriots joined him.

I walked up to the guard watching the first captive tent and stood next to him. He looked up and I nodded quickly. "Serle sent me to watch for you while you get some soup from the mess tent. Something to warm you up."

The Fifteen smiled and wandered off. Marana walked over to the other guard watching the prisoner tents and told him the same thing. When alone we both opened the captives' tents and told the Justices to head south, back away from the mountain. "Wait in the clearing two hundred yards off."

They all slipped away from the camp unnoticed. I had to kill one Fifteen who tried to stop me from walking away from my "post" once the Sixteens had all fled, but that was the only difficulty in the whole operation. Marana and I retied the tent flaps and we followed our compatriots into the night.

Once we had all gathered in the clearing, I told them to strip off their snowsuits and bury them.

"What do you have in mind, Nolan?" Jevin's question was echoed in everyone else's eyes.

I waited for everyone to settle down before I spoke. "I'm tired of playing in the snow. Let's go back—while our tired little hunters sleep—and earn more Imperials than any group of Sixteens in the history of the Talions!"

For the second time in my life I stood before the Master. The amethyst set in the dragonthrone shimmered and sparked with a life all its own. Beneath it the Master sat in shadow, so much shadow, in fact, that I could not read the expression on his face.

Lord Hansur stood at his left hand and His Excellency sat down and to the Master's right. I'd never been that close to the immense Lord of the Services before, and I found him somewhat threatening. His black eyes followed every movement I made. I felt as if I was an animal being sized up before he made an offer to buy me.

His Excellency spoke. "You managed to eliminate one hundred ninety-seven Fifteens."

I nodded. "Yes, sir, but I was not alone."

His Excellency closed heavy lidded eyes for a moment. "No, no, you were not. You had other Sixteens with you?"

"Yes, Excellency, by the end all forty of us were there." I kept my voice low. I was uncertain why I had been summoned so quickly after my return from the mountains. Inside myself I realized there would be concern about the end of the exercise, but I had the distinct impression that I had done something wrong, something very wrong.

The Master seemed to sense what I was feeling and he leaned forward. With a simple hand motion he silenced His Excellency and spoke. "Nolan, the three of us have read the journals of various Fifteens and a few Sixteens, so we have some idea of what happened out there. Still, I would like to hear about the action from you. You might have forgotten something in your account of the past week."

I looked down quickly, because I'd mentioned nothing about Marana and myself in my journal. Just as I'd not told her about the secret treasure room, I believed that our feelings were for no one else so I left them out. Quickly I looked back up. "Where should I start?"

Lord Hansur spoke softly. "I think the rescue would be the best place."

I bowed my head to him, paused, and gathered my thoughts. "Marana and I agreed to free our captured companions. The only way we could get them out was to ransom them, but we did not have enough Imperials. Since the Fifteens had organized themselves the same way we'd done the previous year, I assumed they had one person keeping track of the Imperials for the whole camp. We figured out who that was and, by using the right of plunder, we were able to take his Imperials and ransom the other Sixteens."

His Excellency cleared his throat. "That much we all understand, Nolan. What we wish to discover is what happened after that."

I quickly killed the grin trying to creep onto my face. "Once the Sixteens were free I got all of them to return to the Fifteens' camp. Because Marana and I had killed their leadership, and the two guards before the tents didn't realize their captives were gone, no alarm had been raised. We wandered back into the camp, slew those who were awake, then systematically killed all the others while they slept."

The Master leaned back and tapped his chin with his right index finger. "And then."

I blushed. "Then we kept careful track and rekilled everyone in six-hour intervals so we could ransom them and earn every Imperial they did without letting them back into the Game."

"Amazing," breathed His Excellency. "You split them into groups and harvested them like crops." He turned and said something in High Tal that was to fast for me to catch. The Master nodded and looked to Lord Hansur.

The Lord of all Justices smiled. "Nolan, can you explain why you did what you did?"

I nodded. "The reason we were out there was to learn to survive in a hostile land with people searching for us. During the first three weeks I learned how to survive in the winter, and how to avoid unorganized pursuit. It was not easy . . ."

"Especially when smuggled goods run out . . ." the Master laughed.

I nodded sheepishly. ". . . especially when the simple things I've learned to rely upon are not available, but in those three weeks I managed to survive. Marana and I eliminated enemies, and even mounted a couple of successful ambushes and raids upon them.

"When the Fifteen entered the Game, the situation changed. They were well organized, and if I'd not happened to see a pack of them moving that first morning, I'd have been rounded up in one of their sweeps rather early. Marana and I backtracked them and watched their camp for a full day. By the end of that day they'd brought in twenty-three of us."

I stopped and licked my lips. Sweat trickled down my temples and my heart raced. My explanation sounded like well-thought-out strategy, but I'd pieced things together as I went along out there. Each step just seemed to follow the other, and they all formed a very nice pattern in the end, but it sounded better than it had really been.

"I realized that survival would be impossible in a place where the opposition was so well organized. We had no options. We couldn't leave the exercise area, and I knew we could not hide forever, so I thought coming back and killing all the Fifteens would slow them down. Once we'd done that someone commented that in another six hours they'd be after us again, so we took control of the camp and kept them out of the Game."

I shrugged my shoulders. "Eventually the other Sixteens noticed they were not being pursued and came in to investigate. That's how the rest of them joined us."

His Excellency shook his head in disbelief. The Master looked up and stared at the interior of the dragon's skull, then looked at me. "You know your group of Sixteens brought in nineteen thousand Imperials. That buried the previous record, and, conversely, the Fifteens ended up with a net debt of seven thousand one hundred and eighty-two Imperials. Why did you let three of them keep enough to ransom themselves?"

I smiled. "Marana and I told the two we took in the woods that we would return and pay their ransom so they would give us information. We could not threaten to hurt them, so we threatened them with failure. I did the same with Serle. There was no reason for us not to honor our deals."

His Excellency's chair creaked as he leaned forward and narrowed his eyes. "How much did you want to embarrass the Fifteens for adopting your plan from last year?"

The accusations beneath the question stunned me for a second. "I didn't . . . ah, I, that was not my goal." I looked to the Master. "I'd be a liar if I said that didn't cross my mind, but it was not what I meant to do. I must admit that because they were using our plan from last year—greatly improved by Serle's planning and organization—I knew what might be a weak link. Last year we had four people guarding our treasure, but since there was never an attack mounted against us that detail seldom got brought up when the plan was discussed. I took a chance on that because it was the only chance I had to free the others."

I felt as if I were begging for my life, but no one showed any sign of having been swayed by my plea. I looked from face to face without successfully piercing any mask or reading any expression.

Finally the Master nodded to me. *"Thou art dismissed."*

• • •

Jevin met me in the supply hallway. "What happened?"

I shrugged. "They asked me some questions but I've got no clue about what they wanted. No praise, no reprimand, just nothing."

Jevin smiled. "Have you heard what Lord Eric has done to Serle?"

"No, but I'll bet he's got the same thing in mind for me." My heart sank at the news that punishments for the Game were starting to filter down.

Jevin smiled. "He's assigned him to watch every night."

My shoulders slumped forward. "That's a bit harsh, isn't it? And if that's what he gives blood kin, I can't wait to see what he does with me. Can he get me assigned to a Journey in the Sand Sea Reaches?"

Jevin laughed. "I don't think so, and I also don't think Serle's punishment is light because they are blood kin. The other Lancers just got a lecture. It seems Lord Eric feels Serle dishonored the family, hence the extra duty."

A harsh shout cut my comment off.

"*Nolan!*" The angry Call spun me around instantly and fury exploded inside me because of the involuntary reaction of my body to the Call. Lothar stood in the hallway behind me. His face burned bright red. "*She told me what you did to her.*"

I unconsciously balled my fists. I recognized the threat in his voice, but his words confused me. What I'd done to her? It took me a moment to realize what he was saying, and how Marana must have told him about us. He was so angry that a vision of Marana, lying senseless and bleeding upstairs, flashed through my mind and I dropped into a fighting stance.

Lothar stalked down the hallway at me. Jevin drifted to my right, two steps back and one to the side. "She told me what happened and how you seduced her."

My nostrils flared. "If you've hurt her . . ."

Lothar straightened up and sneered at me. "Such concern for a woman you've used to get at me." He shook his head. "She even believes she loves you. She refuses to come back to me even though I forgave her."

I lowered my fists and narrowed my eyes. "I think you've got this all twisted up, Lothar."

"No!" he laughed. "You used your time together to poison her mind against me. And I counted you as a friend, I trusted you and here you stole my woman!"

"I stole no one, and I never meant to attack you. It just happened!" Lothar's stare went blank as I spoke, and he shook his head as if an adult bemused with the fanciful tale told by a child. I ground my teeth and shouted at him. "Don't you patronize me, you self-important lordling. If you'd paid the attention to her that she deserved she'd never have noticed me. You get so wrapped up in *you*, Lothar, that you think of us as your courtiers, and of Marana as your court consort."

The benevolent peacefulness in his eyes melted as raw anger poured in. Color rose to his cheeks and veins stood out in his neck. "Peasant! There it is, the truth comes out. You're jealous of my bloodlines and the antiquity of my family. You struck out at me through my weakness. You used our friendship to get at me."

"I've never been jealous of you, Lothar, you've got nothing I want."

"I have Marana."

"No, Lothar, had." I sneered at him. "My previous statement stands. You have nothing I want." I regretted my words the second they escaped my mouth, but by then it was all too late.

Lothar lunged forward and buried his left fist in my stomach. I doubled over and reeled against the corridor wall. I raised my hands up into a weak guard and tensed for the blow that never came.

I forced myself to breathe and looked up. Jevin had Lothar's jerkin and held him back. "No, Lothar, you can't. It's not the way of the Talions." Jevin's deep voice filled the hallway. I heard anguish in his voice and knew it was more for the death of my friendship with Lothar than it was over any concern about our fighting.

Lothar fought wildly but ineffectively to escape the Feala-reen's grip. "Let go of me, you demon!"

"Lothar!" Jevin's Call slashed through Lothar's rage. *"This is not done in Talianna."*

I straightened slowly and still leaned against a wall. Lothar calmed a bit and composed himself. Jevin released him and

Lothar tugged his clothing back into proper position, then snarled and stabbed a finger at me.

"Jevin is right. This is not how Talions settle their differences. You have three days. I challenge you to *Cirhon*!"

New pain rippled through my stomach. *Cirhon* is a ritual in which two Talions meet to settle matters of honor. The challenger selects a site, sets a large circle of stones or draws the circle in the dust, and informs the challenged Talion where and when they will meet. The Talions both enter the circle and the fight is not finished until one is forced from the circle or dead. Seldom are the fights to the death, but with Lothar and his wounded pride there would be blood.

I hung my head in a heavy nod. "I accept."

"No." The Call spun all three of us about as if we were weather vanes in a tornado. Lord Hansur strode down the hall like an executioner.

Lothar opened his mouth but said nothing.

Lord Hansur raised his right hand. "I know, Lothar, why you want to fight Nolan in *Cirhon*, but it will not be allowed." He stopped four feet from us and spoke to us as a group. "In two days all the Sixteens will leave on their Journeys." Lord Hansur looked down at his own right hand, then back at us. "And until you return from that Journey, and have earned this mark, you are not true Talions. Until then you will have no right to *Cirhon*."

Lothar and I both bowed deeply and remained with our heads down until Lord Hansur and Jevin left us.

I looked over at Lothar and he at me. We both knew, in that instant, we'd survive our Journeys.

And three days after we became Talions we'd do our best to kill each other in *Cirhon*.

Chapter Eleven

TALION: LORD NOLAN

Allen slapped my stomach with the back of his hand and ripped me out of the past. "Dammit, Nolan, I have to have these measurements right. Stand up straight. Stop tensing. Let your arms hang naturally."

I straightened myself and smiled down at him. "I thought you could size me at a glance."

Allen snapped his measuring string around my bare chest and pulled it roughly tight. It pinched and stung but I was beyond reacting. "I can, for Talion uniforms, but they"—he jerked his head toward the Star—"want you in court clothing, so I have to be more exact. Now stand as you would normally."

I exhaled deeply and tension flowed out of me. I forced myself to relax.

Making Allen's work more difficult would not bring Marana back, and would only make my job of avenging her harder. "I apologize, Allen. I . . ."

The supplies clerk nodded without looking up. "I know, I know . . ." He whipped the string from around my chest and called the measurement out to a novice behind him. "His Excellency uses coercion as you use a *tsincaat*: easily and with deadly effect." Though His Excellency was Allen's superior, his tone clearly said he did not always approve of the Services Lord's methods.

I pressed my lips together and nodded. "His technique was brutal, but he was right. I've got a job to do." I held my arms out so Allen could measure them. "King Tirrell may have conquered my nation, but I am a Talion now. This is my nation, and my duty is to the Master."

Allen turned and tossed me my armored leather tunic. "Because of the war you came to Talianna. In a way you owe King Tirrell a debt, don't you?"

I nodded grimly. "More than one. Perhaps I can pay them all off."

Allen coiled the measuring string. "You can go to your briefing now. I should have enough clothes for you to travel in the morning."

I reached the door, then turned back. "Is it still fashionable, on hunting clothes, to wear a dueling sleeve?" In years past the nobles of Hamis, Lacia, and Rimah had taken to wearing hunting jackets that could double as dueling apparel by having the sword arm made of studded leather armor. They felt it made them look dangerous and rakish. Every bit of armor I could get interested me.

Allen frowned and rubbed a hand back across his balding head. "It is fading in popularity, but should be appropriate for your new identity. By the way, the moustache and goatee look good."

I raised my right hand to my chin. My face still tingled where a Wizard had used magic to speed my whiskers' growth. "Thanks. If you can fix up my hunting clothes with the leather, and perhaps fix me a pair of bracers that could go under some of the wide-sleeved tunics, I'd appreciate it." My request sounded as if such work would be simple, but the novice behind Allen winced and shook his head with resignation.

Allen nodded, turned to follow my gaze and laughed. "And you want your *tsincaat* concealed in your boots?"

"No." I chuckled. "A throwing dagger in each will do nicely."

I pulled my leather armor on again but left the front half-open so I'd not overheat. My walk to the Master's chamber took virtually no time at all. For a moment I wondered if the chamber might truly occupy no *real* space in the Star, but merely appeared in a location most convenient for the person trying to find it. I found the room after two turns off the main corridor, and the doors opened for me before I'd realized I'd reached my destination.

I bowed and seated myself in the chair I had occupied six hours before. The Master, His Excellency, and Lord Eric still occupied the chairs they had when I departed. For a second I thought they'd not so much as breathed since I left, but the color draining from Lord Eric's face and the sweat beaded up on His Excellency's forehead suggested a fierce discussion had occupied them during at least some of my absence.

Since the morning I'd had my hair cut, my face shaved except for the moustache and goatee, had a Wizard accelerate my beard's growth, had been force-fed Hamis history and recent court politics, and got measured for a new wardrobe. Stiffness from the morning's fight had set in, and I'd not managed any food in all that time, so the table laden with fruit, cheese, and wine next to my chair immediately attracted my attention.

His Excellency waved a hand at the table. "I know you've not eaten. Please, help yourself." I hesitated and looked at the other lords first, but His Excellency just smiled and added, "We have already eaten."

I reached out and took up the goblet of wine. The long-stemmed goblet was made of gold, but had no design or precious stones worked into it. I cupped the bowl with the stem resting between my third and fourth fingers. It held dark red wine and I recognized the scent almost immediately.

I sipped. The wine tasted dry but not bitter. I smiled. The wine came from Sinjaria. The grapes grew in an area north of my family's farm on vines transplanted from Hamis. Though it was far better quality wine than my family used to drink, I recalled having drunk this vintage before, a long time ago, at my first Festival.

I set the cup down and picked up an apple. It was small, green, and probably grown in the central valley of Hamis. I took a knife from the tray and peeled the fruit. I carefully cut around it because I didn't want to break the peel.

It was an old game, but one I suppose the wine's familiarity brought back to me. If I could peel the apple, leave the peel intact, and then throw it over my shoulder it was supposed to land in the shape of the initial of the person I was to marry. As a child, all of my brothers and sisters had tried it, and whenever an initial came up of someone we did not like we dismissed the results as Hamisian superstition.

Once I'd peeled the apple—I tossed the spotty green peel into a zig-zag heap on the table—I cut around the core and sliced the apple into circles. I ate the apple rings one at a time.

Lord Eric's restlessness radiated from him like summer heat from a stone. "What is all this foolishness with the food? Cannot you discuss his assignment while he eats?"

His Excellency steepled his fingers above his vast stomach and regarded Lord Eric with a glance that could have melted glass. Then he looked over at me and let a vulpine grin slash its way onto his face. "Nolan, where is the wine from?"

I swallowed the bite of apple in my mouth, then washed it down with a bit more of the wine. "My family only drank the common vintage, not anything this good, but I would guess it's from the Sinjarian province of Yotan?" I took another sip, thought for a moment, and added, "And it's from before the war because it's not as sweet as they like it in Hamis."

His Excellency smiled fully and looked over at Lord Eric. The Lancer Lord remained puzzled, but he said nothing. His Excellency again addressed me. "Congratulations on holding the goblet correctly and how you sliced the apple."

I frowned. My family might have been tied to a farm on an overworked plot of land, but we'd been brought up correctly and knew how to act in polite company. My mother was a merchant's daughter and occasionally, on high holy days before sunfever killed my grandfather, we traveled to his home for feasting. My father's mother always coached us in manners so we'd not be an embarrassment on such occasions.

She wanted to give my mother's relatives no reason to believe their money could possibly make them better than us.

I reached for the wine again and caught the cheese's scent. I sliced a sliver of it off the wedge and gingerly laid it on my tongue. I almost spat it out. "Please, don't tell me this is still popular at court!" The Hamisian monarch enjoyed cheese laden with a half-dozen spices, all masked by an over-abundance of garlic, and I hated it. My mother once made some for market and from the first I'd wanted nothing to do with it.

His Excellency shifted in his chair and, with a hand motion, encouraged me to take a larger slice. "You'd best get used to it because it is as popular as ever in the capital, Seir."

I cut and chewed a larger slice. I followed it quickly with a piece of apple and some wine. That washed most of the taste from my mouth.

His Excellency glanced at the Master and curtly nodded his head. The Master smiled and spoke to Lord Eric. "You see, Lord Eric, Nolan's actions merely confirm his selection as our agent. He grew up in the area and without a second thought performs tasks as only a native could. Take the apple as an example. In Imperiana you might cut it into eighths without peeling or coring it. Such a simple action would mark you as an outsider no matter how carefully you studied the background we have created for you."

The Lancer Lord frowned. "We should be able to impart that sort of training to any Talion we send off to play a role."

The Master narrowed his eyes and, for the first time, I saw displeasure crease his brow. "You know that training is given to others, *when time allows*, which it does not in this case. Still, a native accent or experience is invaluable, and worth more than years of training."

I looked up toward His Excellency expectantly. I had no place interrupting, so I would say nothing, but I did not like the situation developing here. I hoped His Excellency would take the opportunity I was giving him and break in.

He did. "You have a question, Nolan?"

Lord Eric spitted me with a harsh stare—warning me off commenting on or addition to his dialogue with the Master—so I addressed myself to His Excellency. "From the historical reading I was given earlier, I assume you believe King Tirrell will be slain sometime after his daughter's coronation. At that point the King's uncle would be made regent until she was married, at which time her husband would be installed as a Prince and would be given command of Hamis's armies."

The tension between Lord Eric and the Master slowly evaporated, and His Excellency, with jowls bouncing fluidly, nodded agreement with my assessment. "Even as we speak King Tirrell is out hunting a mountain leopard. Princess Zaria, during her Dreamvigil, saw one in a dream. Once the King gets it the coronation will take place. All the nobles from the area are gathering at Castel Seir. The ceremony should take place by the end of the month, but we intend to have you there before the hunt is complete."

He pointed to a folded and sealed piece of foolscap tucked halfway beneath the tray of fruit. I withdrew it, broke the seal, and studied the crabbed writing on it. I realized Lord Eric was watching me closely, and had a puzzled look on his face, so I paraphrased the contents aloud. "I am Lord Nolan ra Yotan ra Hamis, but I do not use the 'ra Hamis' for reasons of family pride. I am the illegitimate brother of Count Evin ra Yotan. He learned of me in his father's diary, sought me out, and accepted me. My mother is dead, but little of her is known and the less said the better."

His Excellency frowned at my addition to the text, so he spoke the rest from memory. "Your family makes wine. Count Evin cannot attend the coronation because it is time to harvest his grapes. It is inconvenient for him to travel. He has sent you to represent him and his family at the affair. A shipment of wine has already been sent in your name."

I nodded—he'd not missed a word. "Isn't letting a Lord of Sinjaria know a Talion will be coming to protect the King a bit risky? I would have thought Sinjarian nobles would be strong candidates in the list of those who engineered this plot against him."

His Excellency looked up at me. "The Sinjarian lords, in general, are, but Count Evin has managed to deal with them and the Hamisians by remaining neutral. He sent us a message suggesting the coronation might be a critical time for any sort of action against King Tirrell, and this was a week before the 'incident,' so we believe him free of involvement."

His Excellency then narrowed his eyes and answered the

question I'd dared not voice. "We did not coerce him, Nolan. We do a great deal of business with him and buy much of his produce. He was more than pleased to help. He wants nothing more than peace. While he resents Hamisian domination, he does relish the years of peace and prosperity since the war's end."

I blushed and looked down. "I meant no disrespect."

The Master stood, stepped from the throne, and walked over to get a piece of apple. "No offense taken, Nolan. Your suspicion of Count Evin was certainly cautious, and that is to be lauded. Still, you must not think everything His Excellency does stands on a foundation of blackmail. There are many people, like Count Evin, or even King Tirrell, who agree to work with us because they appreciate what we represent."

His Excellency continued once the Master returned to the dragonthrone. "You will fly from here to the valley between Twin Mountains. In the western end of the valley you'll find a mount waiting. If the mountain leopard has been taken before you get there, you will have to ride and join the King as soon as possible. The hunt's progress should be slow enough to allow for that easily enough.

"Only the King knows we are sending a Talion to protect him. No one else should know your identity. All the Lords of Sinjaria are suspect, as are many of their Hamisian counterparts. The Rimahasti are backing the Sinjarians with money and have offered to make troops available because they fear King Tirrell wants to add Rimah to his realm."

I ate another piece of apple and nibbled, reluctantly, at a slice of cheese. "What about Janian nobles and Duke Vidor?"

His Excellency ignored Lord Eric's reproving glance at me. "The Janian delegation is made up of nobles you have never met. You cannot trust them with your identity, because of the interdiction, of course, but they have no part of this." He hesitated and focused his gaze on the ceiling. "Duke Vidor is something else again."

I shook my head. "I do not understand. He should be, ah, twenty-six years old now. He signed a treaty of peace with King Tirrell after his father and brother died during the siege of Jolis. Jolis was razed, so the 'capital' of Sinjaria moved to Seir and Vidor was made Duke of the Sinjarian duchy. He was fifteen then and has lived at court since. He's supported King Tirrell in all things."

"The problem, Nolan, is that different people tell different stories about Duke Vidor. He's traveled widely in the area and really shows no interest in politics at all, yet he seems friendly with all the factions at court." The Services Lord held both his hands out palm up. "On one hand he is nothing more than a captive jester at court." His left hand sank slightly. "On the other, he is the man all factions believe will marry the Princess and gain the army. The factions seek to control him for that reason."

He rotated his right hand so it sank, then turned it to face me and show the death's-head we shared. "You cannot trust him with your identity because he might let it slip without realizing what he has said. I think it would be best if you told no one but the King who you are."

Lord Eric cleared his throat. "What of Captain Herman? Shouldn't he be told?"

The Master shook his head. "He will be notified a Talion is coming to replace the one slain, but I want no chance remarks that might expose our deception. Nolan can reveal himself when he thinks it appropriate. We don't want the two of them to be talking over fond memories of Taliana and have Nolan be discovered. I will send the message to Captain Herman with tonight's Elite flight to the east."

That did not please Lord Eric, but he said nothing.

His anger, and my recollection of comments from that morning, made me hesitate in asking my next question because I knew it would provoke a reaction from him. "Do I have leave to slay the nobles behind the plan?"

His Excellency nodded, but before he could add any sort of caution or caveat, Lord Eric shot from his chair. "How can you even ask for such permission? You can't just give him leave to kill off nobles."

The Master turned. "Even if a noble ordered the death of a Talion?"

Lord Eric's open mouth snapped shut and he lowered himself into his seat. More calmly he protested, "We do not know her death was ordered. She might have met the *nekkeht* in combat when she did not expect it and was thus slain."

"It matters not." His Excellency heaved himself to his feet.

"King Tirrell's death would bring instability to that area. There is no clear, strong candidate to replace him and I will not have civil wars ravaging the Sea States because you feel a noble's blood is more precious than that which runs in peasant veins. The death of a noble has no significance."

"Tell that to the ruling family in Jania." Lord Eric rose and stalked angrily from the chamber. The doors opened before him and he just avoided a collision with a Wizard who jumped to the side. The Wizard recovered himself, bowed, and waited in the doorway.

The Master rose and beckoned me to join him. "Lady Cosima is ready for us, Nolan. It is time for you to create a *nekkeht*!"

Our guide, whose name was Catalin, was just a bit smaller than me, both in height and build. He wore his black robe with the hood pulled up, so I could see only the tip of his nose and his mouth. I spotted one hair on his robe—it was short and blond—but I had no real way to even guess what he really looked like.

Silently he led us through dark, narrow corridors that twisted back and forth. I let my fingers brush against the walls, and discovered them to be solid, but the rough blocks my eyes saw contrasted wildly with the smooth, curved surfaces my fingers felt. Goose bumps rose on my arms and along my spine. Magick: I did not like it at all.

Finally we passed through a doorway so dark I thought it curtained, but I felt nothing as I stepped through it into a room white enough to momentarily blind me. I raised a hand to shade my eyes, and saw the Master had done the same. Across the room Lady Cosima bowed her head, and I caught a grin on Catalin's lips.

The Master shook his head. "You do not need parlor tricks to impress me, Cosima."

Her nostrils flared and something flashed through her eyes. It leached the color from them and for a moment her eyes became solidly pearl gray; then they returned to normal. *"I sought not your attention, Master. Nolan needs the impressing. Approve of this, I do not, but that discussion we have played like an old duet many times, you and I."*

The Master shook his head and looked old.

Her Call made each word strike physically and ripple through my chest. I bowed my head. "I am impressed, and I am as reluctant to learn as you are to teach."

"Learn you will, Justice, and well you will learn." She waved me to a table three feet wide and three times that length. The surface—unpolished white marble with some wisps of gray shot through it—had bolts sunk in the side every six inches to which straps could be fastened. An inch in from each edge, a shallow blood groove rimmed the table and led to a hole in one corner, beneath which hung a bronze catch basin.

I looked up and started. Catalin was rummaging around in a cabinet built into the wall opposite the door. He had the doors open and searched for something amid the orderly arrangement of alembics and cups.

This was not remarkable, except in that the cabinet had not existed when I walked into the room!

Finally success rewarded his search. Catalin selected a small cup, barely larger than a thimble, and placed it on the table. Though he took no care in how he handled it, it arrived at the table full of water. I looked up at him and received another shock. As he closed the cabinet, all traces of it *vanished*.

Lady Cosima watched me, then blinked once, slowly. "Dismissed you are, Catalin. Appreciated your aid was." She waited until the Wizard had departed before she continued. "Nolan, what you will be taught is taught over my objections. Understand you must that this magic being handed to you is much like giving a child a vial of poison. Do not imagine that because you can perform this ritual magic, you could control great forces or can defeat great magicks."

Her hand darted out and grabbed my right wrist. She drew my hand forward and twisted it so the tattoo showed. "You have not the training or blood for sorcery. This alone makes you capable of this magic." She let my hand drop and stared me in the eyes. *"If not for that you would be blind in the world of magic."*

As she said that, just for a sliver of time, the white walls dissolved and I saw the room as it must truly be. A vast black void surrounded us, and while there was no light, I detected black shapes within the darkness that moved with purpose and intent. Lady Cosima's form was sharper here, and full of more color and substance than before. Here she was home.

The white walls exploded back like a lightning flash at midnight and I staggered because of the dislocation. I shook my head to clear it and caught the Wizard watching me closely. *"What do you know, Justice?"* she demanded of me.

Her Call made an answer imperative, but I had no conscious choice over the words I spoke to her. "I know, I know nothing." The words came from deep within, from an ancient memory. I saw my grandmother, but she faded faster than the void had. This confused me, and I did nothing to exclude that fact from the expression on my face.

That *thing* flashed through Lady Cosima's eyes again, then was gone. "You are correct, Nolan, you know nothing." A hint of a smile writhed across her lips. "But you will learn."

Lady Cosima turned away from the table, then turned back and laid a gray rat on the table. His wet fur looked clean. It was also very apparent that he was dead, because his neck was badly misshapen. "Since this is only a demonstration, and because none of us could answer your questions while *Sharul*, we will not withdraw the soul from a creature, but we will use one that is already dead."

The Wizard took the rat up in her bony hands and straightened his neck, as if setting a broken bone. She muttered some words, in a low voice I could not understand, and then set the rat back down again. His neck stayed straight. "He was killed in Taltown this morning by a trap, but the damage was simple to mend." As if the rat merely slept, she patted the body gently.

"Nolan, please follow me." She moved off to my left and into a narrow, white corridor I'd not seen before. I did not reach out and touch those walls, though, because after what I'd seen for that one second, if the walls really were not there, I did not want to know. Still I did notice a light blue hue creeping into the walls as we walked.

Lady Cosima paused before a flickering display of rainbow lights on a panel set in the wall. It was only two feet square, and color played across it the way light dances off water and cavorts on the side of a ship or beneath a bridge. The lights twisted and shimmered like sparks racing up from a campfire to join stars in the sky above. They were all different colors and hues, but most were faded and some were bright, pure white. Immediately I knew the white lights were *rhasa* souls.

"Bare your right arm to the elbow."

The armor made Lady Cosima's order difficult to comply with. I twisted within my leather and bared the whole right side of my body.

Lady Cosima turned to the panel and stared at the lights. "Guessed it you have, the lights are souls. I know not what determines their colors, but the white ones are *rhasa*. The panel here holds them back, but you may insert your hand through it. Beware, the souls will settle on your flesh like mosquitoes in the summer. Those with strong color are most recently taken and they hunger for flesh. Hurt you they cannot really. Finally a *rhasa* soul will light on your palm. Draw it in as you would if you were taking it from a criminal."

I wiped the sweat from my palm off on my trouser leg and slowly raised my hand to the panel. I felt nothing, really, except pressure that yielded easily enough as my hand advanced. Once it was through the panel I felt a chill seep into my arm and suddenly, from elbow to fingertips, my arm was as cold as the tattoo.

Immediately a scarlet soul wrapped itself around my forearm like a viper. It's touch stung like the bite of an ant and I tensed. I shook my fist and flung the soul off easily enough, but it left an uncomfortable tingling in my arm. Then, as if the thought had to work its way out through the panel before I could think it, recognition came to me. That had been Tafano's horse!

More timidly, other colorful souls approached. Several soared past my arm, very close, to brush it with a sensation that tickled. They were very pale and it seemed as if part of them wanted to remember why they'd once held flesh so dear. Slowly I got faint impressions of who or what they had been, but most of the memories came from early life so I had no good way to identify them.

Lady Cosima must have read the wonder on my face. "The souls with color have not fully lost their identities yet. Imagine, though, the madness that would result if you had several souls like that chattering and remembering within your mind!"

I slowly nodded my head, then shook my hand again to

scatter the tinted souls. They swirled away like plumes of smoke in a gentle breeze. In their wake came a searingly white *rhasa* soul. It landed on my hand like a butterfly descending on a flower. I pulled it in effortlessly, then withdrew my hand from the panel.

Lady Cosima smiled because I held my hand as if it bore a terribly fragile egg. Without a word she swept past me and led me back to the first room. I forced my hand to relax and slipped half my armor back on my shoulder without putting my arm through the sleeve.

Lady Cosima stood beside the Master and frowned disapprovingly at the book he was reading. The small book had a black binding that looked like lizard skin with gold-leaf lettering, but both were so alien that I was unsure of what they really were. She took the slender tome from him, laid it on the table, then gently pushed it down and out of sight.

My skin crawled, but she ignored my reaction. "Nolan, concentrate and turn inside. Reach inside yourself and seek the *rhasa*. Find it, feel it, learn where it is. The Skull locks them away in a different prison from the one it uses to hold unclean souls."

I filled my lungs and let the breath out slowly. I closed my eyes and withdrew attention from outside impressions and senses. Unconsciously I stabilized my balance, then went in and located the *rhasa*. Searching it out was not difficult, because it burned like a beacon. I found it, touched it, and knew I could call it instantly. Secure in this knowledge, I came back out and nodded to the Wizard.

"Lay your hand on the rodent and gently push the soul into it." She spoke slowly and easily to let me preserve the sense of tranquility in my mind.

I reached out and touched the moist, soft fur. I settled my hand around it and called to the soul. I felt it trickle down my arm and out through my palm.

The rat started breathing!

My hand recoiled as if I'd been bitten. The rat's whiskers twitched and its eyelids fluttered. Muscles contracted and limbs jerked; then it rolled onto its paws and sat up to sniff the air.

"It's alive!" The words escaped me and earned a harsh frown from Lady Cosima.

"Alive it is not! It is *nekkeht*. It breathes because the body remembers how to do that, but it does not need air." As if to defy her, the rat dropped to all fours and waddled to the cup of water Catalin had earlier placed on the table. It drank, then sat up again and watched us.

I narrowed my eyes. "It breathes and drinks."

She shook her head vehemently. "It is not alive, and if you assume any *nekkeht* is alive, you will be slain by it." She flicked her fingers above it, as if passing a knife through unseen puppet strings, and the rat's head slumped forward. She'd undone the healing to its neck, but it did not die again. The whiskers still twitched. It turned and scuttled along. Its body pushed a twisted head before it and one eye stared up at us.

The Darkmaze dread sent a shiver through me. "I understand, it is not alive."

She stabbed a finger into my shoulder. "Understand this: the *nekkeht* you hunt can be hidden beneath the Runt Sea until he chooses to appear. If his neck was broken"—she gestured casually at the rat—"he could repair it in an instant. Deal with it as you dealt with the *nekkeht* this morning and it will destroy you."

She reached down with her right hand, touched the rat, and it flopped lifeless to the table. She raised her right hand and showed me the Skull. She had destroyed the *nekkeht*, and was now *Sharul*. Our audience was at an end, but I understood now, more than ever before, the importance and dangerousness of my mission.

The Master preceded me from the room and brought us back to his chamber by a very short route. "Nolan, do not let yourself be overwhelmed by the illusions and tricks she or Catalin played in there. Despite being Talions, they are Wizards. With many of those who work magick there is a greater allegiance to their art than there is to anything in this world."

I scowled, but the Master barely paused. "Take, for example, teleportation. You have to fly a Hawk to Hamis because the Wizards tell us no living creature can survive teleportation. And I have seen demonstrations, with mice or rats, where translocating the creature from one side of a table to another results in a dead beast frozen solid."

I shook my head. "I don't understand."

The Master mounted his throne, and His Excellency took

up the explanation. "How do we know the Wizards do not just freeze the creature, then move it? How, if teleportation does not work, can Wizards manage to travel great distances in a handful of hours?"

The Master smiled. "You see, Nolan, we can only believe what the Wizards tell us. Your new clothing will be teleported to Hamis while you fly there. Because they tell us teleportation is difficult, and can only be accomplished between certain points on the continent, teleportation is expensive and used sparingly. Imagine, though, what would happen if teleportation worked easily and anywhere."

I smiled with understanding. "There would be no need for ships or caravans. Trade routes would no longer exist and hundreds of cities would die. Wizards would be in great demand, and would spend most of their time teleporting armies behind other armies. There would be utter chaos."

The Master nodded. "There you have it. The Wizards have to protect their world, and they do that by protecting their art." He stepped back down and cut himself a slice of the cheese. "Now, I do believe teleportation will kill living things, but it is important to remember that where magick is concerned, nothing can accurately be described as impossible."

He popped the cheese into his mouth, chewed twice, and swallowed hard. "It must be an acquired taste. I do not envy you this assignment."

The Master looked over at His Excellency, who shook his head, then turned back to me. "Nolan, you leave in the morning. King Tirrell is the bait to trap the *nekkeht*, but I do not want him killed if at all possible. The plotters are expendable, no matter who they are. Spend the rest of the day working in the library on building your background story. I suggest a rumored stint with some Darkesh bandits to explain your weapons skill."

I nodded and rose to leave.

"One more thing, Nolan."

"Yes?"

"Your hand." The Master raised his right palm and showed me his Skull.

I winced, and was very glad Lord Eric had not returned. I almost started out disguised as a noble with a death's-head on his palm. That would fool no one.

As I had done to reach the *rhasa*, I let my body relax. Instead of withdrawing totally inside, I forced myself to feel in and down my arm. I traced a path through muscle and bone, past arteries and veins. There, deep within my palm, lurked an alien blackness.

I forced myself to touch it, and almost jolted away at the frigid shock it sent through me. I persisted and finally it noticed me. It receded into the bones of my hand when it realized its presence was a threat to my assignment, but it promised to come back when I needed it.

My eyes flickered open and my palm lay unblemished. The flesh still felt chilled, but it looked normal. I knew I could touch and seal papers with a death's-head without the tattoo returning, or could summon my *tsincaat* and the mark would remain hidden. Only if I pulled the soul from a body would the tattoo reappear, and then I could not send it away again until after Shar.

I held my unmarked palm up.

The Master nodded and I left.

The Fifteens I'd displaced from their room found me in the library in the early evening. I was almost finished with my background so they had little trouble persuading me to wrap things up and join them back at the room for story swapping. I stopped in the kitchen on the way back to the room to take a few apples with me, because I'd worked straight through dinner.

Each Justice deals with missions in different ways. Some Justices get drunk and spend their last evening wenching in Taltown. Others double- and triple-check everything until they're so tired they can only fall into bed and wake ready to go. I even know of one Justice two years my senior who goes through the Shar ritual before he heads out.

I like to spend the evening with others because I know, so often, I'll be alone on the road. There are few enough normal people who are willing to have a Talion as a friend. I know Weylan's wife accepted me only because I'd known her husband for many years, but if I hadn't know him I doubt I'd have shared a meal or roof with her.

In Talianna I was not a figure to be feared. Here others understood what my life was. They had grown up with me and realized I was more human than the word *Talion* or *Justice* comes to mean. Even in Selia's song the Justice was a faceless killing machine that a rogue had made a fool of; here I was just a man who had experience, and this was especially true and valuable to the Fifteens.

The two Fifteens who lived in the room had invited four of their friends to sit and talk. They dragged chairs in from their rooms and I sat on the bed with my back against the wall. Each of them produced a bag of sweets, from anise seed to sugar rocks, but I declined their kind offers and munched the apples. They waited until I had one apple in me before they started their interrogation.

As usual, in these informal discussions, most of the initial questions were about me. They wanted to learn, as quickly as they could, who I was and tie that into the things they'd heard about me. I remembered pestering a Justice just like that when I was a Fifteen because I wanted to know as much as possible about him in case I had to travel with him during my Journey. I'd have given my right arm to know something about the Justice I was to ride with.

Then they asked questions about the world and I imparted wisdom, generally through an anecdote or joke. I didn't preach at them because I knew they'd ignore preaching and we'd all quickly get bored. The only time I got even the least bit insistent was when I stressed that people work with those they like far better than with those they fear.

Finally, as the evening drew to a close, their questions became pointed and gently steered me in the direction of the story behind the scar on my shoulder. I'd seen it coming, especially after Jevin's prodding them toward it earlier, but I evaded and dodged their questions on that subject. They knew the story already, but I was not going to give them the satisfaction of hearing it from my own lips.

Still they persisted, and had almost pinned me down, when Jevin appeared in the doorway. *"Hast thou nothing better to do than persecute a Justice?"* Jevin combined High Tal and the Call perfectly to demand attention and mildly scold in one breath. The Fifteens, who had their backs to the doorway, all started. They instantly realized Jevin wished to speak with me alone. They stood, thanked me, wished me luck, and departed.

Jevin shut the door behind himself and dropped into one of the wooden chairs. I leaned back on the bed and rearranged the pillow so I was comfortable. I held up an apple, but he waved it off, so I tossed it aside and let it roll to a stop toward the foot of the bed.

"Nolan, I'm sorry about Marana." Jevin's voice lost some of its power as he spoke.

I nodded and shut my eyes for a moment. "Thank you. When did you know?"

"It was not announced until this evening's meal. Still I suspected. She was sent out after whatever had killed three Elites and taken a Black Wagon. I had my doubts."

I was instantly defensive. "She could handle herself." I drew my knees up and hugged them to my chest.

Jevin nodded, reached out, and squeezed my forearm. "That she could. Still you have to remember that Marana used skill and fear to be effective. She was subtle, not powerful. Whatever took the wagon was sheer power. There are not that many Justices who can deal with that sort of power."

I nodded. He was correct. Marana was a hunter. She'd always watched and waited. She'd learn about her prey, study it, and take it when she could strike easily. She often appeared from nowhere to deal justice, then vanished again, just as quickly. And she never used the Ritual.

Jevin continued. "I guess I knew she was dead when you were recalled before you got Morai. You're one of the few Justices who could deal with that sort of power. If they sent for you, Marana was obviously dead."

I shook my head. "Why didn't you say any of this that first night?"

"I had to hope for the best, didn't I, for you and for her?"

I forced a smile and nodded. "Perhaps, between one thing and another, this is best for Marana."

Jevin said nothing, but in his eyes I read agreement.

"What do you know of my mission?"

The Fealareen shook his head. "Rumors. You go out tomorrow and will be in disguise, but that much I could guess from the beard and the time you spent with Allen. And I know it must be a very tough thing they're sending you after. You're one of the few Justices who could destroy something like that. Lastly, it must be in the Sea States because you can assume a role there with little extra training."

I released my legs and leaned back shaking my head. "I bow to your deductive powers, Jevin." I smiled weakly. "Who do they send when I fail?"

Jevin pursed his lips. "Me. You go first because you can pass unnoticed. If there is a need for secrecy you can be secretive. I'm afraid growing a beard would not disguise me."

We both laughed at that thought. "If I fail and you have to come after me, tell them I'll see them in the Seven Hells."

Jevin shook his head and stood. "You'll succeed. You are a Justice."

A lump caught in my throat like a bubble. "Gods, Jevin, I miss her."

Jevin closed his eyes. "Yes, Nolan, and you are not alone in that. But remember, this ends her torment."

He was right. I thanked him for reminding me and watched him leave. I undressed, set the apple on the table, blew the lamp out, and after a short time I actually went to sleep.

I awoke reluctantly. It was one of those mornings when I'd roll over onto my stomach and try to lever myself up on my elbows. They'd collapse and I'd fall face-first into the pillow. Sleep reclaimed me twice, and probably would have kept me except for the Services clerk who entered the room and left me a brown hunting suit.

I took my time getting ready. I lounged in a hot bath and scrubbed myself cleaner than I knew I'd be in the three days' worth of flight to Hamis. When I returned to my room all my things had been packed up and removed. Those I would need on the trip itself would already be down at the Mews; the other things would go back into storage until I returned.

I dressed in the hunting suit and walked to the mess hall. I was late, so I had to eat in the kitchen. I didn't mind that, because I got the chance to supervise my provisioning. I removed the hard biscuits from my food sachel and replaced them with some apples and more jerked beef. The Services clerks certainly knew what food would preserve well, but I was only out for a week's journey, not a march across the continent.

I tried to find Jevin before I left, but, as improbable as it might sound, he was well hidden. I wanted to thank him again for talking with me the previous night. Having a friend around to help you understand the loss of another friend is invaluable.

Jevin, as it turned out, was waiting for me at the Mews. He was dressed in the standard black leather sleeveless jerkin, black cloth trousers, and knee-high boots. His *tsincaat* and *ryqril* rode in their respective sheaths on his hips. He smiled and held a sack out to me.

"Ah, Nolan, there you are. Here, I thought you might like this."

I took the bag and opened it. It contained a half chicken from the Gull merchant in Taltown. I smiled. "Thank you, Jevin, I appreciate it."

The Fealareen smiled and his fangs shone white against his gray-green lips. "I wish you the best of luck on this outing."

I nodded and walked toward the Hawk some Elites were preparing for me. It was Fleet, Tadd's bird. I tied the bag to the saddle. "Jevin, if you are the one sent after me I'll arrange for everything I've learned, up to the point they get me, to be told to you. Someone will speak with you. What do you want for a recognition sign?"

Jevin knitted his brows and thought for a moment. *"Drijen."*

I pressed my lips into a thin, grim line. "Good choice." *Drijen* was High Tal for "revenge."

I mounted the hawk and walked it from the saddling enclosure. Jevin reached up and we clasped each other's forearms. "One other thing, Nolan, you can do for me."

"Yes?"

Jevin looked down. "It's a small favor."

"Yes?"

He smiled. "Can you bring me back some of the court cheese from Seir? I've developed a taste for it. . . ."

I laughed. "As much as you want, my friend, as much as you want."

I waved and Fleet and I headed east.

The three-day flight was totally uneventful, utterly solitary, and felt like punishment. It gave me a long time to think about Marana and reconcile myself to her death. Being alone was difficult, but it helped me face the problem instead of allowing me to be deflected from it by well-meaning people who wanted to help me with the pain. Friends like Jevin could help me *through* it, others would just delay consideration of it.

I remembered my grandmother helping my mother deal with her father's death from sunfever. My father's mother had always been the family historian, the storyteller, and even the political analyst, but in her dealing with my mother's grief she became a caregiver. The image I had of her changed and perhaps for the first time I became aware of the changes, good and bad, wrought in people by great stress.

I wished for the comfort she would've offered me, but settled for bits of wisdom she'd imparted in her life. I'd had experience laying ghosts while traveling alone before. Each mile further I'd traveled from our farm in Sinjaria helped fade the faces and memories of my family. In the same way each mile away from Talianna took me further and further from where Marana and I had spent our time together. Even though I was heading toward where she'd died, I had no mental picture of her in Hamis, or any of the Sea States, so she could not haunt me there.

By the evening of the third day I reached the west end of the Twin Mountain Valley. I landed in a clearing marked by a red blanket and hooded Fleet. Tadd walked from the nearby forest leading Wolf.

We exchanged greetings and immediately looked after our own animals. Wolf looked fit to me, in fact a bit overfed, if that was possible on the long ride from Ell. Wolf nickered as he got a nose full of me. I patted him and turned back to Tadd.

Tadd completed his inspection of Fleet and seemed pleased. "Thank you for taking such good care of him."

"And you for caring for Wolf. Have you had any word about King Tirrell and his hunting party?"

Tadd shook his head. "No one has come and spoken to me. Still I had heard the horns and drums of his beaters over the last few days. They've been working this way but they stopped abruptly late this afternoon. I can only conclude the mountain leopard has been taken and they'll head back in the morning."

I nodded. With the sun going down Tadd would have to stay until morning. I thought it might be best for me to ride on into the camp and start working. "I think I'll leave you here and join the party. Which way?"

Tadd pointed east. "Two, maybe three leagues."

I swung into Wolf's saddle and adjusted the saddlebags Tadd handed me. My *tsincaat* lay in my bedroll and I'd sheathed my *ryqril* at my right hip. The sword would not attract any attention because it looked like any other blade. It would only be "special" if my identity as a Talion was revealed.

I pointed Wolf east and we cantered off. The dying sun gave us enough light to pick out a trail, but by the time we left the valley at the far end I could only see flickering firelights to guide us into the camp. Wolf saw them and we hurried on in the darkness. We found a woodsman's track and made good time on the trail rubbed smooth by the logs hauled down it each day.

The tent community needed to house the hunters and all the servants who accompanied them was the size of a small village. Fifty tents, from large nobles' pavilions and the central tent for entertaining to small tents for servants, formed a rough circle in a meadow. A stream cut through the camp and woods surrounded it. Fires burned before each tent and servants scurried to and fro making preparations for sleep.

Something was very wrong, because there was no celebration going on. The largest tent was dark and I heard no sounds of drinking or merrymaking anywhere in the camp. Furthermore, the servants acted terrified of something. One half was startling the other at any one moment, then everyone would freeze when something common and normal within the forest made a sound.

I urged Wolf forward and we rode into the camp. A young man nearly collided with Wolf, turned, and screamed when he saw me. The loaves of bread he'd been carrying flew up and out and he fell to his back.

I reined Wolf in and dismounted. "Whoa, why so jumpy?" I bent down, helped him to his feet, then squatted to gather some bread up.

He stood there shaking. "The goblins, they have him!"

"Who? Who do they have? Where is the King?" The servant trembled and could say nothing. I Called, *"Where is the King?"*

He held a quaking hand out and pointed to the south. I looked back along the direction he indicated and saw more torches. I handed him the loaves—he promptly dropped them—and mounted Wolf again. In five minutes we reached the circle of torches.

Nobles, hunters, and servants stood looking down into a huge sinkhole in the middle of the road. Large enough to have taken down three ranks of horsemen riding four abreast, it was a riot of dirt, stones, and roots. Off to one side a narrow little hole just large enough for a man to stand upright in broke into the sinkhole's wall. Wolf shied and I knew what it had to be.

Dhesiri. Goblins, the servant had said, and he'd named them correctly.

I dismounted and looped Wolf's reins around a bush. I could not see King Tirrell, so I searched out the noble in the center of things. "I beg your pardon, my lord. I am Lord Nolan ra Yotan. Where is the King? I was to report to him upon my arrival."

The noble was an older man. His hair had thinned without losing any of its black color. His face was florid and full, though neither it nor his middle were as stout as they might have been at his age. From the crest worn over his heart I learned he was Hamisian and I deduced him to be Grand Duke Fordel, the King's uncle.

His black eyes quickly took my measure. I could read his dislike in my crest because it was not surrounded by the blue field meant to acknowledge Hamis. Beyond that, though, he saw something he liked in my stance and how I carried myself. He decided in an instant to deal with me as a peer as opposed to a foolish noble who would only get in the way.

"The King is in there." He pointed at the sinkhole. "Him, Duke Vidor, and my son, Count Patrick. And their horses."

"When?" The Dhesiri love horseflesh, and if the queen was sated by the horses, the King and the others might not yet be gone.

"Two hours ago is when we found the ambush. I saw them

not too long before that." The Grand Duke looked at the other nobles crowded around us and they confirmed what he said.

I nodded. "Have you sent anyone in after them?"

Murmuring started behind both of us. He shook his head, then stopped and stared into my eyes with an unwavering gaze. "Into a Dhesiri warren, are you mad?" He shook his head again. "We've been waiting for them to fight their way out."

I looked hard at him and saw his dilemma. Were he twenty years younger, back in his prime, he would have leaped into the hole and gone after them, but surrounded by young nobles who had never fought in a war, and who probably only dueled to first touch or blood, there was little he could do.

Alone, the job was impossible, unless the person sent in could sneak through the warren, free the prisoners, and get them out before anyone raised an alarm. No one in that lot had those skills and, even in his prime, the Grand Duke would have been hard pressed to succeed.

"They won't get back without help." I walked back over to Wolf, withdrew my *tsincaat* from the bedroll, and strapped it on over my back. My hilt rose at my right shoulder.

Grand Duke Fordel stared at me. "You can't go in there, it's suicide."

I nodded to him and drew my *ryqril*. "It can't be any more difficult than eluding the lords of the Darkesh. Send any after me who have more courage than brains."

Then, for the second time in a week, I jumped into total darkness to do battle with a foe who was at home in it. Certainly, kill anything I find down there. But the question was, in a Dhesiri warren, could I kill enough?

Chapter Twelve

NOVICE: NIGHTMARE

A breeze swept across the dusty yard and swirled the charnel-house scent around me. It knocked me from Wolf's back and onto the ground, where I vomited. Weak knees and unsteady, quivering arms held me above the puddle that had been my breakfast as my body convulsed again and again to further empty my stomach. Bitter bile coated my mouth, sweat slicked my flesh, and tears seeped from my tightly shut eyes.

"That's enough, Talion. *Get up.*" Ring's Call cut through my physical agony but carried no compassion or concern for me with it. He hated me and threaded his words with contempt.

I dug my fingers into the dust and relished the simple feel of each grain of gritty sand. I reached inside to calm my body and stop my stomach from heaving, but a second gust of wind threatened to start the process all over again. I used my rage with Ring and myself to exert iron-willed control over my insides and, for a moment, took refuge in just feeling all the pains in my body. Better that than what lurked outside.

"Now, Novice, get to your feet and tell me what you see."

I rolled back on my heels, kept my eyes closed, and raised my face to the sky so the sweat could cool me before I attempted any more complicated movement. I reached behind me, felt for and found my left stirrup, then dragged myself to my feet. I swayed, both from weakness and a dizzying wave of nausea washing over me. Slowly, dreadfully, I opened my eyes.

I'd seen it before and shook my head hard to flick off the tears welling up in my eyes.

They'd used sod to build their house but, other than that, the farm looked identical to the one I'd grown up on. The smoke still drifted up from the charred ends of roof beams. Fire-blackened ruins and the blue sky filled the empty doorway and windows. Back behind the house, mocking the carnage before it, stood a smokehouse.

Corpses choked the sunbaked yard in front of the house. The men lay on the right and the women on the left as if they had been taken in the midst of a ceremony or celebration. Their animals, all dead, lay scattered around haphazardly, but they looked as though they'd tried harder to escape their fate than the people had.

Several small pits, about two feet in diameter, half that depth and filled with loose, dry dirt, were sunk in a seemingly random pattern throughout the yard. Everyone, everything was dead and had been dead for a few days. And everything had been chewed on.

"Nolan, what do you see?"

I turned too quickly in anger and wavered until the world caught up with my head. Ring towered over me up there on his horse. A silver circlet held back his long black hair. The breeze tugged and played with his hair, but he gave no indication that it brought to him the same scents it did to me. A cruel sneer twisted his black moustache and warped his

250 MICHAEL A. STACKPOLE

pinched face into a mask of disgust. His eyes were merciless, flat, slate-gray chips.

I breathed in through my mouth, then spat to rid myself of the dusty thickness on my tongue. "I see a farmhouse that has been attacked by Dhesiri. I see many dead people. I see evidence of Dhesiri tunnels in the area. I see one male body that might be one of the two men we are chasing." I could not and did not hide the anger in my voice.

Ring narrowed his eyes to gray stiletto points. "Oh, good, little Nolan. You tell me what is there. Now look again and tell me what happened."

Something inside of me whispered the true story of this farmhouse, but I denied that explanation because it hurt too much, and forced me to remember too much. "Dhesiri attacked and killed the family here. It's obvious."

Ring vaulted from his saddle and for a moment I thought he'd lash me with his quirt. "You fool! You are not thinking!" He stood a head shorter than me and carried an open challenge for me to try him any time or place I dared. "You'll need a Journey far longer than a year to make *you* a Justice."

He walked past me and I turned to watch him. "The women are over here on the left, the men on the right. Dhesiri do not segregate prisoners. All the animals are dead, but there is no horse body. They had a plowhorse—there's manure back beside the house—and that's what the Dhesiri would have taken first, but there's no hole large enough to drag even a dismembered horse through. And this man over here . . ." He kicked the headless body of a big man. "He has no head."

I walked forward. "He could be Ahnj ra Temur."

Ring shook his head violently. "No! Look at his neck. It's been cleanly cut with a steel weapon, one blow. His head is gone to make identifying the body difficult, or misidentifying the body, as you have done, easy."

I could not surrender that easily because my transparently wrong explanation was all that shielded me from past ghosts. "The Dhesiri could have taken it, for food."

"Fool. If they wanted the brains they'd crack the skull." He spat in my direction, then skewered me with a volcanic stare. "You're wrong, admit it and stop being stupid."

Inside all hope withered. Vanquished, I bowed my head to him. "Please, Justice, tell me what happened."

Ring turned away, but I knew he did not smile. His hatred ran so deep he could not even take pleasure in a victory over me. "Ahnj ra Temur and Dabir ra Insal came to this farmhouse. They offered to trade labor for food and lodging. During the night they rounded the family here up. They murdered the men, raped and murdered the women. They took the plowhorse and headed off.

"It's all obvious, novice, despite the arrival of a Dhesiri hunting party. The humans have been dead longer than the farm animals. The Dhesiri have sampled the carrion but have not returned to carry it away. The Dhesiri killed the farm animals to make sure they would not get away, then returned to their warren to bring more workers to carry the bodies off. The one body that could be mistaken for Ahnj was decapitated to make misidentification possible."

His voice almost lost its biting edge at the end of his explanation. Everything he said echoed the words I'd heard within my own head. I should have known better than to fool myself, because, successful in my effort or not, the battle inside was lost, and I would suffer the consequences as certainly as life breeds death and sleep breeds nightmares.

In a small voice I asked, "The Dhesiri will return soon, then, won't they?"

Ring nodded. "If you're over your sickness we'd better get started hauling the bodies into the smokehouse back there." He pointed to the small building back behind the house. "We'll have to burn them."

I was almost sick again, but I did not protest the work. I knew a funeral pyre had a particular scent to it and I knew it would bring back the nightmare. But that really mattered little, because after seeing a family lying slaughtered around their farmhouse, nothing could keep the nightmare away.

I lay in total darkness. Even in my feverish state I knew the shadows were my friends. They made sunfever easier and sucked away the searing pain that burned the flesh when light struck it. They made sunfever survivable and, down there, nestled in the cool, dark root cellar beneath my family home, I would survive.

Silhouetted faces came and went. I could not see detail, but the soft, soothing voices—my grandmother, my mother, and Laura, my elder sister—encouraged me and praised my progress. Sometimes I woke when they came to press cool cloths to my forehead, and even forced a smile when they brought me broth. My brothers were not allowed down to see me—they'd not had the fever and it was much harder on men than women—but I heard their joyful shouts as Mother or Laura would apprise them of my improving condition.

Fleeting memories of delirious dreams and pleasant times melted away as the nightmare took hold. My eyes snapped open, painfully wide, and locked open. I could not close them or flood them with tears. I could not move.

I was powerless to do anything but peer through the invisible darkness. The stout wooden beams above me stood out in exquisite, sun-drenched detail, then faded to a misty gray. Slowly, but agonizingly swiftly, they became crystal clear and provided me an unobstructed view of the glassy floorboards above them. Anything and everything that could prevent me from seeing the drama unfolding above me, obligingly and unbidden, became transparent.

Even the tears I tried to summon to blur everything just drained down the sides of my head.

I tried to scream. The sound echoed within my head, but I knew it never made it past my lips. Locked in deathlike immobility I could only watch. Watch and die inside.

Soldiers stood in our house. With harsh voices the two of them demanded information from my father. They'd bound him into a chair and struck him when he answered curtly. My mother screamed and Hal held his twin, Malcolm, back. Grandmother and Laura quieted Arik. My sister Dale, a year younger than me, fingered a knife and, behind her, a friend named Lyel—a boy my age from the next farm over—balled his fists.

The smaller Hamisian soldier, a Master-Sergeant according to the red armband he wore, hit my father again with a backhanded slap and drew blood. Dale rushed forward and stabbed the sergeant in the stomach. He roared in pain and smashed a fist into her face. She flew back and slammed into the wall with a wet thud. Her neck broken like a twig, she slid to the floor. Blood trickled from her nose but lost all color as it washed across the floor.

Hal and Malcolm, too young to join the army, yet old enough to die for their country, closed on the soldiers. Hal kicked the wounded soldier in the stomach, drove him to the ground and completed the job Dale had started. The other soldier wrestled with Malcolm. They crashed through the door and out into the yard.

They rolled to a stop right in front of the eight other men in the Hamisian patrol.

Everyone was screaming. Hal pointed to the door and yelled, "Run, run." Lyel bolted out the door with Arik quickly following. Mother stopped to untie my father. Laura bent to help free his feet. Grandmother picked up a meat cleaver.

Malcolm got to his feet first and kicked the soldier he was fighting in the teeth. The man's head snapped back, and I saw his neck was broken just like Dale's. Malcolm stared down at him, pleased, and oblivious to the danger he was in.

Again a scream blasted through my skull but could not break free to warn Malcolm. My eldest brother half turned as the horseman galloped up behind him. Malcolm's hands rose, not to ward the sabre slash off but to try to catch the wrist behind it and pull the man from the saddle. Malcolm was far too slow and the blade crushed the left side of his head. He was dead before his body, wrenched around by the force of the blow, flopped to the ground.

Arik ran to the left, as fast as his hobbling gait would allow, toward the barn where he'd so successfully hidden many times before. He shot glances back over his shoulder and a smile played over his lips. He was innocent enough to think this some sort of game. Death meant nothing to him, and he was just running off to hide until someone came and told him the game was over and it was time to return home.

The Hamisians balked at chasing him because of his clubbed foot. To them it meant he had been touched by supernatural creatures in the womb. To the Daari mercenary in their midst it meant he was a demon. And, for the Daari, that meant my brother's death was a divine imperative to be ignored at the peril of the warrior's soul.

The Daari chased Arik and herded him. He shouted taunts

at my brother, who, though he did not understand the words, was lashed by the tone and the hatred. Arik turned to run back to Mother or Laura—who he knew would drive his tormentor off as they had so often done before—but he never made it. The Daari speared him from behind. He left Arik's crumpled form in the dust with the Spiritlance standing high in his back—the weapon was now unclean.

Father shook the loosened ropes off and was free. Hope sparked in my chest, but was almost instantly smothered. He drew the family sword from over the doorway and walked out into the yard. The horseman who had killed Malcolm turned his horse and came back for Father. My father dodged the first slash and cut up through the soldier's rib cage. The man fell from the saddle and lay still in the dust.

Lyel ran off to the right. A Hamisian soldier chased him on horseback. Lyel dodged and evaded him until trapped against our pigpen. He got halfway over the fence before the soldier split his skull with an overhead sword blow.

Two men dismounted and engaged my father in a fight. While Father might have been agile and smart, he was no swordsman. He held them off at first by parrying their blows furiously but futilely. Then they seriously started to work and cut my father to pieces.

Hal dove from the house and tackled one of the swordsman. My father, bleeding from a dozen wounds, turned his full attention on the other and crushed his sword arm. My father turned back to help Hal when an arrow burst through his chest from the right. It spun him back to face the archer seated high up on a horse. The second arrow thudded into his chest and pierced his heart. My father fell lifeless and the sword spun from his hands.

A second archer shot at Hal and missed. Hal twisted his foe in front of him so the second arrow killed the swordsman. Hal could not support the dead weight, and as he tried to drag his shield back up an arrow ripped through his throat. Hal fell beneath his dead enemy.

The Hamisians dismounted and, with the Daari in the lead, they entered the house above me. The soldiers smiled when they saw my mother and sister; my mother and Laura were terrified. Grandmother, the cleaver hidden in the folds of her dress, was calmer. She watched the soldier the way she'd watched over us children, and decided the Daari was most dangerous.

"Let us alone!" Mother pleaded. She hugged Laura and pressed back against the wall. Mother was pretty, but the terror in her face made her ugly. She had always been strong and confident—a rock in all emergencies. The soldiers stripped that away from her and reduced her to a scared child.

"Let us live." Grandmother's plea was more reasonable than my mother's.

"Perhaps, for a while," answered the Daari, "but we have our orders."

Grandmother's face drained of color. She knew our secret was no longer a secret; nor was survival an option. The fire of life left her eyes and she struck.

The cleaver chopped into the Daari's throat, spraying blood everywhere. He reeled away with his hands vainly trying to staunch the pulsing geyser shooting from his neck. Grandmother strode forward and slashed at the next soldier. He parried her easily and his riposte took her through the chest as the arrows had taken her son.

She died. And, after several hours of screaming and pleading, my mother and sister joined her.

I lay in the darkness alone and cried. Once again I lay blind to all but the shadows, and deaf to all but the drip, drip, drip of blood leaking through the floorboards from above.

Ring shook me awake. Sweat covered me and my limbs trembled. I blinked my eyes and wiped the tears away.

"Nolan, are you hurt?" The words, while stated in a form to suggest concern, rebuked me for not having told him of any injury earlier.

I blushed from the shame. I shook my head. "Nightmare."

Ring looked at me, and for the only time during my Journey, shared my feelings. He nodded. "Everyone has them. Go back to sleep."

"Sure." I lay back down but I knew, after long years of experience with this dream, sleep would be elusive. I'd long since discovered I could only do one thing to lock the nightmare away: I had to finish it. I lay back, breathed deeply to calm myself, and forced myself to relive that incident.

• • •

I recovered from the sunfever a day and a half after the attack took place. I had vague memories of the sounds, but knew nothing of the sights the dream would bring to me that night and later on. Still, I did know something was wrong because no one had come to see me for a long time, and I heard no sounds from above.

And a puddle of blood lay dried and cracked on the root cellar floor.

I pushed the cellar trapdoor up and came face-to-face with the Daari. My heart leaped to my throat—scarring on his face was hideous, especially bloated as it was after two days of his being dead. I wondered why he lay there, and why my family would leave a dead body in the house. It made no sense!

Then I saw Dale and my grandmother.

I didn't cry; at least I don't remember crying at that point. I walked through the house like a ghost and denied everything I saw. These bodies could not be my family. My mother, my sister would never lie like that. Dale's head could not possibly be at that angle. This was some *jelkom*'s trick, or I was still dreaming mad dreams in the grasp of the sunfever.

I walked into the front yard and saw more I could not believe. I waited for Hal to get up because he was famous for his practical jokes: the arrow in his throat had to be a trick. My father could not be dead because there was so little blood. Malcolm fell with his wound in the dust so I didn't notice it at all.

"It's me, Nolan," I called out. "You can stop now. I'm well." No one moved, but I knew they couldn't be dead because death came to take the old, like my grandfathers, not a whole family.

My denial lasted until I found Arik. Terror perverted his face and deformed it into a mockery of the optimistic expression he always wore. It ripped away his innocence. The lance pinned his body to the ground—the feathers on its end floated gently in the breeze—and served as a concrete reminder of how his body had betrayed the spirit it housed. The scavengers had started on him.

I collapsed and cried. I knelt beside Arik and waited for anyone, or anything, to comfort or kill me. I cried until no more tears could come, and my chest ached from the sobbed

half-breaths. I cried until I realized my tears came more for
me than for my family.

I had to care for them first. I had a lifetime to care for
myself.

Within two hours I dragged all my family's bodies back
into the house. I laid them all out as if they were sleeping and
put my mother and father side by side. I could not dress them
because death had swollen their bodies, so I laid their favorite
clothing over them. I lifted my grandmother into her rocking
chair.

"Yes, Grandmother, I saw the rune you wrote with your
blood. I know what it means. I'll do it." I spoke with her as if
she was alive. She had to hear me. In her last seconds of life
she'd drawn a symbol on the floor, one linked to Hamis and the
evil that had killed her. I remembered the stories she had told
and I knew I had to honor all the bloody rune represented.

Lastly I dragged Lyel into the house. I decided he should
be with my family because he had died for me. They had
come for us and he had been mistaken for me. I put him next
to Dale. I knew he liked her, and she him, though neither one
had discovered that fact about the other in life.

I'd hauled the soldiers' bodies from the house. I also took
the things I'd need on the journey to Talianna, including the
gold coin my family had treasured. Then I started a fire and
burned the house to the ground.

While my home burned, taking my family and acquainting
me with the scent of a pyre for the first time, I had one other
task to perform. I dragged the soldiers' bodies to the trees we
had planted to protect the house from the north wind. With a
mallet and some heavy framing spikes, I nailed each man to
his own tree.

Smoke from the fire lazily drifted around the farm. As if
sentient, it gently pushed me away from the burning house,
and chokingly halted my one suicidal attempt to join my
family. I picked up the satchels of food and clothes I'd prepared for my journey and never looked back.

But before I left our farm forever, just to the leeside of the
trees, I knocked down our scarecrow. I wanted nothing to
disturb the scavengers.

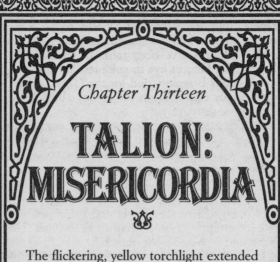

Chapter Thirteen

TALION: MISERICORDIA

The flickering, yellow torchlight extended into the Dhesiri tunnel for just over twelve feet, but everything beyond its pallid circle of conquest remained pitch black. I adjusted a small tab of leather on my right sleeve so it covered the back of my right hand, and secured it by tightening a leather loop beneath the middle and ring fingers on that hand. I rubbed my hand on my pants to dry it, then took firm hold of my *ryqril* and slowly walked into the tunnel.

I'd dealt with Dhesiri a couple of times before, and had spent a certain amount of time with Dhesiri-hunters learning about the creatures. Most people call them goblins, but the hunters eschew that term. As one once told me, "Goblins frighten bad children, but Dhesiri will eat them. Folks that think of Dhesiri as goblins probably don't believe they exist at all. Them's the folks that end up in a Queen's supper dish!"

Dragons supposedly created Dhesiri to be a parody of humans and to give humans something other than dragons to hunt. Most Dhesiri, I've been told, are child-sized, tailless lizard-men. The Dhesiri live in colonies, like ants, with hundreds of workers bringing food for the Queen. The Queen's job is just to lay eggs to keep the colony alive. The colonies live underground in warrens.

About a hundred yards in, the tunnel dropped six feet then climbed back up eight. I kicked some footholds in the tunnel wall and drew myself over the top of the vertical shaft quickly. I knew the dip was just a trap for rainwater, but it provided an excellent place for an ambush. Dhesiri were not supposed to be smart enough to think of such things, but I was and I decided to be careful because I did not relish meeting the Queen while looking up from a stewpot or serving platter.

The narrow tunnel wound through the ground somewhat aimlessly. The workers that dug it must have been following a root or the buried course of an old stream. This heartened me, because the workers only built tall, wide tunnels under the direction of a Dhesiri warrior, and I had no desire to meet one of them in a tunnel, or any place else.

I'd never seen a Dhesiri warrior before, and most of my informants were very vague about them, which I took as a testament to the warriors rarity and ferocity. They are supposed to stand eight feet tall, have a long tail and a powerful build. They mate with the Queen and act as her guardians. Each colony can only support a half-dozen warriors because of their voracious appetites and their tendency toward cannibalism when the workers failed to find enough food. Lastly, they are rumored to possess near human intelligence, which could make them even more dangerous than just their physical size would suggest.

Inching along the tunnel was hot and dirty work. I felt the wall with my left hand and slid my right foot along to test for any pitfalls. I held my right hand out and pointed the *ryqril* off in the darkness like a lance. I moved in bursts, then stopped and listened for any reaction to my movements.

Once I felt safe I'd move forward again and repeat the whole process.

The tunnel split into three smaller tunnels and I paused at the fork. Even though I'd now worked deeper into an inhabited warren than any of my teachers, I felt certain from what I'd learned about abandoned warrens that two of the tunnels would lead out or into traps. The third passage undoubtedly led deeper into the warren.

I crawled about ten feet into the mouth of each tunnel and felt around for any clues that might help me make a choice. The light Dhesiri workers left no tracks, but in the third tunnel I found a ring. In the darkness I could not see it, but by touch I could tell it was a man's ring set with his family crest. I had to assume one of the three men dropped it to point out the correct tunnel.

I struck off through the third tunnel. The roof of this tunnel rose only four feet high and forced me to work forward at a much slower pace. I dropped to my left knee and continued on in that half-kneeling position. My right hand remained extended and my left hand trailed along the wall. I didn't like the reduction in my mobility, but the passage's size absolutely ruled out the possibility of a warrior ambush, so I did take comfort in that.

I got forty feet along into it when a worker came scurrying at me. It's little mind tied up with whatever task it had been given, it did not see me. I heard it and raised my left hand to stop it. I touched its chest and immediately slid my hand up to its throat. I slammed it into the tunnel wall opposite me and drove my *ryqril* into its chest.

The goblin died quietly because I choked off all sound it could possibly make with my left hand. It thrashed a little but, thanks to the armor on my right sleeve, did me no harm. It did send a chill down my spine because it's flesh felt remarkably like Rolf's after Chi'gandir had changed him. The mental picture of Rolf merged with my image of a Dhesiri warrior and it took me a moment or two to get going again.

I dropped the corpse behind me and continued forward. The tunnel broadened and some light leaked into it from ahead of me. I stopped at the edge of the semicircle of light and looked out.

I'd reached the heart of the warren.

Just the sight of the Grand Gallery took my breath away. The Dhesiri-hunters told me how they had once dug down to a gallery in a deserted colony and described it as just a big hole in the ground. That description, while accurate in a general sense, really denigrated the surprising majesty and complexity of the place. From where I squatted in the mouth of a tunnel high up in the gallery, the whole thing looked alive. The entire area below glowed with luminous mosses and fungi that cast the deep hole in shades of green and purple. A four-foot-wide ledge spiraled down through the brown, striated earth around the gallery's interior face and the dark mouths of tunnels large and small dotted the gallery walls.

I guessed I'd want one of the larger tunnels, because the Warriors would need access to the prisoners. That eliminated many of the tiny tunnels immediately. I also imagined the prisoners would be somewhere in the middle of the warren in a place not close enough to the top to tunnel out nor far enough down for the air to get stale and kill them. While workers would eagerly eat carrion, the hunters said the Dhesiri preferred to feed their Queen fresh meat, especially horseflesh.

I cut a diamond in the dirt wall beside the tunnel I'd come in through. Then I left the tunnel and worked quickly around and down a couple of levels. I stopped whenever workers moved above or across from me, but they all stayed hunched over and watched their own feet. Like preoccupied children they noticed nothing and went about their tasks with no concern for the safety of the warren. While pleased that their single-mindedness protected me during my infiltration, I shuddered at the idea of a horde of Dhesiri who had only one thought: "Kill the intruder."

At first, the reptilian odor of the warren almost overwhelmed me. The dry, musty scent laced the air thickly, much like the odor of a stable that has not been mucked out for weeks. Despite the scent, though, the warren was very clean. I suspected the workers carried all refuse to the gallery and pitched it into the darkness below me. I could easily imagine the gallery's central cylinder going deep enough to reach an underground river, both to sweep garbage away and provide water for the colony.

I flattened against the wall beside one of the large tunnels. Two Dhesiri workers trundled out to the ledge with armloads of bloody bones. They did not notice me and, as they threw the bones off the edge, I pushed them out into the darkness. They did not scream, and fell so deep I never heard them hit bottom.

I picked a bone up from the ground. It was a vertebra, fresh, from a horse. I smiled. If they'd fed the horses to the Queen perhaps the prisoners were still alive. I scratched a crown into the wall beside the tunnel, assuming the Queen was somewhere further along that passage, and continued my search for the prisoners.

Despite the thought I'd given to the problem of locating the prisoners, I would have missed them completely but for quick thinking by one of the prisoners. A dozen large tunnels fit my requirements for size and location, and searching each one was impossible. I scratched a number beside each and moved on, but at the sixth I noticed parallel grooves heading off along the tunnel, going away from gallery.

I dropped to one knee and ran my left hand over the grooves. They'd been cut into the hard-packed earth by a pair of spurs. Somehow one of the prisoners had freed his feet and dug his heels in to leave a path for me to follow. I grinned, nodded my head, and ducked into the tunnel.

The tunnel turned gently to the right and sloped down a bit. I worked along it in a running crouch until I saw an opening. Through it I spotted a chamber where three men were tied up and left against the wall like so many sacks of grain. I could see one warrior standing watch, but he faced the prisoners and seemed unaware of my approach.

The warrior stood both taller and broader than Jevin. Like most lizards he had a huge tail and did not have ears, only holes in the sides of his head. I hoped that meant a reduction in hearing, because I had to traverse twenty feet of shadowed tunnel before I could get to him.

Beyond him I got my first glance at the three prisoners. King Tirrell's handsome face matched the profile on Hamisian gold coins. He had an aquiline nose, strong mouth, and high cheekbones. His hair was full and steely gray. He looked strong—clearly a warrior despite his years on the throne. The eyes, though, were dark, brooding circles of midnight, and they reminded me that his years on the throne also made him a politician.

The other two prisoners were younger, my age or slightly older. Duke Vidor had a narrow, slender face as yet uncreased by worries or difficulties. He watched the Dhesiri with dark blue eyes that appraised every movement and sought out weaknesses in the enemy. He reminded me of a cat, both because of how he watched the warrior and because of his generally lean build. I didn't know if he had the skill to be a fighter, but he seemed to have all the instincts, and that counted for a lot all by itself.

Count Patrick, on the other hand, was not a warrior born. He had bright red hair and a slightly chubby face. While his clothes were very much cut along the lines of the hunting suits worn by the other two—and, for the most part, as somberly colored—vibrantly colored bits of cloth trimmed his clothing. If I'd not been able to trace the spur tracks to his boots, I would have supposed him nothing more than a court fop. His body was thick around the middle, unusual in so young a man, yet his blue eyes spoke of intelligence and common sense.

Count Patrick saw me as I padded down the hallway. I raised a finger to my lips unnecessarily. He blinked once then looked at the warrior. "Excuse me, how long must we endure this outrage?"

The warrior lazily turned his head toward Patrick. He eyed the Count like a snake watching a mouse from ambush. "Sssoon you eaten," it hissed out with difficulty.

"I demand you take us to the Queen immediately!" Patrick's voice took on an annoying whine.

The warrior's head backed a bit, then darted forward on the thick neck. "You will see her soon enough, fat one." It hissed out a laugh, forked tongue played along the edge of its mouth. I'm fairly certain that's how he discovered me, by "tasting" the air.

Realizing something was wrong, he licked the air again. He spun on me and reached out a two-finger, one-thumb hand to grasp a huge, knotty club. He filled the opening into the prison and advanced slowly in my direction. He hissed out another laugh because I only had my *ryqril* in hand.

I shifted it to my left hand and waited for him to block the prisoners from my sight. Once they could no longer see me I summoned my *tsincaat*. The blade's magical appearance in my hand solicited a startled hiss from the warrior; then he lowered himself into a more defensive fighting stance.

I sailed in at him. I arced my *ryqril* at him with an under-handed toss that he neatly dodged by pivoting back to the left. The *ryqril* flew past him and landed at Duke Vidor's feet, but the warrior paid it no attention because I slashed at his left leg and forced him to parry my blade wide.

His parry worked, and I let it because I continued my rush on past him and into the prison. I thought I'd made it past cleanly, mainly because his weight rested forward on his left leg, but he managed to bring his club back around and strike me just below the kidneys with a weak return blow. It stunned me for a second, and knocked me off balance, so I flew across the room and smashed into the wall to King Tir-rell's right.

I bounced back from the wall and landed on both knees. I spat out dirt and tasted blood from a split lip. I knew the warrior was coming for me, and I knew I had to move, but the tingle running through my legs warned me they would not respond yet. My injury made me a target, but I knew my survival demanded I be more than that. I tightened both hands on the hilt of my *tsincaat* and a deadly calm ran through my body.

I heard the rasp of leathery footpads on dirt and felt the rush of air as the warrior raised his club for a crushing blow on my head. King Tirrell yelled "Look out, man, move!" and tried to knock me to the side with his body. His impact against me made me sway just a bit, but I returned to my original position and waited. The urgency of King Tirrell's cry and action failed to penetrate the hideous calm that had settled over me.

Feeling trickled back into my legs as the warrior's shadow dropped over me like a cloak. I saw the green flash of his body reflected on my *tsincaat*'s blade. His breath hissed in, his tail scraped against the floor. A groan presaged his strike and without a moment's hesitation when I heard it, I struck.

I urged my body up, and forced my legs to uncoil as I thrust my *tsincaat* over my head. Locking my elbows, I stabbed up and back. The warrior's club smashed down where I had been, and safely within the arch described by his arms, I drove my *tsincaat* up through his jaw into his brain. My crossguard smashed into his chin, pitching him over backward.

I sank back down to my knees, having relinquished my grasp on the *tsincaat*, and turned to face the prisoners. The King had just rolled onto his back, but he joined the other two in staring at me. They could not believe what they'd just seen. The surprise on King Tirrell's face quickly melted into a narrow-eyed appraisal of my action.

At the same time I found myself appraising him as well. By trying to warn me and by trying to knock me out of line with the Dhesiri's attack, he had put himself in danger. That was not how I would have expected him to act, based on all I had been told about him. In his action I began to see some of the reasons His Excellency wanted King Tirrell kept alive.

I reached over and took my *ryqril* from where Duke Vidor was close to slitting Count Patrick's wrists and severed the Count's bonds. "Thanks for leaving me the spur tracks. I'd not have found you otherwise."

The Count brought his wrists forward and rubbed them. "What you just did, it was impossible."

I shook my head and sawed through the ropes binding Duke Vidor's wrists. "Insane, perhaps, just like heading out after you, but not impossible." I smiled, shrugged, then glanced back at the warrior and shivered. "Perhaps," I laughed nervously, "incredibly stupid and lucky would be a better description."

That broke the tension and drained the shocked looks from their faces. Count Patrick smiled as I shuffled behind the King and cut the ropes binding his wrists. "Your crest, you are from Yotan?"

"Aye." I tossed him the *ryqril* and bent to tug my *tsincaat* from the warrior's head. Once I'd freed it, I crossed to the tunnel mouth and watched for any workers or other warriors. "Lord Nolan ra Yotan."

Count Patrick made quick work of the others' leg-bonds. "Lord Nolan, may I present His Highness King Tirrell ra Hamis and Duke Vidor ra Sinjaria ra Hamis."

I turned and nodded to the others. King Tirrell locked

eyes with me and an unspoken question passed between us. I nodded slightly.

The King stood. "I had word you would represent your family at the coronation."

I smiled. "Had I known you were Dhesiri-hunting I would have arrived even earlier."

The others chuckled and quickly picked their swords out of a pile in the prison's corner. Patrick handed me back my *ryqril* and I slid it into its sheath. "Swords are only useful in tunnels this size, so if you don't have a dagger I suggest you take one from that pile." I jerked my head toward the dead warrior. "I don't think he'll mind too much."

Each of them recovered his own dagger and, despite my remark, we all left the prison with swords in hand. I led the others back through the tunnel. We all stopped at its terminus and looked out at the Grand Gallery. "I cut a diamond into the wall near the tunnel we need to exit through. The other symbol I used was a crown for the tunnel leading to the Queen."

"I have half a mind to visit her and repay her hospitality." The Duke sighted down the length of his blade as he spoke, and I saw green mosslight glint from its razor edge.

"You would need just half a mind to go in there." Count Patrick's gibe brought color to Vidor's cheeks even though he offered the comment in jest. Vidor said nothing in return, but glowered at Patrick for long enough to suggest to me the Count enjoyed baiting the Duke, and had done so for some time.

The King laid a hand on Patrick's shoulder. "Good cousin, let us get out before we fight amongst ourselves."

"I agree. Come on." I moved forward onto the ledge, with Vidor, Patrick, and the King following in that order. We moved quickly, but all paused at the entrance to each tunnel before crossing it. Twice I heard Dhesiri coming out the smaller tunnels. Each time the single worker did not see me. I grabbed each of them by the scruff of its neck and pitched it into the Grand Gallery, then signaled the others to follow.

It happened in a second. I heard nothing and signaled the tunnel was clear just as a worker strode from it and collided with the Duke. Vidor tumbled toward the edge and the worker squawked out a cry of surprise as I wheeled and backhanded it off the ledge. Patrick lunged and caught Vidor's wrist. The Duke went over the edge, slammed into the gallery wall, but did not cry out. The King tackled Patrick to prevent his being dragged over the edge and, being very careful to avoid his bared sword, I caught hold of the Duke's other hand.

We pulled him to safety, but other Dhesiri in the Gallery heard the worker's cry. Instantly they filled the central cylinder with echoes of the call. Workers boiled from the tunnels both above and below to advance upon us.

I helped the Duke to his feet and dragged him into the nearest large tunnel, which happened to be the one with a crown carved beside the mouth. "I hope you have something to say to the Queen after all, because we're going to visit her." I shook my head and spat out a little of the blood leaking from my lip. "Count Patrick, I need you and the Duke to act as rear guard." I turned to the King and inclined my head to him. "Your Highness, I'm not much of a diplomat, but I would be honored to lead you to your audience with the Queen."

Cut at an uphill angle, the tunnel to the Queen made any sort of fast assault very difficult. The passage was broken into small segments set off at angles to each other to limit the usefulness of bows or other long-distance weapons. Though large enough for us to use our swords easily, I knew the size was more for the warriors' convenience than ours.

We met two warriors in the corridor. We took the first one by surprise, but he hissed out an alarm despite my best efforts to finish him quickly with a blow to the throat. My decidedly desperate attack forced the warrior to parry it with his club, which left him open to another attack. King Tirrell stepped in and swung a heavy two-handed chop to the warrior's chest. The Dhesiri warrior collapsed, but whatever he'd cried out alerted the second warrior lurking further on.

That warrior waited in ambush and nearly did to me what none of Morai's compatriots could. Slightly ahead of the King, I went wide around one of the corners. The warrior stepped from my blind side and swung a hard blow down at my head. I noticed it at the last second, and twisted enough to face him, but could not ward the blow off.

King Tirrell dashed forward and swung a sword cut from

his feet up toward the ceiling. His sword pealed as he caught the descending club and deflected it back behind my body. The force of the blow he'd stopped drove him down to the tunnel floor and he sprawled between the startled Dhesiri and me.

I gave the warrior no chance to recover. I stepped in toward him and snapped a kick with my left foot at his knee. The joint broke cleanly and the monster dropped away from the King. Even as it fell I planted my left foot on the ground and pivoted to bring a two-handed slash down across his neck. My *tsincaat* swept through his throat and severed head from body.

I looked quickly for any other warriors, then bent and helped the King back up. "Thank you, sire." The words came hard for me, but I forced them out nonetheless. "I owe you my life."

King Tirrell took my proffered hand and stood. "And I owe you my life, and that of my cousin and the Duke." He looked me hard in the eyes. "And, if what *your masters* fear is true, I expect I will owe you my life yet again."

I nodded. "Perhaps, but first we'd best get out of here."

King Tirrell lead the way into the throne chamber. Situated at the top of a long, sloping but straight section of corridor, it looked unremarkable from the outside. The King stopped cold when he stepped through the portal and shifted his grip on his sword. I stopped behind him and swallowed hard.

The chamber was huge and dark and deep. The throne, a squat hill set about twenty-five feet beyond the doorway, rose only fifteen feet above the corridor floor, but it appeared taller because of the fetid moat around it. A narrow causeway, about six feet wide, ran from the doorway to the throne itself.

Lying atop the throne-mound was the Dhesiri Queen. She was an incredibly obese lizard with four stubby legs that could not even touch the ground because of her massive girth. Her flesh was a mottled, grainy pattern of orange, brown, and black. Her eyes were all black and had an opium smoker's glazed look to them.

Workers moved over the throne like a living carpet of flesh. They ferried food—the last of a horse by the look of it—up from the moat to the worker at her head. She opened her mouth, displayed a triple set of triangular teeth, and let a thick tongue flop out to lick the offering. The worker advanced, rotated the raw horse haunch to strip the flesh off the bone and onto her teeth, then actually had to force her tongue back into her mouth before she shut it and swallowed.

At the other end, beneath her stub tail, workers carried away feces and ivory-colored eggs. The grapefruit-sized, translucent eggs showed the silhouette of a Dhesiri within. Workers passed these eggs along and carried them into a side chamber where I could see nothing but moving workers and piles upon piles of eggs that varied widely in size.

A warrior stood between us and the Queen on the causeway. He hefted a club and I knew, on the narrow strip of earth, we could not get past him easily. He hissed something and, for the first time, the workers and Queen took notice of us.

"Don't issue a command to attack." I stabbed my *tsincaat* into the earth and pulled my sling from a pouch on my belt. I fitted a stone into it and whirled it gently. "I will kill her."

The Queen hissed something at the Warrior and he hissed back. The workers left off their duties and threw themselves on her. They grasped each others' hands and formed an interlocking, living armor that left only her eye open. She nictitated a clear membrane up over it and continued to watch us.

I shook my head. "How long can she survive like that? She'll suffocate quickly."

The Dhesiri shrugged. "She will survive long enough for the workers to kill you and your compatriots." The warrior opened its mouth in what I guessed passed for a Dhesiri grin. Its tongue flickered out once, then again. It closed its mouth. "How many warriors have you slain?"

I held up my left hand and raised three fingers. "We'll kill more, and will fight while standing amid the eggs if you force us to do so." I nodded my head toward the egg chamber to the right of the throne and his tongue flipped out quickly, then retreated.

Behind me Count Patrick and Duke Vidor entered the throne chamber. They both stood dumbfounded for a moment, as had the King and I, but the Count recovered himself quickly enough. "There is a horde of them coming after us."

Duke Vidor nodded in agreement. "It is a wall of the little goblins."

My eyes narrowed. "Any other warriors?"

"One." Patrick raised his left hand and touched his forehead. "He had a triangular red blaze on his brow."

Out of the corner of my eye I saw the warrior react to the Count's description. I decided to gamble. "I trade you that warrior's death for our lives. No other will compete with you for the Queen."

I saw the light of intelligence in the reptilian eyes. "That warrior is fruit of my seed." He shook his head slowly. "You have killed all the other competitors for the Mother-Queen."

I shrugged. "Then it's a siege."

The warrior nodded and raised his club as if to attack. My slingstone struck high on his chest plate and ricocheted up through his throat. He knew I'd have to kill him and, one warrior to another, he acted to provide me the excuse I needed to finish him. He toppled over into the moat with a splash and sank from sight.

I turned to the others and spoke to stop the Duke from heading toward the egg chamber. "No, not there." I looked to the King and he nodded. "We'll defend the corridor into this chamber."

The Duke looked up to protest, but the King raised his hand. "The corridor is a superior position."

King Tirrell and I strode through the doorway and into the tunnel about twenty feet. I expected Duke Vidor or Count Patrick to step up beside me, but the King waved both of them back. Using his sword he drew a line across the tunnel. "Let us stop them here, shall we?"

"Agreed, but you should not put yourself in danger this way, sire."

The King raised an eyebrow. "Do you think I would be in any less danger standing behind you?"

"No."

"Nor do I, but I can hope so. I want Duke Vidor and my cousin back there because they are the future of Hamis, I am just its history. I can fight here to preserve the future, and consider it my most solemn duty do so."

I found a smile growing on my face. "For the future of Hamis, then." I toed the line he had drawn and prepared myself to kill for as long as I could stand and saw the same resolution mirrored in King Tirrell's eyes. Count Patrick and

Duke Vidor took up positions behind us to protect us from any workers that slipped between us, or who decided to attack from inside the throne chamber.

The worker army turned the corner down below us and began a slow advance. Their little heads bobbed like so many buoys on a choppy sea. Though they were small, the sheer weight of their numbers would drive us back and tire us until we couldn't strike another blow. We were doomed and all of us realized it as the corridor continued to fill.

I cleared my throat and looked at my companions. "Well, my lords, I'd guess there are only a thousand or so Dhesiri to slay in a colony this size. Shall we say an Imperial a head?"

The Duke chuckled. "And five for a warrior?"

I looked over at the King. "Only if we can count those we've already killed."

King Tirrell nodded enthusiastically. "A most worthy suggestion, Lord Nolan." The Duke and Count nodded their agreement and we turned back to begin our grim work. The horde had reached us.

I won't attempt to recount a blow-by-blow description of the fight because I cannot remember that much of it. Little pieces of it come to mind unbidden—like a lizard face being chopped in half or a worker reeling away with an arm gone. Visions such as those are just enough to remind me I've been in a battle, but everything else just fades from memory. Not that I mind the loss of those memories; such lapses keep me sane.

Any man who claims to remember and can recount each cut, parry, and riposte in a melee like the one we faced is either a liar or did nothing but watch. It was less a pitched battle than it was butchery on our part. The workers just kept pressing forward and gave us no opportunity for the finer points of swordsmanship. I felt as though I was trying to smash out a fire instead of fight an army, because all I did was chop and slash and hack at little green hissing monsters who clawed back at me. I struck with either edge of my *tsincaat* and smashed some creatures with the flat of the blade, but all my blows seemed to have no effect. The workers just kept coming.

I've heard, in bardic accounts of other sieges, of fighters having to push bodies away so they can get at more foemen, but we had no such problem. Before the bodies could pile up to form a breastwork behind which we could hide, the workers dragged their dead and dying comrades away. Because the line of workers lay unbroken as far as I could see, I easily imagined the bodies being hauled the full length of the corridor and being tossed off into the refuse hole in the Grand Gallery.

The King tired a bit before I did—at least before I admitted to myself I was tired—and with a shouted order to his cousin, he withdrew. Count Patrick stepped into the fight and attacked with a vitality I'd not have guessed he had. Both Tirrell and I had been pushed back down the corridor toward the throne room, but Patrick's ferocious attack actually cut into the Dhesiri forces and drove them back. I redoubled my efforts and we won back a few precious feet of the corridor.

My body ached all over. Soaked with sweat on the inside and spattered with Dhesiri blood on the outside, my hunting leathers hung heavily on me like an outsized second skin. My boots were scraped and torn, my trousers were slashed open, and my legs bled from several shallow scratches. Sweat stung my eyes, and I tried to blink it away. I did not need to see to kill Dhesiri.

The King called out to me and ordered me back. I shouted, "On three, Duke Vidor," then counted down. The Duke slipped in past me and roared as he met talons and teeth with bright, sharp steel.

I slumped down to one knee and tried to control my breathing. My chest heaved like a ship on a stormy sea and I felt dizzy. I tried to wipe the sweat from my brow on my left sleeve but all I succeeded in doing was smearing my face with Dhesiri blood.

I closed my eyes for a moment and shut out everything but the sounds of battle. The two nobles grunted and groaned with explosive exertion, then barked out inarticulate cries of satisfaction when a blow was successfully or decisively struck. The Dhesiri squawked and gurgled at the front lines, and hissed expectantly in the ranks behind, as if they were repeating their last order over and over again to themselves. The swords made a thick, moist sound when they hit, very close to the sound of a hoe being raked through wet mortar.

The Duke cried out and my eyes snapped open. He reeled away and clawed at his left thigh. His pant leg was slashed open and a Dhesiri hung on with a dogged single-mindedness. The goblin had his teeth firmly sunk into the Duke's thigh. Vidor dropped to one knee and crushed the Dhesiri's skull with a blow from his sword's hilt, then faced the grim task of prying the goblin's jaws loose.

I darted forward and bisected a Dhesiri leaping at the Duke's back. The whole line surged forward and the King stepped in between Patrick and me to hold them back. We lost a half-dozen precious feet, but managed to check their advance long enough for the Duke to drag himself deeper into the corridor.

In the middle of the horde I saw the colony's remaining warrior. He hissed orders at the workers between him and us, and then back at the workers following him. This puzzled me for a moment, but I really did not have time to figure out the reason behind his action. I did regret the Duke's wounding, though, because it meant I could not stand back and use my sling to kill the warrior.

Then the curious problem of the warrior's orders back down the corridor solved itself. I heard men's voices coming down the tunnel. The warrior moved more toward us, and the Dhesiri he passed turned to face back down the tunnel in the direction of the Grand Gallery. In another minute Grand Duke Fordel came into view.

The King shouted the Hamisian war cry, "My blood for my country," and chopped away with renewed vigor. Count Patrick yelled from the sheer joy of seeing his father again, and the three of us pressed forward. Urgency numbed all aches and pains. Behind the Grand Duke fought other members of the hunting party, and with their support we felt, for the first time, we might actually breathe fresh air again.

I shouted to the warrior. "Stop the workers and we won't kill the Queen. We'll let you move her and make another warren elsewhere."

He looked at me with a hard cold stare. I nodded and King Tirrell joined me. The warrior hissed a command; the Dhesiri stopped fighting and withdrew. King Tirrell shouted an order and the Grand Duke stopped his men.

The workers streamed past our line to the throne chamber. Count Patrick helped the Duke limp toward the Grand

Duke. King Tirrell joined me and we preceded the warrior to the throne chamber.

Even though the fighting had stopped the workers still covered the Queen, and the workers streaming into the chamber joined their companions to safeguard her. The warrior hissed a new order when he reached the chamber and the armor dissolved to once again form the feeding and birthing line we'd seen when we first discovered the chamber.

The warrior stood taller than Jevin and had a darker green to his skin except on the arrowhead splotch of red between his eyes. His scaled flesh shone with a smooth glow and did not look to be cold as I might have suspected from a greater distance. "Where can we move?" he rasped out to the King.

The King squatted and drew a rough map of the area with his dagger. He placed an "X" at our current location then indicated a spot close to the border of Ealla and the Darkesh. I'd flown over it on my way to Hamis and knew it to be a semi-arid grassland that had few people living in it because the soil did not easily support agriculture. "Here no one will bother you, and you can feed on the wild horses that inhabit the plains."

The warrior nodded his understanding, then turned to me. "Why?" Despite the harshness in his voice, he managed to convey a certain disbelief behind the word.

I looked into his flat black eyes. "There was no more need for killing." I turned to walk away.

"Wait." He touched my shoulder. I turned back.

He looked hard at me. "Debt." He offered his club as payment.

I shook my head. "No debt."

He shook his head adamantly and tightened his grip on my shoulder. "Debt."

I nodded. I pointed to the Queen. "Give me a warrior's egg."

The warrior hissed sharply. The Queen hissed something at the warrior, and he hissed back. The Queen produced an egg, but it was larger than the others and reddish brown in color. A worker brought it to the warrior. He took it and held it out for me.

I laid my right palm on it and marveled at the warm, leathery texture of the shell. I concentrated for a second, then

withdrew my hand. A simple black death's head now decorated the shell. The warrior within was still alive; I'd sensed
life but only marked the shell. To draw the life out, which I
did not want to do anyway, would have brought the black
back into my tattoo, and that would have scuttled my mission
almost before it began.

"West of here, in the valley"—I dropped to one knee and
pointed out the spot on the King's map—"there is a compatriot of mine with a large bird. Give him the egg. He will give
it to my masters. Now no debt."

The warrior gently took hold of my right hand with his left
paw. His flesh was supple and as soft as leather, yet very dry
to the touch. His forked tongue flickered out and scraped
across my flesh. "I will remember you."

I nodded solemnly and bowed to both him and his Queen.
Silently, respectfully, King Tirrell and I withdrew and
rejoined our own people.

The servants standing around the pit greeted our return
from the warren with thunderous applause. Someone thought
to bring a cart for the wounded and we loaded Duke Vidor
into it, along with one or two of the other nobles who'd been
hurt in Grand Duke Fordel's party. They sped along ahead of
us while the more hearty rode back to the camp at a pace that
suited our exhaustion.

The servants had a full celebration started by the time we
got there. First to greet the King was Keane, the Earl of
Cadmar. He was a tall, blond, mustachioed man who was well
known as a fierce warrior and able general. "My lord, I am so
glad to see you are safe. I and my party arrived in your camp
just as word came that you'd been recovered from the
Dhesiri."

The King swung from his saddle, as did Count Patrick and
I. Grooms took our horses away and the King turned to intro-
duce me to the Earl. "Lord Nolan ra Yotan, this is Keane,
Earl of Cadmar."

I took his extended hand. "I know of you, sir. You are the
King's champion and were the victorious general at the siege
of Jolis." He bowed his head, and I returned the gesture. "I
take it you still have the Star of Sinjaria?"

I felt the shock run through his hand. The Star of Sinjaria
was a brilliant emerald that used to be the centerpiece of the

Sinjarian monarch's crown. After the siege the King had it reset into a medallion to commemorate the victory and gave it to the Earl. Popular legend maintained that Sinjaria would never be free unless a Sinjarian returned the gem to his homeland.

Keane narrowed green eyes so dark they looked olive and studied me. Instantly he rejected the idea that I'd been at the siege, because of my youth, then let a grin creep onto his features. "I still have it, Lord Nolan, it is quite safe within my baggage at Castel Seir."

The King draped his arms about both our shoulders and started us toward the large tent where feasting had already begun. "Keane, I'll not have you and Nolan at odds with each other. I owe both of you very much, and I would have you be brothers in that concern instead of enemies in any other."

The Earl and I both laughed and accepted the King's truce. Despite the camaraderie and good feeling for me, I felt very ill at ease. I was not wholly ready to be befriended by the men who had destroyed my nation. Worse yet, that part of me that was—a part that basked in the fact that Sinjaria's conquerors found me praiseworthy—grew stronger with each moment and each laugh. The familiarity the King showed me both grated on me and made me seek more of it.

The King swept the Earl of Cadmar and me toward his place at a table on a raised dais toward the north end of the tent. Servants poured each of us a goblet of wine and the King raised his cup on high.

"I toast your bravery, and offer my thanks!" he shouted to the assembly. The nobles cheered and drank, then returned to their feasting on venison and wild pig. I heard incredible war stories shouted out around mouthfuls of meat and shook my head.

The King beckoned a servant over and instructed him to bring us food in the King's personal tent. The Earl, Count Patrick, and I followed the King out to his tent and found a court wizard there already tending to Duke Vidor's leg.

The wizard had cut away Vidor's pants and had washed the wound off with wine. Two slightly rounded lines of fang marks dotted the Duke's thigh top and side, and thin lines of blood traced from the deepest holes.

The Duke smiled bravely. "It hurts, but not as much as it did before I pried the goblin's jaws open."

I seated myself on a bench and a servant pulled my boots off. I ripped open my own pant legs and peeled off my hunting tunic. "At least Dhesiri have no venom."

The wizard nodded. "I will spell the leg numb for several days and help the healing speed up. You will be fine." He turned to deal with the King before he finished with the Duke, but Tirrell waved him off.

"Tend the Duke and then worry about Nolan and Patrick. I've no serious injuries."

The wizard did as he was commanded, enchanted the Duke's leg, then came to me. I winced as he washed my cuts off with wine. The wizard shook his head. "You do not need my healing arts, your cuts will not scar."

I nodded. "No, but I will need a new pair of boots and more clothes until I reach Seir."

The Grand Duke, who trailed in behind the servant carrying food and wine, joined the others in laughter. "You shall have whatever you need, Lord Nolan. And when we reach Castel Seir there will be banquets in your honor."

The King stood. "If my lords will excuse me, I will take Lord Nolan back and find him some appropriate attire. Please," he waved at the steaming platter of venison, "enjoy yourselves until we return." He walked to the back of the tent and held a flap open for me. Beyond I saw a smaller tent.

I preceded the King and sat in the chair he pointed to. It was a comfortable campaign chair made of three pieces that could be taken apart for easy storage or movement. The decoration on it was simple, yet highlighted with gold leaf to add an air of opulence to it. While it might have seemed ostentatious, I suspected the King paid no attention to its aesthetic value; he kept the chair around because it was practical.

The King let the flap drop and walked across the deep blue carpet to a battered old chest. He opened it, took a look at me, and selected a shirt and pair of pants. "They might be a bit large for you, as I have filled out over the years, but I think you will find them serviceable."

I ripped the rags from my legs and pulled the clothing on while the King walked to each corner of the tent and lit a lamp. When the last one was burning he drew his dagger and scraped one of the scratches on his leg until a drop of blood collected on the blade. He held the blade in the flame and suddenly a blood red curtain shot from one lamp to the next and surrounded us.

He smiled at me. "Now no one can overhear us."

I nodded, ignored the fierce itching on the back of my left hand and finished buttoning my new green tunic before I sat again. The King pulled another of the campaign chairs around and sat facing me.

"Nolan, I know you have been sent to protect me. I am most grateful that you arrived when you did. I also realize you may feel that what you did was merely in keeping with your orders, but I want to reward you."

I started to protest but he cut me off. "I'll not reward you for saving me, because I know your Master frowns on that sort of thing. Instead I want to acknowledge your bravery and to thank you for saving the others." He paused for a moment and I did not interrupt him. "In saving Count Patrick you prevented my uncle's heart from breaking. In fact you may have saved all Hamis because both our deaths would have put a devastated Fordel on the throne, and he would not have been able to rule."

I slumped back in the chair and closed my eyes. The King's words were easy to ignore, but the emotions woven through them pounded at me and crumbled walls I'd spent years building. The depth of his love for his uncle and cousin chipped away at the image of him I'd carved and polished since the day I'd left the farm.

Every step I took toward Talianna, with the image of my grandmother's blood-rune burning incandescently in my brain, helped me distill my grief into utter loathing for King Tirrell. Because of him, my country lay in ruins. Because of him, my family lay dead. He was a monster, and it was my duty to someday bring him to justice, return to him everything he'd given me, and take from him everything he'd stripped from me.

Even as I'd agreed to accept the assignment in my desire to avenge Marana, I'd known I'd not leave Hamis with King Tirrell on the throne. All I had to be was careless and I could accomplish my Talion mission along with my personal mission. And even if the *nekkeht* slew me, I'd die happily if I knew King Tirrell was dead before me.

But now my resolve to see him dead slowly dissipated. Once I'd thought him a coward who hid behind armies, yet in the warren he fought beside me and matched me stroke for stroke. I'd believed he was callous and uncaring but now, and in the warren when he sensed my fatigue and called me back, he showed concern for both family and an utter stranger. Twice he had put himself in danger to save me, something the King Tirrell that lurked in my imagination never would have done. He was highborn, and needed to acknowledge no peer within his realm, yet he accepted me, an untitled peasant from a rebellious nation, as though he thought our bloodlines of equal nobility and antiquity.

Try as I might to hug the promise I'd made to my dead grandmother so tightly it could not escape, it shrank away to nothing. What she had believed of King Tirrell might have been true of him in his early days—even up to the moment before he found himself trapped in a Dhesiri warren, but it was not true now. I had wished for the death of a phantom, a construct I'd cobbled together from painful memories and sinister stories. The fury and hatred in the blood-rune had animated it the way a *rhasa* soul animated a dead body. In very much that same way I realized that my image of Tirrell was no more real than a *nekkeht* was alive.

Knowing I had discovered the truth, and hating myself for it, I relinquished my grip on the vow. My only regret in doing so was the fading of my grandmother's image. I saw my mission with new eyes—mine instead of my grandmother's—and I decided that as long as I had life, I would do everything I could to insure King Tirrell would live.

I opened my eyes. "Please, I could name no reward you could grant. Saving the lives is more than enough reward for me. If you must reward someone, reward your cousin. His tracks led me to you."

The King rose and patted my shoulder. "As you wish, then, I will reward the Count. But please understand how indebted I am to you." He snuffed one of the lamps and the curtain curled away as if greasy smoke.

"Come, Lord Nolan, let us join the feasting for at least a

short time. If you are as tired as I am, you'll retire soon. And tomorrow you can join us and hunt the mountain leopard."

Wearily I levered myself to my feet. "Lead on, my king, your wish is my command."

In Hamis succession is strictly figured by order of birth, so both Kings and Queens can and do rule. Still, no child is acknowledged as heir until eighteen years of age. At that time the child is started on a monthlong series of rituals in preparation for coronation as the next ruler of Hamis.

King Tirrell's eldest child was his daughter, Zaria. In keeping with custom, she undertook a Dreamvigil during the first full Wolf Moon after her birthday. After a special meal, priests gave her a sacred Dreampillow, conducted her to the easternmost tower in Castel Seir—the Moon Tower—and locked her in for the night.

That night she dreamed of a mountain leopard, and the priests and sages rejoiced over this excellent omen. They immediately worked the animal into her coat of arms and people predicted great things because the reigns of all other Queens who'd dreamed of a mountain leopard during their Dreamvigil had been long and prosperous.

The King laughed as he explained all this as we set out that next morning. "She was not overjoyed at hearing the other Queens averaged seven children each, but she was pleased by the animal the goddess Shudath saw fit to visit her with."

I nodded and patted Wolf on the neck. He stamped and blew steam, impatient to be off, but we had to wait for Count Patrick and the Earl of Cadmar. The other hunters were not awake—most of them had not yet gotten up from the floor of the feast tent—and the four of us agreed an early hunt might well be for the best.

The other two joined us quickly enough and we set out from the camp. We'd decided to do without beaters because most of them were still unconscious and they'd not been very successful so far in the hunt. In addition Count Patrick recognized our general location from the Princess's description of her dream, so we knew the mountain leopard had to be close by.

Eager to track the cat, I rode in the lead on Wolf. Mountain leopards are known for their power and solitary habits; very few ever get taken by hunters. Unlike the leopards in the plains, this cat's coat is made up of large patches of brown fur bordered by the more common tan fur. In the lowlands the beast is called a clouded leopard and the pelt is very valuable.

Count Patrick directed us toward the nearer of the Twin Mountains and I agreed with his choice of hunting area. I'd flown over it the day before and had seen deer and antelope, which the cat is supposed to hunt, so it seemed a likely area to start. Very quickly Patrick pointed out an oddly shaped rock the Princess had mentioned seeing in her dream, and excitement rippled through our company.

The first sign we ran across was the half-eaten body of a fawn dragged up onto a narrow cliffside ledge. I reached down, pulled from the saddle quiver a small horse bow I'd borrowed from the Grand Duke's huntsman, and strung it. I tested the pull, then nocked an arrow. Though it was smaller than the recurve bows the Archers use, I knew it would certainly do the job at close quarters.

The others brought their bows to hand and nodded to me when they were ready to continue. I draped my reins loosely across Wolf's neck and urged him forward with gentle pressure from my knees. Wolf went another quarter of a mile, then stopped. His ears flattened back against his head. I raised my right hand, taking it from the bow, to signal the others to a halt. That was almost the last mistake I ever made.

I'd underestimated the strength of Wolf's training. He was terrified and wanted to bolt, but he did not. I wish he had, because the reason he wanted to bolt was the leopard crouched to spring from the rocks on my right.

Finding me a sitting target, cat screamed and leaped.

I did the only thing I could. I ducked forward and twisted myself out of the saddle, dumping myself to the ground. The cat sailed and slashed through the air, all screaming fangs and claws, and passed right through where I'd been sitting a second before. I landed flat on my back and tried to renock my arrow so I could shoot beneath Wolf at the cat.

The cat lay on the far side of my horse. She thrashed out her last moments in impotent, nervous fury. Three arrows stood crossed in her chest.

I slowed my breathing, rolled to my feet, and patted Wolf on the neck. His nostrils were flared and his eyes were broadly rimmed with white from the terror, but my reassurances calmed him. "Easy Wolf, it's dead." I turned to the Hamisians. "My thanks to whoever taught you to shoot."

They smiled and dismounted. They huddled around me and I knelt by the body. "All clean shots. Two got the heart the other the lungs." I winced as I rubbed her stomach. "These teats are full of milk. It looks like she's not weaned her litter yet."

No one took that news well, and Count Patrick looked positively tortured by it. Then something dawned on me. "She had enough food for another day or two in that fawn we spotted. I'll bet she attacked because we are near her lair. We must be close."

We spread out and hiked all over that mountainside looking for any hole or small cave the leopard could have used as a lair. The search took an hour, but I finally found the opening. It was a small cave, a slightly tighter squeeze than the first Dhesiri tunnel, but I managed to get inside and found one live kitten.

We brought the kitten and his dead mother back with us to the camp. That night we feasted again, and this time we all joined the other nobles in the large tent for the celebration.

Patrick's concern for the leopard kitten distracted him from the feasting. I watched the Count dip a finger into a bowl of mare's milk and offer it to the kitten so he could lap the liquid off. I marveled at the care he lavished upon the kitten and bristled when one brutish lord suggested the leopard would make good hunting when grown.

I struck out and flattened the lout with a roundhouse right to the jaw. Everyone else attributed my action to the wine, and the close call with the leopard earlier in the day. I let them believe that's why I'd hit him, but deep inside I knew the real reason behind my attack.

The cruel delight I'd seen in his eyes reminded me all too well of Ring.

Chapter Fourteen

NOVICE: BLOODED

The statues towered above me and looked down with sightless eyes like so many forgotten gods. I let Wolf pick his own path among them—he followed Ring's horse—because I was too awed by the stone giants gathered to oppose each other here in the middle of the Tuzist Valley to guide him. I'd never seen anything as magnificent in my life, and nothing quite so sad.

I spoke to the Justice riding before me. "What are they, Ring? Why are they here?"

I half expected him to demand I puzzle out their purpose for myself, but he didn't. In the half year I'd spent with him I noticed that ancient buildings and the sites of legendary battles held a sanctity for him that even dampened his hatred of me. It seemed to me as though Ring wished he could have been part of their history, instead of being stuck in time now.

He reined his horse to a stop. "These, novice, are the Guardians." He pointed south toward a city built of shining white marble like half the statues. "Down there is the city-state of Tuzi, and back over there," he turned and pointed to a northern city built with black basalt stones, "is Zist. The Guardians belong to both cities."

I frowned. "Why are the statues here? This valley's been peaceful since before the Shattering. What do they guard the cities from?"

Ring smiled. "Each other." He dug spurs into his horse's flanks and waved me to follow him. "I'll explain on that little hilltop."

On the hilltop, less than a quarter of a mile from where we had been before, we dismounted and I had enough perspective to see that most of the thirty-two statues stood arranged on a grid roughly defined by lines of wildflowers. I narrowed my eyes. "They almost look like chess pieces."

Again Ring smiled, then turned away from me and spoke as if addressing himself, the statues, as well as me. "You are correct in that observation, novice, because that is all they were intended to be, at first. But then, after the years, they became the Guardians."

With Ring's confirmation of my guess it became much easier for me to identify the various pieces. The white pieces showed a great deal of old Ellian influence in their design. The Emperor, the tallest piece, wore a simple circlet similar to the one on the King of Ell's brow. The Empress, a foot or two shorter than the Emperor, yet still taller than the Star in Talianna, had the broader face and higher cheekbones common to the Boucan Princesses often wed to Ellian nobles. The other pieces, from Lancers and High Priests down to Elites and Warriors, all had their left ears pierced to mark them as the Emperor's loyal servants.

The black pieces, on the other hand, were more individualized and drew on various Imperial provinces for their models. The warriors, for example, were all Daari with Spirit-lances and the Lancers were Imperianan heavy cavalry. The Emperor piece even resembled a couple of busts I'd seen of old Emperors, but I could not identify him by that alone.

Rather fittingly, and perhaps optimistically, the Empress was styled on the women of Sterlos—a nation that paid tribute to the Empire, but one the Empire never conquered.

"Tuzi controls the end of the valley with vast mineral deposits and Zist produces an abundance of food that it exports all over the Empire." Ring stared out at the statutes as if he was seeing them as they had been. "The two cities fought war after bloody war for control of the whole valley, but neither could mount a victory. After a year or two of unsuccessful campaigning the troops would withdraw and the cities would heal up until they had enough men to try again to conquer their neighbor."

Ring pointed at the black Emperor. "Emperor Clekan the Eleventh decided to put an end to this fighting because both cities were important to the Empire. He needed Tuzi's metal and Zist's grain. To prevent a war that could cut production of both, he summoned the leaders of both cities and carefully explained his solution to them.

"He told them ownership of the valley would fall to the city that could defeat the other in a game of chess. The cities were to build the pieces—the Emperor was specific about the sizes and colors—and announced there would be one move a month until the issue was decided."

Ring turned to me and smiled broadly. "He told the leaders there could be no war in the valley until the game was done, and he stationed Talions here to enforce his order. If one city attacked the other, the Talions were to join the defender and wipe out the attacker."

I spoke in a low whisper so I'd not destroy Ring's mood. "Why didn't the cities go out and hire master players?"

"They did, novice, they both did. It took three years to complete the pieces, and another two to prepare the field." He traced the rows of flowers outlining the grid with a finger. "All you can see now are a few of the flowers, but at one time each square on the board had a different flower on it, and tending the board to make sure your squares looked better than those planted by the other city became as fierce a competition as the game itself.

"The game was a classic. Both cities hired chess masters, and after an early decisive move by black the citizens of Zist threw their leader out and installed their master as the new ruler. It took five years for the game to reach this point, and that was over a thousand years ago."

The emotion in Ring's voice peeled away the years for me and I visualized the crowds of people surrounding the board as wizards moved the pieces on the board. Each move would come after a month of waiting and the anticipation had to be incredible. I could almost hear the hushed intake of breath as a piece stirred and drifted forward to supplant another.

Slowly I came back to reality and sadness gripped my heart. The pieces stood waiting for a game that might never end. Pieces driven from the board early lurked at the edges like ghosts watching to make sure their sacrifice was not wasted. A bird nesting in the mouth of the white Emperor took off, and with it all feeling of life fled the field.

"Why was the game never finished?" I took another look at the arrangement of the pieces. "I'm not that good a player, but it looks to me like black wins with the next move."

Ring turned and walked back to his horse. "Black does win in one move, and everyone knew it. Still there had been peace in the valley for ten long years, and no one looked forward to new wars. Zist's leader wrote to the Emperor and requested more time to consider his move."

Ring swung up into his saddle. "The Emperor gave him an unlimited time to think, and twenty years later the champion died without having made his move. In his tomb in Zist they have a board set up in this exact pattern, and a statue of him hunched over it so he can study the board for all eternity."

I smiled broadly. "That I'd like to see."

My enthusiasm hit Ring like a fist. His face closed and hardened. He turned forward in his saddle and Called. *"Come, novice, we have men to kill."*

We'd not been able to pursue Ahnj and Dabir after we found the burned farmhouse because an order came through for Ring to perform a mission off in Solnaria. The mission, which involved escorting a government minister from Solnaria to Thele for talks about the bandits that plagued the border between both nations, irritated Ring.

Ring complained that he got the mission because I rode with him. The journey certainly did take me places I'd not been before, and introduced me to court politics in Solnaria.

I found it very educational, while Ring found it boring and grew anxious to get back out hunting criminals.

Luckily, for Ring, Ahnj and Dabir managed to avoid capture. They robbed a few towns in Ditaan and Lacia but had not pulled a gang together to aid them by the time we cut across their trail upon our return from Solnaria. We saw them once, but they escaped by setting half a town on fire. Although it granted them a day's lead, Ring insisted on remaining until the last victim of the fire—a child—was uncovered in the ashes.

Many people in the town thought he did that out of the compassion for her parents, but I learned the truth after we left the town. I commented on how much the family felt in his debt for his efforts, but he snarled. "Didn't stay around for them, novice. I had to know exactly how many died in the fire so I can make them pay for it."

Ahnj and Dabir tried to escape us, but Ring was too good a tracker to be fooled by their desperate attempts at deception. We slowly gained on them and Ring took great delight in locating their half-hidden campsites. At least twice we actually got ahead of them and Ring set little irritating traps where he knew they'd settle down to spend the night.

"Why not just get them and be done with it?" I'd ask.

Ring would just narrow his eyes and let a sadistic smile curl across his face. "They're not finished paying, novice, for all the crimes they've done."

I hated that cruel side to Ring, but I'll admit I preferred having it directed at Ahnj and Dabir instead of me. Still, the trail we followed was fresh enough that I fully assumed this day would bring an end to Ring's game of cat and mouse with the two criminals.

Their trail headed almost directly east, and a local boy told us the only thing in that direction was a farm. We reached the farmhouse by early afternoon. We'd ridden through wheat fields since morning—the plants just reached our stirrups—but we saw no one tending the fields. We both assumed the worst: I hoped the farmer and his family would be unharmed while Ring hoped Ahnj and Dabir would be preoccupied.

The farm buildings stood in a small bowl-like depression centered amid the fields. Several large trees shaded the wood-and-stone house and two on the right held up a clothesline full of drying clothes. The yard in front of the house was dusty and two dozen chickens scratched through the dirt for any food they could find. The chicken coops and hog pens stood back off to the right behind the house, while the big old barn was set farther back and to the left.

A tired old plowhorse watched us from the corral adjoining the barn. A dog, his long winter coat shedding in patches, lay near the farmhouse door. He lifted his head and looked at us with a low growl rumbling from his throat. He decided we were not worth the trouble and dropped back to sleep.

Ring and I stopped our horses near the well in front of and to the left of the house. A thatched roof shaded a round rock base and was held in place by two stout oaken pillars. A wooden bucket hung from a rope threaded through a rusted pulley and a nail held a ladle up on one of the posts. A medium-sized, cast-iron bell was screwed to the post on the other side of the well, the side closest to the house. A rawhide thong lazily drifted on the wind beneath the bell's clapper.

Ring pulled the bellcord once. The bell rang loud and mournfully; not at all the happy sound of a bell calling the family to dinner. The sharp, explosive peal demanded immediate attention. Somehow Ring had Called with the bell.

The farmhouse door opened slowly and the farmer stepped out cautiously. He pulled the door shut behind him without looking back or speaking to anyone inside. The farmer took a kerchief from his belt and wiped it across his forehead. He smiled weakly.

Because I'd been raised on a farm everything warned me the tranquility I saw was a fraud. There was no way the windows should have been empty of people staring out at the two Talions in the front yard. The clothes on the line told me the family had at least five people in it, and the idea that none of them had work to be done was mad. Clearly Ahnj and Dabir had the family hostage inside.

I looked over at Ring to communicate this fact to him, but Ring ignored me. He sat and stared at the farmer. More sweat poured out onto the farmer's brow and for a moment it looked as though he was melting under the harshness of Ring's gaze.

The farmer forced a smile onto his face. "Do you need

something, my lords?" He walked to the well and kept it between him and us. "Water, perhaps?"

Ring waited. I watched the farmer's hands tremble as he lowered the bucket into the well. Ring's horse stamped and shifted, yet Ring did nothing but stare at the farmer. Then, as the farmer hauled the brimming bucket back up, Ring answered his question in a low, even voice. "Yes, farmer, water."

The farmer's face showed the doom he felt, and his relief at the gentle stay of execution Ring granted him. The farmer knew what we wanted. He could feel the pressure, and it slowly crushed him. If Ring asked for information, the farmer would deny ever having seen or heard of anyone and we would leave. If we did not ask for information, we would stay and all that while the pressure would increase.

Ring took the ladle, dipped out water, and shifted his gaze to the house. He drank, but never took his eyes off the front door. The farmer's eyes darted between Ring's face and the door. Ring returned the ladle to the bucket. The farmer unfastened the rope and brought the bucket to me.

I took the ladle and drank. The cool water washed the trail dust from my throat. I looked down into the farmer's face and smiled as reassuringly as I could. His expression eased. "Thank you, the water is good."

"We are looking for two men."

The farmer spun, faltered, and spilled some water. "Beg pardon?"

Ring stared at the door as if he could see through it. "Are you alone here?"

The farmer stared at Ring and trembled. Terror locked his jaw and stole any words he might have offered in answer.

"Farmer, you have a family?"

"Y-yes. My wife and her mother."

"No children?" Ring's voice mocked the man.

"Two, a boy and a girl." The farmer's face eased. The answers to those questions came easily. For a moment he thought he might survive this ordeal.

Ring disabused him of that notion. "They are in the house?"

"Yes, no!" The farmer stiffened and agony tore jagged lines across his face.

"Which is it, farmer? Are they inside or not?"

The farmer hesitated, then steeled himself for the worst. "They went into Tuzi this morning to trade for things we need." Doom swallowed him whole because he'd just lied to a Talion, and only now noticed we'd come from the direction of the Tuzist Valley.

Ring raised his voice. "We seek two murderers. They are men in form, but are cowards in spirit. We will find them. Have you seen them?"

The farmer shook his head violently. "No, no one. We've seen no one for weeks. Beside you, that is."

Ring shifted his stare to the farmer and froze him on the spot. Ring gathered himself as if a cat ready to pounce. "You would not lie to us."

"No, no, no lie. We've seen no one."

Ring urged his horse forward. He made straight for the door.

Blood drained from the farmer's face. His knees quivered and almost gave way. The bucket splashed to the ground and soaked the farmer's homespun trousers. He stared at Ring's back, flexed his hands, then looked over at a scythe leaning against the house.

I reined my horse between the farmer and the scythe. "Talion, let us leave. They elude us."

Ring rode forward, deaf to my words.

"Talion, thou dost slay his blood."

Ring snapped his head around at the combined High Tal and Call. Pure fury flowed through his eyes. His stare should have wilted me, but my hatred for him and my fear for the farmer's family shielded me from his rage. I held his stare for long enough to convince him I was not afraid of him, then turned to the farmer.

"What is your name?"

"Ben."

"Don't mind my partner, Ben. He's ra Temur and has never taken a good look at a real stone house. Get him into a city, a real city, and he wanders around in a trance." I dismounted and scooped up the bucket. "Do you mind if I water my horse? We've a long way yet to ride today."

I draped an arm across Ben's shoulders and steered him

toward the well, and away from the scythe. "I grew up on a farm myself, Ben. We raised grain like you do."

Ben gave no sign he heard me. He tied the bucket back onto the rope and lowered it into the well.

He drew it back up again and I directed Wolf's muzzle to it. I smiled at the farmer and scratched Wolf between the eyes. It was time to gamble and I hoped Ben would relax enough to see what I was doing, then play along.

"I can remember the good things and, boy, can I remember the bad. You ever have trouble with glutton flies?"

I saw something flash through his eyes, and I hoped he'd stay with me long enough to save his family. Glutton flies are a staple of farm folklore. They are a mythical insect that's blamed for eating everything whenever there is a poor harvest or supplies run out too fast.

I reached across Wolf's muzzle and laid a friendly hand on Ben's shoulder. "Yes, I remember those glutton flies. Had a farm in Sinjaria, my family did, and the glutton flies we got there were the nasty ones, all green with four wings. You know the type I mean." I smiled confidently.

Ben's eyes narrowed and he nodded as if he were in a trance.

I continued. "Bad as they are in the field, have you ever had them in the house? I can remember once we had three swarms in the house. Have you ever had that? What's the most you've had in the house?"

Ben closed his eyes and his lips moved silently, undoubtedly in prayer. "Two."

I smiled, let loose a cautious sigh, and squeezed his shoulder. "Then you've never had it bad. Two swarms is no problem. Have you ever had them in the barn? They go there at night sometimes."

"No, only the house." His voice still was nervous, but the answers came easier as he realized what I was asking. "Horse-flies in the barn, though."

"The glutton flies we had only had small stingers." I dropped a hand to my dagger. "How about you?"

"One swarm is mixed, long and short stingers. The other only short."

I laughed. "I wouldn't worry about them. I've heard they

often pass without causing any real harm, especially at this time of year."

Ben nodded, a weak smile returning to his face. "That's what I've heard, once the weather changes and everything is clear."

"Oh, good. Then you'll have no problem." I pulled Wolf's head from the bucket and swung up into the saddle. "We'll be going. Good luck, Ben. Thanks for the water."

I reined Wolf around and virtually forced Ring to leave the farmhouse. We rode further east, then cut back down into a gully that ran north for a bit, then headed west. We got a mile from the house before Ring spoke.

"Talion I am wont to slay thee."

I reined Wolf to a stop and turned in my saddle to face Ring. "And after me you'll go back, get Ben's family killed, then take our friends?"

Ring stiffened at my tone and words. "Beware, novice, you do not have Lord Hansur or the Master to make sure you win where you should have lost out here!"

Rage flashed through me like lightning and I vaulted from Wolf's saddle with liquid ease. "Now, Ring, right now. You've hated me since the beginning, and I never knew why. Now I've figured it out. Get down and I'll show you I've earned everything I've gotten."

Ring's face softened with astonishment. "You've only now realized why I loathe you? I'd not have you wondering about such an important thing. Let me explain it to you carefully, novice. Since the first day you came to Talianna you've been Hansur's darling and the Master's pet. Without their bending the rules you'd never have gotten even this far."

Words raced through my mind and caught in my throat. I'd struggled for everything I'd gotten—the Master said so himself at our first meeting—yet Ring so easily stripped it all away from me through an acerbic slander tossed off with casual recklessness. *Am I a fraud?* shot through my mind like a hawk stooping on insecurities still hidden deep inside me.

Ring pressed his attack before I had any chance to marshal a defense. "I've known of you from the beginning. Nolan, the boy who walked a thousand leagues. Nolan, the boy who defied Lancers and who always tried harder than anyone else. Nolan, the boy who believed he could become a Justice."

Ring spat at me. "There you were wrong, as you have been so many times this year. No one can become a Justice, it is a job one is born to."

I shook my head and scattered all my doubts. "No, becoming a Justice is not a birthright, it's an honor to be earned."

"You are wrong, novice!" Ring's nostrils flared and his eyes grew wide. He jabbed his own chest with the thumb of his right hand. "My father was a Justice. He died when I was five. He was killed in the line of duty, but I grew up with a tradition. I know what it means to be a Justice. It was bred into me. I was destined to become a Justice."

"Oh, and that breeding makes you a better Justice than I am. I don't think so." I pointed back toward the farmhouse. "What were you trying to accomplish back there?"

"Justice." Ring's eyes glazed for a second. "Ahnj and Dabir could hear us. They were scared. They knew the terror their victims did. That is just a small dose of the justice they deserve."

I shook my head violently. "No, Ring, that's torture. You tortured them, and in doing so you tortured Ben and his family. Ahnj and Dabir were waiting in there with his wife and children, ready to hold them hostage if you entered the house."

"But I never planned to enter the house."

"You knew that, they did not. I didn't know it."

Ring's haughty grin came back to his face. "So you, a novice, decide to step in and help me. You Called me, shamed me, there, in front of the farmer."

"Ben, his name is Ben." I slammed my right fist into my left palm in frustration.

"What does it matter? We are not concerned with him."

I shook my head slowly. I was tired of the fighting and sad there was any reason for it to take place. "Yes we are. Ben is the reason we are here. He is the reason we do what we do. Ben and those like him are *all* that matters."

Ring chuckled lightly and silently. His shoulders rose and fell gently as he shook his head at me. He decided to humor me. "And talking with him about farm pests helped him?"

"No." I pleaded for his understanding. "He was dying

inside with each of your questions. I had to try something, so I gambled, and that gamble helped him. And it helped us."

"How did it do that, novice?" His voice took on the same patronizing and questioning tone as a teacher's voice does when he braces for an improbable and fanciful explanation from a student.

I sighed and turned back toward Wolf. "One of the murderers is armed with sword and dagger, but the other only has a dagger. They told him they would move on without harming anyone once we were gone and they have horses in the barn. I imagine they will head back to the valley and try to lose themselves in Tuzi or Zist."

"How?" He narrowed his eyes and regarded me suspiciously. "How do you know this?"

I hauled myself up into Wolf's saddle. "There are no such things as glutton flies. He realized I was asking about Ahnj and Dabir." Ring's face still was a mask of puzzled disbelief. "Ben was more afraid for his family than he was afraid of you. He felt trapped and I gave him a way out." I started Wolf off down the gully. "I'll wait for them among the Guardians."

Ring said nothing. He sat there and stared off into the distance. His body sagged a bit as if the doctrines he'd used to support himself all these years had crumbled just ever so slightly. Then, before I could ride out of sight, he straightened, caught up, and led the way to the valley.

Ahnj was the one with both sword and dagger. Both men rode into the valley easily, as if they didn't have a care in the world on a path that would bring them right through the Guardians on the way to Tuzi.

Ring rode from behind a black Lancer Guardian onto the road before them and stopped. He raised his right hand and showed them the Skull. "You are criminals and outlaws. I demand you surrender or I will kill you." His words were precise and clipped off; they begged for either man to do something stupid.

Dabir jerked the reins of his gray mare and cut off the road to skirt the Guardians on his way to Tuzi. I let fly with a sling-stone and it smashed him in the spine. He arched his back in pain and rolled from the saddle. He hit the ground, tumbled, and groggily rose to his hands and knees.

Ahnj watched Ring summon his *tsincaat* and turned his horse toward Zist. Ring directed me to follow Ahnj while he leaped from the saddle and stalked toward Dabir. The Insalian had struggled to his feet and, despite the fall he'd taken, crouched in anticipation. He dwarfed Ring but the *tsincaat* dwarfed Dabir's dagger.

I spurred Wolf and he shot forward like an arrow from a longbow after Ahnj. I rode a zigzag course through the Guardians—with blurred glimpses of Ahnj flashing between them—but Wolf ran like the wind and actually gained on the outlaw. I put another stone in my sling, whirled it, and, when I broke from the statues, slung it at him.

I missed Ahnj, but hit his horse behind the right ear. The horse ducked its head and dug its front hooves into the earth. Ahnj vaulted high out of the saddle and crashed to the ground in a tangle of thornbushes, but he rolled up ready for me.

I leaped from the saddle and drew my sword. "Surrender, Ahnj."

Ahnj scowled. His thick black beard soaked up the blood from a dozen crisscross thorn scratches raked across his face. His clothes were full of little holes, and pieces of bush still hung from his clothing. "You are a child. I would never surrender to a mere child."

I swallowed hard. "I don't want to kill you."

He shrugged. "Then I will kill you." His words were spoken as if casual conversation, but they shot icy fingers through my stomach. He stood no taller than me, but he outweighed me by at least thirty pounds. His arms were certainly thicker than mine, but in the tattered robe he wore I could not really tell how much of his size was fat versus muscle. Then he moved, and I realized he carried little fat on his body.

I hung back, which was uncharacteristic of me, because this was the first fight I'd ever had where my foe wanted to kill me. All the other fights during my training were practice. I might be ruled dead because of a good blow, but armor protected me and I got up after the match. Here there was no appeal to a judge, and no penalty for a foul blow struck.

Ahnj attacked savagely and tried, quickly, to finish me so he could escape. He windmilled sweeping cuts at me and had my training not taken over immediately, he would have killed me in short order. I sidestepped the first blows, blocked a few more, and parried the last.

Ahnj's movement fell into a pattern, two high blows and one lower, and that pattern marked him as a poor fighter. I sensed he was unconscious of the repetition and already my mind ran through a number of moves I could make that would use this weakness against him. I could not count on his continuing it, but I knew I could use it to kill him if it appeared again.

His next cut came high. I kept my blade in a low guard and stepped to my left to avoid it. Ahnj raised his sword again and rained it down toward my right shoulder. I blocked the cut high to my right, stepped forward, and slipped my right leg behind his right leg. I hit him with my right shoulder and toppled him over. He fell, sprawled out on his back, and my sword stood poised above my head, to chop through his chest.

My eyes met his and I read the terror there. I hesitated, for just a heartbeat, then struck, but Ahnj had rolled from beneath the blow.

"Well played boy, but the sword's got to stick if the blow is to kill." He tried to make the words light, but his fear betrayed him. He dropped into a defensive posture and waved me on with his open left hand.

I moved forward and tried to consciously recall all the varied sequences of cut, parry, and riposte I'd been drilled in for the last six years, but nothing came to mind. Still my body remembered the training and attacked. I released my thoughts and just flowed into my body's rhythms.

The fight ended sooner than I imagined it ever could. Ahnj parried a feint and riposted while my blade hung up in one of his flowing sleeves. His sword passed between my sword arm and body, then started up to slit the artery in my armpit. I spun back and away from him, raising my arm just quickly enough to avoid his attack, then launched forward and continued the spin.

I'd moved past his flank so, as I spun and he whirled back into sight, my sword bit into his back and tore through his chest. My sweeping slash carried the blade free and sprayed blood all over the white Empress. Ahnj reeled away from the blow and fell heavily to the ground.

I continued the spin, dropped to my knees next to the dying bandit, and vomited.

Ring dealt with the guardsmen from Tuzi and, mercifully, kept them away from me. I could not hear whatever explanation he might have given for me, and I did not care. I felt as if one of the Guardians had reached out and crushed my insides in punishment for defiling the valley.

As a game, novices often spun wild tales about what it would be like to actually kill someone. All the stories were heroic tales about a titanic battle where the novice was all that stood between an evil murderer and a virtuous princess, or was the last hope to defeat an abomination set on destroying the world. In those stories killing was good and right. The odds were always against the novice, but virtue, training, and a valiant heart always won out in the end.

Never did I imagine I'd kill a poorly trained bandit amid a field of wildflowers. The scent of wild roses drifted up to me where I sat on a black Elite's base. I wondered how long it would be before I could smell a rose and not think of Ahnj's death.

Ring rode up and brought Wolf with him. He jerked his head toward the receding guardsmen and their grisly burdens. He wore a self-satisfied smirk on his face. "I told them you had been ill for days. It would not do for them to think a Talion weak."

My dry lips tasted bitter. I licked them with a thick tongue. "They should never think a Talion human."

Ring nodded. "Now you begin to see. Perhaps I judged you too harshly before. Now you're a man, a Talion in everything but formal declaration. This kill should have opened your eyes."

I snorted. "It did."

Ring misread my words and smiled broadly. "Now you see that you have to be as death itself. You have to inspire fear, for without it no one will obey you. They will refuse to aid you." Ring's face lit up and his lust for terror twisted his features into a mask of warped ecstasy. "We can forget what happened earlier."

I shook my head slowly despite the waves of nausea the motion produced. "No. I'll never forget anything about today."

Ring looked beyond me, toward where he'd disarmed Dabir with a quick parry and sucked the soul out of a screaming man. "Perhaps you are right. If you forget the past you might slip back into it."

I laughed gently. The laugh had a note of insanity in it, and that caught Ring like a gig spearing a frog. "You don't understand it, do you?"

Ring stiffened and stared at me.

"That kill changed me, just like this afternoon. I don't like killing, and I don't like terrifying people." I searched for comprehension in Ring's face, but it had less life in it than any of the Guardians. "I don't want everyone to fear me."

"Then you'll never be a Justice." Ring pronounced the words with the same finality he'd used when passing sentence on Dabir.

I pushed myself off the Elite's base and dropped to the ground. "If killing and scaring others is all there is to being a Justice, I guess you're right. But I don't think you are, and I'm going to be a different type of Justice."

Ring stabbed a finger at me. "There is no other way."

I balled my fists and snarled at him. "Yes, there is." I pointed east toward Ben's farm. "I showed you that today. I know his name, I understand his fears, and I don't have to be something he is afraid of. I want people like Ben to know I'll be there when they need someone to get rid of Ahnj or Dabir."

Ring started to reply but I waved his words away and continued. "I've seen it, I've seen what you do to people. I've seen the lightning bolts of fear jolting through those we meet. People turn away when they see us, even the lawful *who should have nothing to fear*! Everyone stops and asks 'Are they here for me?' whether they have cause for it or not. You may enjoy that. Their fear may sustain you, feed you, make you feel important, but it revolts me. We are here to protect those people. They should not be afraid of us."

I looked up at his silhouette against the pink and purple twilight sky. "Perhaps you want to keep everyone back because you're scared. Your father was killed by someone or something he met out here. I'm sorry about that, and I know how much that hurts, but it's over. Perhaps you feel if his killer had been properly terrified he wouldn't have attacked your father. I don't know." I held both hands up, then crossed my arms and hugged them around my chest. "But maybe, just maybe your father pushed his killer too far, drove him like you drove Ahnj and Dabir, then his killer struck back and overwhelmed your father because of his panic."

I swung up into Wolf's saddle and started east.

Ring's nostrils flared. "You cannot leave. Your Journey is not over."

I shook my head and stopped trying to explain myself to Ring. "No, my Journey is not over, but the portion of it I'm spending with you is. There is nothing more you can teach me."

"You'll never be a Justice!" Ring's shout sounded distant and small as if he was lost and screaming from deep inside himself.

I turned to Ring for the last time. "If I gave up, if I became just like you, I'd still not be a Justice."

Chapter Fifteen

TALION: ENTENTE

The journey to the Hamisian capital, Seir, took two days. We set a deliberately slow pace expressly for the people along the route. Word spread quickly that the mountain leopard had been taken, and the peasants wanted to see the nobles returning triumphant to the capital.

We stopped at every village on the Kings' Road and gratefully accepted the simple gifts of bread and wine offered to us. I was more than pleased to see the King take only one symbolic loaf and a solitary cup of wine from the peasants, then offer the thanks of his whole company for their generosity. His action forestalled his entourage from descending on each village like a plague of locusts and eating everything in sight.

The people's devotion to their monarch was painfully plain to see on their faces when they saw him or reached out to touch him. More than one daub-and-wattle house had been painted to resemble the mountain leopard's pelt, and legion were the children held high by parents so the King could touch a hand or forehead. Everywhere we traveled the adoring crowds shouted prayers to Shudath for the health, prosperity, and longevity of the King and his children.

At one time such displays would have revolted me. These were the people who swelled the ranks of his army when Hamisian troops marched into Sinjaria. I should have hated them, but I found my enmity directed more to the shadowy nobles who plotted to kill the King and, once they'd martyred him, use his memory to incite the people and lead them on another war of conquest.

I turned in my saddle to watch noble faces and tried to imagine who wanted the King dead, but before I could select a likely culprit, Grand Duke Fordel edged his horse in beside me and cleared his throat. "Lord Nolan, a moment of your time, if I might?"

I nodded easily. I liked the older man, and respected him for shaming the other nobles into assaulting the warren. I'd been told by the Grand Duke's personal body servant that after I disappeared into the hole the Grand Duke reviled the nobles for their cowardice. "And what will you answer when asked, 'Where were you when our King was in peril!?'" the servant reported his master as shouting. Then the Grand Duke drew his own dagger and leaped into the hole. Slowly the nobles followed him and came to our rescue.

"Lord Nolan," he began timidly, "the accounts are unclear as to what part my son played in my nephew's rescue. If I could trouble you to recount it from your point of view . . ."

I read the desire in his eyes to know his son was indeed brave and courageous. His love for Patrick, offered freely even though he did not fully understand his son, was more than obvious. Gladly I assured him that without Patrick's quick thinking and sword skill the King would now be in the Mother-Queen's belly.

At tale's end the Grand Duke slipped back in the procession, and only approached me once more for clarification on a few points. By the time I answered all his questions the caravan reached a perfect spot to camp. Again Fordel thanked me, then took his leave to organize the camp.

I quickly found Count Patrick and helped him and his servants erect his pavilion. Earlier Patrick learned I had no servants or tent, and despite my assurances that I was quite content to sleep beneath the stars between some blankets, he insisted I share his tent. He read my reluctance and suggested it would be best for "my" leopard, so I surrendered and accepted his offer.

I tossed my blankets on a wood and canvas cot, then turned to Patrick. "By the way, I've forgotten to return this to you." I reached into the pouch of slingstones on my belt and fished out the gold ring that led me in the right direction within the warren. I held it out and dropped it into his hand.

Count Patrick beamed, wiped it on his tunic, and worked it onto his right ring finger. "You must know, Nolan, I thought dropping this ring was the last act I would ever perform in this life." He sat on his cot, reached over to lift the kitten into his lap, and scratched him behind an ear.

I lay back on my cot and laughed. "Imagine my surprise at finding jewelry in a Dhesiri tunnel. Using your spurs to make tracks was brilliant."

The Count's reply was cut off by a servant bringing in a bowl of mare's milk. He set it down and Patrick dipped a finger into it. He raised the finger to the cat's mouth and the kitten licked. Patrick then set the kitten down and let him lap the milk up. His hands free, he pulled a dulcimer into his lap and hammered out a few chords.

"Has my father been after you to tell him everything about the battle?" He played a martial tune with a proper marching rhythm to it. He devoted more concentration to his song than to my reply.

I nodded and laughed silently when he shook his head with resignation. "He asked, I told him you saved the King."

The song shifted to the Hamisian anthem and he shrugged. "I had no choice. Until Zaria is crowned, I am in line for the throne."

I frowned sat forward and propped myself up on my elbows. "You sound as if that is a problem. You do not want the throne?"

The music collapsed into a sour clash of notes. Patrick

looked up in surprise at me and rested a hand on the dulcimer's strings to quiet them. "Take the throne and have to deal with people at court?" He shook his head vehemently. "Not if I can avoid it! I'd rather serve as Ambassador to the Dhesiri Mother-Queen than sit on the throne." Then he paused and looked at me with narrowed eyes. "Of course you do not really know what life at court is like, do you? I mean to say I understand you have not long been acknowledged a noble."

I shook my head and sighed. "I have been called a bastard many times, but that has to be the most polite phrasing I've ever heard." We both laughed. "However, your observation is correct. I have not spent a great deal of time at court."

Count Patrick settled back, picked up the hammers, and began to play again. "There are two types of people at court." A high and low note echoed from the dulcimer to represent each type. "The first comes to ask the King for favors," high note, "the second comes to demand them." He punctuated the second point in his lesson with a low, ominous note. "And both types form alliances or conspiracies to get what they want when they want it." Again the dulcimer produced a harsh din of contrasting notes.

The leopard kitten rolled over on his back, snarled at the sound, and batted at a thread hanging from Patrick's pants. We both laughed.

"So, Count Patrick, I take it you try to avoid both sets of people?" The Count's remarks, and my personal impression of him, removed him from my list of possible masterminds plotting to kill the King. In addition to his disgust with courtiers, if he desired the throne he'd have arranged his cousin's death well before the coronation to avoid any regency he could not control. But, while not a suspect, he had knowledge of the court and individuals that could help me narrow the field, and would increase my chances for success.

The Count nodded his head and concentrated on a simple tune that carried different lyrics in a half-dozen nations. "You have it right, I avoid court as much as possible. Avoiding the conspiracies, on the other hand, is more difficult." He looked up at me with a serious expression on his face. "Conspirators assume that if you are not with them, you are a sworn enemy."

I paused and reached down for the kitten. The beast snarled and curled up in my hands. He sank sharp teeth into my thumb and tried to gnaw it off, but I felt no pain—actually it tickled. "So are there so many conspiracies that you can't avoid them all?"

The Count smiled. "You will find out for yourself, Lord Nolan. Of course, it is possible that you already belong to the Sinjarian group that wants to see Duke Vidor wed Princess Zaria and win freedom for his nation."

"Not me. You must remember I'm newly come to my station."

"Nolan, that will make no difference to the schemers." He thought for a moment, then smiled. "You saved the King's life so you have a certain influence with him. You could be advanced by the Sinjarian faction so the King would repay his debt to you with your homeland's sovereignty. Or"—he stopped playing and rubbed his chin with his left hand—"Keane could win your support and use you as an example of a loyal Sinjarian subject to the Crown."

I stroked the kitten's fur and he slowly dropped off to sleep. I could feel his heart beating beneath my hand and I smiled unconsciously.

"Have I found you out, Nolan?"

Patrick's question brought me back to reality. "No, I'm sorry to disappoint you, but I'm not part of anything. And," I added sincerely, "I'd like to void any entanglements."

The flame-haired noble smiled. "If you want to do that, seriously, I would be more than glad to have you as company. A day or two being seen wandering about with me and everyone will know you are beyond their ability to manipulate." He started to play again as I nodded in agreement. "It will not make the plotters happy, but they will live despite their discomfort."

"Joining them is the only thing that pleases them?"

The Count wrinkled his nose with distaste. "No, you could do what Duke Vidor does, if you had his position."

I frowned and shook my head. "What is his method for dealing with the courtiers?"

Patrick sighed and hammered out a complex tune where each hand had a different rhythm and key. "He curries favor with each by promising to be faithful to all their demands. I think he sees it as a game, and it is common knowledge that he plays everyone off against each other. So, while everyone has a plan to work with him if he supports them, most ignore him and treat him like the fop he is."

The mention of Vidor seemed to anger Patrick, and his tune picked up volume and tempo while he spoke, so I let him calm himself before I spoke again. "Duke Vidor plays the weathercock and favors the direction of the strongest storm on the horizon."

Count Patrick nodded and his playing returned to a simpler tune. "I assume you have gathered I do not like the Duke?"

I nodded slightly. "I had noticed something passing between you back in the warren, and I don't think I've seen you speak to him since we won our way back to the surface."

Patrick smiled. "It is not that I hate him, because I do not, really. It is more that I pity him because he believes, or dreams more correctly, of getting more power than he has. He is, in reality, a newer breed of ulSinjaria. He has no power or control, only a title and the desire to have more than that."

"That was not pity I heard when you chided him about wanting to speak with the Dhesiri Queen." I gently lifted the sleeping cat from my lap, placed him on the cot behind me, and leaned forward. I suspected Patrick would tell me the tale behind their rivalry, but I also sensed he wanted the story kept quiet. My shoulder burned in sympathy.

Patrick set the dulcimer aside and leaned toward me. "When Vidor arrived in Seir he was all of fifteen years old, but full of pride and anger. I am four years his senior, but a Count is an inferior rank in peerage. He demanded preferential placement to me in ceremonies of state, and while I did not care, my cousin absolutely forebade it.

"Vidor protested, 'But I am a Duke, my lord,' and my cousin replied, 'You may choose to stand below my cousin by your choice, Duke Vidor, or you *will* stand below him by my order.'

"The Duke chose to stand below me on his own."

I chuckled and sat back. "I will remember that, my Lord Count."

Patrick fixed me with a more serious look. "Then remember this as well, my Lord Nolan. The difference between the warren and court is that in the warren you know who your enemies are."

By noon of the next day we rode to within four miles of the capital just as the rain started to pour. The drops came thick and heavy. They reduced the road to a muddy flood and dampened everyone's spirits—except those of the peasants who still lined the road to watch us pass.

Count Patrick rode up alongside me. The leopard kitten peeked out from his cloak. "The rain will be no good for this beastie so I thought you and I should ride ahead to the Castel and get him to drier quarters." He looked back toward the King. "My cousin needed a messenger sent to the Castel to ready your rooms so I volunteered. You get to ride as my guard."

I nodded and we let our horses canter off toward the capital. A mile or two away from the caravan the rain slackened and died, but we saw no reason to slow our ride. We rode over the last rise, the Seir Valley rim, before descending into the valley itself, and there I got my first look at the Hamisian capital.

The valley started narrow where we halted at its western end, and spread out as it sloped down to the Runt Sea. Wooded stands of pine and maple and bright stone or wood buildings formed a patchwork covering the mountainsides that defined the valley. The woodlands divided the city into definite wards and, in that way, served both utilitarian and aesthetic services.

A thin canopy of clouds hung above the valley. Lances of sunlight filtered between dark thunderheads and brilliantly illuminated whole buildings and districts in the city. High on the southern valley wall, pinned in place by a sunbeam, stood Castel Seir.

The Castel walls were larger than the Siegewall in Talianna and built of seven towers with thick granite walls running between them. The keep they enclosed—a tall building built into the moutainside—had a tower in each of the four corners and a slate gray roof. It was built of white marble and reflected the sunlight enough to dazzle my eyes. As if a giant squatting amid a toy village, the Castel rose impressively up from the buildings gathered below it.

Even Patrick paused for a moment before riding into the valley. "It'll take your breath away more than once, my friend."

We descended into the valley and I followed Patrick, riding hard on his heels up the winding causeway to the castel's entrance. He identified himself to the guards and vouched for me. We rode across the cobbled courtyard to the stable and turned our horses over to the stableboys. Outside the stable a balding little man waited for us.

"Ah, Halsted, this is Lord Nolan ra Yotan." At Patrick's introduction the man bowed his head to me, and I to him. We moved across the courtyard as Patrick spoke and headed directly for the keep. Patrick fished the kitten from beneath his cloak and held him out. "And this is his cat."

Halsted took the kitten gingerly and cradled him snugly to his chest. The kitten immediately bit a finger but Halsted only reacted with a smile.

Patrick continued. "King Tirrell wants Lord Nolan housed in the Wolf Tower suite. Yes, I know the Earl of Cadmar and his brood are there, but this man saved the King's life so the Earl himself insisted upon the change. How could the King show him less courtesy? Send two boys down to get our things and select one of them as Lord Nolan's personal servant because he brought no staff with him."

Patrick stopped inside the vaulted entrance hallway of the keep. Somehow Halsted had managed to understand all the instructions and busily dispatched other servants to complete them. Patrick watched him leave and smiled. "Actually, had my cousin died, I think Halsted could have kept the kingdom running all by himself."

Count Patrick unfastened his cloak and tossed it toward a youth waiting behind him. "There is only one way to get the wet cold out of your bones," the Count announced, "wet heat."

The servant relieved me of my cloak and I followed Patrick back toward the southern corner of the keep. At the base of the Wolf Tower he opened a door; we descended a curved stairway and emerged deep within the castel's foundation. The map I'd seen of Castel Seir noted this level existed, but contained little or no information about it. That puzzled me, because Patrick acted as if he was about to show me a state secret, yet the lack of description on the Talions' map suggested that whatever lay down here had no military value whatsoever.

Patrick yanked open an ironbound oak door and a cloud of steam rolled into the hallway. He pulled me into the room quickly and hastily shut the door behind us. "Behold, Lord Nolan, this is my court."

We stood in a vast cavern that looked, on most of the walls and ceiling, as if it had not been modified by the hand of man. The torches ringing it cast flickering shadows into half-hidden alcoves cut into the walls, but did little to dispel the snug, warm murkiness of the chamber. For the most part sand covered the floor except at the doorway, just beyond a trough I guessed was meant for washing feet off, where smooth wood heralded the return to the normal world out-side the door.

The steam came from two of the three pools I could see. Heavy curtains cut off two other pools—one hot and one cold—from view. The curtains hung from a rope running the length of the room and provided privacy for the person soaking and splashing beyond them. Patrick indicated we should be quiet and walked to an alcove to remove his clothes. I passed beyond him, sat in the next alcove, and disrobed.

By the time I'd doffed my clothes, Patrick had already sunk himself up to his neck in the nearest steaming pool. I suspected he was used to the heat so I slipped into it care-fully, and was glad I did. It was hot at first, but my body quickly got used to it and I settled back against the naturally smooth sides of the basin.

After twenty minutes of peaceful soaking that reminded me of the Shar Chamber in Talianna, I broke the silence. "You were right, the wet heat has soaked the rain chill right out of my bones." I held my hands up and looked around the room. "I envy you your throne room."

Genuinely pleased, Patrick smiled a big grin. "I spend so much time down here my father believes I have boiled any and all sense from my head. That belief was behind his need for you to reassure him I am really a man in the martial con-text he understands."

"At least, my Lord Count, your father is concerned for

you. To mine I was nothing more than a footnote in an auto-biography." I lowered myself completely underwater to cut myself off from Patrick's hearty laughter. The warm water enfolded me like a blanket and relaxed saddle-sore muscles. Torchlight sparkled on the water's surface and danced like stars in a summer-night sky. I could have stayed below forever had not my lungs protested and demanded a return to more hospitable an element.

I surfaced to discover Patrick kissing a sheet-swathed woman. Her dusky skin, not quite black enough to mark her a full-blooded Sterlosian, did suggest she had kin from that nation. Her unbound, jet-black hair hung just above her shoulders in a style more common here in the East than in the West. Despite the bulky sheet gathered around her, she appeared slender and attractively proportioned.

They broke the kiss and murmured to each other. She rocked back onto her haunches and Patrick smiled at me. "Lord Nolan ra Yotan, this is my wife, Countess Jamila. Her father was my grandfather's Ambassador to Sterlos."

I bowed my head to her. "The pleasure is mine, my lady."

Her radiant smile accentuated the beauty in her delicately sculpted face. Mischief filled her dark, heavy-lidded eyes. "A pleasure we share, then." She leaned behind Patrick and ran a hand through his hair. "If you will permit me, my lord, what happened to your shoulder?"

Patrick spun, caught her wrist, and kissed it. "Leave him alone, woman, he is the man who saved me from the Dhesiri."

She smiled down at her husband. "I can forgive him that, my darling, and I am sure Lord Nolan does not mind so innocent a question." Her eyes flicked up to me and assured me I did not think the question an intrusion.

I smiled graciously. "Not at all, my lady. It was an accident in the Darkesh. I was wounded back in the days before I had access to a court wizard to heal my wounds."

Countess Jamila smiled slowly and lifted her husband's hand to her lips. She kissed it, then looked over at me again. "I thought very few bandits ever escaped the Lords of the Darkesh."

I laughed, which she took as a sign of nervousness, and bowed my head to her. "That is my understanding as well, and even the lucky ones don't escape unmarked."

She meant to continue but Patrick raised his hand to her lips and gently stifled her next question. "That is enough, dearest. Lord Nolan also saved the King. The man is a hero, not a criminal for you to interrogate."

The Countess fixed him with a stare that lowered the temperature of our pool by several degrees. She smiled sweetly at me. "We will pursue this later, my lord, as I am sure it is an interesting tale." She rose, slipped back behind the curtain, and splashed into the other hot pool.

Patrick swam over to me and whispered in low, conspiratorial tones. "Be careful, Lord Nolan. I love her dearly, but what you say to her will make the rounds through court quickly."

I nodded and noticed two servants entering the room with sheets similar to the ones the Countess had been wearing.

Patrick spoke to one of them, then turned to me. "They have put your things in the Wolf Tower suite. That puts you on the same level with my suite and Duke Vidor's suite. Above us is the Princess and above her is the King."

The Count directed a chubby, towheaded youth toward the alcove I'd used earlier. "Adric will take you to your room. You should not see anyone on the way, so you can wear the sheet as opposed to climbing back into your wet clothing. I will call upon you before this evening's reception and see how you are getting along."

I climbed steaming from the pool and wiped myself off before wrapping the sheet around myself. "Tell your wife I much enjoyed meeting her."

He nodded slowly and looked back over at the curtain. "I best apologize or I will never make it to the reception at all. If I survive I will see you later."

Adric carried my sodden clothing and led the way up to my suite. Patrick's prediction was correct and I saw no one on the stairs. We covered the flight up to the main floor, then continued up one more flight and exited into a small, circular central lobby that had three doors off it. Adric preceded me through the southern doorway.

The suite took up one-third of the level it was on and was divided into a large antechamber nearest the door, and two smaller adjoining rooms on the outer circumference of the tower. Smoothly carved stone blocks formed all the walls except for those in the back room, which were carved from the mountainside the castel abutted on the south.

The antechamber was appointed as a library or study. The walls were built up with shelves, and volumes of various sizes, bindings, and ranges of antiquity filled them. The library had four large chairs and a sideboard stocked with a wine pitcher and four silver goblets.

Immediately to the right of the doorway stood a huge fireplace built into the tower's interior wall. Carved in the shape of a salamander's head, it would have no trouble warming the whole suite when a fire burned in it. Above it perched a carving of Hamisian arms. It featured heraldic animals and arcane symbols much older than Castel Seir itself, and while not actually part of salamander, it complemented the stone beast and added a grand air to the chamber.

Beyond the library, through the most eastern of two lancet arch doorways, lay my bedroom. The bed was colossal, though after three nights on a cot anything would look big, and had carved bedposts at each corner supporting a canopy embroidered with choice scenes from Hamisian history. Another coat of arms—this one more recent than that hanging over the fireplace—decorated the headboard, and the quilt had sacred symbols sewn into it to insure pleasant dreams. Situated in the south wall, the one carved from the mountain behind the Castel, stood a narrow washing alcove with a hand-carved basin, a polished silver mirror, a water pitcher, and two small towels.

The third and final room in the suite could have been a second bedroom, but served me as a wardrobe. Adric busily laid out the clothing I'd need for the reception later that evening, then sat down to polish a pair of dress boots he'd pulled from my trunk. He looked up expectantly when I entered the room, but I just smiled and waved him back to what he was doing.

I smiled because I felt as much at home here as I did anywhere in the Shattered Empire. I knew of Castel Seir from the stories I had heard as a child, which gave the place a sense of antiquity. While Castel Seir was not as old as Talianna, it had survived the Shattering and shared with Talianna a long arc of history. Its existence became a manifestation of continuity and permanency which was very important to me. I often felt alone in the world because the people I loved most, like my family, Lothar, and Marana, were taken away from me, but the constancy of Talianna or Castel Seir gave me something to hold on to, something that felt as if it would never go away.

I banished the bad memories and concentrated upon the tricky task of shaving. Adric warmed water for me in the fireplace, then busied himself whisking soiled linens out of sight. I shaved carefully and was quite pleased with the length and condition of my moustache and goatee even though they meant I had to pay more attention when wielding a razor. For the barest of moments I considered keeping them after this mission was over, then rejected the idea in favor of just being able to simply scrape a razor over my face without worrying about where to stop or how to trim.

Adric laid out a blue velvet and silver silk doublet and a deep blue silk tunic. The combination, in addition to being appropriate to the color scheme for the evening, was quite handsome. Alternate stripes of color ran from shoulder to wrist on sleeves loose enough for me to strap a dagger to my left forearm without anyone being the wiser. Allen's seamster had even included a hidden slit in the seam to allow me swift access to the blade

Formality also required me to wear hose, which I really do not like. The stockings make my legs very hot and garters give me more trouble than Morai ever dreamed of. I detest the baggy upper hose—mainly because they are such a contrast in feel to my normal clothing—and the silly little silk slippers needed to show hose off to their best advantage annoy me with their flimsiness.

Adric offered to help me dress but I kindly refused, and asked him to find me some fruit or cheese to take the edge off my hunger before the reception. I dressed myself, strapped the dagger to my forearm before Adric returned, and almost balked at wearing hose. The hose, though, yielded to me and, properly sized, decided to stay in place. They were still warm but they made a nice addition to my suit.

As was allowed by custom I strapped my *ryqril* around my waist. By law a noble may wear a dagger anywhere as a symbol of his status, but only the King's Champion can wear his sword at this sort of social function. On occasion nobles draw their daggers to defend their honor when insulted, but usually the blades are only used for meals. The dagger I had strapped to my arm was strictly outlawed, but I wanted it there in case someone took it for granted I was armed as poorly as the other nobles.

Adric returned, followed closely by Count Patrick. Adric set a tray with an apple, already cut into cored circles, and a small wedge of the King's favorite cheese on the library table. He bowed and backed from the room. I waved Patrick to the food and crossed to the sideboard to pour wine for us.

He was already dressed for the reception. His clothes were more silver than mine and worked in a patched pattern I suspected he chose because it resembled a harlequin's costume. Still it suited him well and really forced him to look more like a noble than he probably desired. A silver circlet restrained his red hair.

The Count cut himself a small piece of cheese and chewed it thoughtfully. "I have to apologize for the trouble I may have caused." A sly smile crept onto his face.

I walked over and handed him a cup of the wine. "What are you talking about?"

He drank before he replied. "You will recall I said my wife is a court gossip?"

"Yes." I bit into an apple circle. The fruit was sweet, but the feeling of impending doom settling about me made it taste like dust.

Patrick frowned for a moment. "Damn, I do not know why I feel guilty over this. It is Duke Vidor's fault, after all."

I shook my head. "I am missing something here. What is going on?"

The Count sighed and seated himself. "My wife spoke with my mother, who spoke to the Queen and it was decided that you would escort the Princess to the reception. Vidor, because his leg is still numbed from the wizard's spell, cannot dance, so he cannot accompany the Princess." A wide grin broke onto his face as I aspirated the apple and coughed it free.

I recovered and glowered at him. "I do not think that would be a good idea."

He just shook his head and tried to compose himself for my sake. "There are two things you must understand in Castel Seir. First, your selection is actually in keeping with tradition. The hunter who bags the animal is always honored at the reception."

"No, no," I laughed gently. "You shot it. You, Earl Cadmar, and the King got it. One of you should have the honor."

"Nonsense, Nolan, you lured it out into the open. You deserve the honor." Patrick leaned back and smiled at me over the rim of his cup. "Besides, the King cannot escort her, I will be with my wife, and Keane's wife will kill him if he abandons her to be so honored."

I raised my left eyebrow and stared down at him. "Do you often honor the bait at a reception?"

Count Patrick laughed. "A fair point, but not one worthy of discussion in light of the second thing you must remember in Castel Seir. You see, my friend, the Queen and Grand Duchess have decided you will escort the Princess. There is no appeal from that sentence." He sipped more wine. "Even the gods have reconsidered actions when those two conspire to oppose them."

I toyed unconsciously with my goatee, then settled my goblet on the tray. "That being the case, I would be more than honored to escort Her Highness, Princess Zaria ra Hamis, this evening."

The Count set his goblet down, rose, and patted me on the shoulder. "That is exactly what I told them you would say."

I had no idea of what to expect when Count Patrick led me into the throne room. The arched roof rose up three stories and a series of stained-glass windows commemorating the more famous Kings of Hamis decorated the tall walls. Laid out in a diamond pattern of polished marble squares, an alternating series of black and white floorstones stretched out, from wall to wall, beneath my feet. The decorations and stonework dated from before the Shattering, but still provided the room with an atmosphere of power and legitimacy.

At the far end of the hall I recognized the King seated upon a canopied wooden throne and the Grand Duke standing below him to the left. Patrick's mother, Grand Duchess Xanthe, had to be the strong, solid, white-haired woman straightening a bow on his father's jacket.

Walking toward the throne I studied the slender, striking

woman seated next to King Tirrell. She had to be his Queen Elysia. The simple coronet she wore flashed highlights into her black hair, yet was appropriate to her demeanor because it suggested rank and power without fanfare or fuss. If the old saying about a husband telling how his wife will look in later years by looking at her mother is true, the man who married the Princess would indeed by fortunate.

A dozen other people filled the room. I recognized Countess Jamila and a dressed-up Halsted, but the others were children and utterly unfamiliar. Patrick described all of them as the Princess's or his younger siblings, with one proud exception. He indicated a small boy attired in a suit modeled on his own. "That is my son Phillip. He is three years old."

Phillip and most of the other children looked as thrilled as I felt about being fashionably attired. Patrick introduced me to all of them, and I quickly abandoned all hope of remembering their names because each had been named after a dozen past heroes and had three or four titles already.

Count Patrick left off his eloquent torture when I'd shaken the last hand in line and then led me to his parents and the King.

"Queen Cousin, and Mother, this is Lord Nolan ra Yotan ra Hamis."

I bowed deeply.

The Grand Duchess watched me like a hawk and appraised me instantly as her husband had. I must have been acceptable, because she bowed her head toward me. "I thank you for my son, and for my Lord King."

I saw the Queen exchange a quick glance with the Grand Duchess; then the Queen extended a hand toward me. I took it and lightly kissed it. I straightened up and she smiled at me. "We wish to thank you for saving our husband, cousin, and Duke Vidor. Our husband tells us you refuse to name a reward for your action, so we will not ask you to name one."

She looked to Halsted and at her invitation he walked to me with a small wooden box in hand. I took it from him and he withdrew. The Queen nodded at me and in a strong, gentle voice said, "Within you will find something I trust will reward you."

I opened the box and my jaw dropped. Nestled amid folds of red velvet I found a gold ring. Despite the slight signs of wear on the edges, the original designs and crest on it stood out sharp and clear in the bright metal. Then I noticed the crest still had an Imperial Hawk perched above it, and I instantly knew the ring dated from before the Shattering because that symbol had been struck from all arms after the last Emperor died.

I stared up at the Queen in disbelief. "I cannot accept this. It is too old. It was made before the Empire collapsed. It must be priceless."

"As is our husband to us." The Queen anticipated my argument and crushed it instantly. "The ring, if the court historian is to be believed, was worn by Prince Uriah back before the Shattering. It is related that he ventured into a Dhesiri warren to save a peasant who had been taken, and this ring was made to honor that deed. We believe he would applaud this reward for your bravery."

I bowed my head and slid the ring onto the fourth finger of my right hand. It fit perfectly and, despite its weight, felt comfortable on my hand. "I thank you, and I am deeply honored by your gift."

King Tirrell, who sat silent through all this, turned to his wife. "Are you finished tormenting my guest?"

The Queen nodded. King Tirrell turned to me. "Lord Nolan, I would like you to meet Her Highness, Princess Zaria ra Hamis."

I turned to my right to watch Grand Duke Fordel lead Princess Zaria into the throne room from a side chamber. My breath caught in my throat and I forced myself to bow so I would not stare at her. She was, quite simply put, the most beautiful woman I'd ever seen in my life.

The Princess effortlessly matched the Grand Duke's martial pace, though she stood three inches shorter than him. Her long black hair washed in waves over her shoulders and all but hid a beaten silver coronet set with a diamond in the center. Her eyes were dark brown and the Princess emphasized their size and beauty with the judicious application of cosmetics. Her nose was straight and proportionate, her cheekbones were high, and lip rouge highlighted her full, sensuous mouth.

Silver and white except for a few deep blue ribbons and bows, her gown tapered down from puffy shoulders to tightly enfold her narrow waist, then blossomed out like a flower with satin petals to reach the floor. Lace trimmed it at the wrists and rose up from bosom to her throat, but could not conceal her charms. Though she would not officially be acknowledged a woman until crowned, her gown served notice that the ceremony was merely a formality.

The Grand Duke slipped her hand from his arm and she held it out to me. I kissed it and looked up. She smiled at me, then at her parents. "I am sorry you were put to such trouble, Lord Nolan, on such short notice."

I smiled slowly and used the time purchased thereby to calm my racing heart. "Escorting you is an honor, Your Highness, and no trouble at all."

"Tell me that when the evening is over." She stepped back and turned to face Halsted. The servant cleared his throat and bowed his head to the King before he spoke. "As protocol demands the Grand Duke and Duchess will lead the party in, followed by the Count and his wife. Then the King and Queen will enter the hall. Princess Zaria will follow behind them alone, and you, Lord Nolan, will walk behind her. Once she has been presented to the assembly the King will look at you and you will lead her to where the Grand Duke and Duchess stand."

When adults nodded their understanding, Halsted turned his attention to the children. "Line up, tallest to smallest. You will march behind Lord Nolan. After he has led the Princess off each of you will be introduced. No clowning or laughing. If there is any, all of you will be sent to your quarters before the bard Duke Vidor has found will perform." Halsted's threat washed over the children like a cold bucket of water. They sobered, looked serious, and sprang into line with no trouble.

Halsted led all of us back behind the throne to a tall bronze door. I saw no handle or hinges amid the symbols and figures worked into the door, but I was only given a half second to wonder how it opened before Halsted gently knocked on it. The door shuddered and then, slowly, slid upward into the wall itself. It rose in pace with the Hamisian anthem and, as if the sun were rising to banish the night, the light from the ballroom washed over the royal procession.

Beyond the King, in the ballroom, I watched the assembled

nobles and guests gently retreat from the base of the stairs we would descend. Everyone was dressed in shades of blue and silver, yet despite the limited choice of colors permitted for that evening, no two gowns or suits looked the same.

The first thing I noticed about the ballroom, after my eyes adjusted to the brighter light therein, was the intricate pattern of stone revealed on the floor as the nobles withdrew. The stonework was made of both granite and marble, yet instead of having simple square blocks, the stone had been cut and shaped like pieces of stained glass. They varied in color from a bright pink granite to a dark black marble and formed a map of the continent. Clearly, from the nations shown, the map had been produced after the Shattering, but had not yet been revised to incorporate Sinjaria within Hamis's borders. Small stars of contrasting colors pinpointed the important cities within each country.

White marble pillars supported a vaulted ceiling painted with scenes from legends and faery tales. A large, glittering crystal chandelier hung in the middle of the room and splashed little rainbows of light onto the walls while four smaller versions of it lit the deeper corners of the rectangular room. Directly across from our doorway stood open glass doors provided access to the Castel's gardens.

Eight musicians gathered together in the ballroom's near right corner reverently played the national anthem with respect and skill. Standing to either side of them, and scattered strategically around the room, tables offered various forms of food and drink, but three tables remained empty to be later filled with meat taken during the leopard hunt.

The procession took place as Halsted had instructed and warm applause greeted the Princess. The younger male nobles double-checked their attire, and a few uncharitable individuals made whispered comments to their escorts about her, but the majority of people seemed genuinely charmed by her beauty and friendly smile.

King Tirrell turned and looked to me as the applause trailed off. I advanced and stopped one step below her before I turned to offer her my left arm. She gently laid her hand on my forearm, did not let her surprise show when she felt the knife, and let me lead her to the Grand Duke. She graced me with a smile that shot a thrill through me and burned envy into more than one noble as we glided past them.

We stopped at the Grand Duke's right and Halsted appeared at my shoulder instantly. "The first dance is the Ceremonial."

I nodded. He took it for granted that I knew the dance, because all nobles had to know it. Fortunately it was common in Sinjaria and my grandmother had seen to it that all of us— save Arik—learned it as children. Somehow I managed to avoid laughing as the image of a Services clerk teaching the step to one of Lord Eric's Lancers burst unbidden into my brain.

Halsted's voice saved me. "You will dance with the Princess. Follow her parents onto the floor."

I nodded and he vanished to signal the musicians that all was ready for the dance. I stiffened for a heartbeat because, although the music started familiarly enough, it shifted as King Tirrell led his Queen into the floor. The Princess half-stepped to the left and slipped her right hand up to take my hand. With her hand resting gently on mine at shoulder height we walked onto the dance floor.

The dance itself really was simple, and my initial concern faded as the steps came back to me. We walked forward three strides, turned to face each other, slid one step back in the direction whence we had come, then turned and stepped forward for three paces while the Princess turned a pirouette. We repeated the sequence and followed the King and Queen in their circuit around the ballroom. Behind us couples fell into line and soon almost everyone was dancing.

In Hamis the dance had been changed ever so slightly. Physically the steps remained the same, but the musicians picked up the pace with each repetition, and the women were expected to turn more than one pirouette as the tempo increased. I adapted quickly by surrendering myself to the music and my partner's skill in the dance.

Light and graceful, the Princess moved fluidly, like a silk pennant in a gentle breeze, and used me for nothing more than guidance and support during the dance. The music consumed her and she spun wildly with her hair flying and her eyes flashing. Her smile was infectious, so I soon found myself grinning like a fool before we'd half finished the dance.

The music raced on and older or timid couples gracefully bowed out of the dance. The Princess reached down, caught her gown with her left hand so it would not trip her, and continued to fly around the room as the crowd thinned. I noticed the King and Queen had withdrawn, but Count Patrick and his wife followed quickly behind us in a scintillating blur of silver and azure.

Princess Zaria winked at the Countess and tossed her head back in a wordless challenge. She whirled four times beneath my hand with that sequence and five times the next. I saw a grimace on Patrick's face as his wife matched the Princess, then spun like a top, swirled six times around, and smiled broadly at her cousin.

The dance ended abruptly as one musician, unable to match the pace set by the royal dancers, faltered and broke his companions' concentration. The Princess twirled to a stop and breathlessly backed away from me to curtsy. I bowed, fully expecting to lose her to the other nobles who already hovered nearby, but she saw them and quickly took my right hand. "You will get me some wine?"

The question had only one answer, so I led her to the nearest table laden with goblets and pointed to a crystal decanter filled with a dark red vintage. Though I did not realize it until I smelled the bouquet, the wine I'd chosen came from Yotan. She sipped and smiled at my choice.

The Princess studied my face and I smiled in a vain attempt to forestall a blush. A small laugh caught in her throat and she slowly turned her goblet between her third and fourth fingers. "I thank you for the dance."

"The pleasure was all mine, Your Highness."

She tilted her head down, studied the light reflecting from her wine for a moment, then flashed her brown eyes up at me. "You dance quite well for a Darkesh bandit."

Her comment took me by surprise and caught me in the middle of a swallow. I narrowly avoided inhaling the wine, but it still took a second or two, and a weak cough, to recover myself. "I have no idea how you would have gotten the idea that I ever was a bandit."

She peered up impishly over the lip of her cup. "Certainly

the object hidden up your sleeve would not have suggested that possibility to me, would it?" She sipped then composed her face with mock sympathy. "Your shoulder does not bother you when you dance?"

I smiled and matched her mischievious stare with one full of innocence and chivalry. "Not when my partner is so lithe and graceful."

Her reply died aborning along with the playful light in her eyes as a man joined us. Shorter than me by an inch or two, his thick muscular build suggested he outweighed me by at least forty pounds. He was easily twice my twenty-three years and wore his white hair in a mane cut. He alone ignored the evening's chosen colors and proudly displayed a white horse rampant device on the left breast of his black tunic. He wore a *ryqril* of sorts at his left hip.

The Princess bowed her head to him just enough to suggest respect without any trace of friendship or warmth. "Lord Nolan ra Yotan, this is Captain Herman ra Tal. He is the Talion in charge of the cavalry here."

I turned and smiled to him. "My pleasure."

"Hast thou been long in Seir?" Herman backed his deep voice with a smile and the words came naturally slow. He set his trap well.

I shook my head and stared at him with an utterly puzzled expression. "Excuse me, I do not understand."

He forcefully renewed the smile on his face. "Forgive me. I had to practice High Tal so often when I joined the Lancers that now I even come to think in it. I asked if you had been long in Seir."

I shook my head. "No. I met the hunting party in the country." Then I turned to the Princess and laughed. "This is rather odd, is it not? You believe me a Darkesh bandit and the good captain here mistakes me for a Talion."

The Princess smiled, then turned to speak with a young baron. He asked and she agreed to join him in the current dance. I reached out to take her goblet with my right hand and openly exposed my unadorned palm to Captain Herman. The Princess smiled at me and thanked me, and Herman frowned. He excused himself, turned away, and wandered off through the crowd.

I gravitated toward Count Patrick because, as the

Princess's escort, I could dance with no one but her. I found him at a table eating grapes and, although we started talking quietly, we soon attracted a circle of people who pressed us to describe our adventure in the Dhesiri warren. I demurred, but Patrick had no qualms about terrifying our listeners with dark and forbidding pictures of an underworld ruled by lizard demons. Once he'd brought them to the point where they believed the King's party was lost, he pointed me out as their savior.

Our audience turned to me for my half of the story, but I shook my head to downplay any heroics on my part. "If not for the Count risking his life to leave me a trail, I never would have found them. His risk was much greater than any I took."

Patrick offered me no refuge. "Blazing a trail is simple, but only a hero could follow it and recover us from certain death."

I glared at him, then smiled. "Honestly, my lords and ladies, my efforts would have been all for naught had the King not led the Count, Duke, and myself through the warren and forced us to hold the only defensible position in the whole underworld. And if the Grand Duke had not brought the others to our rescue there is no way we would be here talking to you this evening."

Patrick guessed what I was doing and helped me deflect our audience. They easily accepted our story and slowly evaporated when they found our tale no longer novel or thrilling. As the last one turned away, Patrick raised a cup to me and laughed. "Nolan, let them see you as a hero. There is no reason you should fight it so hard."

I swallowed a grape and repeated his gesture. "I could say the same to you, my lord. You were as much a hero there as I was." The wine we had picked up was a sweet white from the island of Takkesh. It had a subtle flavor and I enjoyed it.

Count Patrick narrowed his eyes and a self-conscious grin flitted across his lips. "Between us, I will accept that praise. You were there and you know what we did. But we only did what we had to if we were to survive. Is that bravery? I do not think so, but others who are not in that situation might see it that way."

Phillip's arrival cut off further conversation. "Father, up, up. The bard. I want to see." The boy held small hands up and clutched at air until Patrick lifted him into his arms.

I set both Count Patrick's and my cup down, then trailed after the redheaded noble as he cut through the crowd. Everyone moved toward the corner where the musicians had been earlier, and I saw the musicians drifting off toward a wine table. I could see nothing of the bard until I got close, and my first glimpse of the minstrel came through the tall fan-comb one dowager wore at the back of her head. Though I saw a flash of golden hair, I didn't make the connection until I met her blue eyes.

The bard was Selia!

I backed to retreat instantly but the Princess slipped up from behind me and firmly took hold of my left forearm. She led me to an open spot in the circle of nobles surrounding Selia. I knew better than to hope my moustache and goatee would conceal my identity from her, so I smiled like everyone else and nodded to her when she looked at me. My only chance to keep my identity intact was if she could keep quiet until we had a chance to speak together privately.

Selia first sang two songs about Hamisian history. Both praised the wisdom and antiquity of the current ruling family without even a hint of the strife Selia told me about when we were on the trail. I understood it. She had no reason to insult her hosts and another version of these songs that included the bloody start of this House would play well enough in Sinjaria or Lacia.

For her third song she chose, of course, Morai's Song. I had a smile on my face throughout, laughed when the others did, and prayed she'd not embarrass me. I tried not to cringe when she added two new verses to the song I'd heard in Pine Springs, but I had nothing to worry about. They only mentioned me in passing—by title instead of by name since she did not know it—and they concentrated on the lady Morai had fallen for. It changed the bandit's song into a romance and provided an ending that precluded the need for the Talion to pursue Morai any further.

Duke Vidor limped from the crowd behind her as the third song ended and led the applause. Halsted appeared and reverently whisked her lute away. The Duke took her arm and led her straight toward the Princess and myself. Recognition sparked in Selia's eyes.

"Your Highness, I would like to present the bard Selia ra Jania." He hesitated, then corrected himself. "More properly she is Lady Selia as her father is a Janian noble. Lady Selia, this is Princess Zaria."

Selia curtsied deeply. Princess Zaria smiled and returned the gesture. Vidor then turned on me. "Lord Nolan, this is Lady Selia ra Jania . . ."

I interrupted him. "We know each other already." I held my right hand out to her palm up, took the hand she placed in it, and kissed it. Then I turned to the Princess. "Ask her nothing about me. She will merely fill your head with tales of a Darkesh bandit who ran with Morai for a short time. None of it is true."

Selia smiled and nodded her head sheepishly. "My lord, the Duke, says we should discuss the escape from the Dhesiri warren. He says it would make an interesting song."

"Perhaps," I replied, "it can be arranged."

Duke Vidor immediately bowed to the Princess. "Who are we to stand in the way of art? Since these two have something to discuss, could I trouble you to join me in the dance? This one is simple enough I think I can acquit myself admirably."

The Princess looked at me and Selia, then turned away and took the Duke's arm. "Of course." The swirling cloud of silver and blue quickly swallowed them.

Politely, I took Selia's arm and led her around the dance floor to the gardens. In the sky above us the Wolf Moon, half-full, did its best to catch the smaller Rabbit Moon as they raced from horizon to horizon. The night breeze mixed the salty sea air with the fragrant perfume of night-blooming flowers. In a shadowed corner of the garden I found a stone bench and guided Selia to it.

"Selia, I thank you for not saying anything. It is more important than you can imagine that my identity remains secret."

She smiled too easily, then nodded her head. "Perhaps we will work on more than one ballad, then?"

I shook my head solemnly. "Not about this." I grimaced, then dropped to one knee in front of her. I took her right hand and held it firmly, but not as roughly as I had in Pine

Springs. "I need to ask you something and I need an honest answer. Is Morai in Seir?"

She stiffened and looked over my head.

I gently squeezed her hand. "Selia, I'm not stupid. The lady in the last two verses of your song is you. If you've managed to tame his spirit and have convinced him to leave off banditry, I'm all for you—both of you." I reached up, took her chin between my thumb and forefinger, and tipped her head back down toward me. "You must believe I don't intend to bring Morai in, or kill him, and I would never ask you to betray him while keeping a confidence for me. I need to speak with him." I hesitated. "I need to ask him for help."

I stood and stared out at the stars reflecting in the sea. "The one thing no one anticipated when they asked me to come here was a need for information from the streets. I can't get it. I'd be too conspicuous in a ghetto here—if I ever found the time to get to one with all the ceremonies taking place." I turned back to her and folded my arms across my chest. "On top of that, I don't know who to trust here—they may all be involved in plots."

I squatted and smiled at her. "You see, I need Morai."

She paused and, with the moonlight shining silver off her hair, smiled weakly. "Yes, he is here."

"Where?" I asked. Then it dawned on me. I smiled and laughed. "Finally, *I* can surprise *him*."

I silently opened the door to my suite just a crack. I heard some furtive shuffling and a mumbled curse. I stifled a laugh, slipped into the library, and slammed the door shut with an explosive bang.

A shadowy figure, Morai silhouetted himself beneath the arch leading to my bedroom. "Say nothing, my Lord Keane, and you will live to see the Princess's coronation." Morai moved quickly and his sword materialized in his hand as if by magick. "Only a fool would attack an armed swordsman with a dagger."

I let a low, insane chuckle rumble from my chest and summoned my *tsincaat*.

Morai's silhouette jumped.

"Earl Cadmar and the Star of Sinjaria are in a different suite. I was given these quarters just today."

Morai shrugged his shoulders. "Oh." Then he turned his head and peered through the darkness at me. After a second he rested his sword's tip on the floor and struck a pose that was the very picture of indignant outrage. "What are you doing here, Talion?"

I squatted and stirred the coals in the fireplace with a poker. I tossed a small log on the fire and its flame lit the room. "Take a chair, and help yourself to the wine if you haven't already." I pivoted and looked up at him. "I've got something to discuss with you."

Morai looked as dapper and handsome in his night-black thieving clothes as he had when I last saw him. I seated myself across the table from him and took the goblet he offered me. "I'm glad to see you're not letting Selia support you with her singing."

He shrugged and drank. "This is contract work. Some Sinjarian noble wants the stone." He smiled at me. "Besides, I have to stay active or I'll get fat like your Captain Herman."

"He's not mine, he's a Lancer."

"He's a Talion. They're all the same." He drank more wine. "No offense intended, of course."

I snorted out a laugh. "None taken." I waited for him to finish refilling his cup before I continued. "I have a problem I want you to help me with. Oh, don't look so offended. Half the Talions in Talianna think you and I have worked out a deal to trap all the truly mad criminals in the Empire."

"And the other half?"

"The other half know you use me to whittle your gangs down because you only like to split loot with yourself."

Morai chuckled. "Go on, I'll try to keep my feelings and ethical sense under control."

"Most kind of you." I drank a mouthful of wine—a hearty Janian red—and continued. I quickly decided how much information I could trust Morai with, and tailored my story accordingly. "I am here because rumors suggest a power struggle may take place after the coronation. Various factions want to control who the Princess will marry to promote their plans for the future. I need to know who they are and what they have in the way of resources."

I hung my head and watched the fire. "I'm stuck dining and dancing in the company of the men who might be plotting a revolt against the King while I should be out learning who's been hiring troops or"—I smiled at him— "excellent thieves to steal symbolic items."

Morai sat silently and stared off beyond me. He placed his winecup on the table and steepled his fingers. "I've heard nothing substantial, but then I've not been listening. Someone must be hiring mercenaries—there have been enough in the city lately—but I don't know who it is."

"Will you check into it for me? I need that information desperately, and you are the only one who can get it for me."

He laughed and watched me through slitted eyes. "Yes, I will get it for you, and professional ethics be damned. After all, it won't be the first time we've worked together, will it, Talion?" He laughed so hard he fell to the floor.

My shoulder throbbed with pain.

Chapter Sixteen

NOVICE: SOLITAIRE

Leaving Ring presented me with a grand problem. To my knowledge no one had ever done what I did before—I was fairly certain if someone *had* we would not have been told about it—so I had no idea of what sort of reception I'd have in Talianna. The worst possible situation was one where Ring rode straight to Talianna and Lord Hansur sent riders out after me.

I didn't really think Ring would be all that anxious to advertise our parting, and because I still had six months in my Journey year, I decided to travel until that time was up or someone found me and forced me to return to Talianna. I took a small amount of satisfaction in that a solo Journey would really prove my ability to survive in the world, and even if it incurred the wrath of my superiors, it should still count for something in their eyes.

My biggest problem was funding. Ring had been able to get money from the various Lancer and Warrior troops scattered throughout the countryside. If things were really difficult, he could draw up a note sealed with his skull tattoo that could be exchanged by the bearer for local coinage, but I could not produce one of those notes—at least not honestly. I further resolved to stay clear of Talion billets to avoid any recall notice, but that likewise cut me off from a ready source of money.

I resorted to the only solution I could think of: I spent a great deal of time working at farmhouses. In exchange for a few days' hard work I could get lodging and enough food to get me a little further on my way. I rode from Leth into Ell supporting myself in this manner, then got a job as a caravan guard that took me into Boucan and paid me enough money that I could travel more freely.

I rode north from the trail's end and always wore my uniform. I wore it so the people could see me and come to view a Talion without abject terror. I wanted them to know someone out there would protect or avenge them and yet that same person could stop and help with crops or cut wood. Presenting that image of a Talion became very important to me, and I knew I worked hard at it so I could stop Ring's image from winning the day and representing all Talions whether they agreed with him or not.

For the most part the journey was uneventful and the things I was asked to do were simple. In a couple of places I helped find lost children or animals, and in one other I fought with, but did not kill, a tyrannical carpenter who abused his apprentices. I heard rumors of a bandit group running about a week ahead of me, and tried to catch up with them, but they proved very elusive.

In northern Juchar I rode into a village just hours after the bandits raided it. A half-dozen men had ridden in, beaten up the men who dared oppose them, and stolen the money the villagers had collected to pay taxes. While that account did not differ from what I'd already heard in other villages, the scene that presented itself in the village square was unique.

Three burly men wearing the livery of the local Baron had

stripped the clothes from an older man and bound him into a pillory. One of the Baron's men was tying a cestus onto his right fist and chuckled as the bound man sobbed incoherently. For a moment or two I thought these men had captured one of the bandits, but then I noticed none of the gathered villagers were jeering at the captive. In fact, most of them looked terrified.

I rode Wolf into the center of the crowd and pulled some black gloves on. "Hold, what goes on here?" I sat tall in the saddle and tried to look official.

The man tying the cestus on snarled at me, then saw what I was and became a bit more civil. "Leigh says bandits stole the tax money we're here to collect. He's lying and won't tell us where he's hidden it, so"—he shook his fist—"I'm going to beat its location out of him." He shrugged, took one end of a thong in his teeth, and pulled the last knot tight.

Leigh, the village headman in the pillory, had two blackened eyes from the raid. He looked up and saw me. His tears stopped instantly and he shouted to me. "You, Talion, you must find the bandits, you must get the money back. We had a good harvest and had all our tax money until they took it." The pain in his voice shot through me.

The man with the cestus swung his fist through the air a couple of times and smiled. "Stop your lying, Leigh. Lie to a Talion and he's likely to give you worse than I will." The Baron's man looked to me for confirmation.

I shook my head. "Don't hit him."

He stepped closer to Leigh and slowly let the frightened man examine the cestus. "I have my orders, Talion." He never turned to look at me. "I get the taxes, or I administer a beating."

I dismounted and the crowd spread back away from me. "Are you out of your mind? Are you trying to tell me you're planning to beat an innocent man when the bandits that robbed this village and others near here are riding away?" I shook my head in disbelief. "That makes no sense whatsoever."

The tax collector just shrugged. "I just follow orders." He took one quick step back behind the pillory and buried his fist in Leigh's stomach. The headman vomited and sagged.

The thug grinned as he turned to me. "See, I just do what I'm told."

I stared at him. "Then leave him alone."

A wicked grin slithered across his lips. "And what do I tell my master? I tell him I let this man off because a Talion told me to, and he'll say to his torturers, 'Make Marko here talk and tell me where he's hidden my taxes.' Not me, Talion, they won't do that to me 'cause I'll give them no reason to do it."

I peeled the glove off my right hand and held my palm up for everyone to see. "I'm not a Talion yet, Marko, but I'm still telling you to leave him alone."

Marko nodded to his two companions. They closed from both sides and I stepped back just before they reached me. Each man pulled back to avoid colliding with the other. I kicked out with my right foot and caught one in the stomach, then lashed out with my left hand to hit the other on the side of the head. The kicked man collapsed, holding his stomach, but his partner needed another blow to the chin to knock him out of the fight.

I stood triumphant over his companions and stared at Marko. "I know Justices who would kill you simply for setting your friends upon them, and I know others who would repay you with ten blows for every one you give to Leigh." I held my open hands away from my body. "I am far more reasonable. Leave him alone and you need not face me or an angry lord."

Marko watched my face and tried to figure out what sort of trap I'd set for him. "I'm not going after those bandits."

I shook my head. "You don't need to. I'll deal with them and you handle your Baron."

"Fine, a fair deal." He reached over and released Leigh while I crossed to his horse. I rummaged around in his saddle-bags and found a folio with loose sheets of paper pressed between its covers. I drew one out and asked someone to find me ink and a quill pen.

Marko looked over to see what I was doing. The pen scratched out a receipt for the villages taxes and I signed it with my full name and a flourish. "Give this to your Baron, he will know what it means and what to do with it. He will accept it as your money."

"Now your masters will be angry." Marko looked at the

receipt and laboriously read it. His lips moved with every word. Satisfied, he looked up at me. "How will you pay off this much money?"

I smiled without feeling even close to as confident as I tried to look. "I'll just have to get it from the bandits."

I pursued the bandits as closely as I dared and cut their lead from half a day to half an hour by pushing Wolf and myself fairly hard. I felt uneasy, because they made their trail painfully simple to follow. They visited no other villages and made no attempt to conceal their passage. It seemed to me that they wanted everyone to know where they had gone.

We traveled north, which took us close to the border with Venz. I thought, in fact, they meant just to run north and cross over into Venz's western marches, which were known for their lawlessness, when they surprised me and turned west. It wasn't until I crested that last hill and saw them disappear into the forests below me that I believed they'd ever escape me.

From that hilltop all I could see was an ocean of dense forest. My pursuit had taken me through the woodlands of northern Juchar, but they might as well have been treeless plains when compared to the timberland below me. Nothing in the world could match Woodholm.

A few islands of gray granite broke through the treetops, but aside from those barren hillsides, I saw no clearings or open spots from my vantage point. The trees drank in the sunlight for life, but did not let it penetrate that canopy with anything more than token strength. The whole tenebrous forest brooded like a living creature and defied men to enter it.

I could almost hear the bandits' laughter. No one would follow them into that forest. It was Woodholm. Even the Talions refused to follow Kiritan the Mad into those verdant depths. In the Aelven grove's shadow they felt safe from all the dangers they could think of, and probably thought themselves brave enough to deal with anything the forest would beset them with.

Woodholm swallowed the bandits. I waited on the hill and listened for their screams, but I heard nothing. Then I tipped my head back and laughed aloud. "You know, don't you,

Woodholm? You feel me waiting and watching. You won't destroy them until I enter your demesne and join them, will you?" I spurred Wolf forward. "Very well. I accept your challenge."

I grew more and more apprehensive about Woodholm as I rode toward it. Even as far away as Sinjaria I'd heard stories about Woodholm. I knew, like The Forests nearer my home, Woodholm was an Aelven refuge. Even though many stories told of Aelves helping human heroes fight the epic battles of the past, I knew whatever sense of kinship the Aelves once felt for men had long since died, and that intrusions into either Aelven preserve were for the insane or foolhardy.

The Aelves in the stories stand tall and willowy, yet they are lithe and wiry instead of fragile or sickly. Their eyes are slightly enlarged so they can see clearly in the dark forest. Their skin is reported to be very pale because the sun never touches it. All the stories describe the Aelves as very beautiful and, to the consternation of the human heroes in these tales, report Aelves would never consider mixing their blood with that of humans.

In the very center of Woodholm there supposedly grows a massive tree that is home to all the Aelves. They have a city woven into the tree's branches and it is connected to other trees by high, swinging bridges. The Aelves have maintained the tree through powerful magicks, and use those abilities to enhance every aspect of their lives. They always wear silk garments that change color like a rainbow and never get soiled. Their whole life is peace and beauty.

But no human has seen that city, and all attempts to reach it have been savagely repulsed by the Xne'kal.

The Xne'kal are Aelves in reality, form, and blood. Unlike the Aelves, though, the Xne'kal are openly hostile to humans. The Xne'kal dress in skins, and arm themselves with spears and throwing darts. They haunt Woodholm and The Forests in great roving bands that destroy any trespassers into their domain.

No human has ever offered a definitive explanation of the Xne'kal enmity toward humans, but there is one widely held belief that makes more sense than all the others. At one time Aelves were common throughout the lands encompassing the Shattered Empire but, even before Clekan established his empire, their domains had shrunk drastically and men encroached on them everywhere. I believe the Xne'kal chose to oppose men and keep them back so the Aelves could continue to live in peace and practice their arts without human intrusion.

The Xne'kal are known as fierce fighters. Their weapons are often poisoned and many a hero has died at Xne'kal hands. Even so, they rarely attack out of their forests to harry human settlements. Some people even report Xne'kal returning children who have wandered into the forests, but they regularly butcher cattle any farmer releases to forage in Woodholm.

I stopped at the edge of the forest and dismounted. I fished my own paper, pen, and ink from my saddlebags. I wrote a quick letter to Lord Hansur about where I was and what I was doing. I folded it and drew as good an imitation of a Skull on it as I could. I tied the message to the saddle, then pulled my saddlebags from Wolf's back and carefully discarded everything I would definitely not need in the forest.

From that pile of soiled clothing and odd-looking stones, I selected one dirty stocking and filled it with dirt, grass, and a small piece of tree bark from Woodholm. I tied that to the saddlehorn to give the Wizards a means of locating the spot where I entered Woodholm, then turned Wolf so he faced due east and slapped him on the rump. "Go on, Wolf, get out of here. Go to Talianna."

I don't know if he understood me, but he wasted no time getting away from Woodholm. I watched him disappear over the hilltop and laughed, "I wonder which of us is really a dumb animal?"

I picked up the saddlebags and tossed them over my shoulder. I felt lonely without Wolf, but I knew he'd have been of little use in Woodholm. From their tracks I saw the bandits had dismounted soon after they entered the forest. The tightly packed trees had too many low branches to make riding possible. In fact, much of the undergrowth had to be chopped away to make passage anything but impossible. I consoled myself with the idea that I could take one of the bandits' horses after I captured them.

The midmorning sun warmed me outside Woodholm, but it might as well have been midnight, it was so dark and cold within the woods. If the bandits had not cut such a wide path and left it strewn with freshly trimmed branches, I would have missed their trail completely. The trees only allowed enough light in to cast confusing shadows, and more than once I started at what I took for a Xne'kal warrior, but ended up dismissing as nothing more threatening than a pine or oak. Still, the occasional call of a bird or chirp of an insect gave Woodholm an edge over the Darkmaze for feelings of danger and impending doom.

I discovered, totally by accident, a narrow trail running roughly parallel to the bandits' course. I moved onto it and quickly pulled abreast of them without revealing my presence to them. All too clearly I heard them cursing and crashing through the woods.

A mousy little man stopped to catch his breath. "Dav, this idea of yours was not that intelligent."

"Shut up, Giac," the bandit leader snapped at him in a harsh whisper. "We make a little loop through these woods and we're into Venz with no one believing we're alive. We're off free." The leader's voice was strong and confident. The glimpses afforded me through windows in the underbrush showed him to be a strong, bald man with a thick black moustache.

Another man spoke. He wore his salt-and-pepper beard and hair long. He was lean, grizzled, and clearly the eldest of the group. "What about the Aelves? They aren't going to like our little journey through their woods."

A black-haired youth who looked to be about my age answered him. "If we get out fast enough they won't have time to get us. It's a gamble, but one with time on our side. We'll be fine, Elston."

The older man smiled and shook his head at the youth's confidence. "I hope you're right, Morai, for your sake. You've got a lot more living left in you than I do."

Steely fingers sank into my neck from behind and ended all interest I might have had in the bandits' conversation. I dropped to the ground in a crouch and rolled back. That broke the grip on my neck and, even before I could see who my assailant had been, I continued the roll and kicked both my feet up into my attacker's chest. I completed my backward somersault and whirled to face my foe.

My kick had knocked the Xne'kal warrior over and back down the trail a body length or two. The red heelprints from my boots stood out livid on his chest, and two ribbons of blood from where my spurs caught him trickled down between his breasts. He wore a loincloth and armband cut from a mountain leopard pelt. Even before he tried to stand, he reached an incredibly long, thin arm out for the spear lying in the middle of the trail.

I dove on him and landed on his chest, but he backhanded me with a short, sharp blow to the side of my head. I flew from his chest and rolled to a stop at the base of a tree. I flipped myself over to a prone position, pushed off and back to avoid his first spear thrust, and stood quickly enough to draw my sword in time to parry his second attack.

He circled me and his long white hair flew. I caught a glimpse of pointed ears, but concentrated on his wide, black eyes. Erect, he stood only a foot taller than me, but was so thin he seemed much bigger than even that. His hands only had three fingers in addition to the thumb, but the aches in my neck told me those slender digits did not lack for strength.

The Xne'kal lunged straight forward and closed, because he expected me to back away from his attack. Instead I slapped his spear down with my sword, then slashed back-handed without retreating a step. He walked directly into my attack and the blade slit his throat effortlessly.

He dropped to the ground with a muffled thump. I knelt and examined the flint tip on his spear. A green, sticky substance coated it and I smelled it. The sweet scent instantly identified it for me: it was a plant poison that festered in wounds and the amount of the spear tip was enough to kill a man slowly and painfully.

I looked around saw no other Xne'kal, nor could I hear anything to suggest others might be out there, but that did little to make me comfortable. I'd not seen or heard the dead Aelf at my feet sneaking up on me. I ran further along the trail and broke through when I saw the bandits.

As could be expected, having a Talion arrive unannounced in their midst surprised them. One, a rakishly handsome man in well-worn finery, dropped a hand to his sword hilt.

I smiled at him and held my sword up so they could see the dark red—almost black—blood running down it.

"Don't be hasty, there'll be more than enough killing for all of us momentarily." I turned to Dav. "I just killed a Xne'kal back on a trail running beside this one. I'd guess they have us surrounded."

Dav, if nothing else, was a man of action and a leader in every sense of the word. "Morai, you and the Talion here in front. Head due east. Leave the horses. Elston, you and Ivan are in the rear. Ario, Giac, get the gold."

I pointed back the way I'd come. "There's a faster trail just over here."

Dav looked to where I pointed, nodded, and then ordered Morai and the others to follow me. "Morai, if we can make the granite hill we saw before we entered this cursed wood we might be able to hold them off."

Morai drew his longsword and we set a quick pace down the Xne'kal footpath. We wanted to go faster, but we could not because Giac and Ario hauled several sacks of gold along in the middle of the party. Elston and Ivan, a blond giant with a broadax, watched the back trail. "Ivan's a mute, but a demon in battle," Morai told me.

Behind us the horses screamed.

Dav shook his head. "That's it then, mates. Drop the gold and run. The rocks are our only chance."

Giac, a man who was average in every respect, refused. "I'll carry it, and it'll be mine."

"Fine. Let's move."

Elston and Ivan ran past Giac. Giac took one step forward, then pitched over onto his face with a Xne'kal dart quivering in his back. We all panicked and ran as fast as we could through the sepulchral depths of the sylvan copse.

We stopped short of the granite hill and all caught our breaths. Ahead undergrowth thinned and sunlight gleamed through the trees. The open area was a tumbled, chaotic landscape of huge boulders surrounding a naked granite spire twisting up into the sky. It was inhospitable, but seemed like a paradise to each of us.

We waited for Ario but he never joined us. Thankfully Woodholm swallowed his screams as completely as it swallowed him. I turned to Dav and wiped my forehead on my left sleeve. "They'll be waiting in the rocks, you know."

Dav acknowledged the veracity of my comment with a

grim nod, but urged all of us on. He was right because we could not avoid the Xne'kal, but in the rocks we could see them before they struck. We followed him out onto the rocks and into the toughest battle of our lives.

Without Ivan we would have all died. Silent and awful, he surged ahead of Dav. He charged across the open area of rockslide and boulders heedless of the darts flying through the air around him. He leaped from stone to stone with an amazing agility and presented the Xne'kal a difficult target for their darts and spears.

One Xne'kal warrior stood and screamed a war cry that sounded distressingly similar to High Tal to me. He slashed at Ivan with his spear, but the giant dodged the attack and split the warrior's head with an overhand blow. The first warrior crumpled as a companion lunged at Ivan from the left. Ivan laughed silently and caught the spear behind its head with his massive left hand. As if it were a twig, Ivan snapped the spear in half and whipped one end of it across the Xne'kal's face. That Aelf slid to the ground and Ivan signaled for us to advance.

We surged forward and sprinted across the rocks. I ran at the back of the line, followed only by Elston, when I caught motion in the corner of my eye. I twisted back, saw a Xne'kal leap down from a rock and drive his spear through Elston's back and out his chest. My sword crashed into the Aelf's head and blasted him back away from the old man, but Elston was already dead.

I ran on, vaulted a boulder, and landed myself beside Morai. Ivan and Dav hunkered down behind large rocks to our left. We lay in a natural bowl ringed by large stones. It was a place of relative safety, but the Xne'kal superiority of numbers made the outcome of any battle inevitable.

I caught my breath and looked over at Dav. "They got Elston."

Dav swore and Ivan gritted his teeth. Dav tapped Ivan on the shoulder and jerked his head at us. Ivan nodded. Dav turned to us. "We're going to get you two out."

"No." Morai and I answered at the same time.

Dav smiled and shook his head at our foolishness. "Fine. Then get ready because here they come."

We stood as an even dozen Xne'kal clad in mountain-leopard skins ran across the rocks toward us. One threw a spear and without thinking I dodged to the side and plucked it out of the air as I had done before in exercises at Talianna. I sheathed my sword and brandished the spear. The Xne'kal stopped their advance and cheered delightedly.

Dav swore. "If we live through this, Talion, I'll surrender to you."

I shook my head. "I can understand a few of the words they said and I think my action just made us 'worthy' foes. I'm not sure what that means, but I'm afraid it's just made them more determined to kill us." I looked up and set myself because the Xne'kal, having paid us enough tribute, attacked.

The majority of Xne'kal concentrated on Dav and Ivan. Two attacked me, and my skill with a spear clearly surprised them. The first lunged at my stomach, but I parried the blow and riposted to his throat. I twisted the spear free by snapping the butt up to catch the second warrior in the face. The blow turned him half around and my return slash with the spearhead cut a ragged bar sinister across his pale chest.

We successfully repulsed their first attack. Morai had killed one and wounded another. Five Xne'kal lay dead between Dav and Ivan, though Dav just smiled and said, "With Ivan here, all I have to do is keep count of his kills." The other Xne'kal retreated and we waited.

I couldn't understand why they hadn't thrown their darts at us. No larger than crossbow quarrels, the weapons were tipped with a thin, three-inch-long flint blade. A dart rested in the rocks nearby and I saw that its point was thoroughly stained with their poison. It occurred to me that they might have attacked with handheld weapons because we had nothing to throw back at them, but I couldn't imagine that courtesy being extended to us much longer.

Another dozen warriors materialized at the forest edge. They advanced more slowly and were almost stately in their approach. They chanted something I couldn't recognize, but from the rhythm and range it had to be a martial song of some sort.

The four of us foolishly stood and watched them march forward. They continued toward us and I dried my hands against my jerkin. I saw Ivan do the same thing and we shared a smile over it. Then we both sobered because another dozen warriors rose and marched behind the first group.

Dav looked over at Morai and me. "See those tall rocks up there?" He pointed at a circle of stones halfway up the steep granite spire behind us. We nodded. "When they come, get up there. We'll hold them off."

"No." Morai's voice was adamant.

"Yes. Damn you Morai, you'll get up there. We'll buy you that time, you use it to take as many of them with you as possible. You've never followed my orders since I've known you, but do it this one time, please."

Morai scowled. "I'll do it. And I'll kill a dozen for each of you."

Dav smiled. "That's the spirit. Here they come. Go!"

Before we turned to run, I hurled the three spears I'd collected and saw two Xne'kal felled by their own weapons. I spun, scurried after Morai, reached him at the hill base, and scrambled up on all fours behind him. I heard the Xne'kal cry out below us and a spear shattered on a rock beside my head, but that happened at the bottom of the hill. Once we reached our new breastwork the spears stopped, but the screaming did not.

I didn't see any of the fight but from the look of pain on Morai's face I knew Dav and Ivan must have sold themselves dearly. Nine new Xne'kal bodies lay dead beside them, and other Xne'kal carried six wounded warriors back toward the forest.

I turned to Morai and laid a hand on his shoulder. "They made a mistake by not taking us in the forest."

He nodded and shifted melon-sized rocks over between the taller stones that formed our breastwork. "They don't know how bad a mistake it was. I'll kill every Xne'kal in this forest if I have to."

"I'll help."

He nodded solemnly. "Then start piling these rocks in the cracks. They'll figure we don't want any holes in our wall, but I intend these to go crashing down on any Aelf stupid enough to try and come up after us."

We set up the rockslides and took turns watching. I'd just sat down when Morai spotted something. "Talion, come look at this."

I stood and my height betrayed me. A Xne'kal jumped up from the base of the hill, screeched out a chilling war cry, and threw a dart. Morai laughed aloud because, at that distance and up a hill, it was an impossible throw.

"Damn," I said stiffly.

Morai shot me a sidelong glance. "Just another one to kill. See, he's run off. No problem."

I swallowed hard. "Problem." I turned and Morai saw, for the first time, the dart I held in my right hand and the hole in my left shoulder.

I sat down before I fell and tossed the dart aside. "Don't move, Morai, and don't let them think they've gotten me. Keep watching them. Describe to me what they are doing. Anything, just keep talking."

He looked very unsure, but did what I told him to do. "Ah, I count about a hundred of them out there. One is all dressed up in wolf skins and has eagle feathers in his hair. He looks important." Morai stared harder down at the Xne'kal, then cursed. "Oh, no, there's trouble. The one who hit you is up on a rock, dancing around and shouting at the one in feathers."

Morai's voice barely registered. I consciously slowed my breathing, closed my eyes, and dropped into a trance. I drifted inward and instantly located the poison as it spread from the wound. Already it chewed into my chest muscle and I was weakening fast. I had to stop it before I became too weak to fight.

I reached out with my mind and stopped the blood flowing to and from the wound. That prevented any more venom from infecting me, but I already felt the burning tendrils of pain that warned me I'd not been fast enough to get it all. I forced the pain to subside and slowly came back to reality.

I wiped my brow on my right forearm and fished my sling from the pouch of stones at my belt. "Where is the one who got me?"

"He's still jumping around on the rocks. They're near Ivan's body. The one who got you is pointing up here and then pointing at a group of about fifteen warriors. If I had to guess, he's trying to convince the one in feathers to let them take us. The one in feathers is having fun denigrating the other's combat effectiveness."

I nodded and got to my feet. "It sounds like rival clans or warrior societies competing. If the Aelf in the wolf skins hates the leopard warriors, maybe I can help him out." I spun the sling and stepped into the open. I whistled loud and defiantly.

The Xne'kal on the rock jabbered, capered, and pointed at me. He poked a finger at his own shoulder and laughed.

I cast the stone with all my might.

The stone flew straight and found its target. The warrior flipped back as if I'd cut his legs from beneath him. He toppled from the rock and all I could see were his feet but, after a couple of twitches, they didn't move a bit.

Morai turned to me in surprise. "You hit him in the forehead!"

"Sorry." I sagged back against the granite cliffside as a wave of nausea washed over me. "I wanted to hit him in the mouth." I coughed and winced. "Did that stop them?"

Morai looked back at the Xne'kal, then shook his head. "No, one of the other leopards has picked up the argument." Morai laughed easily, "And they've moved back out of your range."

I tore a piece of material from my pants and stuffed it into the hole in my shoulder. "Are they coming?"

Morai turned and nodded with a smile on his face. "Yeah, all fifteen of them, but no more than that."

Morai swam in and out of focus. I felt hot and very tired, but I forced myself up and dropped another stone into the sling. The rockslide killed ten. I killed two more halfway up the slope. They were badly shaken by the rockslide anyway, and were fighting their way up the hill so that was no great feat. Morai killed a pair at the breastwork and finished the last one, who made it all the way into our haven, with a rock.

Morai stood, raised the bloody rock high, then casually tossed it down the hill. "Come on, send more."

Pain shot through my upper body and chills racked me. "Don't antagonize them. We may have eliminated old Wolf Chief's rival for power. He might be grateful." I shivered and collapsed.

Morai spun to catch me, then froze and stopped breathing. I turned my head to follow his gaze and saw a radiant Aelven sorceress extending a glowing hand to me. I reached out and touched her; then an ebon bolt of agony smashed me senseless.

I regained consciousness four weeks later in an infirmary bed in Talianna. My head ached and buzzed fiercely but my shoulder was curiously numb. White gaze swathed my left shoulder. Marana sat at my right and held my hand.

She smiled broadly, leaned over, and kissed my forehead. "Welcome back to the land of the living."

My first words stuck in my throat. Marana poured me a cup of watered wine and I sipped at it. "Thank you, for the greeting and the wine." I looked around and confirmed my location. "This question may sound strange, but how did I get here?"

Marana shrugged. "I only got back two days ago myself, and you were here by then. Rumor has it someone brought you in on a travois. He told Lord Hansur that a bandit brought you out of Woodholm after a battle. The bandit gave you over to him and told him to bring you to Talianna."

A Wizard drifted into the room and smiled politely. "Ah, I'm glad to see you up on schedule. How do you feel?"

I sighed weakly. "Halfway between dead and dying?"

The magicker nodded. "It stands to reason. You were dehydrated when you got here, and you hadn't eaten much according to your guide. We managed to clear up most of those problems, and I would certainly like to meet the person who cast the first spell on your shoulder. It saved the nerves in that arm."

The Wizard grimaced and looked at my medical record. "I'm afraid, despite that first spell, the poison did a lot of damage and you'll have a scar on that shoulder. It will also take some time for you to build that shoulder back up, but other than that you should recover perfectly well. And the other thing shouldn't bother you at all."

"Other thing?" I sipped some more of the wine. "What other thing?"

The Wizard frowned and seated himself on my bed. He gently took my left hand, turned it palm down, and passed his hand above it. I felt magick energy trickle over it and, for a moment, the purple outline of a wolf's-head glowed on the back of my hand. The Wizard shrugged. "No one but Aelves can see it."

I slowly twisted my left hand, but I couldn't see it. "What is it?"

The Wizard shook his head. "In various Aelven rituals a person is marked with the equivalent of a magical brand. As nearly as we can tell it marks you as a warrior in the wolf caste."

"Oh." I smiled to myself and Marana squeezed my hand. "Is the person who brought me here still around? I'd like to thank him."

The Wizard shook his head. "He stayed until we told him you would recover then he left."

I scowled. "That's too bad. I would have liked to thank him."

The Wizard frowned. "I told him the very same thing. But he said he had to be going and that you could owe it to him. That's strange, isn't it?"

It was, but people had odd reactions when involved with Talions. Marana laughed and I smiled. "If I owe him a debt, I guess you should tell me his name."

The sorcerer nodded. "He called himself Morai."

Chapter Seventeen

TALION: LOATH: CHAMPION

I escorted Morai from the Castel, less because I didn't trust his thieving heart than from fear some zealous guardsman might discover him leaving the way he got in and end up worse for the encounter. I turned to head off to the ballroom as a servant closed the keep door behind Morai and found Halsted hovering at my shoulder with a smile on his face. "I had thought, my lord, you might have become lost in the unfamiliar surroundings."

I threw off a quick laugh. "I appreciate your concern, but I was merely guiding someone who mistook my quarters for those of the Earl of Cadmar."

Halsted gave no sign of any suspicions about my explanation. He turned and waved me to precede him. "You are needed in the ballroom because it is time for the presentation of gifts to the Princess."

I hesitated, and Halsted smiled, all-knowing. "I have selected Adric to bear a bottle of your family's wine in your stead."

I nodded appreciatively, then bent and whispered something in Halsted's ear. He backed away and looked me over again, then smiled very broadly. "Yes, my lord, an excellent idea. I will see to it personally."

I thanked him and found my way back to the ballroom. I entered through the main doorway—the one centered in the wall left of the stairway to the throne room—and immediately crossed to Count Patrick's side. He smiled when he saw me and covertly pointed out where I should stand.

A small wooden platform served as a dais at the base of the stairs. Rich, blue-satin bunting swathed its sides and a darker blue carpet covered the top of it. A low-backed wooden throne sat on it, and the Princess was seated therein. She smiled when I appeared at her right hand, but the icy stare that accompanied the smile cut at me like a winter gale.

"We are so pleased you could rejoin us, Lord Nolan." Though the smile stayed on her face, the tone of her voice managed to be yet more cold than her stare.

"Forgive me, Your Highness, but a bandit must take any opportunity available to steal what he can." I placed my hands behind my back and tried to look pleasant. I saw Selia in the crowd standing next to Duke Vidor and I nodded at her. She smiled.

The Princess apparently saw my nod and Selia's reaction. Her voice seethed with anger. "You, my lord, are a rogue and a scoundrel."

I turned my head and stared down at her. "The Lady Selia and I finished our conversation in the gardens quickly. You certainly marked her return alone. I may be a bastard, my lady, and I may have been pressed into this duty, but you should know that only something of grave importance would carry me away from acquitting myself honorably in your service." A smile remained frozen on my face while I spoke in whispers and I'm sure only the most unkind court gossip even suggested anger in our words.

Princess Zaria looked straight ahead and ignored me as the first Ambassador presented his gift to her. He approached, introduced himself and his wife, then stepped aside so the servants bearing his nation's token could bring it forward. The servant stood while the Ambassador explained the significance of the offering; then they all moved to the right and deposited the gift on a table.

Incalculable wealth passed before us in a parade containing gifts from every corner of the Shattered Empire and beyond. Many of the gifts were traditional, like twenty of the finest stallions Kartejan had to offer, or a pearl necklace from Takkesh. Each Ambassador made it clear in his description of the item that it represented the hopes of his people for the Princess's long and prosperous life, and a renewal of the good relations between their two nations. The most obsequious speeches came from Hamis's neighbors, while the most interesting gifts came from far away.

The Temuri Ambassador offered a set of eight goblets and a golden pitcher. Each goblet differed and represented the tribe whose artisans had created it, while the pitcher represented the capital of Betil. I had to smile at the arrangement, which subtly implied that without Betil the other tribes would be useless, and wondered if similar thoughts ran through the minds of any Temuri subjects at the reception.

The Daari Ambassador offered the strangest and most chilling gift of the evening. It was a mask of beaten gold that looked exactly like the Princess, and truly matched her beauty from the position I first saw it resting there on a servant-borne velvet pillow. Then the Princess picked it up, letting blue satin ribbons dangle from either temple, and started. She turned it toward me and I saw that delicate and intricately convoluted scrollwork scarred the left profile. At once gorgeous and hideous, it shot a cold lance of lightning through me.

The Princess made no attempt to hide her pleasure with the gifts, and greeted each with wonder and joy. The only exception to this rule was when Lancer Captain Herman appeared before her. As he strode boldly up to the dais and dropped to one knee with military precision that left the other courtiers looking careless and sloppy, she shivered and her smile dulled.

"As you know," he intoned in a deep voice, "Talions acknowledge no ruler other than their Master, and our Ambassadors are simple soldiers, like myself." He smiled, rose, and took from his lieutenant a circular shield with the Lancer crest on it. "We, the Lancer troop in your father's service, present you this shield as a symbol of our pledge to defend your sovereignty and honor your nation."

I saw muscles twitch in her jaw; then she thanked him and nodded to his aide. She did not extend her hand to him to be kissed, and Herman withdrew as if he did not even notice the affront. He turned with razor sharpness and marched away. The only unmilitary thing about him was the trace of a smug grin on his lips.

Once the independent nations finished their presentations, the time came for the gifts from Hamis. The King led the procession bearing the mountain-leopard skin. He knelt at his daughter's feet and laid the pelt out. He smiled at her proudly and brushed away the tear coursing down her right cheek before he withdrew.

Grand Duke Fordel followed his nephew and gave the Princess a key. It opened the door to a villa on Lake Tamar, which lay deep within his demesne. "Because you so enjoyed spending summers there when you were younger, I cede it to you. May the future Kings and Queens of Hamis enjoy it as much as you did." His remarks were relayed back through the crowd and everyone nodded approvingly as the Princess stood and kissed her grand-uncle on the cheek.

Because Count Patrick stood at Princess Zaria's left hand, he could not present his gift to her in person so, as with me, a surrogate took his place. His son, Lord Phillip, nervously carried a toy boat up the Princess, and mumbled something out. The Princess graciously accepted the gift while Patrick translated for his son. "The boat is a model of a sailing ship I have built for you to sail on Lake Tamar, in remembrance of your times there when you were but a child."

The other counties, baronies, and marches in Hamis and Sinjaria followed the royal family and presented gifts that could not match the opulence of the free nations' presents, but were more heartfelt and given to honor her instead of furthering diplomatic aims. The last gift to be offered the Princess was the wine Count Evin had sent, and she received it as graciously as she had any other gift.

As my surrogate turned away I stepped down and stood before her. "I realize, Your Highness, that each of these gifts was given by a people, not by an individual. I have a gift to present to you, and as it would be unseemly for me to give it from myself, and you have already accepted a gift from Yotan, allow me to entrust it to you as an offering from your people, the subjects of Hamis." I turned, pointed to Halsted, and smiled as the elder servant carried the leopard kitten to the Princess.

I took the beast from him and laid him in her lap. "The kitten's mother is dead. Care for the leopard as you will care for us."

I took her hand, kissed it, and looked up. She said something in a small voice, but I didn't hear the words. Recovered from their stunned silence at my action, the nobles burst into spontaneous applause and drowned out her words.

The King stepped up behind his daughter and rested his large hands on her shoulders. "In my daughter's name, and that of a nation, I wish to thank you all. Stay, enjoy the bounty provided by the nobles who hunted with us." He smiled and spread his hands to take in the parade of servants carrying steaming platters of meat to the previously empty serving tables. "But I caution those who would participate in the coming tournament: a full stomach tonight may well presage a short ride tomorrow."

Count Patrick, Phillip, and I wandered the tourney field early that next morning. Brightly colored pavilions had sprouted up like giant rainbow mushrooms all around the field below Castel Seir. Servants and squires trotted over the field carrying everything from food and wine to armor and decorative pennants. Nobles, many of them the same men who followed Grand Duke Fordel in the Dhesiri warren, stood outside their tents in full armor and graciously invited the wandering ladies to sit and watch them spar against their squires or other nobles.

The tournament field stood beyond the forest of pavilions.

The royal box sat in the center of wooden stands on the north end of the field and was situated perfectly to watch the combat. The field itself was level and sown with grass, though the patchy center's brown grass gave way to small areas of golden sand.

The three of us watched two combatants go through an elaborate routine of parries and thrusts. They executed each move with far more flourish than was necessary, but their actions amply thrilled the small group of women standing nearby. I found it mildly amusing, but Patrick frowned.

"I hate this, Nolan, it is so pointless!" He shook his head and waved a hand as if a sorcerer attempting to make all the tents vanish. "The sons of the highest-born lock themselves in tin carapaces to batter each other for the right to be the Princess's Champion during the coronation. Most of them have had little training, and they will limp around court for the next week."

I shrugged as if it he made too much out of a little thing. "That just means there will be less competition for the ladies at the balls to follow the coronation." I nodded my head toward two fighters who fought with more fire and less show. "Besides, if they do learn something in a Grand Melee it might save their lives in the event Hamis goes to war and calls upon them."

The Count smiled in a most evil manner. "In that case, half of them should already have their surrogates fighting for them."

I laughed and we continued our stroll through the tents. The conversation naturally drifted to fighting tactics and strategy and I realized Count Patrick possessed a superior grasp of combat theory, both on an individual and army level. We watched various fighters practicing and discussed the flaws in their styles. Over and over the Count noted one thing that disturbed him. "Most of these nobles just play at fighting. You and the King were deadly in the warren because you were fighting to kill, not to first blood."

I frowned. "Your criticism is not fair. In the warren we, you and the Duke included, had no choice, and we knew we had to kill our foes because they wanted to kill us." I paused and pointed to the nearest fighters. "Most of their fights are to first blood. They are not out to kill, they fight for honor, and that demands a bit of skill, not a death blow."

A bass voice commented from behind us. "That is quite a wise insight, Lord Nolan."

I narrowed my eyes, but forced a pleasantly surprised expression on my face by the time I'd completed my turn. Captain Herman snapped a quick head bow at me by way of a salute and smiled easily. "The question you are wrestling with is this: Would a highly trained warrior defeat these duelists in a battle today?"

I pursed my lips and pondered the question for a moment. "Since you posed the question that way, I assume you have an answer."

The Lancer nodded confidently. "I have no doubt a trained and experienced warrior would tear through the nobles assembled before us."

Count Patrick spoke up with a challenge in his voice. "Perhaps one of your Lancers will enter the lists and prove your theory?"

The Captain smiled and shook his head. "No, I am afraid that is not possible. No Talion could ever participate in such a display because of the politics involved. For a Talion to be chosen the Princess's Champion he would have to ignore the most basic and important dictum Talions live by. We are, at all times, impartial and never become entangled in politics." The Captain turned to me, and a look of surprised joy lit his features. "But Lord Nolan here could prove my theory. By all accounts he is quite skilled at arms."

Before I had a chance to answer I felt a delicate hand slip onto my left forearm. The Princess's hand felt gently for the sheath I'd worn last night, then smiled up at me when she found it. She smiled coldly at the Lancer Captain. "You need not question Lord Nolan, Captain. The rumors of his having been a bandit in the Darkesh are baseless inventions."

Captain Herman smirked self-confidently. "On the contrary, I merely remarked to Lord Nolan that I felt he would do very well in today's combat, and would prove a point I had made to the Count."

The Princess looked at me. "Will you fight for me, Lord Nolan?"

The Lancer froze for a half second like a cat spotting prey.

I smiled graciously and rested my right hand over hers on my arm. "I would gladly do so, Your Highness, but I have no armor." I nodded toward both the Count and Captain Herman. "And even if, as these sage men suggest, I would fight well enough to become your Champion, doing so without armor would be impossible."

Captain Herman clasped his hands together and brought them to his chest in an overdone gesture of joyous discovery. "Why, since none of my men are fighting, I am certain one of my Lancers would lend Lord Nolan armor."

My heart sank, but the look the Princess gave me buoyed it again. "Then if you give him armor, I will give him a shield." She squeezed my arm and turned to the Lancer with an icy stare that appeared to physically impact him.

Captain Herman bowed deeply and turned away. He marched off proudly and shouted orders to his subordinates. The Princess snorted and shivered irritably. "Good riddance."

A frown flashed across my face. "You do not seem to like him very much, do you?"

The anger drained from her eyes and she smiled up at me. "It is not just him, it is all Talions. They are so arrogant and superior. I wish one of his Lancers was in the lists so you could trounce him as well as the others."

"How many Talions have you known, Your Highness?" She shrugged and held up four fingers before I continued. "I think your judgment is rather harsh with such limited experience to back it up. Your father seems to tolerate them well enough. He has not banned them as Jania has."

Princess Zaria's eyes narrowed. "I never expected a Darkesh bandit to be an apologist for the Talions."

I forced myself to laugh easily. "I have learned, over the years, to respect Talions. They train well, fight bravely, and prevent madness and evil from spreading too far."

She smiled and nodded. "Your argument has merit, Lord Nolan, and carries more weight coming from you than it does from Captain Herman or any of the other Talion officers I've ever heard in court. Perhaps, when I become Queen, I will allow the Talions to stay on, but"—she smiled—"only if they send a leader who is not so proud of himself."

For a moment I thought her father had revealed my identity to her, but her last comment plainly told me he had done no such thing. "Until a civil Lancer arrives here, though, may the Goddess rot all Talions."

The Princess disengaged her hand from my arm gently and joined a circle of her handmaidens—which included Countess Jamila. Count Patrick laughed gently and slapped me on the back. "Well, my Lord, it appears you have impressed, or at least interested, my cousin and she wants you to be her Champion."

I scowled. "I would have thought she wanted Duke Vidor to be her Champion. Everything I have heard has linked the two of them. Almost everyone supposes they will wed after she is crowned."

The Count shrugged and led me off toward a black pavilion graced by a Lancer pennant. "I cannot tell you truly why she is so taken with you, though I can guess. Apparently your good looks, the rumor about you being a Darkesh bandit, and your reluctance to confirm or deny that tale have all contributed to your allure." He held the black tent flap aside for me and I preceded him inside the Lancer pavilion. "As for Vidor's fall from favor, I would guess both of them share a weariness for the stories wedding them to each other, and I know the Princess is uneasy with the way Vidor curries favor with all the different power factions at court."

The lone Lancer straightened and rose from the floor. He smiled easily and did not recognize me. I took his offered hand and shook it. "I am Lord Nolan ra Yotan, this is Count Patrick ra Joti ra Hamis and his son Phillip."

The brown-haired, brown-eyed Lancer shook hands with each of them in turn. He stood as tall as me, and had my general build. His grip was firm, his smile easily offered and gladly returned. "I am Lieutenant Slade ra Tal. You'll be using my armor."

I nodded and we all stepped forward to examine it where he'd laid it out on the ground. I knew from his accent he'd been raised in Talianna, from his general appearance and rank I guessed he was four years my senior. Chances were very good we'd never seen each other but for a second or two at mealtimes in Talianna.

He nodded toward the armor. "As you can see Talion armor is constructed a bit differently than the armor used elsewhere in the Shattered Empire. Strips of steel are bound together with cords so they overlap, like slate shingles on a roof, to form the armor itself." He picked up one of the armor strips meant to cover the shoulder and upper arm. "By binding the strings to a piece of leather we get an armor that is flexible and considerably lighter than most conventional armor."

Patrick took the armor, turned it over, and then, when it was right side up again, gently punched it. The overlapping plates stopped his fist soundlessly. "I am impressed. But why are Talions the only people to use this armor?"

Slade smiled. "The design is an old imperial one that was widely used before the joust became part of tournaments. This armor is not as effective as the normal plate when hit by a lance so it fell out of favor. Still," he smiled, "I'd rather have it than nothing."

I smiled weakly at that remark and stripped my doublet off. Slade dropped to one knee and fastened a braced mail greave onto my right leg. I almost asked Patrick to pass me a piece of the armor, which I knew quite well how to don, then stopped prudently. "I think this is the first time I've gotten into armor when not in the midst of some confused attack."

Both men laughed at my comment and started a conversation that buzzed around me without my participation. I felt tension growing within me, and quickly identified the source. Lancers, and in fact every branch of the Talions aside from Justices, all wear face masks sculpted for them alone. It is part of their graduation from novice to Talion in much the same way as the *tsincaat* and *ryqril* are personalized for a Justice when he completes the Ritual. Justices wear a plainer mask of a death's-head design, but I did not have one with me, and could not have produced it even if I had. Unfortunately, since I could not wear Slade's mask, it looked as though I would have to fight with a bare face and, no matter what Patrick or Captain Herman thought of my opposition, I did not want to do that.

I slid the mailed and braced sleeves on and Patrick helped tie a padded doublet in place while Slade fastened around my waist the armored apron meant to protect my thighs. I slipped the back and breast armor on over my head and discovered Captain Herman had entered the tent in the second or two of my blindness.

"I am glad to see the armor fits so well." The Captain smiled at Slade and the Lieutenant placed the bowl-shaped helmet onto my head. A sheet of cord bound steel strips hung down to protect the back of my neck.

Slade swore. "Captain, Lord Nolan cannot use my mask. We cannot send him out without a face mask."

Captain Herman smiled. "We would never do that. Lord Nolan is fortunate. We have a mask like the ones Justices use. It will fit."

He held it out to me and I took it. I noticed a long, black hair tangled on the thong used to tie the mask in place and my mouth went dry. This was Marana's mask!

Slade didn't notice the change in my expression, and thankfully stepped between me and both Captain Herman and Count Patrick. The Lieutenant tugged on one of the shoulder plates until it dropped to the same height as the other one. "There, it's perfect." He smiled at me. "I wish you luck."

He gave me the time I needed to recover. "Thank you, Talion, I appreciate the loan of the equipment." I thumped a gauntleted fist against the breastplate. "I would hate to ruin your armor, so have you any words of advice for me?"

Slade nodded emphatically. "I suggest you avoid the Earl of Cadmar if possible. He is a superior fighter, as you might expect the King's Champion to be, but . . ." He hesitated.

I leaned my head forward and prompted him, "But?"

"The Earl is getting old and tires after a while. When he is tired he is not as quick with his shield as he should be." Then Slade's eyes narrowed. "But that only holds for the Grand Melee. If you have to joust him, forget all that and prepare to be unhorsed."

"Is there nothing I can do to best him in a joust?"

The Lancer smiled. "Perhaps, but I wouldn't want to drive spikes through my legs into the saddle just to become the Princess's Champion."

The selection process for the Princess's Champion was simple and involved only two stages of combat. All those battling to become her Champion would meet in a Grand Melee. The combatants would be divided into two "armies" and would line up in the west or east ends of the field, alternating sides as they were introduced to the spectators. Once everyone was in place, King Tirrell would signal us and both sides would charge toward the other and meet in the center of the field.

The Grand Melee would continue until only two fighters remained on their horses. Those two men then would be set to joust each other, then the victor of that match could be challenged by any of the nobles who had fallen previously, and would have to defeat the challenger in a joust to remain Champion. The first two jousters both put up a personal prize, chosen by their foe, for the victor. Then, to prevent spurious challenges, the champion could demand, and would be allowed to keep, a "ransom" if he defeated the challenger.

Outside the Talion tent I met Adric. He led Wolf, already saddled and encased in armor lent by Count Patrick. I took my swordbelt from the saddle and strapped it around my waist. With Adric's help I mounted and he handed me the shield Captain Herman had given the Princess the previous evening.

The round shield was large enough to cover me from waist to chin. I was quite accustomed to using a shield of this design and slipped my arm through the strap running from top to bottom. I gripped the handle just inside the forward edge and worked the shield up and back. The skull mask hid my satisfied grin.

I waited in line until a page nodded at me, then I urged Wolf forward. Because the mask was tied in place I could not remove it as I stopped before the royal box, but everyone there knew who I was. The tournament consul announced my name and I bowed my head to King and court. They all returned my gesture and I reined Wolf off to take my place in the eastern line.

The wait for the rest of the introductions was short, but it gave me time to mark the absolute paradox of the tournament. The gaily dressed spectators in the stands sat there enjoying a boxed lunch of fruit, cheese, and wine. They looked peaceful and content, as if somehow unmindful of the chaos about to explode before them.

The combatants, on the other hand, exuded nervous energy. Horses stamped and started, while warriors whispered to each other and pointed out members of the other group to avoid. I studied the opposite line and only saw two men who inspired caution in me: Keane and Duke Vidor. I drew my *tsincaat* and set myself because, despite the calm in the stands, this would be anything but a summer holiday.

King Tirrell rose after the last introduction. "My lord, ladies, and esteemed guests. Here, arrayed in all their armored splendor, are the boldest and bravest men on the continent. I commend them to you." Mild, polite, applause erupted from the stands, then died quickly enough. "To you, the men who battle to become the Princess's Champion, I wish the best of fortune. Fight well, brave men, so only the most courageous of you wins the day."

The King turned and took a lace kerchief from his daughter. He raised it high above his head and it fluttered in the gentle breeze cooling the field. He opened his hand and the kerchief gently floated earthward to unleash the expectant warriors.

Men and horses surged forward in a glittering wave of martial ardor. Wolf wanted to burst in among them and out-strip the other horses, but I held him back. I knew the forces unbound when both lines of fighters collided would blast fully a quarter of the men to the ground, and would leave the rest shocked, confused, and disoriented.

I charged Wolf into this secondary pandemonium to smash left and right with both *tsincaat* and shield. I hit the first men I reached and battered them aside while Wolf forced his way between them, then broke through the other line by spilling a small knight to the ground. I jerked the reins firmly shieldside and Wolf responded with a tight turn and lunge that carried us back into the milling disorder. Again we won through and unseated a trio of fighters.

On the other side of the line I took Wolf further out of the fight before we turned again. Huge dust clouds choked the center of the field and made visibility very poor. I cursed softly because I'd not thought to wear a bandana over my nose and mouth. The dust could easily make me sneeze, and the moment that took could be my last in the saddle.

I looked over to my right and saw Duke Vidor waiting for the dust to clear before he charged back into the battle. I raised my *tsincaat* in a salute to him, and he did the same to me. At the same time we shrugged as if we'd each read the other's mind, and closed with each other.

We passed shieldside the first time. I slashed at his head and he blocked the blow with his shield while I stopped his low thrust with my shield. We swept past each other, turned—though his turn was not as tight as mine—and raced at each other again.

I ducked his head-high cut and leaned into him behind my shield. I felt the jarring impact and felt him give way, but the shield punch did not unhorse him. With gentle pressure from my knees I spun Wolf around and prepared for another attack, but the Duke, still unbalanced, had trouble turning his mount. Then he tightened his shield hand's grip on his reins and we charged at each other for the last time.

I feinted high, then slashed lower when his shield rose to defend his head. Because his shield blinded him he didn't see me shift my attack, and only became aware of the cut that sliced through his reins when a two-foot length of each hung limp in his left hand. Wolf whirled again and I knocked the Duke from his saddle with another shield punch before he could turn his mount and adequately oppose me.

Wolf and I swept forward, and into disaster: three knights assaulted us. Two hit us, one from each side, simultaneously. I blocked the sword blow of the one on my left with my shield, but could not parry the attack of the other knight. He wielded a flail and the smooth ball on the end of it smashed down on my right bicep.

Pain burst through my arm, and for the barest of moments, numbed it entirely. The third knight passed on my right and slashed at my head. I leaned away from the blow, avoided the cut, but did not escape untouched. His sword twisted my *tsincaat* free and sent it spinning back over my right shoulder.

I let Wolf race forward before I turned. Someone in the crowd shouted that I was disarmed, but I barely heard him over the thundering sound of hoofbeats as the trio attacked. They came in line this time and expected to unseat me easily.

I drove Wolf straight at the knight with the flail. Wolf responded to my knee pressure and moved so that knight would pass on my right. He rose up in the saddle, whirled his flail above his head, and smashed the ball downward. Wolf, as directed, rammed his horse with a shoulder. The knight leaned toward me to regain his balance and complete the attack, but he failed at both tasks. I smashed a mailed fist into his gorget, then caught at his breastplate and hauled him from the saddle just in time for him to shield my right side from the next knight's attack.

I trapped his right arm against my body, between my shield and breastplate. I dragged him along just far enough for my right hand to pull his flail free; then I dropped him. Even though I'd recovered a weapon, and could once again fight, I knew I'd taken too long and that the third knight's attack would batter me from Wolf's back.

That attack never came. Wolf carried me clear of the fallen knight and I turned. I spotted the third knight lying in a tangled and dented heap. Keane, the Earl of Cadmar, saluted me from horseback above the fallen warrior. I returned the salute and rejoined the fray.

The flail served me well, and, in fact, better than my *tsincaat*. With the blade there was always the chance, in the heat of the moment, I'd twist or cut and find a chink in the armor by instinct. The nobles fighting that day were not as bad as Count Patrick or Captain Herman thought, but I could have slain most of those I fought relatively easily.

The flail had a longer reach than my *tsincaat* and the chain linking ball to haft allowed the ball to bend around shields to hit the knight hiding behind the shield. The ball hit with a harder impact than the *tsincaat*, and I knew better than to carelessly bash away at a head because the weapon was more than capable of denting a helmet and crushing the skull beneath it. Instead I used it to crunch bracers, dent breastplates, or tear weapons and shields from weakened fighters.

Soon masterless horses and crumpled fighters filled the battlefield. Wolf deftly stepped around groaning piles of metal and bones to carry me to the outer fringes of the battlefield where the bodies were not packed so densely. Squires and loyal retainers dodged horses and helped their masters from the field while grooms chased after horses and led them back to the appropriate pavilion.

Although it generated enough stories for that night and the next day to suggest it had lasted a month or more, the Grand Melee ended somewhat quickly. Little by slowly the dust settled and unvictorious aspirants limped and clanked from the battlefield. The only two men still in their saddles turned out to be Keane and me.

The two of us rode up to the royal box. Keane lifted the visor on his helmet and I removed my mask. We looked over at each other and smiled. "I thank you, Lord Earl, for rescuing me when I lost my blade."

King Tirrell stood and cut off any reply from Keane. "You have done well, my lords. Which of you shall be my daughter's Champion?" Already, behind us, servants pounded posts into the ground and strung a rope linking the tops of each from one end of the line to the other. In no time at all they had a barrier sufficient to serve as the center strip for jousting.

The Earl smiled. His broad blond moustache drooped with sweat. "I have an odd request to make of you, sire."

King Tirrell's brows knitted together. "Yes, Keane, Earl of Cadmar, what is it?"

"Because I am your Champion, my King, I would surrender my claim to the same office for your daughter to Lord Nolan." I started and looked over at him, but he just smiled at me. "In addition I will not suffer the indignity of falling beneath his lance."

I shook my head slowly in disbelief. "I think my Lord Earl grossly overestimates my skill."

He smiled. "But I do not underestimate your youth."

The King nodded. "If this is what you wish, I will permit it although I had wished for jousting this afternoon."

The Earl laughed heartily. "I believe you can be granted your wish, my liege, if you will permit me to make the announcement."

The King nodded and Earl Cadmar turned his horse to face the knights who had once again assembled themselves into a ragged line of challengers. "I concede to Lord Nolan. He is the Princess's Champion. And any who wish to challenge him with a lance must defeat me first."

I remained and watched some of the joust, but left when Halsted arrived to assure me that no one would defeat the Earl and suggested I should prepare for the first ceremony that evening. He hinted I would want to rest through the afternoon and into the evening, which I did. Later, after I'd bathed and dressed, I received a visitor.

I warmly welcomed the Earl of Cadmar to my rooms and invited him to sit in front of the fire. He dropped somewhat heavily into one of the chairs and gratefully accepted the offered goblet of wine. Firelight danced along the broad silver circlet encircling his brow. The sapphire set in the coronet matched the blue of his eyes.

I sat. "Why did you concede to me today? I watched you until Halsted came for me." I shook my head ruefully. "Even with spikes driven through my legs to keep me in the saddle, I would have fallen to you, sir."

Keane smiled with my description of the Lancer's final advice. "Thank you, Lord Nolan. I had three reasons for my action today. They vary in import, but all contributed to my decision." He sipped more wine before he continued. "The first reason, the bulk of my decision, is that you are good. The rumors making you a Darkesh bandit do not do you justice. I have fought against those bandits and while they fight like the devil, they are not as good as you. If you were once a bandit, that is not all you were. I salute your weaponmaster, and I believe you would have defeated me"—he smiled coyly over the lip of his goblet—"eventually."

I laughed. "We disagree about our respective abilities and skills. What was your second reason?"

The Earl set his cup down and wiped red wine from his moustache. "In the initial fight we could demand of each other a prize. I would have asked you for the ring the Queen gave you. As a Sinjarian you could have demanded only one thing from me as my prize for you."

I smiled and half nodded. "The Star of Sinjaria."

"Exactly!" Some of his jocularity drained away. "You know of the various plots to win Sinjaria's freedom, I assume?"

I shook my head. "I am too new a noble, and perhaps seen as too close to the Hamisian royal house, to be considered trustworthy by my countrymen."

He nodded. His lips sank into a thin, grim slash across his face. "Many of them, backed by Rimahasti money, seek to promote Vidor as the new King of Sinjaria and offer promises of fealty to King Tirrell in return for independence."

I grimaced. "Then, by conceding to me, did you not play into their hands by allowing victory for a Sinjarian?"

Keane smiled broadly and his face lit up with pride. "Not at all. You are the Sinjarian who saved the King's life. I am the King's Champion and I unhorsed thirty challengers this afternoon. That event will live in stories and songs for a long time, and every time a traitorous plotter hears it he will be reminded that Hamis is as strong as ever." He drained his cup and set it down gently, but I noticed the white tension beneath his fingernails.

He rose and bowed to me. "You are an honorable man, Lord Nolan. I am glad you are the Princess's Champion." He strode to the door, but I stopped him before he could escape.

"My lord, you said you had three reasons to concede. What was the third reason?"

He chuckled and smoothed his moustache with his right hand. "The most important reason of all: my daughter, one of the Princess's handmaidens, and my wife threatened me with horrid tortures if I kept you from serving Her Highness as Champion."

I smiled and sighed as he vanished through the doorway. Apparently the Queen and Grand Duchess were not alone in their ability to manipulate the court.

The first part of the coronation ceremony was scheduled for midnight, so I sent Adric into the town and had him bring Morai to me. He found the thief in a tavern where Selia was performing and brought him back swiftly. I dismissed the youth and asked Morai to bolt the door behind him.

"Congratulations to the new Champion," Morai said as he poured himself some wine. "It was a very close thing, wasn't it?"

That remark raised an eyebrow. "Were you there?"

Morai nodded and a lock of black hair fell across his forehead. "I escorted the Lady Selia. I thought you were in trouble toward the end, when you lost your, ah, *ziinkac*, is it?"

"*Tsincaat*," I corrected him. "I thought that was the end as well. Have you learned anything?"

Morai nodded and set his goblet back down. "If Seir were an open market, and plots to control the throne were for sale, they'd go cheap because there are so many of them." Morai fished a gold coin from his purse and flipped it to me. "Rimahasti gold funneled through Sinjarian hands is buying up half the mercenaries and cutthroats in town." He shook his head and barely stifled a laugh. "The rest of the mercenaries are being bought up by lots of little lordlings to form their own private armies in case someone is plotting against them."

I nodded and toyed with the coin in my hand. It was from Rimah, with King Egan's profile on one side and the image of a warship on the other. "What are the local lords doing about troops?"

"Lots of loyal Hamisians have flooded the city for the ceremony. I've noticed several taverns have been taken over by contingents from the various parts of Hamis, excluding conquered Sinjarian provinces, and they're run very much like military camps."

I stood and walked toward the fireplace. "Is there a sense of expectation in air?" I groped blindly for words to frame my question accurately. "Does it seem to you something is going to happen soon?"

Morai's eyes narrowed, then he nodded cautiously. "I think I know what you mean. Most of the mercenaries have been paid to stay through the ceremonies and masquerade tomorrow night on into the middle of the week . They've been promised more money and service after that, but I would assume anything that will happen will take place at the masquerade." Then the thief shrugged. "But this place will be sewn up so tight tomorrow night no one will be able to get in or out, despite the fact everyone will be in costume. If I hear anything I'll send word, but I won't be visiting."

"True, security will be as tight as possible, but I don't know if that will be tight enough." I grimaced. "I need an edge and you're it, Morai. Watch me, and remember the word *drijen*. If I get killed someone else will come, a Fealareen Talion. You'll have to tell him everything you've told me so far, including what I'm about to show you, *and* anything else you learn. *Drijen* is a signal I've worked out with the other Talion. It will identify you to him as someone he can trust."

Morai's expression faded to grimness. He licked his lips nervously. "*Drijen*, got it."

"Good, that's it." I reached up to the stone shield above the fireplace and pushed a crescent moon in the design. The stone rasped and slid in. I heard a click and the shield swung out to the left on hidden hinges. It revealed a small alcove barely a foot square or deep.

Morai smiled. "I know about that already, Talion. I paid my sources here very well. I expected to find the Star in there; it was the first place I searched last night."

I smiled. "No surprise you knew of this." I ignored the alcove itself and, from the back of the shield, removed the stone disk that had the crescent on it. As large as my palm, only the top half of it, about two inches in depth, was carved to form the crescent moon. I carried it into my bedroom and over to the washbasin. Morai followed me wordlessly.

I set the stone down and removed the mirror from where it hung. A round wooden plug with a hook in it was sunk into the wall. I worked it loose, then picked the stone up and fitted it into the hole so the crescent did not show. A half inch of the disk still stuck out of the wall. I grasped it and twisted it around three times, then stepped back.

The whole wash area scraped along the floor and twisted open to reveal a passage into the mountain behind Castel Seir.

I turned to Morai. His mouth hung open in shock. "Talion, there's no way this passage exists. My sources were the best"—he pounded his right fist into his left palm—"the best, dammit, and I paid them as if they were. They said the Castel had no secret passages in the Wolf Tower."

I smiled weakly. "Remember, I'm a Talion. I have sources that considerably predate anything you might obtain through bribes. This passage leads down to the old family crypts and fell into disuse soon after the Shattering." I pointed back behind him, "Grab a candle, light it, and follow me."

Dust blanketed the passage and rippled like fog as we walked through it. The passage circled the tower and passed through double thick walls where it left the cliffside. Narrow stairs led to the upper two levels, and another passage ran off into the mountain. We followed it and descended quickly.

Morai rubbed his nose and sneezed. "Well, at least we know no one has been through here in ages."

I nodded and stopped. The flickering light from the candle revealed a cave-in blocking the passage to the crypts. The walls had collapsed and solidly sealed the passage except for a narrow space up by the ceiling.

I took the candle from Morai and held it up there. The flame did not waver. "No draft. The passage must be sealed again further down."

Morai nodded in agreement. "Not only that, but I've seen the entrance to the crypts you're talking about. It's all overgrown with vines and half-covered with dirt. It would take ten men a week to clear it away and unseal the tombs."

"No one is coming through here." I nodded. "Since you seem able to get into the Wolf Tower at will, you can at least use this passage to move unseen within the tower."

"Or the passage can be used to evacuate the tower if there is trouble."

I smiled. "Good thinking."

"You inspire the best in me, Talion." He pried a rock out of the earthen pile and pitched it through the hole. "Any idea when this tunnel was last used?"

I returned the candle to him and toyed with the ring on my finger. "I believe it was when King Roderick dumped Prince Uriah's murdered body in the crypts. In fact, legend has it that King Roderick collapsed this tunnel himself because the breezes running through it sounded like ghostly moaning to him. At least that's one of the scariest tales I heard as a child."

"And you believe it?"

I nodded slowly, then smiled. "At least enough to check and make sure this avenue wasn't open."

We marched back up through the darkness. The shadows swallowed the tunnel below us, and even the sound of our footsteps vanished within the gloom. Morai got a bit excited when he noticed the washstand had closed behind us, but I reached up above the doorway and pressed a block to open the doorway again.

Once safely ensconced in the suite I reset the door and crescent. Morai finished the goblet of wine he poured to cut the dust in his throat and stared at me. "You surprise me, Talion, very much. Perhaps, someday, you'll see how your talents and knowledge are wasted chasing after me, and you will join me."

I smiled and shook my head. "I think that is unlikely,

although we are," I said, raising my left hand and showing him the back of it, "brothers within the wolf caste."

He smiled. "Then you won't mind telling me, brother to brother, how many people know about that passage?"

I turned and stared distractedly at it. "You mean other than us? No one. All the others who know that secret are dead."

I summoned Adric and had him escort Morai from the castle. Morai's report worried me. The masquerade would be the perfect place for the *nekkeht* to strike. The costumes worn to a coronation masquerade, while always beautiful or striking, traditionally represented evil and malignant creatures. At midnight everyone unmasked at the newly crowned person's request in a symbolic banishment of all evil from the kingdom. Certainly more than one Lurker would be among the guests, in addition to demons, *jelkoms*, and a host of terrifying creatures.

That alone, though, could not be the reason factions braced for tomorrow night. Each group wished to place its puppet in a position to further its aims, but what would change that night to make that happen? Even as I framed the question, the answer dawned on me: Duke Vidor might take that opportunity to propose marriage to the Princess! And if he'd informed all the factions of his plans, each would be ready. . . .

Halsted's arrival interrupted any further analysis of Morai's information. He was not alone and moved out of the doorway so a priest dressed in a robe of forest green could enter. Clean-shaven and bright-eyed, he wore his long brown hair in a braid that dangled over his right shoulder to his waist.

I rose and bowed to him. "Welcome be the Hand of Shudath."

"And to you Her blessings." The priest signed a blessing with his right hand. With only two fingers erect he brought his hand up in a wavy line, symbolic of a new plant shoot growing up to the sun, then opened his hand full up like a blossom. He smiled kindly and folded his arms across his chest. His hands disappeared into the large sleeves of the robe.

I invited him to sit, but knew better than to offer him

wine. My family had worshipped Shudath the All-Mother in Sinjaria, as did most of the farm families that made their living off the land. Though I no longer practiced after I left Sinjaria, I'd grown to respect the simple, majestic religion that held both nature and the family sacred. I felt very much at ease with the priest.

Halsted looked at me. "Lord Nolan, Hand Fial will explain your role in this evening's vigil." Halsted bowed and retreated from the room.

Fial smiled easily. "Your part in this holy mystery may seem simple, but it is of the utmost importance. As her Champion you will guard the Princess so nothing can disturb her vigil in the Moon Tower."

I nodded. "I am at your service. Tell me what I must do, and I will do it."

"Good, good." The priest reached out and gently patted me on the forearm. "This evening is the completion of the ritual that began with the Princess's Dreamvigil. In that dream she saw a mountain leopard and now that it has been slain, to directly testify to the veracity of her dream, she will await a visit by the Goddess Shudath."

The priest got to his feet as if in a trance and paced the room silently. "Your part may not be easy to play. The visitation may take different forms. Often a child has emerged from the tower after nothing more unsettling than a night's rest, but occasionally we have unsealed the chamber to find both child and Champion aged unto death."

He spoke with a distracted tone, but that did nothing to soften the impact of his words. Still, he did not invite comment from me, and continued on as if I barely existed. "Your role this night is to protect the Princess if she needs it; otherwise you are to do nothing but observe. The Princess must not be disturbed in her meditations, and unless she is threatened, you must do nothing. Above all, you may never reveal anything you see or hear, and you may not address the Goddess except in the unlikely event she first speaks to you."

I nodded my head to indicate I understood; then I inserted a question before he could speak again. "Has that ever happened? Has the Goddess ever spoken to the Champion?"

Fial's face regained some life and he shrugged. "Clearly, Lord Nolan, I have no way of knowing. The Goddess comes to the children in the royal line to remind them of their connection to the nation. If they treat the nation kindly and attend to the problems therein, their reign will be smooth and long. If they are tyrannical and cruel, their time on the throne will be very difficult, and though short, will seem like a very long time indeed. If the Goddess has ever chosen to speak with a champion we do not know because they have never spoken of their experience, as I expect you will not either."

I nodded and pressed my hands together palm to palm. "Your requirement of secrecy would seem best served by having no one with the Princess at all."

Pain narrowed the priest's eyes. "That was once how it was, but disturbed vigils caused instability and the nation suffered for it."

I thought for a second, then looked down at the fire. "The Rodericks."

The priest smiled warmly. "I see you understand."

I nodded gravely. "Nothing will disturb this night for the Princess."

Another Hand of Shudath knocked and entered my suite. He communicated with Fial through hand signals, was rewarded with a hearty nod, then presented me with a package. I untied the twine and unwrapped the leather covering. Within I discovered a robe cut along the same lines as those worn by the priests, but mine was blood red.

Fial pointed to the robe. "It is the color of the blood you are willing to shed in her defense. You must put it on, and then bring your sword to me."

I stepped into the wardrobe room and changed quickly. I brought the priest my *tsincaat* and he slipped it from the sheath. "You take very good care of your blade, Lord Nolan."

I smiled. "And it does the same of me, Hand Fial."

The priest passed his hands above and below the blade, then wiped it once with a red silk cloth. He passed the *tsincaat* back to me and indicated I should follow him. I did and, with the second priest following behind, I climbed the stairs to the Princess's suite.

Only the lurid red light coruscating from the boar's-head hearth in her antechamber illuminated the room. Another priest, armed with a censer, stood behind the Princess. Smoke curled up from the censer and filled the room with a fragrant haze.

The Princess wore a white silk gown—sleeveless, and really little more than a sheet of soft fabric. A simple silver pin securely fastened it at her right shoulder. The gown hung to the floor and a white cord belted it at the waist.

Her hair hung loose, without even a coronet or comb in it, but was brushed so it cascaded over her bare left shoulder. Her brown eyes were almost entirely pupil, more so than called for by the subdued light in the room, and she stared unwavering at something I could not see. She already seemed to be communicating with the Goddess.

Hand Fial gently guided me to my spot beside the Princess; then the priest with the censer walked around us three times. He chanted in a voice so low that the sound of the censer ringing off the impact with the chain on which it swung stole half his words. He paused once to let smoke enfold my *tsincaat*, then Hand Fial led us from the chamber and on through darkened corridors to the Moon Tower.

The priests opened the Moon Tower and preceded us in. The leading priest bore the censer, and thick smoke hung in the air to mark the way for us. Then one priest with a candle headed up the stairs before the Princess, and Hand Fial followed me as I walked behind her.

We climbed up and around the tower until we reached the uppermost chamber. Smaller than I might have expected, the room had four arrow slits to serve as windows, and had unadorned walls and floor of stone and wood respectively. The mountain-leopard skin lay already spread out in the center of the room, but, aside from us and it, the room stood utterly empty.

I took up my station to the left of the door at the place indicated by Hand Fial; the candlebearer and the censerward flanked me. The Princess knelt on the leopard skin. Hand Fial took the censer and walked around her three times. The censer belched out great gouts of smoke, but they dissipated in the light crossbreeze coming through the windows.

Hand Fial stopped behind the Princess and bowed to something in front of her. "Oh Wise and Wonderful, Giver of All That Is Life, Mother of the World, I present to you your Daughter, Zaria ra Hamis. She is of the Age, and Openly Accepts Your Divine Mission for Her."

He bowed again and turned toward the door. He took the candle from the other priest and placed it on the floor at the Princess's right side. The other two priests left the room before him. He did not acknowledge me with more than a flick of the censer in my direction. I moved away from the wall and shut the door.

I had no bar to drop into place, nor a key with which to lock the door, which made me somewhat uneasy. Aside from that, though, the room was secure, so I envisioned little difficulty keeping people from disturbing the ritual. I set my back to the door and I faced the Princess. I trusted my hearing to warn me of any intruders, and the uncomfortable position in which I stood to keep me awake enough to react to them.

I watched the Rabbit Moon travel from the southern arrow port to the western one and knew two hours had passed—so far in complete and utter silence. My heels and shoulders began to protest but I ignored them because the Princess stayed on her knees, barely moving, for all that time and never shifted to make herself more comfortable. I watched her shoulders rise and fall with her breathing. The motion was even and regular enough for her to be asleep, but I knew she was awake. She stared straight ahead and watched the spot Hand Fial had bowed at earlier.

Then I saw it. It started as a spark, then flared into a blossom of fire. I raised my left hand to shield my eyes because of the brightness and saw the wolf symbol burn with purple flames on its back. The light died quickly and in its wake stood a woman, or so it appeared. One look at her eyes, though, and I knew she was more than human.

She was naked, after a fashion, because although she wore no clothing, she covered her body with the soft fur of a mountain leopard just like the pelt upon which the Princess knelt. Animal flesh made her no less beautiful or seductive, but there was something about her stance and demeanor that set her beyond all sexual considerations.

She smiled lovingly at the Princess and reached out to stroke Zaria's cheek with a lissome, furred finger. "I welcome you, Daughter, and I have for you a prophecy." Her words echoed upon themselves a thousand times over, but were not loud. The sound sent an eerie chill down my spine because I could hear my mother and grandmother in her voice. "Your reign will be long. You will wed the Duke of Sinjaria and bear him children. Through you a wrong will be righted, and by your hand many wrongs will be made right. You will please me."

The Goddess stroked Zaria's silky black hair, then closed the Princess's eyes. The Princess gently slumped to the ground unconscious and slept peacefully.

The Goddess looked up at me and her voice hissed like the cat whose skin she wore. "And now for you, Talion, Nolan ra Sinjaria." She snarled and called me by another name.

Remorsefully I shook my head and dropped to my knees. "I am no longer known as that."

She laughed and ridiculed me in a million voices. "I know you in all that you are. Do not imagine that because you have abandoned your true self others have."

Old feelings bubbled up inside me, but I strangled the child's cry they invoked. "There is no one else who knows, and I have not forsaken my true self. I have changed and grown beyond what I was before, not shed that identity like a snake would a skin."

The Goddess watched me and weighed my words. "No prophecy for you, Talion, only warnings. Remember them, heed them. Death stalks Seir, and you are one he waits to claim."

In speaking, she began to change. Her body bloated and twisted to mock her previous beauty. Open sores ruptured her flesh and coated it with a thick, translucent green liquid streaked with scarlet. Scarab beetles crawled from the gaping holes in her skin to chew it and strip her to the bones. Her stomach burst open and I saw maggots writhing there to burrow deeper and consume even more of her. A bony finger pointed at me, and her voice rasped in a funereal parody of her message to the Princess. "Listen to me, Talion."

Her scalp split and the flesh dropped to either shoulder, but instead of the ivory bone I expected to see, something else rested atop her neck. Her skull was pure crystal, like the skull in Talianna, and the light it projected dissolved away everything below it. I stared into the empty sockets but all I saw was a distorted reflection of the room.

Disembodied, the Goddess's voice filled the tower. "Mighty though you are, Talion, able to crush the living," it said, the crystal jaw moving and ringing with each word, "you cannot defeat the dead!"

Chapter Eighteen

NOVICE: JUSTICE

I stood nervously just inside the doorway to Lord Hansur's chambers. The Justice Lord sat at his desk, and seated across from him was the Wizard who had been overseeing my recovery. Although I'd regained consciousness three days before, the spell numbing my shoulder was still in force and my left arm hung in a sling.

"Come in, Nolan, and please be seated." Lord Hansur pointed to the chair next to the Wizard. "Wizard Adamik and I have been talking about your recovery. Because of some things he has said I have reached a difficult decision and I wanted him here to answer any of your questions."

I nodded. My stomach tightened. The one thing I'd feared since I'd awakened was about to happen.

Lord Hansur steepled his fingers and frowned. "I am afraid you will not be able to test with the other Seventeens, nor undergo the ritual of the Skull with them."

My stomach flopped the pain spread form it like the poison had spread from my shoulder. "Do you mean I am dismissed from Talion service?" I forced the words past the lump in my throat, then ground my teeth together to keep my jaw from trembling.

Lord Hansur smiled kindly and shook his head. "No, Nolan, not that at all. Your shoulder is just not up to the rigors of the test at this time." He looked to the Wizard for confirmation, and the white-haired magicker nodded gravely.

I hesitated, then nodded to the Wizard. "Please do not take this question as any my doubting your ability in any way, because I do not, but can't you just, um, *fix* my shoulder?"

The Wizard smiled benignly. "No, Nolan, I cannot just repair the damage with magick. You suffered a serious injury. The poison destroyed a great deal of muscle tissue. I can use spells to stop infection and to stimulate growth of new muscle and flesh, but the spell's effectiveness is in direct proportion to how soon it is cast after the injuries occur." He frowned and spread his hands in a gesture of helplessness. "My spells could regenerate a severed limb, if I could summon enough power and direct it at the wound the instant the limb was struck off."

I nodded, but Adamik saw I still had reservations so he pressed on. "You know the Archer Seventeen in the bed beside you?"

"Dyre, the one with the broken leg?"

The Wizard nodded. "That was a nasty break. Dyre snapped both bones in his left shin and one poked through his flesh." The Wizard turned to Lord Hansur. "He was out on a survival exercise and fell into a gorge. It took several days to find him." Adamik faced me again. "The people who found him set the bones, but did a poor job. Healing had already begun by the time he came to us, so we had to break the bones again and reset them. Our spells can only aid his recovery, like yours, and both you and he will have to do the rest."

Lord Hansur rose. "So, Nolan, I expect you to design a full regimen of exercises to speed your recovery, and fit that into a full training schedule. Wizard Adamik tells me it should take you six months to fully rebuild your damaged muscles. By the Festival I expect you to be ready for your final test."

I realized I was dismissed. I stood and bowed to both men, then walked from the room. Outside, in the hallway, Marana and Jevin detached themselves from the shadowed walls and fell in beside me. Marana slipped her left hand into my right hand.

"So, Nolan, what did he say?" Jevin's deep voice revealed none of the nervousness I knew he felt.

I smiled. "Well, I won't be tested with the rest of the Seventeens and I won't go through the Ritual with you." Marana's hand jumped within mine, but I just smiled at her and slipped my right arm up around her shoulders. "But I am not discharged and, once my left arm works well enough, I will be tested."

Lord Hansur decided, and Wizard Adamik concurred, I should live in the infirmary until my recovery had progressed to a level to be determined later. This kept me apart from the other Seventeens, and that was a good choice because it kept me from distracting them in their final preparations for the Ritual, and saved me from depression as I watched them move further and further away from me.

During the evenings Marana, Jevin, other Seventeens beside Lothar, and I did get together, but my days were so full I saw virtually no one from my old group. The time I spent pushing and training myself were not happy times, because I drove myself very hard, but they did satisfy me.

Adamik kept my shoulder numb for a full two weeks after I awoke, and that caused a certain problem with my training. Until I had some use of that arm I could do nothing to build it up, so my first two weeks' exercise consisted of long runs in the morning and evening, and an interesting research project in the afternoons.

Lord Hansur had never spoken to me about my Journey. I knew better than to imagine he'd forgotten, though it did occur to me he might have put me aside while the others prepared for the Ritual. Whatever the case, and whatever he planned to say to me, I decided to salvage something out of my final adventure and perhaps prove I'd not been as foolish as I felt.

I sought out and conspired with a heavyset, square-jawed Services armorer by the name of Gilbere to produce a dozen of the Xne'kal throwing darts. I described the weapons to him as best I could, and under his thorough interrogation I recalled more details than I realized I remembered. He rejected immediately the idea of a flint needle, and by the next afternoon had made a triple-edged triangular needle and sunk it into the body of a featherless crossbow quarrel.

I smiled as he pointed out a target in the back of his shop. "Go ahead, Nolan, you'll be the first to try it."

I flipped the dart at the target as I would have tossed a knife. The dart spun end over end, slapped flat against the target, and fell to the ground. I tried it a dozen more times, and as I got used to the weight I got better, but still could only stick the six-inch-long needle into the target about half the time.

Gilbere and I both shrugged and I offered him the dart back. He waved it off. "I can make more. Perhaps you can practice while running or will figure something out."

I practiced with the dart during my evening run, but the results, if anything, were more discouraging than earlier that day. I left the dart on my bed and snuck out of the room so I'd not awaken Dyre—he was asleep in the next bed over. I walked to the baths and soaked myself until my hands and feet looked like prunes, then reluctantly returned to my ward in the infirmary.

Walking down the hallway I heard thunk, *creak*, thunk, *creak* repeat itself several times over. I burst into the room and saw Dyre sitting up in bed throwing the dart into his footboard. Thunk. Then he leaned forward, *creak*, and pulled it free. The footboard was peppered with little holes and the two throws I watched sank into the wood perfectly.

Dyre looked up when I entered. "Hope you don't mind." He smiled sheepishly and shrugged. "I was bored. This thing is pretty neat. What is it?"

I stabbed an accusatory finger at his footboard. "How'd you do that?" A look of horror passed over his face as he realized, for the first time, the damage he'd done to his bed, but I shook my head. "No, not the bed. How did you make it stick so often?"

Dyre shrugged his shoulders. "It was easy. This thing needs some more weight up front, but it flies fine." He brought the dart up by his ear, held it in the middle of the quarrel, and threw. The dart spun from his fingers, never flipped end over end, and stuck perfectly in the footboard.

I let my breath out. "Oh, you're throwing it the wrong way." I plucked it from the footboard and flipped it at the wall across the room. True to form it slapped the wall and bounced to the floor.

Dyre narrowed his eyes. "Don't they teach you Justices anything? Give me that dart." I picked it up and handed it to him. "I'd have put it into the wall long ago, but then I couldn't get to it." He tapped the dart on his numbed leg.

Dyre once again threw and the dart flew straight to the target. As I stared in astonishment, Dyre chuckled. "The most important thing is a *spin*, Nolan. Why do you think we fletch arrows? It makes them spin so they fly straight."

I thought for a second, then crossed and pulled the dart from the wall. "Fletching. I hadn't thought of that because the Xne'kal didn't do it."

Dyre snorted angrily. "They don't fletch their darts because they don't need fletching. You give the dart a spin when you throw it. Think of it as a javelin and try again."

Slowly what he was saying got through to me. I held the dart as he had and threw. It wobbled a bit in flight but stuck in the wall. I smiled broadly. "And fletching would make it turn in only one direction, right?" I pulled the dart from the wall and held it down at my side with the needle pointing toward the ground. "But that spin would be wrong for an underhanded toss, like this."

I whipped the dart forward and spun it hard. I released as my hand swept up above my waist and the dart stuck into the wall two feet above and to the left of Dyre's rapidly sinking head. I laughed at the expression on his face when he looked up at the dart, but then he joined my laughter.

"I think," he sighed, "you understand the principle, Justice."

• • •

Because of that night's revelations I introduced Gilbere to Dyre and the two of them took over the whole process of designing the darts. They never gave me any advance notions of what they'd have cooked up by the time I returned from my morning run, and I'd spend most of the afternoon trying different prototypes. After I'd completed the series of tests they gave me, they mercilessly interrogated me and nodded conspiratorially when I said something that pleased or angered them.

Adamik finally lifted the spell on my shoulder and the stiffness and weakness appalled me. My first impulse was to shift away from all other exercise and just work on my shoulder, but Adamik advised against that and I saw the wisdom of his warning. All I needed to do was tear the muscles up worse by overworking them. If I did that I might never recover.

A week after I regained use of my arm, Wolf reappeared in Talianna. He no longer wore my saddle or bridle, but he looked fit. His Excellency took charge of the tack he arrived with—I would not have wanted to be identified as the person who kidnapped a Talion horse—and I made his care my responsibility.

Wolf's return, and the growing strength in my left shoulder, shifted my training regimen again. I still ran in the morning, and now included exercises along my run to strengthen my arm. My afternoons changed so I could train with other novices and regain my battling skills. I abandoned my evening run and spent much of that time with Dyre and Gilbere working on the darts.

The two of them decided on a final design. The needle design Gilbere came up with originally survived to the finished product. A lead ring crimped the wood in around the needle tang and added weight to the dart's front half to increase its tendency to hit needle-first even with a poor throw. Finally twelve inches of hardwood made up the weapon's haft and had three-inch long grooves, eight of them, carved parallel into the base of the shaft. They acted as very simple neutral fletching and stabilized the dart in long flights.

Once they gave me the final darts I started training with them in the evenings. Dyre's initial observation, that spin was all important, still held true. I discovered that no matter how I threw a dart, if I gave it enough spin, it flew straight and usually hit the target I aimed for. I practiced hard with the darts, at least two hours a night for five months, and became more than proficient with either hand.

The new weapon attracted a certain amount of attention. Dyre was finally up and around and his enthusiasm for it intrigued a number of Archers to try it. Because I'd practiced with it a great deal, my ability dwarfed theirs at the start, and that discouraged many of them. Still, the few who did remain quickly learned to use the darts very well, and the evening training sessions usually ended up with a contest and wagering to see who could hit whatever improbable target we selected that night. Overripe tomatoes topped the list of favorite targets because of the way they exploded when hit dead center.

Interest in the darts prompted, about a month before Festival, an official demonstration of the weapon. The Master wanted the weapon evaluated as a possible addition to Talion arms. As his judges he chose Lord Fletcher, Lord Hansur, and His Excellency. They spent the early part of the day questioning Gilbere and Dyre about the weapon's design and manufacture. Once they'd satisfied themselves about technical details, they invited me to demonstrate the weapon in a practical combat simulation.

The demonstration range occupied a small portion of the training yard southeast of the Star. Four Justice Fifteens and I waited at the start of the range. Each of them carried a pouch of overripe tomatoes to use as missiles against me and wore a different color armband. I was armed with a dozen darts and could take one of them out of the fight by hitting one of the dummies scattered over the course that corresponded in color to their armband. The only difficulty stemmed from the condition that I could only hit a dummy if the appropriate Fifteen was in sight, and there were plenty of barricades for them to use as cover.

Lord Hansur waved the Fifteens into the range and waited until they'd hidden themselves before he signaled me to hunt them. I turned and ran into the range with one dart in each hand. I caught a flicker of motion in the corner of my right eye and dove forward. A tomato burst behind me and I saw a trace of blue before the novice vanished.

I grimaced and rolled to my right. That Fifteen, a dark-haired, gangling kid named Alf, would be the toughest to get. I rose to my feet, then crouched and rolled back left. Two Fifteens, yellow and red, stood and threw tomatoes through where I'd stood. I threw with my right hand and sank a dart into the red dummy, but Yellow ducked away too quickly for me.

I ran forward and stopped in front of the barricade where the red Fifteen had hidden. To my right I heard a rasping sound and turned just in time to see White rise up and throw. I twisted aside and the tomato exploded on the barrier. White dropped back out of sight as the fruit drenched me with seeds and pulp.

"Damn," I swore aloud and raised a dart beside my ear. White popped back up to see if he'd hit me, and recognized his mistake. I launched the dart and hit a white dummy square in the chest.

I shifted the dart from my left to right hand, wiped tomato from my face, and reached up with my empty hand to the top of the barricade. I jumped up and pulled myself over the three-foot-tall wooden breastwork, but the second my feet touched the ground I had to push off and flip myself back over it again.

A tomato flew between my spread legs and smashed into the wood. Alf dropped from sight again before I could throw, but while I was falling, and in midair, the chances any shot I took would be accurate were extremely long. I slammed rather hard into the ground, but continued to somersault backward to make myself as small a target as possible.

On my left Yellow stood and threw three tomatoes in rapid succession. The first two splashed the ground behind me, but the third was thrown perfectly and dead on target. I leaped up from a crouched ball as the last tomato liquefied beneath my feet. I swept my left hand out the side and arced a dart at the nearest Yellow dummy. The dart hit home before Yellow safely ducked behind cover.

Now Alf and I were all alone. I ran from barrier to barrier and watched for any movement at all. I saw nothing, then, as I worked myself around toward the east, a small wisp of dust curled out from behind a barricade and betrayed Alf. Beyond his hiding place stood a blue dummy.

In an instant a plan sprang to mind and I acted upon it. I could only throw at the dummy while I could see Alf, and he was far too quick to expose himself for the time it would take to sight and throw. Determined to keep him in sight for long enough to hit the target, I rose up and ran directly at his position.

Alf never moved as I charged. I sprinted across the open ground, ready to throw the second I saw any part of him, but he remained concealed. It was a war of nerves, and neither of us was going to give in.

I laughed and leaped up to the top of his barricade. I kicked off it and jumped yet higher into the air. Alf, lying flat on his back, grinned at me and snapped a tomato past my left ear. Chuckling, I spun slowly and threw the dart in my right hand. It sailed into the blue dummy's head at the same time Alf's second tomato burst on and drenched my chest. I collapsed to the ground and laughed until my sides ached.

My mirth died when Lord Hansur's shadow fell across my face. He stood flanked by Lord Fletcher and His Excellency. I climbed to my feet at once, bowed deeply, and heard Alf scrambling to do the same behind me.

Lord Fletcher spoke first, and addressed himself to Lord Hansur. "Your novice's weapon does seem to have some use, which is more than I can say for his tactical sense." Offered lightly, the latter half of his comment put me at ease.

His Excellency pulled the dart from the white dummy and turned it over in his hands. He frowned. "It penetrates flesh well enough, but does not have enough force to penetrate bone. It would have to be poisoned." Lord Hansur nodded and His Excellency looked over at me. "The Xne'kal poison their darts?"

I nodded. I knew the idea of poison was not well liked in Talianna, but I'd taken some time to read about poisons in the library. "If you will permit me, my lords, I've read of a plant poison—not the one the Xne'kal use—used by the Harashu in the Green Desert beyond Sterlos. It paralyzes without killing when used in diluted enough form." I looked down. "It is called *kutarai*."

Lord Hansur bowed his head toward me. "Thank you, Nolan, and you Alf, for this demonstration. Alf, you are dismissed. Nolan, clean yourself up and report to my chambers within the hour."

Lord Hansur already sat at his desk by the time I reached his chambers. For some reason I felt prompted to wear my uniform—the sleeveless black leather tunic and black leather breeches over riding boots—and felt very nervous at this meeting. Lord Hansur invited me into his room and indicated I should sit in the single chair before his desk.

"Nolan, I have spoken with Ring. I wish to know why you terminated your Journey with him."

His voice gave me no clue as to Lord Hansur's feelings about Ring, my actions, or me, but I stiffened nonetheless. While having read my journal, he had postponed the evaluation of my Journey until Ring was available to him. I forced my fears back into their little box and spoke as a man willing to take full responsibility for his actions. "I will not blame Ring for what I did. I left him because I believed I would learn more apart from him than with him."

Set in a mask of concentration, Lord Hansur's face revealed nothing. He leaned back in his big chair and stared past me. He weighed every word I said, and I knew he wanted to hear more because he'd not stopped me. I complied with his unspoken wish.

"I know the Journey year is especially important for a Justice because we travel and learn about the world, and we have a chance to practice our deductive and detective skills. I know we travel with experienced Justices who show us the world, and show us how a Justice must survive in that world. I understand that part of our Journey, and I value the time I spent with Ring for what of that he did teach me."

I grimaced and thought for a moment. "But with Ring I was unable to answer questions I had, about myself, and about how I wanted to survive in the world. Before I came to Talianna I knew what it was like to feel the fear Ring used to goad people, and I did not like that feeling then. By the same token, I could remember hearing stories about a lone Justice scattering bandits from an isolated homestead, and that type of life I did want."

Lord Hansur nodded slowly. "So why did you leave Ring?"

I thought and slowly exhaled. "Ring's belief in his way of doing things is incredibly strong. It makes him very effective, and I'd certainly not like to have him after me, but it also keeps him back away from the world. He would not be incapable of helping someone in a dangerous situation, and when we searched burned ruins for the bodies of children he worked as hard, if not harder, than anyone else. It's just"—I searched for the correct words—"his method never lets him *care* for anyone.

"In the half year I spent with Ring I learned how he worked, and I knew I could work that way, if I *had* to. I also knew working that way would eat me up inside. Perhaps it comes from being raised by a family before I came here, I don't know, but cloaking myself in shadow and terror would kill me. I need people, and I need their respect and friendship instead of their fear and loathing."

The Master of all Justices' expression lightened and he looked at me. "So, novice, what did you learn during your Journey?"

I sat back and unscrambled the emotions racing around so I could see what I had learned. "I've learned that people can accept a Justice as someone to be welcomed instead of feared. For some people a Justice is an authority who can intervene and prevent an injustice from taking place. For others a Justice is a guarantee that evil actions will be punished, or their misfortune will be avenged. I agree with those views, and I learned to present another Justice face: that of a friend who was willing to help."

I closed my eyes and rubbed them for a second. "I remember times, when I was a child, when all of us had to go out in the middle of the night and fight a wildfire or fight to destroy as many locusts as possible before they ate all our crops. I remember hunting for lost animals or children, and I remember my father going out to help hunt down cattle thieves. All those things are part of daily survival for the people living in the lands we patrol, yet Justices can be so far removed from that reality that they can ask a family for food and lodging and hand them a slip of paper in payment. That paper is valueless until the tax collectors come, and paper will not feed the family when food runs low. That's not justice."

I sighed. "I guess what I learned is that justice, for me,

must be tempered with mercy and common sense. Chasing after murders can rob that from a Justice. When I rode into that village in Juchar and Marko set his two henchmen on me, I could have killed them, and him, then gone after his master because of the affront to me. And I cannot say, here and now, that in the future I might not do that, but at the time that was not important. The *just* thing for me to do, I believed then and believe now, was to solve the village's problem as simply as possible."

Lord Hansur narrowed his eyes. "You cannot always befriend everyone. There are those who will try to use you for their own ends."

I smiled and nodded. "I understand that, my lord. I know the only solution to the problem of an insane murderer is his death. I accept that. I also know the image of implacable Justices falling upon criminals deters people from petty crimes. I realize Ring's image of a Justice has its places and uses, and I will not shrink from adopting that image as I need it.

"To the felons I am sent after I will be remorseless and unstoppable. Those who try to advance themselves at my expense will find they are as vulnerable as anyone else. Ring taught me about coercion and fear, but for me they are only tools, not the sum and total of my being."

A smile spread across Lord Hansur's face. "You are, Nolan, unique in my experience as a Talion. You are, to my knowledge, the only Justice accepted beyond infancy since the Shattering, and you have surprised many with your hard work and dedication. More than one person believed you would quit soon after you joined us, and whenever you did something worthy of notice you were criticized for it because you had not been here since birth.

"You may have wondered why I selected Ring to be your guide on your Journey. It was not a decision I arrived at easily. . . ." Lord Hansur looked up toward the doorway and fell silent.

"He chose Ring because I urged him to."

I turned my head, then immediately bowed from the waist to the Master. He returned my salute with a slight nod of his head, then seated himself on a stool by the door.

"You have me to thank for a year with Ring, or"—he smiled—"your half year with him. Ring is merely one of a legion of Talions who believe we, as Talions, know how the world should be run. These Talions were overly critical of your every move." The Master barked out a half laugh. "When your group of Sixteens captured the Fifteens' winter camp and held it I was besieged with demands that you be discharged and that all record of what happened be expunged from the journals and minds of those involved!"

My jaw dropped. "I do not understand, sir, why?"

Lord Hansur spoke softly. "They saw you as a threat. You came from outside, and you were better at things than Talions trained here for their whole lives."

"Worse yet, Nolan," the Master interjected, "your ideas spread easily. Lothar was never respectful enough in the minds of many, and between his arrogance and your unorthodox thinking, Marana, Jevin, and others from your group have broken free from the rigid role 'mold' many have come to cherish and hold sacrosanct."

Lord Hansur nodded his agreement. "We did not agree with them that you were unsuitable for material for a Justice, and both the Master and I were certain, given a chance, you would prove yourself more than worthy during your Journey. We merely differed in choice of arena for you to prove yourself." Lord Hansur nodded a salute to the Master, and the Master smiled in return.

"I suggested Ring to Lord Hansur because I knew him to be one of the staunchest supporters of the faction that believes we should reestablish control over the world. I had hoped you might influence him as you did others in your group, but I did not expect it. I did think you would remain with him, and return here as opposed to his faction as they feel threatened by you, but your departure did not surprise me." He frowned. "It did, however, cause some trouble."

The Master leaned forward. "When Ring reported you had left him, I was told I should send someone after you to kill you, and I had enough volunteers for that job to send a company after you."

I sat back and gasped for air. "What did they say?"

The Master smiled. "They suggested you were a coward and should be executed as an example to anyone else who thought he could wander into a Festival and become a Talion. Of course this talk increased when you were brought in by that young man, but between his story and Adamik's discovery of the mark on your hand, well, no coward enters Woodholm and escapes it again."

Emotions soared through me like clouds boiling windwhipped through a stormy sky. Fear gripped me that enemies I did not even know lurked in Talianna and hoped for my downfall. Anger at these faceless foes ripped up through the fear. Who were they that they dared demand my life? But the anger was swallowed, in turn, by the pride I had in myself. I worked hard for everything, and if that threatened them, it also marked them as petty and small. That made them no less dangerous, but it made them vulnerable, and I knew I could defeat them in time.

Both Lord Hansur and the Master stood. Lord Hansur surprised me and offered me his hand. "Welcome, Nolan ra Sinjaria. You have passed your final test. Get your weapons and go to the Shar Chamber. It is time for your Ritual."

The Ritual of the Skull is the single most important test given to any Talion. Each Talion repeats the Ritual whenever he undergoes Shar, but that first time each action, each step, quickens the breathing and tightens the stomach. That first time, with an unblemished and warm right palm, is the most difficult experience a Talion has faced so far in his life.

Because the sword and dagger I brought to the Ritual had never been used, the Services attendant took them from me before the Ritual. Unblooded, they did not have to be cleansed. After the Ritual I would only refer to them as *tsincaat* and *ryqril*, and they would remain unbroken and unmarked as long as I lived.

I was proud of the weapons I'd chosen to be my tools as a Justice. Gilbere worked with me to make the sword, and he put his heart and soul into it. The blade, long and slender, was broader than a rapier, but still had two edges and was lighter than a broadsword. Gilbere balanced the sword perfectly so I could fence with it easily, yet the sword remained heavy enough to deliver solid chopping blows to heavily armored foes. Gilbere fitted a simple crosspiece to it and created a grip perfectly sized to my hand. I wanted a basket hilt, but Gilbere reminded me that such an addition would make summoning the weapon problematic and I thanked him for his foresight.

The dagger, on the other hand, was selected for me by someone else. Jevin and I agreed, before we left on our Journeys, to provide each other with daggers. I'd purchased one for Jevin in Ell and had it sent to the nearest Talion outpost for delivery to him without revealing who it was from. It arrived well before I did, and was given to Jevin when he came back from his Journey.

The dagger he gave me was a masterpiece. Its overall length was seventeen inches with eleven of those inches formed into double-edged blade. The antler hilt was capped with steel. The dagger, though not suitable for throwing, had the right weight for both parrying and stabbing. It matched my sword's style and was very special to me.

I cautioned the Services attendant to be careful with them; then I slipped into the unadorned, white ritual loincloth and followed him to the Shar Chamber. He reached out and touched the doors. They swung open and smoke engulfed me.

I stepped into the Shar Chamber for the first time and proceeded to the black slab door. My heart pounded in my ears and I felt sweat condense on my flesh. I stared at the gold skull inlaid in the night-black stone and trembled. Once I said the words, once it slid open, I could never be anything but a Justice.

I nodded. I accepted that fact. I welcomed it. *"I, Nolan ra Sinjaria, come to thee with clear heart and mind. If it be thy will to accept me, I will serve thee for all my life."*

The shadowstone responded to my words. It rose silently into the ceiling as a fog lifts before the sun. I felt as if the veil between life and death was opening. Light blazed from the room beyond the slab, and I knew inside there Nolan ra Sinjaria would die.

And in his place, I hoped, there would be a Justice.

I walked forward on stiff legs and knelt carefully before the skull. I could not look directly at it, because the light streaming from it hurt my eyes, but I did notice the hilts of my sword and dagger locked in place behind it. I took a moment to slow my breathing, and as I did so the skull's light subsided.

I lifted my right fist up and forced it open. Sweat poured

from the palm and trickled down my forearm. My fingers trembled despite my efforts to calm them. Terrified, I reached out toward the skull and the light brightened as my hand grew nearer. The glow increased as if the skull hungered for my flesh. The light shone through my skin and I could see my bones. That scared me, but I refused to let fear conquer me. I pressed my palm to the raised death's-head on the skull's brow.

I heard the hiss and smelled the acrid scent of burning flesh, but I felt no pain. Instead I felt something shoot into me through this fused union of flesh and stone. It blazed up my arm and filled my body with energy. It washed over me and examined every part of me; then it twisted itself into a ball and shot up my spine to explode in my brain.

Every memory, every thought, every experience I'd ever had flashed through my mind at once. Sights and sounds, odors and textures battered my consciousness as this mental whirlwind spun on and sifted through everything I'd ever known or dreamed or felt. I clutched at images of my family that had faded over the years, but my grasp on them was too weak and they vanished within the maelstrom rioting through my brain.

Then all motion stopped and I heard myself saying, "Justice, for me, must be tempered with mercy and common sense," over and over again. The words echoed within my skull until they became nothing but an unintelligible buzzing, but I heard them again and realized my lips formed the words and spoke them aloud. The buzz died, but I still repeated the phrase.

The presence dropped down my neck and through my arm to the skull. My body slumped with exhaustion, but I could not free my right palm. No pain rippled through the flesh, but my hand remained stuck.

The skull spoke. The glass jaw did not move, but I knew the words came from the skull. "Justice must be tempered by mercy and common sense. Justice is your *gift* to the world, *not* your right or privilege. Remember this and live by it. In this you will serve well. If you forget, if you betray this dictum, you betray yourself, and I will kill you for it."

The skull's light died and my right hand dropped free into my lap. I stared down at it because of the numbness in it. On my palm, in contrast to the pink flesh, a simple black line tattoo of a death's-head stared back up at me.

I knelt there in shock, and then I smiled. I'd won. I'd succeeded. I was a Justice.

I summoned my *tsincaat* and drew my *ryqril* from the altar behind the skull. The doorway into the corridor slid open and a Justice stepped into the world.

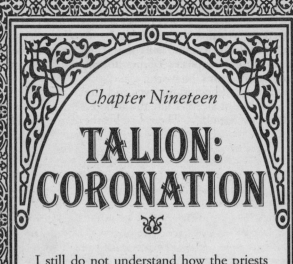

Chapter Nineteen

TALION: CORONATION

I still do not understand how the priests knew the Goddess had come and gone, but they knocked at the door within a half hour after her light faded and the skull evaporated. I cracked the door open after I smelled the incense and admitted Hand Fial. He nodded to me and indicated with a wave of his hand that I should leave.

I did not acknowledge his gesture, but I drifted from the room nonetheless. The Goddess's first warning to me made sense. I never imagined my mission would go unopposed and I'd lived in Death's shadow before now. That part of her message did not frighten me as much as it reinforced the need for caution. That I understood and could deal with adequately.

The second half of her message, "You cannot defeat the dead," formed a puzzle with myriad solutions. The most obvious, especially when coupled with her first warning, described my death at the *nekkeht*'s hands. But she said she had no prophecy for me, and that broke the connection between those two pieces of her message. What did she intend me to believe?

Pain throbbed behind my eyes and although I felt tired, I knew I could not sleep. I left the Moon Tower and walked directly to my chambers. There I resheathed my *tsincaat*, tore a sheet from my bed, and left again for the baths.

I stripped the robe off and sank myself into the hottest pool. Only one torch burned in the room, and it flickered beside the door so I soaked in shadowed peace. Thick steam billowed up in gray clouds to cut me off from everything but the voices in my head.

I focused my mind on the problem of stopping the *nekkeht* from getting to the King. Even if I could not kill it, there had to be a way to prevent it from assassinating King Tirrell. Fire might work because it would burn away the body, and dismembering it might also be effective. Even if the *nekkeht* could recover from so grievous a set of injuries, healing would deplete its energy and make it easier to hurt again and again.

A scenario crystalized in my mind. At the masquerade, before midnight, Duke Vidor would take the first step toward fulfilling the Goddess's prophecy and ask for the Princess's hand in marriage. She would accept, and more than likely would do so with her father's blessings. All the guests, the nobles of the Shattered Empire, would hear King Tirrell condone and praise the union. It was the stuff of faery tales and would play well in that august assembly.

Then, when the city's clocks struck midnight, the Princess, by custom, would order all evil creatures to flee the kingdom. The nobles would all unmask themselves and even cheer the Princess for freeing them from the powers that ensorcelled and changed them into the monstrous forms they'd inhabited all night.

Only one creature would not change to a docile form. It would leap forward and try to attack the Princess. The *nekkeht* would sweep aside Duke Vidor or Count Patrick if they sought to oppose it. Only the King would stand between the *nekkeht* and the Princess. The King would stab the creature, but it would kill him before it ran off howling into the night. It would never be found.

The King would lie dead in his daughter's arms. Her fiancé would try to console her, and would sustain her through the funeral and her ascension to the throne. They would marry, he would be given control of the army, and his masters would begin to pull his strings.

Desperation rose in my throat like ebon vomit. I slammed my fist into the water, then imposed control on myself. *No!* I would not, I could not, let that scenario run its course. If I could not destroy the *nekkeht* I'd make sure Morai knew enough that Jevin could slay every one of the lords controlling Duke Vidor. Even if I had to die to see it happen, no one would control Queen Zaria's court but her. My blood would insure her chance to fulfill the rest of the Goddess's prophecy.

My anger and fear evaporated and suddenly I realized I was very, very hot. I stood up and walked over to the nearest pool of cool water. I carefully tested it with a toe, and involuntarily jerked it back out of the frigid liquid. Then I steeled myself for the shock and leaped into the pool.

I touched bottom and shot myself straight to the surface. "Yeow!" My shout echoed from the walls, and I immediately waited for a reaction, then realized no one was near enough to hear me.

Or so I thought.

"That pool is especially cold, my lord."

I turned. Captain Herman sat huddled in one of the alcoves closest to the door. Fully dressed, he also wore a sword. "I find it quite refreshing," he added. "I've always thought of it as the Tal River in the middle of winter. Wouldn't you agree?"

I looked at him with wide-eyed innocence. "I am afraid, good captain, I have never visited your Tal province. Besides, I thought outsiders were only allowed in during the Festival, and that is during the spring, is it not?"

"The summer, my lord, as if you do not remember." He smiled as if we shared a secret. "We are alone here, Lord Nolan, you can drop the pretense. I know who you are."

I blinked my eyes and brushed water from my face. "You do?" I crossed my wrists in front of me for him to bind them. "I should have realized I never could fool the Talions, Captain Herman, but I did not. I had hoped to complete my role as the Princess's Champion, but if you must lead me away, it is your right and duty."

Captain Herman smiled. "You've a glib tongue, I'll say that much for you. I've been told to expect your arrival, and I stand ready to assist you if I can."

I dropped my hands with a splash, then raised my right hand to cover my embarrassed laugh. "Oh, you still believe I am a Talion." I sighed loudly and forced a look of relief onto my face. "Oh, Captain Herman, you gave me quite a start there. Whew, your discovery of my identity right now would not do at all."

The Lancer raised his hands in surrender and stood. "Very well, Lord Nolan, or whoever you are, if you want to remain anonymous, I will respect your wish. But"—he smiled and bowed his head—"I stand ready to help you when you need the aid."

"Thank you, Captain Herman. Few men can say they have a Talion's offer of assistance whenever they need it." I bowed my head to him and sunk myself in the pool once again when he finally closed the door. Then I emerged, wrapped myself in my sheet, and struggled up the stairs to go to sleep.

Adric woke me gently by making just a little bit more noise than he had to in laying out my clothing. I waded through dreamlees and blinked my eyes open. Adric smiled and poured a cup of steaming, black tea for me. He set it on my night table and the aroma saved me from sinking back to sleep.

I pulled my knees to my chest and then slumped over onto the pillow. I saw some movement at the doorway to the bed-chamber itself and looked up at Count Patrick's cheerful face.

"And how is our Champion this morning?"

I mumbled something at him, then sipped the tea. It was enough to wash the thickness from my tongue and I tried again to speak. "I am alive, and I think I will be much better when I finish this tea." I felt more alert already and traces of my dreams about a ball where everyone unmasked to reveal faces marked with the Lurkers' diamond tattoo around their left eyes faded quickly.

Patrick nodded and brought his right hand from behind his back. In it he held a foot-long rectangular wooden box. "I want you to know I fought through crowds this morning to get this." He smiled and held it out to me. "Only because she asked, and because it is meant for you."

I set the cup down and took the box. It was somewhat heavy, but not overly so. I looked up, puzzled, and asked, "I do not understand?"

"You are the Princess's Champion. It is traditional for the Champion to be presented a gift from his patron as a symbol of favor and appreciation." He pointed to the box. "Open it."

I did as he instructed. Inside, swathed in white linen, I uncovered a dagger and sheath. The dagger, like my *ryqril*, had an antler hilt. The blade was slender and straight—six inches of thick steel that made the stiletto both balanced for throwing and strong enough to punch through ring mail at close quarters.

The sheath prompted me to laugh. Laces hung from both top and bottom so it could easily be bound to a leg or forearm. I slid the blade into it and smiled up at Patrick. "It's beautiful."

"Good. I spent most of the morning trying to find something that would match your other dagger. And the Princess noted it would be very poor manners for you not to wear her token during the ceremony this afternoon, and the festivities thereafter, no matter what the laws say about concealing a dagger on your person when escorting royalty."

Patrick excused himself and I settled back to finish my tea. Once I'd emptied the cup, I threw back the bedclothes and got dressed. My clothes were similar to the ones I'd worn to the reception except that the colors shifted from blue and silver to purple and black. Adric helped me tie the sheath to my left forearm and took great pains to see that the slit-seam on my sleeve was placed correctly for an easy draw.

The ceremony scheduled for that afternoon was broken into two time-consuming halves, but I did not expect them to be as difficult as the tournament. I first had to escort the Princess to join the rest of the royal family in a reviewing stand. There we would watch the ambassadors and their national contingents parade into the Shudathi Temple. At the temple, the second, and potentially dangerous, part of the afternoon's activities would take place.

The Shudathi Temple hosted the coronation because of its long association with the Hamisian royal house, and because it was the largest temple in Seir. The priests of Shudath and the Sea Serpent deity Aroshnaravaparta would jointly preside over the ceremony. Priests from the other temples would be accorded status as guests, but only the two patron deities of Seir would consecrate the coronation.

I carried my sword belt with *tsincaat* and *ryqril* hanging from it. An open carriage would carry the King, Queen, Princess, and me to the reviewing stand, and wearing a blade while seated in a carriage is not an easy or comfortable thing to do. Later, in the stands and temple, I would strap the weapons on. Aside from the King, his guards, and the Lancers, I would be the only person in the temple allowed to wear a sword of any type during the coronation.

I joined the Princess in the throne room. The Princess smiled when she saw me and quickly took my arm. Her fingers confirmed the presence of her gift on my forearm. "Do you like it?"

I nodded. "I like it very much. I thank you; you have superior judgment." I glanced side to side and exaggerated the motions of a surreptitious search for enemies. "I hope I will not have to use it."

Halsted ushered the two of us out into the Castel courtyard and pointed us to our coach. The King and Queen had already seated themselves with their backs to the coachman. I helped the Princess into the coach and she sat opposite her mother. I slid my *tsincaat* upright into a set of brackets at my right hand and nodded to King Tirrell.

He smiled benignly and wiped sweat from his brow with his right hand. "I believe I was more comfortable when we first met, Lord Nolan."

I chuckled and nodded my sympathy. The sun blazed near its zenith and the day was unseasonably warm. "I understand what you mean, but you will forgive me I do not wish to be back there right now."

The King smiled, took his wife's hand, and kissed it gently.

"Nor would I wish to be anywhere else, but I could wish for lighter clothing or a heavier breeze."

The King wore heavy robes of gold and purple satin and velvet. A thick gold chain hung around his neck and supported a large gold medallion engraved with a map of his kingdom. He wore eight rings: one for each of the seven Hamisian provinces and the last for Sinjaria—that ring had belonged to Duke Vidor's father until his death. Seven golden panels formed his crown. Each rose to a point and a gem glittered from the top of each. Ages ago the greatest craftsmen in each province labored hard to produce the parts of the crown. It was magnificent.

The Queen and Princess both wore gowns of purple and gold as well. The Queen's dress had a single stripe of gold satin running throat to hem that accentuated her slender beauty. I knew the Hamisian crown jewels included a Queen's crown that complemented the King's, but Queen Elysia eschewed it in favor of a beaten gold crown featuring seven simple spires.

Princess Zaria's gown was a swirl of purple and gold velvet and satin stripes that started narrow at her shoulders, twisted around her body, and broadened out at the hemline. The tailored dress hugged her torso and swathed her legs. The diadem encircling her brow was a slender gold band.

The coachman cracked his whip and our coach rolled from the courtyard on into the streets lined with humanity. The Princess smiled broadly at the crowd and waved heartily. The crowd responded, cheered her, and shouted her name. Many people threw flowers and others lifted children high so they could see. People waved back to the Princess and excitement coursed through the crowd as we passed.

My enthusiasm for and enjoyment of the parade faded as I saw three pickpockets working their way through the crowd. I knew that for each clumsy one like them, there had to be ten I missed. I saw crippled beggars who were not maimed or marred in any way, and "farmers" who stood watch like soldiers as we passed. I studied dark windows and closed doors and wondered how many conspirators and plotters lurked in the shadows to laugh derisively at the outpouring of love for the Princess.

Somewhere out there, waiting for this evening, the *nekkeht* bided its time.

A woman broke past the horsemen riding along the street edges and ran toward the coach. My right hand shot to my *ryqril* and I slipped my left hand around the Princess's shoulder so I could pull her back. Tears streamed down the woman's face, yet she smiled and looked deliriously happy. She raised her hands and I leaned forward with *ryqril* half-drawn, then I stopped.

The crying woman presented the Princess a bouquet of freshly picked wildflowers. The Princess kissed her on the cheek and brandished the flowers like a conqueror's sword. The crowd screamed even louder than before and the woman drifted in a daze back to the outstretched hands of her friends.

My heart obediently dropped from my throat to its proper position and I settled back down in the carriage. I caught the King's eye and acknowledged his nod of thanks. I forced a smile onto my face and shook my head. Neither the Queen nor Princess even noticed how close to dying the woman had come.

I watched the roofline for an attacker with a crossbow, but the parade ended without incident. We left the carriage, took our places in the stands, and awaited the others' arrival at the temple across the street. Count Patrick, his wife, and his parents stood behind us, and the other royal children spread out on either side of the canopied royal box.

We stood to watch the nobles and their companies pass by. As a rule, house troops had to wait outside the temple during the coronation, but they made colorful and fascinating additions to the parade. The local nobles and their troops marched past us first, and the spectators cheered the nobles and troops from their home provinces the loudest.

Sterlos lead the pagent of nations. A dozen black warriors clad in animal skins and carrying spears and shields surrounded the Sterlosian Ambassador. Their oiled ebon skin shone in the sunlight. Each of the warriors, adorned with teeth and claws from various jungle animals, exuded confidence and domination. Only the Ambassador himself, with a gold and lapis lazuli pectoral, white kilt, and staff even vaguely resembled the sorcerers Sterlos was famed and feared for.

Imperiana's contingent was equally impressive. An Imperianan Prince led a dozen men in full suits of glittering, gold-gilt, plate armor. They swathed their warhorses in vibrantly colored silks. None of the men shared Tafano's size but they still dwarfed most men present. Each carried a lance stabbing high into the cloudless blue sky. The lances on the left flew a pennant bearing the Imperianan crest, while those on the right flew pennants in Hamisian blue and gold.

The Lancers came last and followed the Daari demon-dancers as if they meant to drive them from the streets. Without a doubt, and in spite of my prejudicial feelings about them, the Lancers were the most impressive of all the companies in the parade. Captain Herman led three dozen of them, all on matched black stallions. The Lancers wore black leathers akin to my Justice uniform, and had polished them until they glowed. Each rider and horse faced forward and did not acknowledge the crowd at all. The ranks stayed absolutely even and stopped before the box without word or sign passing from Captain Herman or Lieutenant Slade.

Lancers drew their swords at the same time and, snapping them up in front of their faces in a salute, turned to face the Princess. The hiss of steel on scabbard echoed deafeningly from the temple façade, and the sunlight sparkling from the silver blades blinded me for a second. Their precision took my breath away and I had to admit that Captain Herman kept his men well trained. I'd seen Lancers at practice hundreds of times, and I had worked through their drills myself, but I'd never seen such a degree of unity as I did in the Lancers stationed in Seir.

I was not alone in my appreciation of the Lancers' skill and discipline. The crowd fell silent and gaped in awe. The swords fell and were resheathed in so smooth a motion that very few who watched could be certain exactly how the Lancers had homed the blades so quickly. Not one rider missed his scabbard and not one horse quivered or reacted as the blade played so close to its neck.

Then, as a unit and without visual or verbal sign, the Lancers trotted their mounts forward again.

The crowd always clapped, politely, for each group passing in front of it, but applause for the Lancers exploded from their hands. Children laughed, giggled, and clapped their hands above their heads. Patrick's son Phillip tugged at his own hair so it might stand up like the manes on the Lancers, and King Tirrell bowed his head to me respectfully.

Hamisian house troops cordoned off a pathway from the viewing box to the temple doorway. The King and Queen preceded the Princess and me along a royal blue carpet woven with a gold diamond design. We passed into the temple and down a long aisle between the backed benches where the nobles and guests sat. The carpet ended at the altar, which stood beneath a giant statue of Shudath and was flanked by the High Priestess of Shudath and the High Priest of Aroshnaravaparta.

I guided the Princess past the bench where her parents had taken a seat and stood with her until she knelt at the foot of the altar. I backed off to her right and stood on a black stone square sunk flush with the gray granite temple floor. Across from me, on the other side of the carpet, I saw a white stone square. The sight of it sent a shiver through me, so I looked away and, instead, studied the statue of Shudath.

The stone idol looked nothing like she had the previous night, though it really differed little from other statues of the Goddess I'd seen in my youth and travels. The statue depicted a pregnant woman of an indeterminate but youthful age. Here she bore three stalks of wheat on her right hand, because her statues usually held products raised in the local region. Oddly though, especially with a temple to Aroshnar-avaparta in the city, the fingers of her left hand supported an actual fishing net.

An older woman served as the High Priestess of Shudath in the Hamisian capital. She'd braided her thick, white hair and it hung over her right shoulder. Still very slender, only her bony hands, her hair color, and the line around her blue eyes betrayed her age. She looked out at the assembled crowd and smiled warmly to welcome them.

She raised her hands to shoulder height and spread them out to include the whole temple as she spoke. "We are here to formally acknowledge this woman Zaria as daughter of and heir to the throne of Hamis." Her voice, clear and loud, reached every corner of the building without growing shrill or losing any of its power. She spoke like a mother explaining a family tradition to a visitor and set all of us at ease.

The Priest of Aroshnaravaparta was a fairly young man. He stood as tall as I did, but was far more slender than I am. A sharkskin thong gathered his long black hair at the back of his neck and, while he did not wear a sailors' beard, his right earlobe did support a thick gold earring. I understood that he had been raised in the temple his whole life and was believed to be the reincarnation of the last High Priest, so I accepted that as the explanation of how so young a man had risen to so high a station this early in his life.

He looked at King Tirrell with deep, compassionate, brown eyes. The King stood. "Do you, King Tirrell, acknowledge this woman, Zaria, as your daughter?"

The King's voice rang out crisply like the peal of fine crystal. "I do."

"Do you designate her as your heir, to succeed you on the throne, to defend it against any claims by a pretender?"

"I do."

The King seated himself and the High Priest walked over to stand beside me. Shudath's High Priestess laid her hands on Zaria's head. She looked up, watched the crowd and focused on the yet open temple doors. "Is there any person here who disputes her bloodline?"

No one replied. The High Priestess clapped her hands once sharply, then gently returned them to Princess Zaria's head. "Does anyone present dispute her claim to the throne?"

Again silence answered her question. The High Priestess clapped a second time, but I detected a quiver in her hands as she pressed them to the Princess's head. That tremor seeped into her voice as she asked the final ritual question. "Is there anyone present who would press a prior blood claim to the throne?"

The white square across from me drew my eyes to it. For a thousand years the ruling house of Hamis dreaded this third and final question. Through it an ulHamis could claim the throne in repayment for Prince Uriah's death. Any ulHamis aspirant had until the third clap to make his presence known and step into the white square across from me.

If an ulHamis warrior did appear the ceremony would continue no further until I'd killed him, or he'd slain me and earned the right to wear the crown of Hamis. I dropped my hand to the hilt of my *tsincaat*, watched the crowd and waited.

The clap I thought would never come echoed like thunder through the silence. I smiled. From this point forward nothing short of divine intervention could stop the coronation and deny Princess Zaria her crown. The cheers of the crowd outside faded as the temple doors closed.

The High Priest returned to the Princess and laid his right hand on top of the High Priestess's left; then they both raised their free hands to shoulder height. In one voice they asked, "Do you, Zaria, vow to obey your father the King and renounce all claims to the throne before his death or willful abdication?"

The Princess swallowed before her reply. "I do."

"Do you acknowledge and accept as your Master and Mistress the nation, lands, and people of Hamis; to do what is right for them to the exclusion of others' wishes, even if it means pain or death for you and your family?"

"I do." More strength and conviction poured into Princess Zaria's voice with this reply.

The High Priestess smiled. She turned and lifted a golden crown from a blue satin pillow on the altar. She and the High Priest held it between them while the Princess removed her own coronet and handed it to me.

The High Priest smiled proudly and looked down at the kneeling Princess. "Let this crown be a symbol of your bond with the nation. Surrender it to another only if you believe they can rule the nation more beneficially than you are able to do. In the names of Shudath and Aroshnaravaparta, we proclaim you heir to the throne of Hamis."

At the same moment they placed her new crown on her head, I twisted the old one entirely out of shape. I dropped it to the floor and it rang out the child Zaria's death knell. King Tirrell stood and strode boldly to his daughter's side. He guided her to her feet; then they turned and faced the gathered guests. "I give you my daughter and heir, Princess Zaria."

As odd and unimportant as it might sound, I spent the three hours between our triumphant procession back to the Castel and the masquerade in serious contemplation of what I would wear that night. Allen had included a highwayman's costume for me in my trunk, and it was a good choice. It fit well with the background I'd built up for myself, and certainly would create a stir, but it didn't feel right. I toyed with the idea of adapting it into a Tingis Lurker costume. In their confusion a plotter might confide something to me that he shouldn't but, I conceded, what that costume would do is attract undue attention to me and might mark me for elimination when the *nekkeht* struck at midnight. I even considered attending dressed as Morai, but only Selia and I would ever know how close to the real thing I got.

Throughout the afternoon one idea kept putting itself forward, and my arguments against it got weaker and weaker as the masquerade drew closer. In a technical sense the costume was utterly inappropriate because I'd not be an evil creature, but I'd certainly make people feel uneasy. In addition the costume fit well with my cover story, and seemed the unorthodox sort of thing I'd be expected to do. In the final analysis, though, one factor tipped the scales in favor of this new disguise: it would annoy Captain Herman terribly.

I wore my Justice uniform to the masquerade.

I salvaged a black domino mask from the disguise Allen had intended I wear that evening. I got my sleeveless leather tunic and leather breeches from a false panel in the bottom of my clothes chest. I boldly wore the Princess's present on my left forearm. With my boots, *tsincaat*, and *ryqril* on, I felt I presented a close picture of what a true Justice might well look like. Only my bare right palm decried me as an impostor.

My entrance caused quite a stir. Halsted, who had learned from Adric what I was supposed to wear, was visibly shaken until I smiled and lifted up the mask to peek at him. "I am supposed to be in costume, not the clothes I might wear every day, am I not?"

He swallowed visibly and smiled. "Yes, sir, though I fear Her Highness will not like your choice."

I lowered the mask into place and shook my head confidently. "She gave me the idea, Halsted, when she lent me the Lancer shield yesterday. Why, between her efforts and those of Captain Herman, they practically turned me into a Talion."

The absurdity of Lord Nolan the Darkesh bandit and bastard nobleman appearing as a Justice finally seeped through to Halsted and he smiled more easily. "Then, if you are ready, I will announce you."

I stood at the doorway and Halsted nodded to a trumpeter at my right. The servant blasted out a fanfare and everyone turned toward the doorway. "Presenting the Princess's Champion, Lord Nolan ra Yotan ra Hamis!"

Dead silence spread through the room. The assembled company of ghouls, goblins, Lurkers, *jelkoms*, and pirates stood in stupefied quiet. Content to lampoon monsters and legends with their costumes, none of them had the audacity to consider doing what I did. No one could believe my choice, and the momentary self-evaluation I'd seen so many times before in utterly innocent people swept across all the faces I could see.

Then one woman worked her way through the crowd. People parted to let her past, then dropped to one knee when they saw who she was. Princess Zaria stopped in front of me and, instead of the rage I feared I might find in her eyes, I saw boundless mirth. She threw her head back and laughed aloud to shatter the fog of tension strangling the room.

"Come with me, my roguish Champion, I wish to see how your Talion training serves you in the dance." She took my offered left hand and led me through the chuckling crowd of nobles.

Slow and graceful music paced me through a simple yet elegant dance step. Princess Zaria and I moved as one around the floor. I held her close and smelled the perfume in her hair, but we said nothing to each other. Somehow, even though I knew scheming plotters and treasonous nobles surrounded us and that a monster waited to slay the King, I felt at peace.

I sensed the return of emotions I'd hidden when Marana changed, and had forgotten when Marana died, but I forced them away. Princess Zaria attracted me very strongly and I already found myself mourning her loss to Duke Vidor. But therein lay the first steps on the road to madness, because I could never claim her. I was a Talion and that made even the most whimsical dream of winning and marrying her utter foolishness.

Nobles throughout the Shattered Empire tolerated His

Excellency's covert manipulations. Some of them never noticed what he did, while others understood and appreciated his skill, but no one protested because he acted so subtly. In return for this acceptance, the Talions stayed out of overtly political situations, and no Talion could hold political office. A blooded Talion on a throne, many felt certain, was only a short leap away from the reestablishment of the Empire.

The Princess sensed my withdrawal and frowned as the dance ended and we split apart. She voiced no question, but I forced a smile to reassure her that I was fine. She returned my smile; then a noble dressed as a pirate came and spun her off into another dance.

I worked my way through the crowd back toward the doorway. I smiled and thanked the nobles, who now understood the irony of my costume and congratulated me on it. As quickly as I could I found Halsted and pulled him aside.

"Halsted, I have a friend in town who may try to visit me here tonight. Adric knows him by sight. Could you have Adric wait by the front gate and bring him directly to me?" The servant frowned, but I squeezed his arm reassuringly and pressed him. "Please, it is of vital importance that I speak with him the moment he arrives."

Halsted read the urgency in my words and bearing. Though he agreed reluctantly, I knew the second Morai arrived he'd be escorted to me. I thanked the servant and returned to the masquerade. I found an open space near a table stacked with wine goblets and rounds of cheese.

Captain Herman, dressed in his uniform, materialized at my shoulder. "I see you chose to reveal yourself."

I'd anticipated him. I smiled broadly and then frowned at my right palm. "Captain Herman, you must tell me how the Justices get that skull to remain on their palms." I shook my head. "I tried ink and some paint, but both sweated right off. How *do* your Justices do it?"

The Lancer stared at me and narrowed his eyes. "That is an authentic Justice uniform. Where did you get it?"

I smiled. "It was a most curious thing. I went out to buy a costume and a man, about my height with blond hair and blue eyes, suggested I attend as a Justice. He said he had an uncle who had been a Justice, and just happened to have his uniform available." I laughed and shook my head ever so slightly. "Of course, I did not believe his story, but the uniform looked good and fit, so I bought it."

Captain Herman fought to contain his anxiety. "Did he have a mark on his palm?"

I stopped and looked down for a moment. "Why, that is curious." I frowned and looked into Herman's brown eyes. "He wore gloves the whole time!"

The Lancer's eyes glazed over for a second; then he started and stared at me. "You will excuse me, my lord."

"Certainly."

The shifting crowd swallowed all traces of the Lancer's line of retreat. For an instant I regretted sending Captain Herman off on a fool's quest for a phantom Justice, but I decided it was just as well that he and his men were out searching the city. If they were present when the *nekkeht* attacked, they would defend the Princess valiantly and could do nothing but die in the effort.

No, the *nekkeht* was my responsibility, and I had to find a way to stop it without killing anyone else in the process.

I set the goblet down and drifted out into the garden. I stopped at the sculpted granite railing and stared down the valley toward the sea. Both moons splashed silver crescent-caps on the swells undulating in the darkness below. Strains of music from behind me matched the lights' rise and fall.

Thunderheads hovered on the northeastern horizon as if loath to spoil the celebration. Instead, lightning flared through them and sprayed them with shades of yellow and red from the inside. They hung just beyond reach like the paper lanterns bobbing on strings throughout the city below me, and promised everything would be soaking wet by morning.

I felt a light hand touch my shoulder. I turned, expecting to find Morai standing behind me, and instead stood facing the Princess. She offered me a goblet of wine and I obligingly accepted it.

She lifted the twin to my goblet. "I propose a toast to you, Lord Nolan." She smiled. "To my Champion; I will regret the day you leave me."

We touched cups, but, as is the custom, I did not drink to a toast in my own honor. When her cup again fell from her lips I raised my cup. "Not a toast, my Princess, but a promise: I will do whatever I must to safeguard your nation." I drank.

Princess Zaria sighed and turned to stare out at the sea as I had. "Lord Nolan," she began quietly, "something will happen this evening."

A deep sensation of dread and loss stole my voice. I'd not allowed myself to feel this way about any woman since Marana, the *real* Marana, had changed. Marana had needed me, and I could never betray her that way. Even now, dead and reduced to ashes, I still felt something toward the person she had been. I realized that was a waste, but I grasped onto those fading feelings for the old Marana because, no matter what, love between the future Queen of Hamis and a Justice would never be tolerated by my masters, and had been ruled out by Shudath's prophecy.

"Something very special will happen to me tonight, Lord Nolan."

I smiled. "I know." I visualized Duke Vidor hugging and kissing her when she accepted his proposal.

Surprise and puzzlement flashed through her eyes. "You do?"

I nodded confidently. "I've watched the signs and I've figured it out." In my mind's eye King Tirrell hugged both of them to his chest and pronounced his blessing over the union.

Her lower lip trembled. "I am a bit frightened by the responsibility, and I have drawn much from your strength over the past couple of days, whether you realize it or not." She shrugged. "All I remember of last night's vigil is feeling secure because you warded me."

I smiled and laid my left hand on her shoulder. "You did very well, rest assured of that, Princess Zaria."

She tilted her head and squeezed my hand between it and her shoulder. She straightened up and watched the wine swirl in her cup. "I want you to be there tonight, at midnight. Will you?"

I closed my eyes and nodded because I could not speak. In my mind I saw the *nekkeht* charge at Vidor and the Princess. I stood between them and it. It grabbed me and lifted me from the ground in a bear hug that made Rolf's grip feel like a loose belt. As I drew the souls from its body, it crushed my insides and burst my heart.

The sound of Halsted's steady tread across the crushed stone garden pathway brought me back. He bowed apologetically to the Princess. "Excuse me, Your Highness." Then he turned to me and handed me a folded and sealed note. "The messenger said it was urgent. As you requested, I brought it immediately."

I turned it over in my hand and swore. It was from Morai.

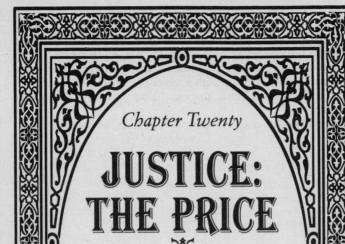

Chapter Twenty

JUSTICE: THE PRICE

A Services clerk appeared at my door to carry off the Ritual clothing I'd worn less than a quarter of an hour earlier. "Lord Hansur would like to see you immediately."

My heart pounded. A novice who completes his Ritual is a full-fledged Talion, but no other Justices consider him a full *Justice* until he returns successful from his first assignment. I'd not expected to be given a mission so quickly, and I regretted not being able to celebrate my Ritual with Marana or Jevin, both of whom had arrived in Talianna the previous week.

I strapped on my *tsincaat* and *ryqril*, then hurried to Lord Hansur's chambers. I had to fight to keep a smile off my face, and I calmed myself so I would not appear to be a novice running through the hallways.

I stopped in the doorway and had bowed to Lord Hansur before I noticed he was not alone. Jevin filled the chair I'd sat in just hours before, and Marana sat in a smaller chair with her back to a wall lined with shelves containing dark rows of musty, leather-bound histories. "You sent for me, Lord Hansur?"

Lord Hansur nodded, returned my bow, and waved me to the chair next to Marana. "I will begin before His Excellency gets here to outline your mission. Nolan, I know you are aware of the tradition concerning a Justice's first mission. Usually he is sent out on his own. I would apologize for breaking that rule with you, but you spent the last twelve months alone. I trust you will not mind working with your friends." He nodded toward Jevin and Marana.

I smiled and shook my head. "I welcome them and will be more than happy to work with them."

"Good." He seemed genuinely pleased I did not mind company on my first assignment. "This job would be difficult for one person alone, and the three of you have trained together, so uniting you into a team should work well." I was too happy to have complained about anything. Besides, I was a Justice and he was my lord. I did what he told me to do.

Behind us, His Excellency walked through the doorway and shut it after himself. We rose and bowed to him. He returned our bows with a curt, preoccupied, nod of his head, then waved us back to our seats. He wedged himself into a chair and cleared his throat. "Three days ago, in Temur, a group of West tribe warriors, dissatisfied with an ajudicated settlement of war claims, kidnapped one of the Emir of Betil's wives. The woman they took was his favorite, and he is not pleased. She is young and from the South tribe. The kidnappers left Temur and were last reported in Zandria."

I noticed Marana's interest pick up when His Excellency mentioned Temur and the South tribe. I recalled that her researches suggested she might be from that tribe, and this could be her chance to learn a little more about where she might have come from.

His Excellency continued. "The Emir, at the urging of the local Elite Colonel, decided to let us handle the kidnappers.

He knows he cannot send troops into Zandria without igniting a border war. The Colonel, with the Emir's blessings and support, sent an Elite requesting our help in the matter. We have decided to grant him that help."

Sweat poured from my palms in excitement. The critical time factor meant we'd have to fly Hawks after the kidnappers. Since they had a hostage we'd need to be very careful and stealthy in our approach, and had to insure the woman's safety and freedom before we worried about ourselves. But first we had to find them, and I frowned because the Temur-Zandria border stretched for many miles and hilly woodlands covered the whole area.

As if he'd read my mind, His Excellency produced a woman's ring from his robes. "The Emir sent this along. It is one of his wife Bethany's rings." He handed it to Marana. "Our Wizards enchanted it especially for you. While you wear it you will know in which direction the woman lies. As you get closer to her you will get more specific directions, and might even establish some sort of telepathic link with her."

Marana slipped the simple gold band set with a ruby on her right ring finger. "It fits perfectly!"

His Excellency raised one eyebrow. "Indeed, how fortunate."

Marana's face blanked for a moment, then she nodded. She pointed her right hand off toward the south-southwest. "I feel a faint pull in that direction." She smiled. "It works. We will find her."

Lord Hansur narrowed his eyes, looked at His Excellency for something, then, when His Excellency made no reply, he stood. "Six kidnappers took her from the palace, but later reports have suggested nearly that many more individuals, including three women, have reinforced them." He walked from behind his desk and pointed to a map hanging on the wall over beside Jevin. "We think they are heading to Ell, but we cannot be sure. You will take Hawks and fly southwest, following Marana's directions. Once you locate Bethany your job is to get her out safely."

His Excellency cleared his voice again. "The Emir would like the kidnappers, but will understand if you take no captives. We do not care what happens to them."

Lord Hansur wished us luck and dismissed us with a wave

of his right hand. All three of us wore broad grins as we left his study. The rescue mission was important, and could make a major difference in the world. If we did our job correctly, we would prevent a war! We knew we could not fail, and smiled proudly because we knew we would return victorious.

That mission was the last time I heard Marana laugh happily.

Marana lead us on a south-southwest course from the time we took off until we camped that first night in Wara at a point very close to the Daar border. We stooped the Hawks at a herd of antelope and I, flying Erlan's Valiant, got a buck. Marana and Jevin broke off their attacks because we needed no more than one animal to feed us and our birds.

We set up three watches so no one or nothing would sneak up on us during the night, though out there in the wilderness, that was unlikely. I got up a bit earlier than I needed to spell Marana, and we talked for a couple of hours before I urged her to get some sleep.

Our talk gladdened me because I'd not seen much of Marana in the past year and a half. Between being separated for our Journeys and my injury, we'd had virtually no time together. I'd been afraid that would force us away from each other. After losing my family and alienating Lothar, I did not want to lose her, too.

But talking that night it seemed as though we'd not been apart at all. She still knew my thoughts, hopes, and fears, and had been afraid that my feelings toward her had changed during our time apart. We both laughed at that and, with a forbidding urgency, tried to tell each other how we'd grown and changed since the month we spent together as Sixteens.

The next day we made very good time. A tailwind sped us along and we flew farther into Zandria than we'd expected. Still the flight tired us, and despite the closeness to our destination Marana reported, night fell before we could reach the target. We agreed to get up at dawn and head out immediately to complete our task.

We reversed our watches and Jevin suggested to me that I might want to show Marana a clear river pool set below and behind our hilltop campsite. The mischievous glint in his dark eyes belied the innocent way he made his suggestion. I ignored his grin and accepted his advice willingly.

Water flowed gently down the valley between several hills and filled a broad, dark pool. The warm evening breezes swept the insects away. Marana and I lay back on a soft bed of ferns and talked for what seemed like hours on end. We listened to the water and laughed at nothing at all. Happiness filled us both with giddy energy, and everything felt right and perfect.

Carefully and slowly we removed each other's clothing. We made love beneath the stars and reaffirmed in each other the discovery of our ideal counterparts. To me Marana offered the love and support I'd once known before the war destroyed my family, and I gave her the love and unconditional acceptance of the family she'd never known.

I returned reluctantly to the campsite and relieved Jevin. Marana offered to stay up with me, and tried to convince me she couldn't get to sleep because of the ring. I kissed her and wrapped her in my blankets. She fell asleep soon enough, and was very much rested when I woke her to take the final shift.

I sat on my blankets and kissed her. "Be sure to wake us before dawn, Marana. We want an early start."

She stood and smiled. "I will, my lover, now get some sleep."

I dropped off quickly and enjoyed very pleasant dreams.

Jevin nudged my ribs with the toe of his boot just once. I sat bolt upright, and before he could tell me, I knew what was wrong. Marana was missing!

I swallowed hard and shook my head to disperse the dreams. "When did you notice she'd gone?"

Worry scored his forehead with black gashes. "Just now. It's an hour after dawn. She couldn't have left before then."

I kicked my blankets off and wriggled into my leather breeches. "Why didn't she wake us?" I wanted to scream. My family had died while I slept and now I slumbered while someone stole my Marana away.

Jevin's lips curled back in a grim snarl. "The ring, it has to be the ring." He looked over at me and his black gaze bored through me. "Never trust magick."

I shuddered and broke eye contact. "I agree." I stood and pulled my tunic on over my head. "Look, Jevin, get your Hawk up. There might be an off chance you can spot her

Hawk in the air. We were dead line heading south toward the Hatu River Valley."

The Fealareen nodded. "What will you do?"

I buckled my swordbelt in place. "I'll fly Valiant in a circle around this camp to see if I can spot her. The kidnappers might have passed by here and Marana headed off after them, intending to get back to us." Jevin knew I was clutching at straws, but he nodded. I forced a laugh. "If Valiant is half as good as Erlan says he is, catching you should be easy."

Jevin mounted up and took off. I followed after I killed our fire. I untied, mounted, and unhooded Valiant. He screamed at Jevin's swiftly receding Hawk. Valiant spread his mighty wings and in seconds we soared above the Zandrian countryside. I guided the Hawk in a grand circle around our camp, but I found nothing.

My heart sunk. The lush landscape below held as much interest for me as a desert because it bore no sign of her. I wanted something to tell me Marana still lived. If her Hawk had broken a wing or she'd slipped from the saddle, I knew I could find her and make her well again. She had to be alive, I needed her to be alive.

In my panic it never occurred to me that she might have been better off dead.

I turned Valiant south and on the horizon I saw Jevin's bird as a black spot against the pale wall of clouds encroaching on the green valley. I urged Valiant forward and tapped him on the back so he'd fly faster. He complied and we soared ahead to slowly gain on Jevin. By the time the spot had grown to the size of an Imperial, Jevin's Hawk circled once and headed to the ground.

Valiant felt my anxiety and pushed hard, but it felt to me as if the air had thickened to slow us. It took me another five minutes to reach the area where Jevin landed. I circled once and saw Jevin's Hawk clearly enough. A hundred yards in front of his position I located tents hidden among the trees on a river sandbar.

I landed Val next to Jevin's Hawk and noticed Marana's Hawk hobbled and hooded beneath the nearby trees. My spirits picked up—at least she'd landed safely. I hooded Val and followed the trail Jevin left for me. I found him lying on his stomach atop a hill overlooking the kidnappers' camp.

He waved me down and I lay beside him. "It's bad," he whispered.

I reached forward, carefully parted the long, green, summer grasses before me, and watched the camp. I counted a dozen men and four women. They had Marana bound to a stake and had piled wood all around her feet. Marana appeared awake and unhurt, but I could not tell for certain because she alternated between being defiant and terrified. The former was Marana through and through, but I'd never seen the scared woman bound to the post before.

My fear drained all the color from my face. "What do you think?"

Jevin grimaced. "We go in fast. You get to Marana and cut her bonds. She's been in and out since I've been watching."

I frowned. "Do you think she's drugged?"

Jevin shrugged, then shook his head. "I don't believe so." He folded some of the grasses down and studied Marana's struggle. "I still think it's the ring. If she has a rapport with the Emir's wife, she's reflecting the woman's terror."

I nodded. That made sense. "The first thing to do, then, is to free Marana and get the ring off her hand. Then she can help us free the Emir's wife. Do you know where the hostage is?"

The Fealareen shook his head. "No, not assuredly, but Marana stares at the blue tent when she's herself. I'd guess the hostage is in there."

I nodded and rose. We crept down the hillside to the river's edge. We avoided all fallen branches and skirted all dry leaves. At the base of the hill the river reeds hid us, but the slow, muddy river cut off any further stealthy advance. All we could do was spring across and hope our very presence would be enough of a surprise to give us an advantage. I reached out and squeezed Jevin's shoulder.

We were off.

I splashed through the shallow river with high steps that sprayed water everywhere. I reached the sandy islet before any of the kidnappers had time to react and summoned my *tsincaat*. Mercilessly I chopped through the first man I saw.

My first victim fell and another man darted toward me. He made to draw his slender scimitar, but never completely pulled it from the scabbard at his hip. I swept past him and slashed him across the stomach. He spun away, but before he fell to the ground, my return cut tore his face in half.

Beyond him, I reached Marana. She writhed and screamed. I touched her to let her know I'd come to save her, but she recoiled from me and hissed like a cat. I looked in her eyes and saw hatred flash through them. I did not know this woman.

I sliced through her bonds with my *tsincaat* in one, clean stroke. With my left hand I pulled the ring from her finger. Almost instantly her eyes cleared. "Nolan, thank the gods. Look out!"

I ducked and twisted away as she summoned her *tsincaat* and blocked the cut intended to remove my head. Marana riposted through the man's throat, then darted toward the blue tent. A women opposed her with only a dagger, but Marana slew her remorselessly. I marked her action and it made me uncomfortable, but I never could have guessed what it meant.

I had no time to consider it then because two enraged warriors charged me. I blocked the first man's overhand blow high above my head, then retreated to the right so the first man blocked the second. I feinted a lunge at the first warrior to back him off, then switched my *tsincaat* to my left hand and slashed low to that side. I caught the second man advancing and opened a gash across his thighs. He fell and I stabbed his compatriot through the chest while he hesitated, and watched his companion thrash painfully on the ground.

Suddenly the fight ended. Jevin stood amid five surrendered, wounded or dead fighters. Two men stood on the edge of the camp with firewood piled where it dropped at their feet and their hands in the air. One woman lay in a pool of blood between me and the tent, and no one offered us any resistance.

Without warning a scream pierced the blue tent from within and ripped through the camp. I instantly recognized Marana's voice in the shriek, but it echoed upon itself and terrified me. I dashed toward the blue tent, leaped over the dead woman, and threw back the tent flap. Stunned, and utterly unable to believe my eyes, I sank to my knees and let the flap enshroud me.

The cry came from two throats that shared identical bodies.

An old woman knelt beside me. "Thank the gods you have come, Talion." She pointed a trembling, bony finger at Marana. "You must kill the demon before she kills us all."

Jevin separated the twins and took Marana back to our camp. The people we'd attacked were Temuri kinsmen of the Emir who trailed out after the kidnappers all by themselves, and had not been discovered missing until after the Elite had been dispatched to summon us. They'd found the kidnappers, killed most of them in a battle nearby, and were heading home when we fell upon them.

I slowly recovered from my numbed shock and returned Bethany's ring to her. I helped as best I could to bind up the wounds I'd caused, and that was taken as a good omen by the Temuri, though it did nothing to ease their pain or bring back their dead comrades.

The old woman heated some water and made me some tea. It was hot and must have been fragrant because it rose through my head, but I'd not know it again. The sight of two Maranas screaming in terror at each other haunted me.

The old woman sat across from me and rested a liver-spotted hand on my leg. "I was present when they were born."

I nodded. I knew from her tone that what she was telling me was vitally important, but I had trouble focusing my mind on anything. I sipped more tea and swirled the leaves around in the bottom of my bronze cup.

"I helped Bethany from the womb first." She smiled with the recollection. Beyond her, back in the shadowed part of the tent, the Emir's wife slept restlessly. "She was a strong and happy baby, too happy to have a demontwin." The old woman spat and twisted fingers in a sign to ward off evil. "That woman, she came second, and was left out on a hillside to die."

The old woman pulled on my arm. "You have to slay her. She is a demon. It is unnatural for her to be alive. You must slay her!"

I pushed the old woman away and stared at her as if she'd lost her mind. "You don't know her, she's not a demon!" I set my cup down and stood. "I've known her for the last five years and I know she's as normal a human as you or I."

The old woman narrowed her eyes. She reached out and took up my teacup. She swirled the liquid, then splashed it out on the ground. "Ah!" she cried triumphantly. She pointed at brown bits of leaves and how they lay on the wet, golden sand. "Slay her, Talion, slay her today." She stared up at me with eyes as deep and dark as the night sky. "If you do not, she will be the cause of your death!"

I flew back to our camp and Jevin met me before I could see Marana. He looked very tired. "She's sleeping, Nolan, finally."

I nodded grimly. "Marana has to return to Talianna. She can't go to Temur. They think she's a demon and they'll kill her."

Jevin shook his head. "She can't travel alone. She said she was inside Bethany's head." The Fealareen looked up at me with eyes full of pain and tears. "She's not well."

I felt cold all over. I nodded. "I understand, Jevin." I turned and looked back toward the Temuri camp. "You should fly with the Temuri and guide them back to Betil." I faced him again. "I'll get Marana back to Talianna."

I watched Jevin until his Hawk faded to nothingness against the horizon, then walked to the camp. Jevin had done his best to make her comfortable. Marana lay swathed in blankets, but only slept lightly. Her tan flesh had faded to a deathly pale ashen color and pockets of shadow hung beneath each eye. She looked more dead than alive.

I squatted next to her and her eyes popped open. She took one look at me and started sobbing, so I sat and dragged her into my arms. I hugged her tight and rocked her. I told her stories my grandmother and father had told me when I was a child, and somehow managed to keep the fear and pain out of my voice. Her tears mingled with mine, but some of her pain drained away and she slept again.

I lifted her up and carried her from our campsite and down to the pool. Gently I laid her where we'd lain together the night before. The soothing gurgle of the stream coursing down into the pool reached her even in her sleep. Her breathing became more regular and she slumbered on more peacefully.

I wandered around the woods—never straying too far away—and found a medicinal plant I remembered from childhood. The plant was an herb called *vila* in Sinjaria. I discovered a fair-sized patch of the pale green-leafed plants and harvested several of them. I used the leaves to brew a narcotic tea that I fed to Marana so she could sleep more soundly.

I estimated, based on the amount of tea she drank, that she'd sleep through the afternoon and evening, and perhaps into the next morning. I built us a lean-to and gathered rocks to build a fireplace.

I didn't like staying down at the base of the hill when the Hawks were up above, but I realized anyone or anything that got too close to them would get what they deserved. Besides, everyone knew only Talions kept the giant raptors, and that should be warning enough for even the most mad of men.

I carried Marana over to the lean-to and undressed her as the sun sank behind the Ell mountains and splashed the sky with shades of purple and red. I wrapped her in blankets and settled her into a comfortable position. Then I stripped off my tunic and lay down next to her.

I did not plan to sleep, but the day had ground me down more thoroughly than a mill grinds grain. I lost consciousness faster than a drunken sailor beset by alley-bashers.

A sharp kick in the ribs shot pain through me and snapped me awake instantly. Five Temuri, different from the people we'd attacked, surrounded us. They wore blood-soaked bandages and looked exhausted, but seemed surprised and pleased at finding us.

Their leader had kicked me. He turned to the others and laughed. "Look, they thought they'd run off and lead us away from Bethany with a false trail. They left one boy guarding her." He had an old scar running from cheek to cheek across his nose.

I clenched my fists in anger and frustration. I slowly realized these were the kidnappers who had escaped the Emir's kin. I shook my head. "This is not Bethany. Leave her alone, she's sick."

The leader dropped to one knee, grabbed my throat with a

greasy hand, and forced me to look up at him. He licked his lips and ran his other hand across his stubble-bearded cheeks. "Boy, your life is in my hands. Don't make me kill you before I want to."

His men laughed and he slowly tightened his grasp on my throat. These were the men we'd come after, and we'd slain brave, noble people because of them. *Why?* a voice screamed in my brain. *That is not justice!*

One of the others tore the blanket from Marana's naked body. Fury flooded my sight with a blood-red haze. My nostrils flared and I lashed out with my right fist. I smashed their leader in the groin, rolled to my feet, and raised my left hand to stop the others.

I pleaded with the four of them. "She is not your Bethany. Leave her alone. I don't want to kill you, there's been enough killing already." My chest heaved with labored breaths. I concentrated and summoned my *tsincaat,* but none of them understood the true significance of a sword appearing in my hand that way.

"A magick sword, I want it!" one of them cried aloud, and they rushed me.

The Temuri people, as Marana had told me so long ago, were known for their skill at archery. As swordsmen, these four men made better archers, and came at me as if they wanted to die. But I did not want to kill them. I parried and backed several times to show them they stood no chance against me, but they blundered forward, absolutely convinced they had me on the run.

Finally they trapped me and, cheering their good fortune, they forced me to slay them.

I beat the first man's lunge down with a ringing slap to his blade with my *tsincaat,* then eviscerated him with a backhanded slash. He dropped to his knees and tried to scream, but only managed a weak whimper. The second Temuri cut down at me and I sidestepped his attack. He'd thrown himself off balance and I split his skull with diagonal slash to his head.

My anger over the useless slaughter of the morning and my worry about Marana combined to numb me. The third man tried to spit me with a straight thrust, but I parried his blade to the ground. Grinning like a demon, I trapped his sword beneath my right boot and slid my *tsincaat* through his chest in a lethal imitation of his attack. I twisted the blade, then tore it free.

The fourth man had seen enough to be scared and tried to scurry away. He raised his hands to hold me back, and dropped his dagger, but only his death would sate me. I chased him back over the ground he'd laughingly conquered with his companions, and stood above him gleefully when he tripped and lay on his back begging me, like a dog, to spare him.

I nodded sincerely, and when he smiled hopefully, I lopped his head from his shoulders with a single, sharp stroke. He stared at me disbelieving until the last of his consciousness slipped down and out of his neck with his blood.

I howled maniacally and closed on the scar-faced kidnapper still writhing in agony near the lean-to. I drank in the cloying, sweet scent of blood and reveled in the acrid stench of his fear. I stalked slowly toward him and unmanned him with a hideous, barked laugh.

I squatted just out of his reach and leered at him like a gargoyle. "It has occurred to you, has it not, that I am a Talion?" I lifted my right palm and showed him the tattoo for a brief look, as if playing a game with an infant. "Worse yet, I am a Justice." I tossed my bloody *tsincaat* aside with my left hand and opened my right hand more slowly this time. "You know what this is."

The man nodded and blubbered. Tears rolled from his eyes and ran along his scar.

I mocked him in a voice meant for scolding children. "And you know you are going to die."

He nodded again and wet himself.

I crouch-hopped forward, reached down with my left hand, and grabbed a fistful of greasy black hair. I pulled him up into a kneeling position. "Silly man. If you had gone, I would have let you live." I looked back at his dead companions. "I would have let them live, but you would not let me give you life." I smiled simply at him. "Now I have to kill you."

I ground my palm into his forehead and slowly breathed in. I willed his soul into me and I felt him shudder as it tore free and his life dissolved. Every one of his thoughts and fears, hopes and desires, trickled through me and across my brain. I watched it all and I laughed at him. I looked down as the light of life faded in his eyes and I laughed so he knew *I knew* his failings.

I ridiculed his vanity and scoffed at his lofty hopes. My mirth reduced everything he'd ever done to insignificance. His life did not pass before his eyes as he died, it flashed through mine, and he saw his life had been a battle against the obscurity that swallowed him in death here in the Zandrian wilderness.

He wanted everlasting fame and monuments.

I gave him ignominious death and a scavenger's stomach for a sepulchre.

He slumped over as his soul sloughed his body off. I straightened to my full height. I clenched my bloodstained hands like claws. I studied him for any further sign of life I could steal from him, but he was dead.

I stared down at him in scorn. He had been a fool, and had paid the ultimate price for his stupidity. He had not deserved to live.

Then a quiet voice whispered inside my head. *Neither had he deserved to die.*

I staggered to the stream and knelt in the water, but no matter how long I washed my hand, it refused to feel clean.

The next morning Marana awoke, but said nothing about the dead bodies scattered nearby, and did not notice me even though she practically stepped on me as she drifted toward the pool. I stood, stripped off my clothes, and slipped into the water with her. Then she marked my presence, clutched her arms modestly to her breasts, and rebuked me sharply.

I froze. She spoke in flawless Temuri, and did not know me.

Marana shuddered and would have collapsed, but I lunged for her and caught her. She recoiled as she had in the camp, then threw her arms around my neck and started to cry again.

I carried her back to the lean-to and tried to make her drink more *vila* tea, but she refused. "Nolan, sleep does not help me. My dreams are not my own."

I read the horror in her eyes and crushed her to my chest. I hung on tightly and wished I could absorb some of her pain, but she had already begun to drift away. I could not reach her, and I could not share her pain.

Gently she pulled away, but the second I released her she jumped up and summoned her *tsincaat*. She stroked it across her own left wrist, then leveled the bloody blade at me. "Nolan, if you love me, don't stop me. You don't know what it's like to have someone else in your mind. I don't know who I am anymore, but I do know that if I'd been left to die the way I was meant to, those people back in that camp would still be alive."

I stared horrified as her blood traced a scarlet line from her wrist to elbow and dripped off with fluid regularity. With each heartbeat one drop drummed away on rock or leaf. Her *tsincaat* hung there, motionless, and pointed straight at my heart.

I clenched my fists, but could not stop the tears from burning parallel tracks down my face. I nodded toward her wrist and fought to force words through my thick throat. "You might as well kill me now and get it over with, because you're killing me in pieces with each drop of blood."

She shook her head and veiled her shoulders with long black hair. "No, Nolan, my life is over. I killed those people because I am alive when I was never meant to be. I know I am a demon." She choked back tears. "I am, Nolan, I am a demon. I was inside Bethany's head, and I saw myself as she did."

I stood slowly and opened my hands. "No, Marana, you are not a demon. You are no more a demon that my brother Arik was. Just because some fool chooses to believe the sun is purple, that does not make it so." I took one step forward so Marana's *tsincaat* hovered an inch away from my breastbone.

Her jaw trembled. "Don't, Nolan, don't try anything. I don't want to kill you."

I stepped closer yet and felt the tip of her blade against my flesh. "Then bind your wrist because the moment you die I will too."

Pain lanced through her face. "Nolan, I have nothing to live for."

I smiled gently, lovingly, and slowly raised my right hand toward her left wrist. "Live for me, Marana, live for me."

She fought against it, but life won and she dropped her *tsincaat*. "Help me," she whimpered, then fainted.

We stretched our journey back to Talianna over four days. Slowly Marana's condition improved. Nightmares still plagued her, but she never spoke to me in Temuri or tried to kill herself again. I spent my nights just holding her and hugging her until she succumbed to exhaustion and I felt safe enough to drift off to sleep.

We reached Talianna in midmorning and I convinced Marana that she should land first and go through Shar. I knew she'd taken no souls, but I thought the time spent purging herself of this mission might finally break the link and erase the memory of her sister. I hoped Shar would give me back my Marana.

I kept Valiant aloft while Marana landed and circled the valley. I'd had no time to think about what I'd done to the kidnappers because I dared not leave Marana alone after she tried to kill herself. That night's actions burst back into my brain in harsh black-and-white tones. I saw their faces and felt their terror all over again.

Inside me anger flared. Why had they been so driven to force me to slay them? Why had I allowed myself to get out of control? Why had Marana suffered so, when she was only a vessel, a conduit, for the magick used to find the Emir's wife? "Why," I screamed furiously, "why did it have to be Marana?"

Suddenly my rage focused itself and bored through my confusion to answer my questions. *His Excellency!*

I'd been used; Marana had been used. I remembered Lord Hansur waiting for His Excellency to add a remark back when he gave us the assignment, and I recalled His Excellency's forced surprise when Marana announced the ring fit perfectly. I recalled Marana saying His Excellency would give her no information about who she was or where she was found.

He knew all along what would happen! My body itched as if I were a chess pawn and I could feel his hands moving and positioning me. Marana was a piece to be sacrificed in a gambit and nothing more. He'd allowed her to be taken and removed from the board but, unlike the Guardians waiting for another game in the Tuzist valley, Marana could not play again. She was shattered, and he'd permitted it.

I flew Valiant down to the Mews and didn't notice Erlan until he grabbed me by the arm. "Nolan, what's wrong?"

I turned toward him and gaped openmouthed until his voice worked through my anger, and his face swam into focus. I grabbed him by both shoulders. "Erlan, you must do something for me."

The worry didn't leave his face but he nodded emphatically. "Whatever you need . . ."

I rubbed my left hand against my forehead and concentrated. "I'm *Sharul*, Erlan, but I'm not within Talianna's shadow yet." I trembled, then recovered myself. "Erlan, I need you to find His Excellency. Tell him I'm waiting out behind the Mews."

The Elite frowned with worry not skepticism. "What do I tell him when he asks why you're waiting."

I just shook my head. "He won't ask."

In the five minutes it took His Excellency to find me, my rage blossomed from a blaze to a full conflagration that nearly caused me to wait in ambush for him. I watched him pick his way up the hill toward the Mews and my right hand tingled in anticipation of closing about the hilt of my *tsincaat* and driving it through him. But I did not call the blade; I'd been trained too well to do that.

He stepped into the meadow and opened his mouth, but I never gave him a chance to say anything. "How could you, you fat spider? You knew who she was and what would happen!" I stabbed a finger at him and tears blurred his image beyond humanity. "You sent Marana out there not caring what would happen to her."

He stopped, folded his arms across his chest, and rested them on his distended belly. I screamed in inarticulate ire and ground my fists into my eyes. "Damn you! Seven people died, seven innocent people, because you did not warn us how the Temuri would treat Marana! Because you didn't tell us she and Bethany were twins I was forced to butcher five other men. Because," I sobbed, sinking to my knees, "you didn't tell us, Marana is mad."

Drained of my anger, I cried, then looked up at him. "Why?" I wanted to ask him why I shouldn't kill him, but I was sick of killing. I wanted him to justify Marana's sacrifice. I wanted a reason for my pain.

His Excellency spoke evenly and allowed no trace of emotion to creep into his voice. "Yes, Nolan, I knew Marana's identity, and I knew she might suffer because of the magick and from meeting her twin. Once, years ago, even before you joined us, someone remarked on Marana's resemblance to a Temuri girl pledged to wed the Emir. I checked and because I know Temuri custom, I was able to surmise who she was."

He looked down at me. "Yes, I put her at risk, just as I did with you and Jevin." His Excellency turned away.

"No!" I pounded my right fist into the ground, rose, and grabbed his left shoulder. "Jevin and I risked our lives, but you risked her sanity! What gives you that right?"

His Excellency spun with an agility that surprised me. He locked my arms in a granite grip and lifted me from the ground as if I were a child. "I have that right, Talion, because I hold the fate of dynasties in my hands. You kill men and women; I destroy whole nations. I have that right because I can devastate empires with an error in transcription of a coded message!"

He released me and I fell at his feet. "If you had not gone to retrieve Bethany, the Emir would have sent troops into Zandria. Zandria would have counterattacked and Boucan would have swallowed both of them. Ell would have been threatened and war would have erupted along that border. Other nations would have joined the battle and the world would have returned to the days of the Shattering."

His eyes narrowed. "You are smart, Nolan. I saw your doubt at ever being able to find one woman in all of Zandria. You knew the task was not merely difficult, it was impossible. I knew that, but I also knew what would happen if we failed. Faced with the choice between one Justice's mind, and war wasting thousands of square miles, I had but one course. To prevent that widespread a conflict I would gladly send you or a hundred like you to a certain death. If I needed an excuse to withdraw support for a regime to forestall a war, I might even arrange the death of a Justice within the capital."

Uncontrollable sobs wracked me. "It's just a big game, isn't it?"

His Excellency shook his head slowly and his steely

composure cracked. "No, Talion, a game it is not. There are times I wish it were. If this had been a game I could reset the pieces. Marana would not hurt and you would not question what you know in your heart of hearts is right. The innocent people you speak of would still live.

"But it is not a game. Do not misunderstand my words. As willing as I am to expend lives, if the situation demands it, I mourn each death, each injury."

I stared up at His Excellency with tear-flooded eyes. For the first and only time saw the human hidden within that massive frame. He was a political mastermind who formed and caused to be executed nearly perfect plans to combat the world's tendency toward barbarism. Even though he had supreme confidence in his actions and knew them to be vital and correct, he regretted every bit of pain his plans caused. I knew in that instant that I might understand him, but I could never call him *friend*.

His Excellency turned away, and this time I let him go unmolested.

The black slab slid upward in the Shar Chamber and I stared at the blazing skull in the hopes it might blind me, but it did not. I walked forward and knelt slowly. I felt physically purged, yet, despite my careful and diligent effort in the rest of the cleansing ritual, I never expected to be clean again.

I raised my right hand and pressed my palm to the skull's forehead. As before, something stole into me and slipped along my arm, up through my neck and into my brain. It strung battle images together with my emotions and forced me to watch them over and over again.

A voice spoke within my head as I watched myself slaying the Temuri on the sandbar. "Here you have no cause for regret." The picture of Marana bound and struggling amid wood gathered for a bonfire hovered before me. "You fought to defend your friend and lover. That they were not those you first sought means nothing. Do not doubt your actions here."

Those macabre memories dissipated like smoke, and the battle against the four kidnappers flowed in to replace them. I heard the men laugh as they pursued me, and I heard my voice begging them to leave as I retreated. I relived the moment of horror when I realized I could run no further. I even recalled slaying each of them.

The voice's appraisal in that instance did not rebuke me either. "You warned them and tried to leave them their lives, but they only gave you a choice between your death or their deaths. Blood was to flow that night, and you chose correctly."

Then it took hold of the lead kidnapper's soul and lashed it across my mind like a whip. I heard my laughter as it rang in his ears, and I felt myself crumbling inside. I shared his hopelessness and utter humiliation. I died with him and realized what I had done: I'd crushed and tortured his spirit until I stripped him of his humanity.

"This, Talion, this should never be done." Fiery white hot lances of pain stabbed through my brain. "Steal his soul, destroy his body, kill him, but never shred his spirit."

The pain faded, and the voice fell silent as the leader's soul trickled down my arm and into the skull to vanish in a twisting stream of blue light. "Had you not already regretted what you did, your soul would have followed his. Remember, Talion, justice is your gift to the world, *not* a right to demand from it."

It withdrew from me and released me so swiftly that I fell back and lay too weak to rise from the floor. The stone radiated cold up through my sweat-slicked back and I shivered. I lay there and breathed heavily as the skull's shimmering light died. Then, in utter darkness, I rose and staggered to my *tsincaat* and *ryqril*. I pulled them from the altar and, as the exterior panel rose, I stumbled into the corridor.

A tear rolling down her left cheek, Marana stood waiting for me. She extended a note toward me. "He said it was important. I brought it immediately."

I turned it over in my hand and swore. It was from Lothar.

Chapter Twenty-One

TALION: TERMINUS

I slid my thumb beneath the flap, broke the red wax seal, and unfolded the coarse sheet of paper. The note was short:

"Lord Nolan, I've found someone you'll want to hear for yourself. I'll keep him here. Come to the Gallant Fox, knock twice on the door. When challenged answer, 'Lord Nolan.' " The note was signed "Morai."

I refolded the brown sheet and stuffed it inside my leather tunic. Princess Zaria looked at me, and her expression reflected the concern etched into my features. I gave her a heartening smile and looked up for Halsted, but he had already vanished.

She frowned, more from worry than anger, and nodded toward where the note resided. "What does it say?"

I stripped off my mask and shook my head. "More than it was supposed to, I think. A friend of mine is in trouble." Disappointment shadowed her face and I reached out to squeeze her shoulders. "Do you remember what I said the other night?"

She smiled weakly and nodded. "You said only something of grave importance would carry you away from me."

I nodded solemnly. "I meant it. My friend's life is in danger. I must save him." I stepped away and headed toward the ballroom, then turned back. "And I promise, nothing will keep me away at midnight."

I stalked quickly through the ballroom and tried to hide my anxiety beneath a blank smile. I nodded and laughed when complimented on my costume, but I did not stop or linger in one place. Finally I saw Patrick dancing with his wife and waited nervously for the music to end.

I pounced on the two of them quickly, and for a moment the Count thought I wished to steal his wife for a dance. I shook my head, "Not that I would not be honored, my friend, but right now I need your help." I gave him the note and he scanned it quickly. "A life is in danger. I need you to tell me about the Gallant Fox."

Patrick's eyes narrowed. "This note does not indicate danger."

I nodded solemnly. "Yes it does. Morai is illiterate."

It took the Count a moment to absorb the significance of that fact; then he stared at me. "If he's in danger, then so are you." He nodded toward the main entrance to the ballroom. "Come, we can be there in minutes."

I shook my head twice. "No, I have to go alone. Just tell me where it is."

He scratched his head, thought for a moment and, after the hurt of my rejecting his offer of help faded, nodded. "I remember where it is, but it's been closed for six months." I leaned forward and prompted him. "Head off down the road we took to get to the temple and take the second right. The road goes uphill past the old cemetery and curves around toward the sea. About a mile along it you will come to the Gallant Fox on the right side of the street." He shook his head regretfully. "Are you sure I cannot help?"

I shook my head more slowly this time and extended my

hand to him. "No, Patrick, I cannot risk your life in this." He took my hand and we shook firmly. "If you really want to help me, watch the Princess and be her Champion until I return."

He nodded wordlessly and I left him. I stopped at my room before I left the Castel. From the false panel in my trunk I withdrew and strapped to my right hip a pouch of the Talion-made Xne'kal darts, and freshly coated each needle with a full dose of *kutarai*. I strapped spurs to my heels even though I would not ride to the Gallant Fox, then stole into the streets and smiled grimly when I realized no one at the Gallant Fox would find my costume the least bit amusing.

The Gallant Fox was nothing but a ramshackle two-story, weathered-wooden building. A tin-covered, wood-framed awning shielded the worn and warped boardwalk in front of it from harsh weather and moonlight. Boarded-over windows stared blindly down at the street, and I detected no silhouetted motion behind them. Pinpoints of yellow light poured through the cracks in the window coverings and around the wood-plank door. The twisted steps creaked as I climbed them to the boardwalk.

I crossed to the door and vaguely I wondered if they had Selia inside as well.

I knocked twice on the door and flicked fallen paint chips from the back of my hand. A gruff voice from the other side of the door barked, "Who is it?" I mumbled something, then knocked twice again. The challenge gained volume, as did my mumbling. I knocked a third time and took one step back from the door.

I heard the wooden bar scrape against rusty brackets. As the door opened just a crack, and freed a thin sliver of light to stab through the night, I kicked the door hard with the heel of my right foot. The door caught the man behind it in the forehead and bowled him over as it flew open. I burst through the doorway before he'd stopped rolling, and dropped my right hand into the dart pouch.

I looked up and spotted two crossbowmen on the second story balcony across the room from me. I ducked behind a balcony support pillar immediately to my left and launched one dart as they sighted in on me. Their bowstrings hummed like badly tuned mandolins and whipped quarrels forward. One splintered the wooden post by my head and the other burst through the door's upper panel behind me.

My first dart hit one archer in the shoulder, and I sped a second at his companion. The first archer dropped to his knees, and his thigh-stuck partner joined him a second later, but I'd turned away from them to deal with the two men waiting on either side of the open door. The one closest to me, a tall, gaunt, blond man, still recoiled from the bolt that hit the door, but the second had already drawn his sword and lunged at me.

I let my momentum carry me further to my right so his sword slipped just wide of my left flank. I brought my left knee up and smashed it into ribs. He groaned and doubled over. I hammered him to the ground with a left hand to the side of his head, then drew a dart and tossed it underhand into the gaunt man's stomach. His painful bellow dwindled and stopped as the poison sped into his body.

I turned again as he slumped to the floor behind me, but no one else offered any resistance. The man who'd opened the door sat up and rubbed at his head. He smeared blood across his brow, and swore.

Still beneath the balcony, I dropped to one knee beside him, grabbed his chin, and tilted his head up so I could look at the wound. "It will bleed, but you won't die from it." I tightened my grip and forced his head back until he couldn't swallow. "The wound may not kill you, but I will if you don't tell me immediately where you have Morai."

He looked over at the dusty, blocky bar. "Morai?" I called out. An excited thumping sound boomed from behind the bar.

I released the ruffian's chin and he rubbed at his throat. "Do not move." He nodded earnestly, so I threaded my way through the tangle of dirty tables and broken chairs and around behind the bar. Morai lay there trussed up with enough rope to hold even Jevin captive. I squatted quickly and cut him loose with my *ryqril*.

The thief wriggled free of the ropes and tore off the dirty rag they'd used to gag him. He scraped his tongue against his teeth and spat. "Yuck."

I smiled. "How did you get yourself taken?"

He shook his head. "I don't know. Someone learned I worked for Lord Nolan, and kidnapped me to attract your attention. The six of these guys were supposed to hold you . . ."

"Six?!" The word exploded from my lips as I heard my captive scramble to his feet and I stood. He darted toward the door, only to fly back in, unconscious, courtesy of a blow to the face from outside the tavern. Above him, on the balcony over the door, a third crossbowman rose from ambush and shot at me. In one motion I dove to my left and arced a dart at him.

His bolt ripped a ragged furrow across the bartop. My dart slammed into his chest and he sagged against the balcony railing. The rotten banister disintegrated with a loud crack and he flopped down to the common-room floor amid the rain of debris with a heavy thud.

"By the gods!" Count Patrick stared beyond the man he'd knocked back through the doorway at the bodies scattered around the room. "Nolan, you did this by yourself?"

I frowned angrily. "Yes. Why did you come here?"

The Princess, her coronation finery hidden beneath a dark blue cloak, swept past him. "He is here because I asked him to bring me here."

"No," I slammed my fist into the bar, "no, no, no! You shouldn't be here."

My reaction puzzled her. "Why not?"

I held my open hands out to her in supplication. "Because you are in danger here."

She looked at me for a second, then shook her head. "No, you cannot be one of them." She stared at me in disbelief. "Tell me now, Lord Nolan, that you are not one of the plotters from Sinjaria, or I'll have the guardsmen who escorted us here slay you where you stand."

I closed my eyes and almost laughed. "Morai, please tell the Princess who I am."

"Your Lord Nolan is a Justice, Your Highness."

Her laughter pealed through the room. "Lord Nolan, I think your costume has fooled him."

I stared her in the eyes. "He tells the truth."

That stopped her laughter, but she still did not believe.

"You may be a fine fighter, as these fallen men attest, but you are no Talion."

I closed my eyes again and brought my breathing and heartbeat under control. I reached within and forced my mind to touch the thing I'd exiled from my right palm. It felt as cold as ever, but answered my call willingly. I hesitated before I gave it the command freeing it to flood my palm with ebon lines.

I knew she was lost to me. Shortly Duke Vidor would ask her to marry him, and she would accept. I acknowledged the fact that I had no chance to love her; I'd hoped I could have remained her friend. But the deathmark on my palm would drive her too far from me for even that to be possible.

Still, there was no other way. I released the thing and it filled my palm with black ice.

I opened my eyes and held my palm out for her to see. "I am a Justice, and I am here to prevent your father's death."

Two guardsmen entered the room and took charge of the unconscious prisoners. An officer followed them and looked to the Count for instructions, but Patrick just turned and looked at me. "What should they do, Lord Nolan?"

I thought for a moment. Since they'd addressed Morai's note to Lord Nolan the chances were excellent that these men knew nothing about the *nekkeht*. If they'd meant to kill me I would have been attacked on the street, and Morai would not have been left alive. I was almost certain his abduction and this ambush had nothing to do with the *nekkeht* plot; it probably stemmed from someone planning to hold me and use me later as the power factions settled out after the King's death.

I frowned. "Take them to the nearest jail and hold them apart from other prisoners. Search this place and bring all documents you find to the Castel without reading them."

The officer looked at Patrick, and the Count nodded.

"And Sergeant," I added, "use all your men. We will escort Her Highness back to the Castel."

Morai, strapping on his hastily recovered swordbelt, Count Patrick and the Princess followed me out into the cobblestone street without saying a word. I waited until we were fully clear of the guards, and I checked to make sure the

Sergeant had not assigned someone to follow discretely before I turned to speak.

The Princess raised her hand to my mouth and stopped me. "Why did you keep your identity a secret?" Betrayal played through her eyes. "You told a common ruffian who you were."

I ignored Morai's reaction to being classed as a common ruffian and gently shook my head as her hand fell away. "Do not imagine, either of you, that I distrusted you. My instructions were to reveal my identity as needed—even Captain Herman does not know who I am." That mollified the Princess, and the Count nodded with comprehension. "As for Morai, ah, he is *the* Morai from Selia's song, and both of them already knew who I was."

I nodded toward the bandit. "Morai has been gathering information for me so I can try to puzzle out who is behind the plot to kill your father." I turned to Morai. "Is the situation still tense and set for tonight?"

Morai nodded and the purple shadows falling on one half of his face made his expression very grim. "The factions are waiting, and they'll all fall upon each other when just one takes some sort of action."

Count Patrick frowned. "You know there is a plot to kill King Tirrell, but you do not know who is behind it?"

I nodded my head as we continued slowly toward the Castel. "According to Morai, every Sinjarian noble has purchased an army of mercenaries with Rimahasti gold. The Hamisian nobles have their house troops in town for the coronation disguised as peasants." I opened my hands, spread my arms, and shrugged. "Everyone is convinced something will happen, and they're all ready to profit from it, but we can't find the gloved hand with the dagger in it." I frowned with frustration. "Someone will strike because they're all caught up in enough seditious schemes to earn each and every one of them a noose."

The Princess laughed. "Not after midnight."

A cold pang ripped through my stomach. At midnight the assassin would strike, but I realized the Princess did not know that. "What do you mean by that, Your Highness?"

She smiled with relief. "Tonight, at midnight, my father and I will sign an amnesty for all the plotters and truly banish evil from the kingdom! That's what I wanted you to be at so you could witness it." She turned to the Count, who looked stunned by the news. "I am sorry, Patrick, but my father only wanted the witnesses to know before the announcement was made during the unmasking." She turned back to me. "Because you were from Sinjaria, and most of the treasonous lords are likely to be Sinjarian, I wanted you as my witness."

Morai laughed aloud. "That neatly dissolves the only thing holding most of these conspiracies together! Without the threat of betrayal everyone can pull out of a very risky business." Morai slapped me on the back. "Well, Talion, that knocks the spokes out of the rebellion wheel."

I stopped. "Damn, Morai, we've been looking at all the spokes for the key, but we need to look at the hub. Who's the one person talking to every faction in this madness?"

Count Patrick laughed, "Duke Vidor? Impossible. He's a tool!"

Ice flushed through my guts. "A tool is just a tool, unless it does the job by itself."

"No!" The Princess went pale. "My father asked Duke Vidor to be his witness. . . ."

I grabbed the Princess by her arms. "Where were you to sign the papers?"

"In my father's study in the Wolf Tower."

I looked up beyond her and saw the dark silhouette of the tower against the cliffs behind it. One pale yellow light burned in the highest level. The Wolf Moon hung above the tower itself and I knew we did not have much time.

I turned to Morai. "You climbed the cliffs to enter the Castel that first night I found you?"

He nodded and pointed toward the cliff. "Beyond the graveyard, next to the old crypt entrance, there's a narrow crack in the rock that goes up far enough to reach a ledge. From there the walk is simple."

The four of us cut south along a narrow street that twisted its way up toward the overgrown cemetery. The Princess pulled off her slippers and held the hem of her gown up so she could run through the streets with us. Morai led our band, and quickly plied his skills on the cemetery gate's lock. The gate opened with a creak—we raced through it and rounded a hillock built of paupers' graves.

I led the party and I stopped instantly. The massive granite slab sealing the crypts had been torn aside and leaned against the cliff face like a wooden door handing from warped hinges. Broken vines hung like thick ropes silhouetted by the light glowing from within the tomb.

I shook my head. Only the *nekkeht* could have opened the crypt that way. I held my left hand out to stop the others. "Go no further."

Morai took one look at the crypt and drew his sword.

I shook my head. "Listen, all three of you." I pointed to the crypt. "There's something in there I have to stop, and I have to do it alone. I have to use this on it." I showed them my right palm.

The three of them nodded and I continued. "You three must hurry back to the Castel. Get to the King and get him out of the tower. Get him away quickly, don't trust anyone, and don't look back." I turned to Morai. "If you don't see me by morning, send a message to Talianna, and remember that word."

Morai nodded. *"Drijen."*

A voice rang out from the crypt. "Come, Talion, I wait for you. Tell your friends to hurry off on their tasks because it will do them no good." The voice trailed off into laughter and the Princess looked visibly shaken by it.

My eyes narrowed. "And burn every Lurker you see."

I stepped toward the crypt, but the Princess grabbed my shoulder. "Lord Nolan, Talion, you can't go in there. It'll kill you."

I took her hand in mine and kissed it. I remembered what His Excellency had told me so many years before. "It's better I die to destroy it than let it return the world to the days of the Shattering." I pulled Prince Uriah's ring from my finger and closed her hand around it. "Remember me as your Champion."

I stepped away and Count Patrick dragged the Princess back. Leaden feet carried me forward, but I felt no fear. I knew I was dead, the Goddess Shudath had told me as much. Perhaps she had been right, perhaps I'd die regretting my actions, because my grandmother would have relished King Tirrell's death. In that way I would be defeated by the dead, but that did not matter to me.

I was a Justice. Justice was my gift to the world. I had no other task, and could have no nobler purpose. Acknowledging myself already dead, I summoned my *tsincaat* and entered the Hamisian royal tombs to slay a creature that could not die.

I cautiously stepped into the crypt's antechamber and marveled at the lack of decay. Though faded by the years, the colors used on the wall murals still gave life to the artwork. The ornate stonework around the archway into the tombs themselves still had crisp lines and maintained the strength the artist first charged it with. It gladdened my heart to see such beautiful artistry before I died.

The pristine interior of the large crypt room mocked the neglected cemetery behind me. Niches carved high in the walls ringed the whole rectangular chamber. Whereas once they had glowed with magic flames honoring the dead, now they possessed only the jaundiced light of the thick, black candles the *nekkeht* had set burning within them. Back on the left side, in the farthest distant corner, I saw the blackened archway that led up through the valley wall to the Wolf Tower, and enough dirt carpeted the ground near it to suggest it had been cleared to permit passage between the Castel and the crypts.

The central chamber lay broader than it did deep and rose to a height of fourteen feet above the floor. A forest of evenly spaced pillars blossomed upward to support the vaulted ceiling. All across the floor, in an orderly pattern that terminated two-thirds of the way through the chamber, stone coffins rested upon tall biers. The rulers' stone effigies graced their coffin lids and lay staring blindly at the mountain above them.

The *nekkeht* sat and meditated in the very center of the chamber. His left eye, the one surrounded by the black-diamond tattoo, popped open. Thinning black hair did its best to cover a head too large for the gaunt body supporting it. A small man, he looked more like a scarecrow than a human being.

He smiled and spread his hands as if welcoming me to his home. "I am Gyasi ra Tingis, Talion. In these humble and forgotten environs I have waited a long time for you."

MICHAEL A. STACKPOLE

I kept my *tsincaat* before me and walked along until only a dozen feet separated us. I passed by the tombs of a hundred Kings and Queens of Hamis and, in doing so, I felt strangely calm. It struck me that no defender of the royal bloodline could fail amid these coffins.

I looked down upon the *nekkeht*. "I am a Justice. I, too, have waited long for our meeting."

Slowly and easily the Lurker rose from his cross-legged position without touching his hands to the ground. "This tomb is a dreary hidey-hole, but, for an evening, it isn't that oppressive. It certainly offers more diversions than I've had available so far in this endeavor. While waiting for you I did find a way to amuse myself, however." He swept his right hand around his head with a flourish and the candles surrounding us brightened. "I hope you do not mind my decorations."

I noticed the back of my left hand itched, but I attached no importance to it. "They do not concern me. I am here to destroy you."

The *nekkeht* giggled, pirouetted, and leaped deeper into the crypts. His supernaturally enhanced jump carried him away from me with blurred speed. He landed on a sarcophagus, turned, and squatted like a gargoyle on top of it. He clung to the stonework like a squirrel on a tree and leered at me, but before he could taunt me with some childish comment, the dart I'd flung after him hit his right shoulder.

He snarled and ripped the dart free. "Ha! You expect this toy to stop me?" He tightened his left hand around it and I heard it crack. His hand opened and the splinters dropped away, but, as his right hand writhed at them, they burst into flame before they ever hit the floor. "Oh, Talion, your death will be my pleasure."

He sprang from the coffin like a frog, vaulted off the granite floor and tackled me. I'd half twisted to my left to avoid the full impact, but he battered me down and knocked the wind out of me just the same. We rolled and I shoved him off. He flew and slammed into a bier, but didn't even notice the collision.

He dove at me and, on my back, I lashed out with my right foot. I caught him beneath the chin and kicked him over the top of me. He hit the ground awkwardly and then rolled to a jerky stop. He spat and I heard pieces of a tooth rattle on the smooth granite floor. Blood trickled from his split lower lip and he wiped it into a red smear with the back of his right hand.

He laughed, then mentally turned inside to repair the damage and show me his power. The second his eyes rolled up so I could only see the whites, I rose, dashed forward, and thrust my *tsincaat* through his chest.

His eyes popped down and he pivoted. His twist tore the *tsincaat* from my grasp; then he punched me in the chest with an open-handed blow from his right hand. Agony burst above my heart and I heard my breastbone crack as I flew back. Out of control, I somersaulted backward across the stone floor. I smacked my head against a bier, stars sparked before my eyes, and I lay stunned.

The *nekkeht* laughed like a madman. A thin river of blood poured from his mouth with each word as he scolded me. "This cannot stop me, Talion." He ripped his shirt halfway down and looked at the *tsincaat* transfixed in his chest. He wrapped his hands around the blade. "You cannot stop me."

He slowly pulled the blade free. Inch by inch it slid from his chest and the hole around it closed. The bloodflow from his mouth stopped and he smiled at me with a mouthful of scarlet teeth. "I am invincible." He discarded my *tsincaat* and stalked forward.

He obviously expected me to summon the blade and attack him again with it, but I already knew it would have no effect on him. I rolled to my stomach, pushed off the floor, and fought against the pain radiating out from my rib cage. I glided forward and feinted a blow at his eyes with my left hand. Invincible or not, he'd spent a lifetime reflexively guarding his eyes and raised his hands to save his sight. I jerked my knee up and smashed it into his groin.

His hands shot down, but instead of grabbing himself, he caught my left leg and tightened his right hand around my kneecap. He held me motionless, then crushed the bone as he had the dart.

Argent torments washed away my sight and geysered up through the roof of my skull. Agony swirled through my body and raked red-hot talons across every nerve and fiber in my being. I felt myself falling and felt the grinding click as my left knee hit the ground, but that new pain could be nothing more than a shadow of what I felt twisting and ravaging my body.

His laughter swallowed the echoes of my scream. The *nekkeht* walked forward and stood above me. "Are you hurt, Talion? How can that be?" He stepped over and straddled me. "You thrust your sword through me and I am not hurt."

He dropped into a crouch and grabbed up my left hand. He trapped my little finger between his thumb and forefinger. The candlelight sunk his eyes in shadow and made his head into a skull. "I will enjoy this, Talion." He grinned, squeezed, and pulverized the bone in that finger.

I jammed my right hand against his forehead and clawed his scalp with my fingers. I hoped he might think, just for a moment, that I meant to tear at him and hurt him. I needed just a second to start pulling his soul from his body, then we would battle will against will, and his extra souls would count for nothing.

I breathed in . . . and nothing happened.

The *nekkeht* roared with laughter! He poked his face down to mine and spattered me with mirth-driven spittle. "They tried that once on me, Talion, but I've worked a counter-spell. Your magick won't work here." He looked up and I saw pinpoints of candlelight reflected in his black eyes. "I've got an hour until my candles burn down, but you'll be dead by then." He looked down at me. "But you won't have been long dead."

I tried to summon my *tsincaat* but felt nothing. It lay behind him only ten or fifteen feet away, but it might as well have been back in Talianna. Flat on my back I could not reach my *ryqril*, and he held my left hand, which made a grab for the stiletto sheathed on my forearm impossible.

He nodded slowly at me and selected the middle finger on my left hand as if choosing a key from a ring of them. "I know all your secrets and I have countered them. There is nothing you can do but die, Talion."

My eyes narrowed. I stared into his midnight eyes and carefully pronounced one word with the finality of a headman's ax hitting the block. *"Leoht!"*

Gouts of incandescent gold and orange fire exploded within each niche and rolled out to lick at the ceiling in an obscene caress. The brilliant light washed all color from the *nekkeht*'s face, and etched every twisted line of uncertain and confused terror on it in ebon.

My *tsincaat* leaped to hand the instant I willed it do so and swept through his neck. I twisted and flung his headless body off my chest. On my left side, I curled up and grabbed his head by an ear with my left hand. His jaw still worked but no sound came out of his mouth; it hardly mattered because I knew what he wanted to ask.

"Some Talions have more secrets than others, Gyasi." I dropped my *tsincaat*, pressed my right hand to his forehead, and breathed in. I felt the *rhasa* souls pass into me; then the resistance began. I pulled harder, but he fought.

"No, Gyasi, your time is ended. You failed. It is over for you."

He gnashed his teeth impotently because he could not bite me. His body thrashed around blindly but he could not command it because he did not know where it lay or in what direction it faced. He could do nothing, and he sensed that. The instant that doubt crept into his mind, I had him.

His soul flowed into me quickly. His body twitched a time or two down by my feet, then it lay still. His eyes closed and his jaw hung slack. I had killed the *nekkeht*.

Slowly, painfully, I pulled myself to my feet. Bone fragments shifted in my knee and I almost fell, but caught hold of a coffin and righted myself again. I leaned against the stone sarcophagus and trembled. Then I tossed Gyasi's head aside and started to giggle madly.

"There, Most Holy Shudath, I did it," I laughed aloud. "I defeated the dead!"

The flicker of motion I caught in the corner of my right eye was no warning. The thrown *ryqril* pierced my right side and its sharp, steel blade found my heart. I looked down in surprise and shock because, even before I wrapped my left hand around the hilt and pulled it free, I recognized the *ryqril*. I sank to my knees and jammed my right hand against the hole pouring blood from my side in a vain attempt to staunch the flow. I half smiled as I fell forward on my face because I'd mocked her warning and paid the price for my audacity.

The *ryqril* belonged to Lothar.

Chapter Twenty-Two

JUSTICE: CIRHON

Lothar knelt with eyes closed amid the beauty of the Haunted Circle. The short, green spring grasses bowed before the same gentle breeze that tugged playfully at Lothar's white-blond hair and the loose ends of his white silken headband. The grumbled roar of the Tal River racing through a gorge thirty feet below the cliff at his back sounded like distant thunder. Lothar, it seemed, did not notice it and only concerned himself with rubbing a scarlet cloth along the polished, gleaming length of the *tsincaat* lying across his thighs.

I looped Wolf's reins around a tree branch at the edge of the clearing. I tried not to disturb Lothar, but I knew nothing I did could escape his attention. I untied the laces of a saddlebag and withdrew the bread and wine from its dark interior. I knew I'd wasted my money when I purchased them, but I had to hope Lothar would consider my debt settled without one or both of us dying.

I slowly shook my head. If he'd intended no blood be spilt, he never would have chosen the Haunted Circle for our *Cirhon*.

The Haunted Circle sat only a few hundred feet above the valley floor on the southern face of the Tal Mountains. Located on top of a cliff overlooking the Tal River, it commanded a beautiful view of the valley and Talianna. Low stones described the circle, except where it became one with the cliff edge. The twenty-foot diameter of the ring made it a large arena for just two fighters.

I walked to the edge of the circle and knelt just outside of it. I bowed to Lothar and placed the bread and wine within the gray stone border. "I have come, and I offer this bread and this wine in the hope we can end this madness."

Lothar's eyes opened slowly and he stared at me without saying a word, but his body betrayed his mind. His hand stroked the *tsincaat* more lovingly and his nostrils flared ever so slightly as his breath quickened. Finally his anxious anger consumed his sense of propriety. "I see you finally dare meet me. I have waited for you half the day."

I shook my head. "Even in your bitterness you know I am not a coward."

A demonic snarl leaped from his throat. He bared his teeth, as if to frighten me, in a sneer. "If you are not a coward, why did you bring an offering for me to accept in lieu of your life?" He hunched forward and dispelled the last hint of tranquil nobility in him.

I clenched my jaw and gave myself time to calm down. In an even voice I answered him. "I brought these gifts because I do not want to fight you. You waited for me because Marana did not return quite whole from our mission." I hoped for a reaction from him when I mentioned Marana, and I got one, but it was not quite what I wanted.

Lothar's eyes narrowed as if he'd bitten into a tartly sour fruit. He raised his *tsincaat* and studied its edge as the sunlight glinted from it. Then, like a cat caught being watched, he quickly turned his head in my direction and fixed me with a harsh stare. "How dare you mention her to me when you poisoned her mind against me? She is not the cause of our fight, Nolan the Unhomed, your seduction of her is! Do not imagine I will let you live because your death would sadden her." He shook his head regretfully, as if already standing over my dead body and remorsefully lamenting the waste of such a young life. "Fight me yourself, do not use her against me."

I balled my fists and dug my fingernails into my palms. "Damn you, Lothar! I care not that you unman me with such accusations, but you suggest I care nothing for Marana, and that I cannot tolerate." I stabbed a finger at Talianna. "Marana needs you, she needs Jevin, she needs me. She needs every friend she has ever known. She tried to kill herself, Lothar; Marana tried to commit suicide!"

I regained control of my runaway emotions and opened my hands. "I brought the bread and wine so we could both return and stand beside her. Challenge me again when she is well, in a week or month or year. I will never refuse your challenge, but I do not want to take someone special away from her right now."

Lothar heard my words, but ignored their intent. He reared his head back and laughed. "Do not worry yourself, Nolan, you will not kill me."

Lothar stood and walked calmly forward. He bent and picked up the jug of wine, then used his *tsincaat* to spit the bread. He turned with military precision and marched back beyond where he'd been sitting. He stopped at the cliff edge.

"No, Lothar, please." I reached forward and implored him not to discard the offering. "Marana needs you."

Lothar carelessly pitched the wine and bread over the edge. "And she will have me, Nolan, after I have killed you."

I nodded and stood slowly. I reached into the pouch on my belt and drew out a slender length of black silk cloth. A white skull on a circular red background marked the center point of the three feet of cloth. I smoothed the silk out, flipped it over so the circle faced the ground, and raised it to my forehead. I touched the rough painted surface of the skull and, when satisfied it rested exactly in the middle of my forehead, I tied the headband off with a knot over my right ear.

Lothar watched me and chuckled to himself. He'd knotted

his headband—white because he had demanded a *Cirhon* of me—on the left side of his head. He would only accept my death as the finish to this fight, whereas by knotting my headband on the right, I offered him a bloodless way out of the fight. "Nolan, do not be foolish, you will never drive me from the circle."

"Lothar, please, this circle has drunk enough Talion blood over the centuries. Enough ghosts are bound to this spot. Let us not do this to each other."

The Janian noble strode stiff-legged back to the circle's center. He drew his *ryqril* and crossed his arms over his chest. "I, Lothar ra Jania, do claim of thee a blood debt. You were as my brother, yet you betrayed me. In the *Cirhon* this matter will be settled."

I unbuckled my swordbelt, drew my *ryqril*, summoned my *tsincaat*, and similarly crossed my arms over my chest. "I, Nolan ra Sinjaria, do reject your claim, and seek neither your blood or your life in doing so. I have not betrayed you. In the *Cirhon* this matter will be settled."

I took one fateful step forward and entered *Cirhon*. If I drove Lothar from the circle, it would be ended. If one of us managed to disarm the other and he summoned his *tsincaat* from beyond the circle, the fight was over. If one of us killed the other, the fight was ended.

Lothar stood tall and waited for me in the center of the circle. He struck a loose guard, with *tsincaat* in his right hand and *ryqril* held easily in his left. Unlike mine, his *ryqril* was balanced and could be thrown, but I knew he would not do that. I could parry it and that would leave him at a disadvantage.

Suddenly I realized that, after the return trip from Zandria, and the Shar ritual, I could not fight a long battle. I felt too tired, and Marana's illness threatened to distract me. I needed to end the fight quickly, but, looking over at the tall, strong, implacable Janian, I knew that would not be easy or without risk.

I drove at him with long strides. I came in straight toward him with both *tsincaat* and *ryqril* held low at my sides, more like a brawler than a trained fighter. Lothar planted his left foot and lunged at my chest. I twisted my torso back to the left and swept *tsincaat* and *ryqril* up to cross and catch

Lothar's blade. I kicked out with my right foot and hit Lothar in the chest.

Lothar flew back and tumbled in a groaning heap. His *tsincaat* remained trapped between my blades and I took a step toward the circle's stone border to fling it clear, but my right leg collapsed. Pain drilled up through my leg, yet I forced myself to throw his *tsincaat* from our arena before I looked down.

Blood covered my right calf. My brown boot gaped open from just below my knee to where the muscle started to taper back down toward my heel. Already sticky warmth filled my boot and squished between my toes, but, even so, I knew I could still hobble. I'd not lost my mobility completely, and that meant I still had a chance.

Lothar slowly climbed to his feet, brandished his blooded *ryqril*, and laughed at me kneeling there. "A tool is just a tool, eh, Nolan. Well, this time the tool got broken." He looked down at my *tsincaat*. "I'll kill you even with your advantage." The muscles at his jaw bunched but did nothing to banish the confident grin on his face.

I stood and quickly tested how much weight my leg would support. It held even when I leaned on it heavily, but that did not surprise me. Because of the wound the leg would not respond well to quick and agile moves, and it bled too freely to give me much time to somehow defeat Lothar.

Again Lothar grimaced and I noticed he held his right arm tight against his side. I'd cracked some ribs with my kick, and Lothar struggled against the pain. He'd not paled, and no blood flecked his lips, so I'd not punctured a lung, but that put us closer to even than he wanted to acknowledge.

I looked down at the *tsincaat* in my hand, then tossed it from the circle. "No, Lothar, I'll have no one say we took unfair advantage of each other." Something flashed through his eyes, and he smothered it with furious hatred fast enough, but I hoped he understood, just for that second, that I never wanted to hurt him.

Lothar dropped into a low stance and I matched it as well as my leg would let me. He came in from his left and tried to keep most of his body between me and his damaged ribs. Unfortunately his advance came at my right side, so I continued to back in a circle to keep him away from my weak spot. I shifted my *ryqril* to my right hand and made short, slashing feints to keep him back.

Frustration exploded in him. He launched himself and tackled me on his left shoulder and I fell back. I felt his *ryqril* bite into my back and I screamed. My left fist jerked down, driven more by a spasm of pain than intent, and slammed into Lothar's ribs.

Lothar's back arched in agony and he rolled off to my right. His left hand still held his *ryqril*, but both lay pinned beneath me. I hammered my right elbow down into his left forearm and heard a bone snap; then I twisted to my left and curled up into a kneeling position facing him.

I coughed convulsively and tasted blood. I shifted my *ryqril* back to my left hand and gingerly probed my back. I felt the hilt of his *ryqril*, but from the angle I knew the blade was not planted firmly in my back. Instead, the slice ran parallel to my waist and my roll had twisted the blade free so only my leather jerkin held it to my flesh.

I withdrew it and cast both *ryqrils* from the circle. I coughed again and raised my left hand to my mouth to cover it. When I pulled it away I saw droplets of blood sprayed against my palm. Lothar's stab had cut my lung and, without help, the wound would kill me.

Lothar looked no better off. He slowly pulled his legs up underneath himself and used his right arm to lever himself into a kneeling position. He'd paled badly. His coughing brought blood to his lips and pain to his face. He weaved unsteadily and reached his broken left arm across his body to hold his right side.

His body convulsed and wracked a wet cough from him. He pointed a trembling finger at me. "I will kill you, Nolan."

I forced myself to my feet and backed to the center of the circle. "Then come. Let us finish this." I opened my bloody hands and waited. I knew I had only one chance, and I wanted to stop the battle without killing Lothar, so I had to risk it.

Lothar rushed forward and did not realize my intent until I fell back before his attack. I grabbed the lapels of his tunic and rolled onto my back. I posted my left leg in his stomach and pushed up and off even as my impact with the ground ignited new pain in my back. I released his tunic and let him fly away.

I hoped Lothar would land hard enough to jar him into unconsciousness, but even as I let him go, he tucked his right shoulder under and kicked his legs toward the right to start his body rolling. He hit the ground on his right side, and screamed in pain, but did not black out. Still the pain did rob him, for a moment, of any conscious control of his body. Instead of rolling to his feet and attacking back at me, as he had done in countless practice battles between us, his roll continued and carried him off the cliff edge.

"Lothar!" I forced myself to ignore the throbbing waves of torment threatening to suck me down within death's black undertow. I rolled to my stomach and dragged myself toward the circle's open edge. He could not be gone!

Nearer the cliff, I focused on a pale spot amid the grasses at the cliff's edge. I lunged forward and locked my right hand on it. I felt flesh!

"Lothar, I've got you, I've got you." I pulled myself closer and looked over the edge.

Supported by his right hand, Lothar hung there. He reached out with his right foot and just managed to reach a toehold. I felt the tension ease in his forearm, but I did not slacken my grip. Beneath him the Tal River swirled itself into a froth among the rocks and shot a thousand boiling bubbles through a pool. The rocks reminded me of teeth and the water ran through them like saliva through the fangs of a starving beast. It wanted Lothar, but I would defy it.

The Janian looked up at me utterly puzzled. He said something, but the river's howl gobbled up the words.

I shook my head. "I will not let you die." I reached down with my left hand and grabbed the left shoulder of his tunic. "On three."

I must have counted because I remember pulling with all my might, and I felt Lothar rise above me, but there my memories end. The effort wrung too much pain from me, and I succumbed to the black shroud it dropped over me.

I awoke in the infirmary, in a bed I knew all too well, and felt absolutely no pain. My eyes popped open and I focused on Marana, Jevin, and Adamik. The latter two smiled, but

Marana's expression did not change. Only a single tear rolling down her right cheek even suggested she'd noticed me.

I looked at the Wizard. "How long have I been here?"

"Four days."

His reply took my breath away. Assuming they'd gotten to me quickly, that was a great deal longer than I'd have expected to heal two knife wounds. I suddenly realized how close to death I must have actually been. "Why so long?"

The Fealareen's brow knotted and his smile faded. "You lost a great deal of blood. If Marana had not headed out there to try and stop you two, help would have arrived too late." Jevin nodded at Marana and I smiled in her direction.

"I owe you my life." I reached out and took her right hand in mine.

"I live for you, Nolan, I will not have you abandon me." She delivered the words flatly, as if stating a law.

I squeezed her hand, and felt a flicker of response. "I will be here for you always."

I released her hand, eased myself up into a bit more of a sitting position, and looked around the room. Something struck me as very wrong. All the other beds were empty. I fought the coldness in my stomach, and turned to Jevin. "Where is Lothar?"

The Fealareen's face closed up. "You do not remember?"

I shook my head slowly because the only obvious conclusion I could draw from Jevin's question stole all words from me.

Lord Hansur appeared soundlessly in the doorway beyond Jevin. He nodded at all three Talions and they filed from the room to leave us alone. He took a deep breath, then exhaled slowly. "Nolan, Lothar ra Jania is dead."

I shook my head vehemently. "No, he cannot be dead. He was hurt, yes, badly hurt, but I helped him back over the cliff. I know it." Tears poured from my eyes and tasted salty on my tongue.

Lord Hansur stared at me, then reached out and rested a hand on my right shoulder. "You tried to save him, I am certain, Nolan, but he must have blacked out and fallen back. It is not your fault."

I fought with myself and squeezed my eyes tight to stop the tears. I reached down and threw my covers off. I wiped tears from my face with my left forearm. I sniffed, then cleared my throat. "Please tell me you have not buried him. I wish to see him." I swung my feet around and sat on the edge of the bed.

Lord Hansur gently pushed me back onto the bed, and I was too weak to resist. "You cannot see his body. He fell into the river and his body has not yet been recovered."

I tried to speak around the lump in my throat but I could have more easily brought Lothar back from the dead. If they'd not found his body in four days it would never be found. I had killed Lothar. I loved him like a brother and he died by my hand.

No Shar could ever take the stain of his blood from my soul.

Lothar's death, while not a crime according to the Talions because it happened within *Cirhon*, infuriated the Janian royal house. They reacted poorly when told of his death and demanded I be put on trial for murder, but that was no more or less than they would have asked of the government of the place where one of their nationals had been killed. It seemed, for a week or so, that the incident would quickly be forgotten once Lothar was buried in the family crypts.

When His Excellency informed the royal family they could not have Lothar's body, they renewed and strengthened their demand for a trial. The Master himself drafted a missive to them that explained the fight had been a lawful duel and, consequently, I would not be tried or punished.

Jania reacted harshly. They expelled all Talions from the country, and recalled all Janian Talions. They tried me in absentia and imposed a death sentence on me. Because the verdict and sentence only named a Talion—neither His Excellency or the Master named me to the Janians—all Talions were instructed to stay clear of Jania, and thus began the Interdiction.

In spite of the fact that Lothar had not been rational when we fought, it took me months to come to grips with my guilt. I had been the instrument of his death, and he certainly meant to slay me, but I had to hope those last words he spoke, the ones I never heard because of the river, told me he forgave me. I read that intent in his eyes, or, at least, I imagined I did, and I had to hope he died knowing I loved him despite our differences. Lothar had died by my hand—my bungled rescue attempt dropped him in the river and proved deadlier than driving a broken rib into his heart. There was no way for me to avoid claiming his death as my own. I accepted that.

During that time, though, I learned why the place where we fought aptly bore the name the Haunted Circle. It was not for the countless Talion shades tied to that spot. It came from the memories of the fight that haunted everyone who ever survived a battle there.

Late one night, under a full Wolf Moon, I carried a silver bowl made in Jania down to the Tal River. I filled it with water and carried it to the grove of trees overlooking the Talion graveyard. I carefully selected the tree I imagined growing closest to the secret entrance into the treasure trove beneath Talianna. I muttered a funeral prayer I half remembered from childhood, poured the water on the tree, and carved Lothar's name in its bark with my *ryqril*.

I knelt there in silence, then smiled and whispered gently. "This is for you, my friend, for the person you were before we fought, and for the Justice you would have been."

I stood; then, satisfied, I walked away. I left the tree as a living monument to the Lothar I had known. In my mind, he now guarded Vaughan's secret. It was honorable duty, to guard that secret; duty worthy of a noble.

I thought Lothar would be proud.

I hoped I would be forgiven.

Chapter Twenty-Three

TALION: REVENANT

The cold kiss of the tomb floor sank into numbness along with the warmth of the blood pouring from my chest. The shackles of pain binding me fell away. I felt lighter and, as mad as it seemed, I knew I could stand. I wasn't dead.

I stood, then looked down and saw myself standing above my body.

I heard mild laughter from behind me and turned. The stone effigy carved from the coffin lid on a Queen's tomb sat upright, then twisted to sit on the coffin's edge. The statue's blank eyes darkened and became windows to infinity.

I bowed reverently and knelt. "I praise thy name, Most Holy Shudath."

The granite eyebrows tilted in a frown.

"Seconds ago you mocked my warning, now you praise my name. You are fickle, Talion."

I shook my head. "Not fickle, foolish."

Her laughter again played from the stony throat, but my attention was drawn to a spot behind her. I saw a dot of light flare and expand until it became a round doorway into a realm of only light. It drew me as a candle draws a moth, and though I sensed peace within that brilliant realm, I dreaded it.

I looked at the Goddess. "It is done?"

The statue shrugged carelessly. "Your mission? Yes, the *nekkeht* has been stopped."

Again the circle of light commanded my attention. I saw shapes moving within it, much as I'd seen shapes moving with the dark void I'd experienced in Talianna. I counted eight of them, grouped together, who appeared intent upon me. Slowly they took shape and became more solid. I recognized my parents first, then my grandmother and my brothers and sisters. All my dead waited for me beyond that portal.

I stood and walked toward them with faltering steps. "My family, they are there."

The statue nodded solemnly. "Indeed they are. They have waited for you. If you wish to surrender to the peace, you will be reunited with them."

Her words stopped me. I turned. "You said my mission was complete." I spat the words from my mouth. "I have earned my rest."

Divine laughter lashed out and burned me like vitriol with its scorn. "Have you, Talion? Have you earned anything? Think about your family, then what has happened here. Tell me, after you consider that all, tell me you have earned eternal bliss."

Facts I'd known, but ignored, congealed within my mind and gave shape to a horror that had lurked in the background since this mission started. I'd been assigned to destroy the *nekkeht* and anyone outside Talianna who knew of it. I'd been lucky enough to stumble over the mastermind's identity, but I'd not discovered how he first learned of *nekkehts*.

Only Talions knew *nekkehts* existed, and the Duke's knowledge of *nekkehts* meant someone was a traitor. Stopping the Duke's plot meant nothing if the traitor escaped to continue his actions. But only I knew a traitor existed, and that information had to be shared.

I suddenly realized that if Talions were involved in the Duke's plot, the *nekkeht*'s destruction meant nothing toward stopping the plot. Assassins could slaughter the whole royal family and support the Duke's assumption of the throne. Any lord who did not back the Duke would be destroyed outright by the Talions, or would be devoured piecemeal by loyalists.

The picture of armies swarming over Hamis crawled into my mind. I saw a lone farmhouse and a renegade patrol stopping to rape and murder. I heard the screams of homeless orphans, and I recognized my own voice as the loudest amid the chorus.

My family faded from sight beyond the Goddess and I focused on her. "It would have been so nice, so appropriate to die here."

She shook the stone head slowly. "Appropriate for burial, Talion, but not a place for death." The effigy lay back down and the eyes drained of color. "Save yourself."

Agony lanced through me and tore like a series of barbed hooks across my consciousness, but I did not scream. As much as I hurt, worse than I ever had before, I was not dead, and that was cause enough to hold me together so I could act. I *had* to act.

I retreated within and touched the *rhasa* souls. As I had done before in Talianna when I made the mouse *nekkeht*, I coaxed them out and forced them down my arm. I felt them gather in my hand, all expectant and filled with eagerness. Then, with the cold numbness of death nibbling at my face and feet, I pushed them into my body.

They rushed into my side and defiantly banished death. They devoured the pain and filled me with a buoyant joy. They soothed every ache, calmed every nerve and fortified every muscle. Death was the absence of life, but the *rhasa* souls crowding my body were pure life.

I reached inside and monitored my injuries. The *ryqril* had pierced my heart and the punctured chamber still pumped and leaked blood into my chest. I touched a *rhasa* soul and directed it toward the wound. It swirled around the laboring organ and sealed the hole without scar or seam.

Another soul, sensing my desire to be whole, sank into my

knee and pieced the bone back together as if it were nothing more than a broken plate. It took joy in sliding each bone fragment into the correct position. It could have just melted it all into a bony putty, then reshaped my kneecap, but *this* was the right way to accomplish my goal.

Healing naturally is a function of life.

The other souls sought out the injuries to my ribs and lungs and finger. The hole in my side closed without effort or a scar, and the lung the *ryqril* had punctured reinflated without pain. The bruise over my heart from the *nekkeht*'s blow to my chest vanished, ribs reseated themselves in my breastbone, and the swollen lump on the back of my head shrank.

Their tasks complete, *rhasa* souls awaited my next command. Did I want them to fill my muscles so I could shatter stone with a kick or armor my flesh so swords or fire could not hurt me? They offered to end my need for air and food. They would do anything for me, all I had to do was ask.

I thought about the portal beyond which I'd seen my dead. I commanded the souls to gather in my right palm, and I opened it. "I want you to do one more thing for me. Carry a message to those I have lost and tell them I still love and revere them."

Five otterlike threads of light drifted like smoke from my palm. They waited until all had left me, then cavorted, twisting and turning, through the air. Then, after only a second or two of celebration, they coalesced into a brilliant, living white ball. It imploded upon itself and disappeared without sound or trace.

The *nekkeht* had cleared enough of the collapsed tunnel roof to let me squeeze through. I stumbled along in the darkness and cautiously felt my way up the tunnel. The lack of a light made the journey difficult, but I did not regret for an instant destroying all Gyasi's candles by using the ancient magick command that rekindled the flames that once burned to honor the Hamisian dead.

I reached the tower itself quickly and climbed the stairs to the upper levels. I knew the secret entrance to the King's level was behind a washstand like the one in my suite, though the King's study was located in the same spot as my suite's library. I hoped nothing obstructed the door, because I wanted to enter the upper floor unseen. The Talion who had thrown the knife—my mind reeled at the thought of Lothar having joined with Duke Vidor—clearly had preceded me into the Tower. I had to assume the others had not gotten the King to safety and act accordingly to save him. My only advantage lay in the fact that Lothar believed I was dead.

I reached above the lintel and pressed the panel that released the washbasin. It slid forward and grated, but the sound could never have been heard over the Duke's irate shouting in the King's study.

"How could I do this? Ha! You sound offended, my King, that I could have betrayed you so. You slew my father and brother, then brought me here and made me a court pet. My vaunted rank of Duke meant nothing because I was the Duke of Sinjaria, not of Hamis. I ranked below a Count in your court. How long did you think I would suffer this insulting treatment?"

I slipped from behind the washstand but did not shut it. I saw Morai standing with his back to the King's gryphon-fireplace, but the bedroom wall blocked everyone else from view. I knew the bandit spotted me, but he kept all evidence of his discovery from his face.

I heard Count Patrick laugh; then the sound of fist striking flesh exploded through the room. Morai winced and I heard the Princess cry out, but no one else reacted until the King spoke.

"Enough, Duke Vidor. If you wish to have him pay for his 'insult' strike him yourself. Do not have your pet Talion do it for you." The King's voice lapsed, then sounded again. "I understand why you acted, but I wonder what the Talions' broader plans are, and what motivates them? Tell me, Talion, why are you part of this?"

Her answer plunged an ice-dagger into my heart. "I did it for Sinjaria."

I stepped from the King's bedroom and faced her. "No, Marana, no."

Her eyes blazed with insanity. "Nolan! Thank the gods you are alive!" She smiled at me and waited for praise.

The Duke frowned. "I thought you said he was dead!"

Marana shrugged and let her head loll to the side like a child in a daze. "I was wrong."

The Duke growled. "Then kill him now!"

Marana's left hand blurred as she struck. She plucked the Duke's dagger from the sheath over his right hip and, without moving from beside him, drove it through his right shoulder. The backhanded blow carried him backward, and Marana moved with it but did not release the hilt until the blade pinned the Duke to the wooden shelves behind him. The Duke screamed and stood on tiptoes to ease the pain.

To her right the King, seated at a mahogany desk, stared at her. Kneeling before the desk, Count Patrick gawked at the Duke's dangling form. Princess Zaria, standing between the Count and Morai, hid her pale face in her hands. The Duke moaned and screwed his face tight against the pain.

Marana giggled. "I didn't know you were the Talion the *nekkeht* was waiting to kill. I didn't want to kill you, Nolan, but after you killed the *nekkeht* I knew you would spoil everything if I didn't." Her singsong voice filled the room with childish tones. "I wasn't going to do what they wanted, no," she smiled at me, "I did it for you." Her left hand stroked her flat stomach. "I did it for our child, your heir."

Stunned, I could think of no reply.

The Duke struggled against the shock of his wound. "What are you talking about?"

Marana reached over and ripped the dagger from his shoulder. He tried to catch himself before he fell, but she forced him to the ground with an open-handed slap. "Kneel, peasant." She threatened the others with the bloody dagger. "Kneel, all of you! Kneel before your King."

"No, Marana, no!" I swallowed hard as my friends yielded to her threats and sank to their knees.

She stood tall and gloated. "Kneel before Nolan *ulHamis* and let justice reign!" She turned to me and smiled. "Which one shall I kill first for you?"

I shook my head. "None of these, Marana. It is over."

She laughed. "No, Nolan, it just begins. Since you are alive you will be made King of Hamis. Our child will be your heir. We will take our troops—*Talion* troops—and forge a new Empire! What better monument for your family, and for the

Prince this branch of the family usurped and murdered? Who will die first?"

All my emotions sank in a sea of pity. "No one will die, Marana. There will be no new empire. I do not want a new empire. It is over before it begins."

Marana frowned petulantly and dropped the Duke's dagger. "No, Nolan, there must be an empire and you must be King. You told me long ago to live for you, and I have. I have built you a kingdom. I did it for you." Her arms snaked around her torso, holding her confusion in.

I licked my lips and tasted my tears. I'd shared the terrible secret of my family, the fact that we were descended from Prince Uriah of Hamis, with a Marana who was so different than the creature standing before me. Only sixteen at the time, I still wanted to avenge my family because I'd not yet realized their deaths were part of the mindless fabric from which all wars are cut, not a deliberate act by King Tirrell to finally destroy the only threat to his House. Indeed, final confirmation of that came as I stood ready to defend Princess Zaria against any ulHamis who might come to oppose her—if all the ulHamis were dead, why would that opportunity for them to reclaim the throne still be part of the ceremony?

Marana's face brightened hopefully. "Are you angry that I did not let you know I lived? I know it hurt, and I wanted to tell you, just like I wanted to tell you I killed Lothar, but it would have spoiled everything." Her fact slackened and she clutched her hands on her stomach. "I wanted everything to be perfect for you, and for our baby. I wanted you to be happy."

I held my hands out to her. "You have pleased me."

Marana drifted into my arms and I hugged her tightly to my chest. She must have felt the dart blade slip into her leg, but she did not react and did not slacken her hold on me until the poison loosened it. I held her up so she'd not flop to the floor, then lifted her in my arms.

I looked to the others. "Please, Your Highnesses, please go to the ballroom. Announce your amnesty, but say nothing of the Duke. Morai, go with them." I looked down at the Duke. "You will remain here until my work is done."

I carried Marana into the King's bedchamber and gently laid her down. Her eyes were closed and she slept with little difficulty. I caressed her cheek, then affectionately pressed my right palm to her forehead. I steeled myself; then I called her soul.

She knew what I was doing and did not resist me. Instead she showed me all she'd done because she loved me, and my chest tightened. Duke Vidor had come to her and had enlisted her aid. Marana knew Vidor had intended to set her up for an ambush by the *nekkeht*, but her agreement to help him saved her life and put her in a position to restore my family to the throne it had lost centuries before.

I felt her joy as she dreamed of the grand empire we would build together. It would be a spectacular enterprise that would prove that she, too, had value. We would join in creating a dynasty to rival that of Clekan the Just and that led her to imagine, somehow, she had conceived and carried my child even though we had not been together in over six months.

I deflected her into other memories. I watched through her eyes as Lothar turned my unconscious body over at the edge of the Haunted Circle. His right hand pressed to my throat to check my pulse, but Marana thought he meant to strangle me. She threw her *ryqril* and hit him in the head with the hilt. Both Lothar and the *ryqril* spilled off the cliff, and Marana chose his blade to replace her own. Then she lifted me to Wolf's back and got me to Talianna before I could bleed to death.

I felt her love for me in all she had done, but her sense of right and wrong had been so twisted by her discovery of her sister that she could not distinguish between them. She did as she was told, and admirably completed her missions, but all the time she sought a way to comply with the first order in her new life: my request for her to live for me. It shaped everything she did.

I forced her back beyond that point. I held her mind so she had time to relive the month we spent together as Sixteens, and the night we again loved beside the pool. I felt the old Marana return with those memories, and I wished I could stop right then and there, but that was impossible.

My tears splashed down on her face. "I loved you, Marana. Rest well." I drew her spirit into me, straightened her limbs, and stood.

I walked back into the King's study. The Duke looked up at me. He laughed. "You will kill me?"

I nodded solemnly. "If I do not you will face a trial for treason. You will be tried in spite of the amnesty offered this evening, and that will anger many of the people in Sinjaria. There will be riots and people will die."

He swallowed. "And if you kill me?"

I smiled. "You will die defending the King from a Lurker assassin. Only your action will have saved the King. You will be remembered as a hero."

He nodded. "I think I would have prefered being remembered as an Emperor."

I summoned my *tsincaat*. "Settle for being remembered at all."

Captain Herman waited for me in a *Cirhon* roughly described by the bare spot in the midst of the tournament field. Torches burned at various intervals around us where the good Captain had thrust them into the ground. A slight breeze toyed with the flames and caused our shadows to flicker.

The Lancer Captain looked at me. "I was sure it was you."

I nodded. "It must have been simple with Marana to identify me."

He laughed unkindly. "She was so crazy we never let her see you. I could not risk her tipping my plan to you. You played the game well." The Captain's horse shivered and stamped. "How did you find me out?"

I urged Wolf forward and stopped just outside the *Cirhon*. "Someone who knew about the *nekkehts* had to be behind this. I was told no one even five years my senior knew of *nekkehts* and every Talion here in your garrison is within that grouping. That left you."

He pursed his lips. "You are correct. It was very sloppy of me to assume you would believe Marana was the traitor. I won't be that careless again."

I nodded in agreement. "You actually believed you could use Hamis as the core of a new Empire?" I shook my head at his foolishness.

The Captain nodded. "There are prophecies, Justice, that predict it. But they are not the only foretellings about a new

Empire. After you are dead, I will just shift my base of operation to another country. This continent boasts many men who wish to be Emperor."

I dismounted and drew a white headband from Wolf's saddlebags. I pulled it on and knotted it over my left ear. "You will never help them. You have offended me, and I, Nolan ra Sinjaria ulHamis do claim of thee a blood debt. In the *Cirhon* this matter will be settled."

Captain Herman swung down from his saddle, obtained a black headband from his saddlebags, then slapped his horse on the rump and drove it from the *Cirhon*. He tied his headband on and also knotted it over the left ear. "I, Captain Herman ra Imperiana, do claim of thee a blood debt. In the *Cirhon* this matter will be settled."

The Lancer drew his sword and struck a guard. I summoned my *tsincaat*, and also dropped into a fighting stance. The Captain watched my sword and came in slowly. I shifted my *tsincaat* to my left hand and drew the Princess's stiletto, but the Captain refused to be distracted by my ruse.

I stepped forward quickly and feinted a low lunge at his right leg. He parried and I disengaged to continue the lunge at his stomach. He windmilled his sword around and twisted aside so the lunge missed. He allowed himself a cry of joy at his success.

Then he felt the pain in his back where, with my skull hand, I'd thrust the Princess's stiletto. He stiffened and tried to deny the numbness seeping into his flesh. His knees buckled and, vanquished, he fell forward on his face.

I pulled the dagger from him, but left him lying there in the dust. I left his plans for an empire with him.

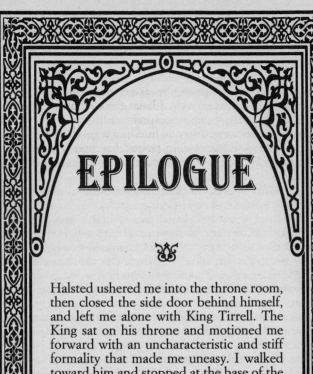

EPILOGUE

Halsted ushered me into the throne room, then closed the side door behind himself, and left me alone with King Tirrell. The King sat on his throne and motioned me forward with an uncharacteristic and stiff formality that made me uneasy. I walked toward him and stopped at the base of the throne-dais.

I bowed deeply and respectfully. "Your Highness wished to see me?"

King Tirrell nodded wearily. "I wanted to speak with you before you left." The King carefully chose his words and spoke them as if they were barbed and refused to come easily for him. He approached his topic very reluctantly, and I thought I read fear in his eyes.

I cleared my throat and gave him a

chance to delay his discussion. "I would, given leave, Your Highness, report to you what I have discovered over the past three days since the Duke's death."

The King waved me to continue and took refuge in my report.

"Captain Herman apparently acted alone in making his arrangement with Duke Vidor. I have elevated his lieutenant, a man named Slade, to brevet-captain until someone can be sent out from Talianna. You will find him a good man. He has already, at his own suggestion, posted his men in conspicuous places and given ample evidence that the Talions support you fully." I looked down at my gloved hands. "The Lancers posted here would have followed Captain Herman's orders to support the Duke, if it had come to that, as willingly as they demonstrate support for you now."

King Tirrell nodded. "I have let it be known that Duke Vidor worked as my agent to determine who plotted against me, and that tale has been widely accepted, especially in light of his death preventing my assassination." The King pulled a sealed letter from his robes and extended it toward me. "This is for your Master."

I took the message, looked at the seal of Hamis outlined in red wax, and tucked it into my tunic. "As nearly as I can tell no one, aside from your family, the Lancers, and those who knew me previously, believes I am a Talion."

The King smiled easily. "What happens to Lord Nolan now?"

I shrugged. "I do not know. He will probably return to Yotan, or perhaps return to the outlaw trail and get killed in the Darkesh. That is up to His Excellency."

Worry seeped back into the King's face. He stood, took the crown from his head, and rested the crown on his throne. He descended to the throne-room floor and looked me straight in the eye. "Nolan ulHamis, take the crown. It is yours, by right and blood." He waved a hand to the throne, smiled and added weakly, "I would be proud to serve as an advisor to you."

I stared at the golden crown sitting before me. The child in me, the Nolan who so ached for retribution, urged me to lunge forward, grab the power, and exact my revenge. The goal I had dreamed of so long ago, the glory my grandmother had insisted we were entitled to, lay glittering just a few feet before me. All the hours and days spent listening to my grandmother describe Castel Seir's secrets, including the passage to the tombs and how the sacred memorial flames could be kindled with a word, could be rewarded with a few casual steps up to the throne. The greatest wrong of the Shattering would be made right.

I shook my head and drew a document from my tunic. "I took the liberty of preparing this last night." I handed it to the King and he unfolded it. I pointed to the "X" at the bottom next to my signature. "That is Morai's mark as my witness. With this document, I, as the last surviving member of Prince Uriah's bloodline, renounce all claims to the throne of Hamis, but I do retain the right for me or my descendants to defend the throne if ever it is imperiled."

King Tirrell nodded as he read the paper, then folded it and tucked it inside his robes. "The throne is still yours, if you want it. I will destroy this document."

I shook my head and waved him to his throne. "A long time ago I would have taken the throne and, with the power it gave me, I would have redressed all the wrongs I felt you had done to my people."

The King's eyes slitted. "Do you not still have that desire?"

I paused, then nodded solemnly. "I do, but over the years I came to realize that, as a Justice, I can help people everywhere. Sitting on that throne, beneath that crown, I could only help the people in Hamis and Sinjaria. I am afraid, my King," I laughed, "my vaunted ambition to aid everyone leaves you your throne."

Slowly the King climbed the steps back to his throne, but instead of putting his crown back on, he set it on the chair beside him. "I will miss you, Lord Nolan. As you requested I have sent a wheel of cheese to Talianna for your friend. I have also written out a pardon for Morai, though I am curious why you asked for it to come into effect only after he reached the border of Seir province?"

I shrugged and laughed. "That was his request, I merely relayed it. From what I know of him, though, he's taken gross advantage of both of us in it."

The King joined my laughter, then grew more serious. "And you are certain Morai will not reveal you are ulHamis?"

I nodded. "He gave me his word, and I accept that. Besides, that information would only benefit Sinjarian nationalists who might want to use Lord Nolan as a rallying point for rebellion, and Morai wants nothing to do with them. We still have not determined which of them kidnapped him. On that basis alone he's decided none of them are worthy of his aid."

A grin spread across the King's face; then he looked more seriously at me. "I realize we went through this before when you rescued me from the warren. I wish you would let me reward you for what you have done."

I smiled. "You have. You mentioned yesterday that you intended to renovate the tombs and install a crypt for Prince Uriah's remains. That is my reward. I could ask for nothing that would please me more."

Again the King descended from the throne and offered me his hand. "I will regret your departure, and look forward to any visit you have a chance to make."

I took his hand and shook it firmly. "I will miss you and your court. Please remember me to the others."

King Tirrell nodded. "My daughter is waiting for you in the garden."

I smiled and walked from the throne room, through the ballroom, and into the gardens. The sun shone brightly from the colorful blossoms lining the crushed-stone walkways. I made my way through the flowers and found the Princess staring out at the sea.

I gently cleared my throat. "I will be leaving before noon."

The Princess turned. She wore a light blue gown and a blossom of matching hue held her midnight hair back over her right ear. She extended her right hand toward me and opened it. The gold ring I'd given her outside the tomb rested there. "My Champion cannot leave without his ring." As I reached out and took it from her, she added, "Remember me as your Princess."

I sighed heavily. "I am a Talion, Your Highness, not Lord Nolan ra Sinjaria, I . . ."

She stepped forward and gently laid her right hand on my lips to stop me. "I know who you are, Nolan ulHamis, and what you are. I know you are a rare man, and I take pride in your service to me." She lowered her hand. "I do not want you to ride from here and forget me."

I shook my head slowly and chuckled. "You underestimate yourself if you think I could do that, Your Highness. You do both of us a disservice, if you think I would want to forget you." I hesitated, thought, then continued. "But I have no idea where I will be sent in the future and I have ghosts I must lay to rest."

The Princess set her hand on my left forearm and squeezed. "You must have loved her very much."

I nodded. "Perhaps too much. She would have been happier had she died long ago."

The Princess eased my guilt with a shake of her head. "She lived on the love you gave her. What could be a happier life?"

I took her right hand from my arm, raised it to my mouth, and kissed it. "The light of your wisdom makes the storm passable. Your nation is blessed."

She smiled. "That wisdom will not let me surrender you, my Champion, to distance or your Talion Master's wishes. I will reach you."

I bowed and withdrew respectfully. She turned to watch the sea, and I turned back, throughout my retreat, to gaze at her until the garden finally stole her from my sight.

Adric held Wolf's reins for me in the Castel's courtyard. I mounted up, then thanked Adric for his service to me and rode from Castel Seir. Wolf, anxious to be back on the open road, hurried through the city despite the uphill climb. Regardless of his sense of urgency, however, I stopped at the valley rim and looked back down at the city and Castel Seir.

"You'll not see her from here, Talion," Morai laughed as he rode from a thicket at my right. "She left the garden after you did and watched you from the Wolf Tower until you left the city."

My eyes narrowed. "To what do I owe this pleasure?"

The bandit shrugged. "I felt a need for a change. Besides the roads are dangerous and I thought I'd be safer traveling with a Talion."

I laughed, reined Wolf around, and invited Morai to join me on the road west. "Why didn't you wait and travel with Selia?"

Morai hesitated momentarily, then shrugged with a little too much forced ease. "She and Count Patrick are working on ballads about the Dhesiri warren and the brave death of Duke Vidor. I'll wait for her in Jania." He smiled at me broadly. "They have a much better class of people there, you know."

I flashed a smile at him. "I'll have to visit and find out, won't I?"

"I'll tell them you're on your way." Morai yawned nonchalantly. "By the way, on that matter of the pardon."

I patted my vest. "The King signed it, as per your instructions, my friend."

"Excellent." The bandit smiled distractedly. "How long will it take before we reach the border?"

Suddenly I remembered the particulars of his pardon. "Of Seir province?"

He looked back at the dust cloud on the horizon behind us. "Yes, at the closest point."

I squinted and looked northwest. "Four hours at our current pace."

Morai looked shocked and disappointed at me. "What, ride slowly and delay a Justice's return to pursuit of horrid, *unpardoned* criminals? I'll not hear of it!" He spurred his horse to a gallop.

Laughing as a golden bauble on a chain hung around his neck flopped from beneath Morai's tunic, I set Wolf to match his horse's gait. And, despite the added weight of the Star of Sinjaria, we raced across the border before Keane could catch us.

Author's Afterword

There is some confusion about my two fantasy novels **Once a Hero** and **Talion: Revenant**. I hope this afterword can clear the problem up. At conventions and in articles I have mentioned that my first fantasy novel was too long to be published as a first novel—that is, as a first novel by an author with no reputation as a writer and no commercial track record. After six years and eleven novels, Bantam Books published **Once a Hero** and a number of people assumed **OAH** was the book to which I referred.

It was not. **Once a Hero** was my first *published* fantasy novel.

Talion: Revenant was my first novel and first fantasy novel. It was completed in 1986 and while the editors who read it liked it, at 175,000 words it was seen as being too long to come out from an unknown author. Luckily for me the editors who read it thought highly enough of it to give me other work—my BattleTech novels from FASA Corp.—and, through Janna Silverstein, Bantam hired me to write **Once a Hero** and the best-selling **Star Wars® X-wing** series.

The text of **Talion: Revenant** is ninety-nine percent the same in this edition as it was in 1986. The changes my editor, Anne Lesley Groell, asked me to make in the manuscript were fairly cosmetic—adding that last bit of polish to it before it saw print. I also caught two errors that had lurked in the manuscript since 1986. I'm not sure I *could* write this same story today, being older and hopefully a bit wiser, but I'm very proud to have written it. I like the story as much now as I did when I wrote it and I'm happy people are finally going to get to read it.

About the Author

MICHAEL A. STACKPOLE is an award-winning game and computer game designer who realizes that "About the Author" pieces tend to add context to a work, but he's not certain how valid that is concerning a work of fiction. For example, how does the fact that he was born on the same day as Caroline Kennedy influence the content of this novel? Perhaps more on point is his history degree from the University of Vermont. Directly applicable was his reading of Stephen Howarth's history of the Knights Templar, which planted the seed for the creation of the Talions. The development of the Shattered Empire comes out of his years spent working on fantasy worlds within the roleplaying game industry.

Talion: Revenant is Mike's twentieth published novel since 1988. He writes approximately three novels a year. That's a pace that is hard to keep up, but it also prevents boredom. If he's bored with a project, he assumes the readers will be too, and since his goal is to entertain, boring is not good.

In his spare time he plays indoor soccer, watches too much television and, recently, has taken to riding a bicycle for exercise. This has lead to the discovery that hills are steeper when you're going up them, unless your brakes aren't working, in which case the opposite is true.